A JACK STEEL THRILLER

STEEL JUSTICE

BOOK 3

GEOFFREY SAIGN

Books by Geoffrey Saign

Jack Steel Thrillers

Steel Trust

Steel Force

Steel Assassin

Steel Justice

Alex Sight Thrillers

Kill Sight

Interior design by Lazar Kackarovski

Printed in the United States of America
ISBN: 979-8-652038-36-6

There is a special offer for a free book
at the end of this book for readers.

~ Geoff ~

For Mom and Dad…

"Injustice anywhere is a threat to justice everywhere."

~ Martin Luther King, Jr. ~
(1929-1968)

PART 1

OP: GENERAL MORRIS

CHAPTER 1

JACK STEEL SAT IN the lobby of the Richmond Marriott Hotel not looking at anyone in particular, but watching everyone. He was a half-hour early, but he wasn't busy today and felt he owed General Morris the benefit of the doubt. The lobby was cool, like its marble floor, so it made wearing his black shell jacket comfortable. Black jeans, a black T-shirt, and soft-soled hiking boots completed his outfit.

He picked up an outdoor magazine on a small nearby table and found an article on bison regenerating grasslands in western states. That interested him. He had a deep abiding love of nature and the current global warming and environmental degradation bothered him. He also wanted to appear occupied.

In a half-hour, precisely on time, General Morris strode into the lobby, ignoring Steel as he walked to the check-in counter. The tall, ebony general was dressed in a long black coat for the February weather and carried a single small suitcase. Graying hair and glasses gave him a distinguished appearance.

In minutes Morris left the front desk, and Harry Thorton arrived via the front hotel door. Six-three, broad-shouldered and lean, he was built like a linebacker. Wearing jeans, boots, a flannel shirt, and an insulated black shell jacket similar to Steel's, he strode to another lounge chair and sat down, not looking at Morris or Steel. His easy-going face appeared calm and relaxed.

As General Morris carried his overnight bag to the elevators, Steel got up and walked a half-dozen steps behind him. He ended up standing next to the general in front of the elevator doors, but didn't look at him.

An elevator opened, two guests exited, and Steel followed Morris in. When the doors shut, Morris looked at him, his hand extended with car keys.

Steel took the keys and nodded. "Just as a precaution, stay in your room tonight, sir."

Morris nodded. "Will do. I appreciate this, Steel."

"Glad to help out, sir. Anytime." Steel turned to him. "I appreciated the help from Colonel Jeffries last September. You authorized that and it made a difference."

The general said softly, "I was glad to help, Steel. We owe you for what you did."

The elevator stopped at the third floor. Before the general exited, Steel checked the hallway in both directions, and then led the general down to his room. Morris unlocked the door, and Steel pulled his unregistered Glock 19 and entered the room, quickly walking through the two-room suite, checking closets and the balcony outside. All empty, as expected.

Finished, he returned to the living room and looked at Morris. "No one knows you're here, so any visitors are suspect. Don't open the door for anyone, general."

Morris smiled. "I can do that."

Steel returned a brief smile. "I'll check in and keep you updated. Call if you need anything."

Morris set down his bag and looked at Steel. "Do you believe my theory is possible?"

Steel regarded the general. He liked and respected the man. "You oversee Army Intelligence for a reason, sir. Your concern is enough for me to take it seriously." He didn't add that he owed Morris help if he needed it, regardless of his feelings.

Morris stared at him. "How much do you believe in justice, Steel?"

Steel hesitated. "Sir?"

"How far should we go to ensure justice?" Morris' voice was calm.

Considering the question, Steel said, "You know what I've done in the past, sir. It depends on what's at stake."

"Some feel they are above the law. That justice doesn't apply to them." Morris stepped closer. "How can we win if that's true? If the law can't touch them?"

"We have to do what's right, sir. No matter what the cost."

Morris nodded. "That's why I picked you, Steel. We agree on that. No matter what the cost."

Steel asked a question that had been gnawing at him. "Why not bring in CID, CIA, or Army intelligence?"

Morris frowned. "I don't know who I can trust inside."

"Hell."

"You're lucky, Steel. You have a family. Take care of them. Keep them close." Morris shrugged. "I have a grandson I see too little of, along with his mother."

Waiting to see if the general had anything else to say, Steel said softly, "See you soon, sir."

"Goodnight, Steel."

Steel exited the room and walked down to the elevator. For ten minutes he casually stood there. The hallway remained empty except for a few couples in their fifties that exited rooms and disappeared down the hallway corners. A few took the elevator in front of him down.

General Morris' words about justice had set him on edge. He wasn't sure what the general was implying or what he wanted. Morris had a lot on his mind and perhaps had just wanted a sounding board. Maybe it was just a conversation.

Letting it go, Steel finally rode the elevator down to the lobby. Striding to the front door, he noted Harry rising to follow him out. Once outside, Harry split off from him and headed to Steel's nearby Jeep, where Christie was waiting. Steel didn't glance at Christie—though he was tempted to. The sun was setting—it was five-thirty p.m.

Steel strode to General Morris' car in the lot, a black sedan with tinted windows, and got in. No one would be able to see who was driving, and the evening lack of light would make it even harder to ID who was behind the wheel in the general's car. Still, he pulled his Glock and set it on the passenger seat and pulled a Lycra hood over his head.

In thirty minutes he pulled into General Morris' attached house garage, one hand on the steering wheel, the other holding the Glock just below the dash. The garage was empty, but he checked to the sides and in the mirrors. When the garage door closed, he pulled on non-latex surgical gloves, pulled a rag from his pocket, and wiped down the steering wheel and car door.

He had visited Morris' large house earlier in the week. This time he entered it from the garage, his Glock leveled. Stepping into the hallway running from the front door to the back, he looked right. Harry and Christie were already entering through the back door, also wearing Lycra hoods.

Harry carried a Glock along his thigh, Christie a Sig Sauer P320. Both also wore surgical gloves. Christie wore jeans, a gray light jacket over a black blouse, and soft-soled shoes. Her brown-and-blond streaked hair was hidden by her Lycra hood. They nodded to him and he pointed up.

Christie led Harry through the living room entrance to the right and up the stairway along the wall, guns up, while Steel remained downstairs, carefully going through all the rooms and closets.

Finished checking the house, they all met in the living room. Steel shrugged. "Now we wait. Stay sharp. Stay on coms."

Christie winked at him, and Steel smiled.

"You got it, Steel." Harry nodded, his voice and expression also on the light side.

Steel watched Harry leave out the back door, while Christie climbed the stairs. All alone in the living room, he decided it was going to be a long night.

CHAPTER 2

STEEL STOOD IN THE front corner of the darkened living room. He felt comfortable without having any lights on. Years of spelunking had given him almost a second sight in the dark. Another advantage over enemies.

It was nearly midnight and he was tired of sitting, so he was standing for a change, squeezed in between two bookcases. From his corner vantage point he could fire through the front entryway between the hallway and living room if anyone came through the front door. He also had a clear view of the far side of the room, where a second open entryway connected to the main hallway.

The stairway across the room led up four steps in the far corner opposite him to a small landing where the stairs turned and ran up along the side of the wall to the second-floor bedrooms. A wall at the top of the stairs blocked any view of the second floor.

The house was dark and Steel's clothing blended in. He had attached a silencer to the Glock, which was holstered. The surgical gloves on his hands ensured he didn't leave prints anywhere in the house. He also wore a throat mike and earpiece.

On-the-hour check-ins were all he permitted, so at midnight he murmured, "Harry?"

"Quiet," came the whisper back.

"Christie?" he murmured.

"Quiet." Her voice was calm.

Steel wondered about General Morris' theory again. Two weeks ago, on a Saturday, the acting Secretary of Defense, Marv Vonders, had died in his bathtub from a blow to his head as the result of a fall. Bathrooms were still the most dangerous place in a house, and the man had been sixty-eight, his death ruled accidental. A week ago, on a Sunday, Senator Seldman—a high-ranking senator on the Senate Intelligence Committee—had died from carbon monoxide poisoning. The seventy-year-old had accidentally left his car running in his garage, and his townhome bedroom was above it. He was found dead in his bed, his death also ruled accidental. Suicide had been ruled out based on the absence of a note, and the fact that Seldman had seemed engaged in his life.

Now a week later, on Friday, Steel was in General Morris' house to spend the weekend, to satisfy Morris' suspicions that the previous deaths were not accidental.

Besides heading up U.S. Army intelligence, in the past General Morris had also overseen the now sidelined Blackhood Ops. Morris had called Steel last week and asked that his protection agency, Greensave, guard him for one weekend. For some reason Morris didn't want to go through Army or any other security channels.

Morris had only said to Steel, *I trust you and you're anonymous in this*. The general hadn't offered Steel any intel that the previous deaths were anything but accidents—and Steel hadn't asked for it. Nor did Morris give any explanation about why he thought he might be linked to the other deaths and next in line for a murder. The elderly general was also paying cash so nothing could be traced.

As obsessive as Steel was with details and security, he still doubted the general had anything substantive to back up his concerns that two high-ranking government officials had been assassinated. However, Steel always operated on gut instinct so he couldn't discount the general's hunch.

Protecting Morris was the first protection gig for his company, Greensave, since the cartel business five months ago. They had all been a little banged up, especially Harry and Christie. But now his core team was healthy and eager to take on any assignment. Harry and Christie had spent the last months limited to exercising and practicing drills in the VR station to get themselves back into shape—something he had insisted on before taking on any new assignments.

His thoughts drifted to Christie, who troubled him more than General Morris' assassination theory at the moment. The question he had been pondering for months was whether or not to buy her an engagement ring. She hadn't asked for one, never even hinted at it. And he didn't need a ring to guarantee how he felt about her. But he still thought about it. They had been together for a year and a half and he couldn't see his life without her in it. He knew she felt the same way about him. They were both happy.

He considered his daughter, Rachel. She had just turned thirteen, and was doing well. However, a two-year kidnapping that she had survived always made him careful about any decisions involving her. Rachel liked Christie, so he didn't think his daughter would mind if they got married, but he didn't want to ask for her opinion—a teenager shouldn't have to make that kind of decision. It was up to him.

He could always ask Christie how she felt about a ring. But he didn't want to pressure her either. The choice of getting a ring seemed more difficult than planning General Morris' protection Op. He smiled over that. Not a bad problem to have.

"We've got company." Harry's voice was barely a murmur from the backyard. "Single male approaching the rear door. No weapon in hand."

"Copy that. Everyone hold positions. No coms unless necessary." Steel tensed and drew his gun, while edging to the front window to peer out past the drawn blinds. No one was visible in the street, front sidewalk, or at the front door. Yet a half-block down a car was parked on the side of the road, lights off. It hadn't been there earlier. That bothered him, since in this neighborhood everyone had their cars in garages and driveways. Especially at midnight. "Car in the street," he whispered.

He strode across the living room to the hallway, which ran from the front door to the solid wood back door. Bringing up the Glock, he aimed it at the back door. Deciding something, he quietly ran down the hallway and ducked into a den doorway near the back door, pressing his back against the inner wall, waiting.

A very faint scraping came from the door. Glass being cut. No alarms went off. Steel had asked Morris to turn off the house alarm system for the three-day weekend. He didn't want motion or sound detectors scaring someone away.

To make the deaths of Secretary of Defense Marv Vonders and Senator Seldman look like accidents, their security systems had to have been bypassed and then turned back on by potential murderers. The intruder here could be a burglar, but the chance of that on the weekend Morris was worried about being murdered was highly unlikely. Yet the fact that the man was cutting glass, which would leave evidence of a break-in, didn't fit the pattern of the other two deaths.

"The man just pulled a gun." Harry's voice was still a murmur.

"Hold positions." Steel abruptly decided General Morris had been right. Which meant someone had assassinated the Secretary of Defense and a senator on the Senate Intelligence Committee. Professionals. He felt a needle of worry for Morris, but he let that slip away to focus. "Everyone watch your six," he murmured.

The back door opened and someone stepped inside, quietly closing it. Steel tightened his trigger finger. There were some sounds of a door opening, followed by a soft metallic scraping. The closet door and the alarm system box. The intruder had to be disarming the security system. Morris had it installed decades ago and hadn't bothered putting it on the second floor, which would have made it harder to find and get to before the alarm went off. Still, someone had to have been in the house once already to know where it was. This had all been carefully planned.

Soft footsteps quickly passed his doorway, and Steel slid out halfway, knowing Harry would warn him if a second man was coming in the rear door. Speaking softly, he said, "Don't move or I'll put a bullet in you. No talking. Raise your hands."

The man stopped near the living room entryway and raised his hands, his right holding a pistol. He appeared six feet, average build, wearing a black leather jacket. At a lean six-two, one-hundred-ninety pounds, Steel wasn't intimidated by most men. But he knew in fights size often didn't matter and he preferred caution. Remaining six feet back from the intruder, he said, "Slowly throw the gun into the next room."

The man complied.

Steel added, "Hands on top of your head, slowly, then drop to your knees, then to your stomach."

The man placed his hands atop his head, and then bent his knees.

The front door opened quietly and another man entered. Steel saw the glint of a gun in his hand.

In a flash the man in front of him rolled sideways through the entryway.

Steel fired once, sure he hit the man's left shoulder. Squatting and moving sideways to lean against the hallway wall, he fired twice at the man crouching at the front door and hit him in the chest and head. Ducking, he rolled through the den doorway, rose to a knee, and fired half a dozen times through the den doorway into the opposite hall wall, about waist-high. No sounds, no gasps, no falling body.

Bullets came through the living room wall, hitting the hallway wall. Steel rose and stepped to the side of the den doorway. When the shots ended, he glanced out and looked at the bullet holes in the two walls to estimate the position of the shooter. Stepping out, he fired another five shots into the wall while swiftly moving sideways toward the living room entryway.

Squatting low, gun extended, Steel peered past the doorway. The intruder wasn't on the floor. He edged farther out. No one on the upper stairway either. The man was likely on the first landing, four steps up, just around the corner before the staircase turned. He didn't hear any footsteps or creaking steps—and he had checked earlier—they creaked. But the gunshots might have disguised those sounds.

Gun up, he slid fast along the wall. The man still didn't come into view. Once past the doorway, he ran lightly to the front living room entryway. The man at the front door was dead. Crouching, then sliding to his belly, he silently crawled into the living room behind a sofa he had positioned there earlier. At the far end of it he slowly peered around it. He wanted to see if the intruder had a serious injury and if he could risk approaching him to question the man.

Three bullets bit the furniture and he ducked back. Crawling backward, he reached the hallway and stood up. Shifting his gun to his left hand, he stuck it around the corner and fired a half-dozen rounds into the far corner of the stairway landing.

Silence. He crouched, peeked around the corner, and saw a body slumped on the staircase. "Two intruders down. Hold positions. Check in."

After loading a fresh magazine into the Glock, he crossed the living room, his gun aimed at the man who was lying on his back. In seconds he bent over, pressed his gun into the man's neck, and took the gun from the man's limp hand. He ejected the magazine and round in the chamber and tossed them to different parts of the room. Then he quickly checked the man's pulse. Dead. Shoulder, neck, and chest wounds.

Something glinted from inside the man's partially open jacket. Pulling it open revealed a machete held against the inside lining of the jacket with elastic straps. That startled him. After ripping the man's button-down shirt apart, he quickly checked the man's neck, arms, back, and chest—no tattoos. Made no sense. The violent street gang, MS-13, hired out to kill, and they used machetes. But a Caucasian with no tattoos didn't fit the MS-13 profile of a Central American ethnicity with tattoos, which often included *Mara Salvatrucha* or *13* for MS-13.

It also worried him that no one had checked in.

Simultaneously shots came from upstairs and outside. Outside it was a muffled machine gun.

Steel swore under his breath and ran up the stairs. "Christie!" he murmured into his throat mike.

CHAPTER 3

HARRY CROUCHED IN A rear corner in the backyard, a fence at his back, an evergreen in front of him. Early February temps were above freezing, but chilly. Richmond, Virginia also had a rare foot of snow on the ground. Harry had dressed for it.

He wore hiking boots and wool socks for the cold and snow, and the flannel shirt and insulated shell jacket kept him warm. He held a silenced Glock 17. Steel had offered to buy him a Glock 19 as a wedding present, but he had refused. The slightly larger gun felt better in his hands. He also liked the two extra shells of the 17.

General Morris' backyard was a five-acre lot, with ten-foot-tall wooden privacy fences on the sides which began ten feet out from the rear corners of the house, running seventy feet back into the yard. Harry had decided to squat behind the row of Thuja Green Giant evergreens that paralleled the privacy fence. The hardy trees grew fast as narrow cones and provided good cover for him. The scent of pine filled the air. Across the yard was another row of the same trees.

He was thinking of Isabella. She had texted him before they had arrived at Morris' house, sending a photo of a simple wedding dress she had found on eBay. She also was going to try on her mother's wedding dress while she was in Mexico and text him a photo. Colombian, lean with black hair, chiseled features, a high forehead and narrow chin, Isabella was beautiful to him even in jeans and a tee. She was in Mexico for the next two weeks to visit her father and tell him of their plans to marry. She hadn't wanted to do it over the phone.

Harry understood that. Her father, Carlos, had almost gotten them all killed five months ago, and Isabella wanted to see what her father's reaction would be to her marrying one of the people he had targeted. She also wanted to spend time with her two brothers, Mario and Pedro.

Harry was supposed to marry Isabella in two months, if Isabella's father could attend—they had decided it was best to do it in Montana, where Harry's parents lived. The wedding was a somewhat hasty decision, but Harry knew it was right because all he felt inside was a glow. Isabella didn't want to wait either. They weren't eighteen-year-old kids; he was thirty, she was twenty-nine.

His inner glow was quickly replaced with cold caution when the man appeared. He spotted the intruder on one of his scans of the backyard with the night vision monocular glued to his eye. The MNVD gave him a fifty-one-degree field, which was enough. The intruder was sidling along the back of the house, coming from the south. It was dark, overcast with no moonlight, so he was glad he could give Steel a warning.

Steel's request to *watch your six* made Harry wary. Steel expected more operatives outside. The man was cautious to a fault, which was a good thing. Caution kept you alive. Harry had the skillset of an ex-marine, but Steel's abilities were at another level, which he hoped to match someday.

He peered between two of the evergreens. He had a good view along the north side of the house and across the backyard. Steel had felt the three of them were enough. But the sudden appearance of the intruder made Harry wary.

Once the man had entered the back door, Harry stood quietly and made his way closer to the house along the fence, remaining behind the row of evergreens. Steel had asked them to hold positions, but something about that didn't feel right; and Steel always advised following your instincts. Someone could be coming in the front door too. And if he had to charge the house to help Steel and Christie, he wanted to be ready.

He almost bolted to the back door when he heard the exchanges of shots, but he forced himself to hold back. He was glad he did when Steel asked them again to hold positions. That was hard to do when one of his best friends and his sister were in the house. Christie was as capable as himself, but he still felt protective toward her. Brotherly love.

Adding to his tension, five months ago in the cartel mess he and Christie had lost their brother, Dale. It had shaken both of them, and had made them even closer. They spent a lot of time together at Steel's house, training, sharing meals, joking. It made the loss of their brother much easier to handle than if either of them had been on their own.

Still, he found himself sweating over Christie's safety. He consoled himself with the fact that Steel was in the house. The man loved her as much as he did and would take a bullet before he let anything happen to her.

Steel's comment of *intruders* meant a second hostile had come through the front door. He decided not to check in. If someone was nearby, he didn't want to risk even a whisper.

Pausing, he glanced east and west along the fence. He didn't see any movement. Nothing across the yard. He considered things. There might have been more operatives in the parked car that Steel had mentioned, and thus a third hostile might be preparing to enter through the front door. He made his way quickly along the fence.

Reaching the end of the privacy fence and the last evergreen, he glanced around the fence to check the north side. Nothing. As expected.

Moving fast, he sidled along the north side of the house to the front corner. Peering around it, he didn't see anyone near the front door. He spotted the empty car a half block south of the house, parked on the opposite side of the street. The monocular didn't show anyone in the car. That made him nervous. The driver could be anywhere. It seemed possible that two men had come to kill General Morris. But he would expect at least a lookout in the car.

Pulling back from the corner, he crouched and listened. He had excellent hearing.

Silence.

He waited a few seconds more, and heard a barely detectable crunch of snow. What tensed his back is that it came from behind him. Not thinking, he leapt sideways, twisting so he would end up on his left side, facing the backyard. With his Glock in both hands, he began firing while he was falling, before he even had the man in sights. Another skill Steel had forced him to practice.

Silenced bullets chewed their way across the siding of the house where he had been squatting.

Harry caught a blur near the east corner of the house. The man pulled back out of sight, and Harry stopped firing after the third shot.

Rising quickly, he scrambled around the front corner of the house and crouched. Whoever was behind the house must have tracked his movements. The hostile might have come from the adjacent wooded lot behind General Morris' house. Harry took a deep breath. He had come close to being ambushed. Moving forward had probably saved his life.

He wasn't sure what the next best move was. Steel's code for problem-solving situations ran through his mind: *Stay calm, assess options, look for a solution.*

Taking a risk, he bolted across the front yard in a southwest diagonal, across the street, and toward the parked car. All the front yards on the block had a few large oak trees, and he ran from one to the next until he was closer to the car. He viewed its interior again with the monocular. Empty.

Settling on a position behind a tree, he waited. The killer was either going to run on foot out the backyard or return to the car.

In a whisper he said, "Third intruder, machine gun, backyard. I'm across the street watching the parked car."

Gripping his pistol hard, it bothered him that no one came back on coms. What if more operatives had entered the house? He'd kill them all if they hurt Christie. His older brother Clay would help him hunt them down if need be.

He took a deep breath to calm his racing thoughts. His back was stiff, his hands clenched on his gun. Shaking his head, he sagged against the tree and waited.

CHAPTER 4

CHRISTIE STOOD INSIDE THE bedroom walk-in closet, its sliding door open six inches. Keeping her body mostly concealed behind the inner wall, she could view the bedroom door and the north bedroom window. After two hours she was feeling warm. The nonsurgical gloves on her hands didn't help. Morris kept his house temperature at seventy-eight. Maybe because he was older.

Steel had put her in the bedroom, because out of the three positions for the Op it was likely the safest. That didn't annoy her. In fact she found it endearing that he cared about her. However it had made her smile earlier when she reminded him of who had saved who's butt in the cartel mess five months ago. He had smiled at her and winked. With his curly brown hair and light olive-colored skin, she thought he was handsome. His skin tone was from his Cajun creole heritage—Spanish, French, Native American, and Caribbean. An American mutt.

Lately he had been acting a bit weird around her. As if he was nervous. And his smile was off. He had something on his mind. Patient, she had decided not to press him. She knew he was head over heels about her, in a good, solid Jack Steel way. So whatever was bothering him wasn't something major, like an impending breakup. But she couldn't figure what else it might be. His daughter Rachel and his ex-wife Carol were doing well, and she and Steel were doing extremely well. She was getting along comfortably with Rachel, and the dogs were healthy. As much as she tried, she couldn't think of anything else that might be troubling him.

Sometimes Steel just made too big of a deal out of small things. His obsessive nature led to his excellence in black ops and protection work, but it also put more stress on him in simple relationship issues. She almost chuckled out loud over that. His issue. And he never made it hers, so she would just wait out the mystery.

The first shots from downstairs revved her pulse, but she held her position.

More shots downstairs.

She turned rigid, but forced herself to remain calm. It was hard at times not to be worried over Steel, but the last mess with the cartels had also taught her that worry wasn't a bad thing. Carelessness was. Still, in the back of her mind was the gnawing thought of her brother Dale dying only five months ago...

She slid the door open and stepped out of the closet, her SIG Sauer P320 compact aimed at the bedroom door. Quickly she crossed the room. On coms Steel requested they hold positions again so she paused just before the door. She debated if she should return to the closet. That didn't feel right.

Carefully she opened the bedroom door, peeked left and right, and stepped into the dark hallway. To her left the hallway led to more bedrooms. To her right the hallway ended in twenty feet, where it turned left to the top of the stairway, which was hidden by the wall. Stepping out, gun still up, she slowly walked right.

Faint whispers of sound made her glance over her shoulder. She barely glimpsed the dark figure rushing her, swinging something. The intruder must have come out of one of the bedrooms. With no time to turn, she collapsed and rolled forward on her side, aware of pain on her upper back. Something had cut through her Kevlar.

She had the gun up, but whatever glinted in the dark was swung back the other way at her. Jerking her hands back, the shiny object still hit her gun barrel, driving her arms to the side. Kicking out at her attacker's legs, she hit his knee, then scrambled back on her butt, swinging the gun up again. He kicked her hands, knocking the gun free, and she kicked her heel at the man's crotch. She missed, but not by much because the man groaned and retreated from her into the bedroom, partially bent over. The door was immediately closed.

Scrambling back, she swept her hand across the floor until she found the SIG. Her upper back was burning as she rose to her feet. Cautiously she approached the closed bedroom door.

Blows sounded from inside.

She quietly opened the door, knelt, and stuck her gun and one eye around the corner.

The killer was already whirling, releasing whatever was in his hand in a sideways motion. Jerking back, she heard the object thump into the door near her head—a machete.

She slid down to her shoulder onto the wood floor, arms and gun extended now, and fired at the kneeling man. They both exchanged shots. Bullets thumped into the door above her head, but the man collapsed and didn't move.

More shots outside. A machine gun. Brother Harry. Her heart raced. She wanted to run to him, but Steel would be ahead of her. And she wanted to make certain her target was down for good.

Rising, she stepped forward, gun still aimed, and sized the killer up—something she was good at. He matched her height at five-eight, thirty-five—four years older than her—and a fit one-seventy pounds. Thirty pounds over her. Caucasian. Dead.

CHAPTER 5

STEEL TOOK THE STEPS up three at a time, gun ready, sweat on his brow over his worry and not the exertion. Slowing at the top to make sure he wouldn't be blindsided, he carefully peered around the corner. Empty hallway. Striding to the bedroom door, he glanced inside.

Christie was crouched over a body, her back to him, her Lycra hood rolled up to her forehead. His shoulders relaxed, but then tightened again when he hit the bedroom light and saw the machete and bullet holes in the door, and the slice across her back. He swallowed. She hadn't held her position. That unnerved him, but he shoved the emotion down. She knew what she was doing.

She rose quickly, facing him. "Harry?"

Harry's voice came over their coms from the street. "The intruder is making a run for the car."

Christie frowned, but Steel said, "I'll go. Check the upstairs and find out how this one came in. Make sure it's clear."

"All right." She winced slightly.

She had to be seriously hurt, but he couldn't wait any longer. Hustling back to the stairway, he took the steps down two at a time, at the bottom deciding on the front door. The inside solid oak door was still partly open. Stepping over the body, he glanced out. Lights were on in houses up and down the street. They had to get out before the police arrived.

A man ran from the southwest corner of the house toward the solitary car parked in the street. Steel felt an urge to let the killer escape and try to follow him, but their car was parked a block away and they wouldn't be able to get to it fast enough.

He aimed at the man's legs and fired twice. Falling in the street, the killer twisted and sent a spray of bullets at him. He ducked back into the house as the door took hits.

Two single shots were fired. Harry.

Silence.

Steel whispered, "Harry?"

"Hostile down," answered Harry.

Steel stepped out as Harry walked into the street, his gun targeting the killer. Steel remained on the front stoop to cover him.

Harry was soon beside the body and squatted. "He's finished, Jack."

Steel said quickly, "Grab his phone, a facial photo, and any ID. Check for tattoos. Hurry."

Steel checked the body by the front door. No phone, ID, or tattoos. But he found a machete. He snapped a quick photo of the man's face with his phone, and then hustled back through the house to check the body on the stairs. No phone or ID. After taking a photo, he hurried up the stairs three at a time, back in the bedroom in seconds.

Christie was sitting on the bed and didn't look up at him as she studied a phone in her hands. "The killer climbed up on the south side and cut through a bedroom window. Skilled."

Steel finally holstered his gun, got out his phone, and called General Morris—on speed dial. While he waited for an answer, he rolled up his hood and walked around the foot of the bed so he could see Christie's back. Her brown and blond streaked hair barely reached the slice across her upper back. The machete had cut through her Kevlar. He couldn't see how badly she was hurt, but the machete attacks on the dummy they had stuffed beneath the bed covers were all deep. His stomach tightened. He couldn't help it.

"It's just a scratch, Steel. No worries." She turned to look up at him, her green eyes steady. She winked. "The dummy had it worse. Both of them."

Heaving a breath, he kept his voice even, professional. "You didn't hold position."

She swung farther around to face him, a slight touch of humor in her eyes. "If our positions had been reversed, would you have held your position in the closet after hearing all those shots fired?"

"Obviously not."

"My point exactly, Steel."

He didn't see any concern on her heart-shaped face and her eyes were calm, which further relaxed him. Morris wasn't answering and there was no voice mail. That bothered him. Maybe the general had gone to bed and shut it off. They would have to check on him immediately, which meant a very late visit to the hotel. He hung up. At least they had thwarted Morris' killers. That made him feel good.

"I found this in the killer's pocket." Christie held up a small plastic bag of white powder. "With the machete and coke, they were trying to make it look like MS-13 was hired for a cartel revenge hit from last September. But my guy here has no tattoos and he's very white. Yours?"

Steel lifted his chin. "Same for both. Machetes. Caucasian. No tattoos."

Harry appeared in the doorway, his hood rolled up too. "Same with the guy in the street. Caucasian, no arm, back, or chest tattoos. Got his phone, no ID. He made a call to someone though. Blocked."

Steel nodded. "All pros. Morris was right about the assassinations."

"Why send four men to kill an elderly general?" Christie looked at them.

"They knew he might have protection." Though Steel didn't know how that was possible.

Harry lifted his chin to Christie, his face showing a rare moment of strain. "You okay, sis?"

"I'm good, little brother." Christie looked up from the phone she was holding, her brow furrowed. "You?"

Harry nodded. "I'm okay." His voice lowered. "You got cut?"

"It looks worse than it is." She turned to Steel. "This phone calendar has four dates marked with latitude and longitude. The first date and location are for here tonight."

"We'll turn it all over to General Morris." Steel turned to leave. "Let's get out of here."

The phone in Christie's hand vibrated. Steel frowned and hesitated.

Christie looked up. "The caller's number is blocked."

"Put it on speaker." Steel put a finger over his lips as Christie answered the phone.

Silence.

After three seconds Steel was going to have her cut off the call, but a voice came through. Steel couldn't place the dialect. American, with a hint of Caribbean.

"Given that I am not hearing the agreed protocol response, I have to assume that whoever you are, you have killed my associates. Thus I am informing you of two things. The first is that you have failed. I have General Morris. You can save his life by giving us your names."

Steel became rigid, his hand clenched. He glared at the phone. Christie stared at it too, and Harry moved closer.

Steel had to work to keep his voice calm. He didn't want to admit that Morris was already as good as dead. "Let me talk to the general."

"You will understand that he has a hard time talking now. He lost some teeth and had some other unfortunate things occur so he's not as coherent as he was when you last saw him. He is loyal though. He hasn't given you up."

Steel didn't reply, his eyes glued to the phone. Morris had already been tortured—Steel felt responsible.

Christie bit her lip. Harry squatted, staring at the cell with narrowed eyes.

The man continued, "The best I can do is pass along two approved sentences. Morris said this will verify for you that he's here and alive."

Steel tensed. "Not good enough. I won't know if he's still alive."

The man's voice remained calm. "You don't have a choice, do you? I'm a professional, like you. I have no need to lie."

Steel grimaced. "Give the sentences to me."

The man recited Morris' sentences; "Hey, Buddy, give him your name or you're going to get me killed. Jay would never do that."

Steel winced, his hands fists. He wasn't sure what Morris was trying to tell him, but he decided to verify it as accurate. The message felt too odd for the killers to make it up. "Let's say I believe the general is still alive, now what?"

The man continued. "If I don't have your full name in three seconds—and I have to assume *Buddy* is not your real name—I am going to kill him."

Steel didn't want to give the man his name. They could come after his daughter or Carol—his ex. He also doubted giving his name would keep Morris alive. He kept his voice level, deciding to give them a common surname from Louisiana. "Pete Comeaux. If you set up an exchange for Morris' release, I'll gladly meet you."

"Comeaux is Cajun, correct? You don't sound it."

Steel didn't hesitate. "I was born in Louisiana, but I moved north when I was very young."

"Ah. It sounds plausible, but I don't believe you. I have a very good sense of when someone is lying and I didn't expect to get your name. So General Morris will die as originally intended. You know how. And I'm certain you will not report it, because if you killed four men, without the general to verify your story you are not very credible, are you? And how can you prove a dead man hired you?" The man paused. "Don't bother returning to the hotel. The room is clean. We're elsewhere. We don't leave trails."

Steel stared at the phone. "What else can I give you in exchange for the general's life?"

"Unfortunately I have lost all trust in your words," replied the man.

Steel squatted next to Christie, his hands sweaty. "Look, there has to be a way to resolve this."

"There isn't. It's not personal."

Steel disagreed. It was very personal to him. "Wherever you are, whoever you are, if you kill General Morris, I will find you."

The man replied, "Which brings us to the second thing I wish to inform you of. We will find all of you and kill you. Maybe tomorrow. Or in a few days. Weeks. Months. Whenever. You'll never be safe. Look over your shoulder. We'll be there. The men you killed tonight were amateurs. We're not. Enjoy the rest of your life. You have little of it left to live."

The line went dead.

CHAPTER 6

SIRENS SOUNDED IN THE distance.

Steel rose, drawing his gun. "Let's get out of here. Hoods down."

The three of them hustled down to the back door and Steel peered out, using Harry's monocular to scan the grounds. Satisfied, he handed the monocular back to Harry and led them out into the night, pointing left and right.

Harry ran right, disappearing behind the evergreens, and Steel led Christie left, toward the opposite row of evergreens. Gun up, he ran between the fence and trees across Morris' rear lot, and into the wooded side lot of a big house on the next block over. His Jeep was parked on the street ahead of them.

Ten yards from the street, still in the trees, Steel stopped and whispered into coms, "They might have someone else watching Morris' house to verify the kill or for backup. Harry, scan the area."

Harry came back in seconds. "Nothing moving that I can see."

Steel motioned to Christie to go wide of him and whispered, "When I get in the Jeep, count to twenty. If nothing happens, we'll leave."

Steel walked slowly to the edge of the trees, eyeing the street and nearby houses, while Christie and Harry moved to the sides of the lot. Nothing suspicious appeared, so Steel quickly walked up to the Jeep, squatted, pulled out a small flashlight, and checked the undercarriage. Clean. The enemy had time to attach a bomb or tracker to the vehicle before the house attack so he didn't want to take any chances. Rounding the back of the Jeep all the way to the front, he checked beneath it several more times until he was satisfied. Hurrying to the door, he unlocked it and got in, again giving the interior a quick check. In twenty seconds Christie and Harry joined him.

Without turning on the lights, he drove down the street, quickly exiting General Morris' Richmond, Virginia neighborhood. Turning on the lights, he headed home, north toward Fredericksburg and beyond. He finally pulled off his Lycra hood and gloves, as did Christie and Harry.

Steel glanced at Christie, her eyes steady on his. He didn't want any part of whatever this was, but he was committed now. General Morris would die horribly, and that bound him to track down whoever was responsible. He remembered Morris' comments about justice, what he would do for it. But he didn't want to bring Christie or Harry into it. On the other hand, it was their decision and he would respect it.

Christie's voice was soft. "I want to put a bullet into the SOB, Jack."

Steel glanced into the rearview mirror at Harry—who looked like he wanted to punch someone.

Harry nodded once. "I'm in. All the way."

They didn't talk further. Everyone was tired.

Steel chewed over what Morris had told him earlier. And he reviewed his actions repetitively to see if there was anything he could have done differently to save the general. They had put Morris into his Jeep, and Christie had driven the general around while Harry had followed her discreetly in his pickup to look for tails. Certain they had not been followed, they had taken Morris to the hotel for the night. Steel couldn't find anything wrong with the plan. But Morris was dead. That was on him.

"You did everything right, Steel." Christie eyed him.

"Not everything." He could have talked to Morris more, perhaps done more groundwork beforehand. Taken the general's concerns more seriously.

Christie rested a hand on his shoulder, her hand sliding down his arm to his hand. "You didn't let Morris down. You placed him in a safe hotel and we took out four killers. No one tailed us when we drove Morris to the hotel."

"No one," chimed in Harry.

Steel gripped the steering wheel. "Then Morris must have called someone. And it had to be someone he trusted." The killer had Morris' cell phone so that was a dead end too. The man on the phone was a professional, had an organization, and had assets. Steel wanted the man dead and his organization destroyed.

Christie squeezed his hand, which relaxed him. But it didn't take away the guilt over Morris' torture and death, nor the rising anger at whoever had killed the general and threatened them.

It wasn't until he was much closer to home, past busy streets and on a quiet highway, that he was able to detect the tail.

CHAPTER 7

KARBU MOELLER SAT ON a lounge chair on the flat rooftop of his villa in north-central St. Croix Island. Dressed in a colorful short-sleeved shirt, white linen slacks, and sandals, he was very comfortable. At eight hundred feet altitude, when he faced north during the day he could see the Virgin Islands and Puerto Rico in the distance, the deep blue of the Caribbean Sea between them. The wet season was over, the air warm, the winds light. Comfortable.

Long ago he had planted frangipani, hibiscus, and bougainvillea around the estate, many of the flowers in pots on the four-foot-high, one-foot-wide rooftop wall. The scent of the frangipani was his favorite, and the color of the yellow and pink hibiscus were pleasant on the eyes. Jungle and trees surrounded his villa. Strangler fig, a few mahogany, colorful flamboyant trees, cacao, wild orchids, and calabash. His was the only house at the end of a narrow dirt road. He had given enough money to local government to ensure that no one else could build around him. He loved it. It was past midnight, and the multitude of stars above created a beautiful scene that he could stare at for hours. Quiet. Peaceful. It was his favorite place in the world.

Ironically, his estate was also protected by two security guards at the locked gate a hundred yards down from the villa, with another two security guards two hundred yards down the road. Multiple and redundant sensors and camera feeds placed in the surrounding forest would give them enough warning should anyone try to attack him by coming up the mountain. He doubted he had to worry about something like that, but his business demanded he be careful.

Usually all that security added to his sense of peace.

But right now he was tense. His stepbrother, Jiri, was on his mind. He had heard the phone ring, and Ivelisse's voice drifted up to him from the stairway leading to the rooftop. Ivel was always kind to Jiri—she tolerated him but did not trust him. In some ways Karbu didn't trust Jiri either. But Jiri was family.

In a minute Ivel came up, wearing a knee-length yellow summer dress, her black hair on her bare shoulders, her tanned face worried. Puerto Rican, she had a beautiful complexion. But Karbu really loved her spirit, empathy, and kindness. She sat on the chair next to his and handed him the phone, giving a small shake of her head. Karbu knew what she was saying—Jiri was in one of his moods. He put the phone on speaker. He kept no secrets from Ivel. Besides being his wife and business partner, she was also his deepest confidante and friend.

"Jiri." Karbu tried to keep his voice calm, but he could feel stress bubbling up inside.

"Relaxing on the rooftop, right brother?"

"Guilty as charged. Good to hear your voice, Jiri." Karbu tried to think of some way to ease into the issue, to make it pleasant, but that seemed impossible.

Jiri's voice remained casual. "You sound worried, brother."

"I am worried about you, Jiri."

Jiri's voice sharpened. "Why did you demand I end my contract? You couldn't even call me to tell me that? You send me a text as if I'm some underling you can order around."

Jiri's anger was evident even from fifteen hundred miles away. Half Norwegian like Karbu, with the rest a mix of European ancestry, Jiri was six-two, muscular, and wore a moustache and trimmed beard. Karbu preferred no facial hair and was a few inches shorter, but thicker in build. At forty, he was two years older than Jiri. They had both picked up a little of the Caribbean in their accents.

Karbu couldn't keep the edge out of his voice. "We agreed long ago no American government targets. Then I hear we're doing just that."

"Who told you the contract involved American targets?" Jiri's voice was hard.

"It's my company. My employees talk to me." Karbu stood up, his free hand flying. "We don't want to become a target, Jiri! We have a nice life. Simple. The CIA uses us, foreign governments use us. It's enough. Why are you doing this?"

"Money. Lots of it. And we're insulated. I hired outside our organization. It can't be traced back to us."

"We're U.S. citizens, Jiri. If any of this is linked to us, they'll come for us."

"You worry too much, brother."

Karbu waved a hand. "Of course I'm worried! Your recklessness and greed are putting everything at risk! Our business, me, you, Ivel!"

Silence. Karbu knew Jiri would be angry, and surprised—it was rare that he yelled at him.

In a few moments Jiri said, "I'm very careful, you know that. I would never let anyone harm you or Ivel. My life on that."

"How many more targets?" Karbu pursed his lips.

"Three."

"Who are the targets?" snapped Karbu.

"Better you don't know, brother."

Karbu tried again. "Who hired you, Jiri?"

Jiri's voice remained steady. "I promised my employer that I will be the only one with his name."

Karbu calmed himself. "I want it finished, and no more contracts without my approval, Jiri. None."

"Brother, I built this business with you. We went from special ops to special mercs to special projects. You call it your company, but what does that mean? I control all of the field work now so you don't tell me what to do."

Karbu stared at the ocean. Sometimes when he heard the anger in his brother's voice, as he did now, he felt threatened. They both were very good fighters, and Jiri always carried a knife at his ankle. In a fight between them, odds would favor Jiri to win. His stepbrother was fast. But he had more strength. Speed often determined fights, but he wasn't scared of his brother. He shook his head. He would never fight Jiri. "When will it be over?" he asked sharply.

"Two weeks."

Karbu waved a hand. "That's not good enough! I heard four of our operatives already died."

Jiri sounded confident. "The man that did that will soon be dead. I am taking three of our primaries to finish the main contract. They are better trained and won't make mistakes."

"One man killed four of yours?" Karbu didn't like it.

"First, the four men were not ours. I hired out. Second, we were given information that the recent target hired a small protection agency to watch over him. It wasn't just one man." Jiri hesitated. "They won't go to the police. They have no proof of anything related to us, and they just killed four people. I will find them."

Karbu thought on that. "That protection agency could put us in jeopardy. Leave them alone. You kill them, someone will be looking for you."

"It's better not to leave loose ends, Karbu. You've always told me that." Jiri paused. "Who told you we lost four operatives?"

Calmly, Karbu said, "You will not take any action against any of our people, Jiri."

"You mean against the one that betrayed me to you."

Karbu felt his anger rising again. "They are professionals, and if you kill our employees, you are a threat to the company, Jiri."

"Is that a threat, brother?"

"It is a fact." Karbu hesitated. "How do you think our employees will react if you kill one of them?" He clenched his fist, working to get his frustration under control. "When this contract is over, let's talk. You can buy me out, and then you can do whatever you want."

"I need your skills, Karbu."

"We get paid by direct deposit into a Swiss account and operate in a black cloud. You can find someone else to help with that. You're good enough to do it yourself." Karbu waited, hoping his brother would say yes.

Jiri spoke decisively. "I'm often in the field, and prefer it. I don't think you can leave something like this, brother. We're family. Talk soon."

The call ended.

Feeling trapped, Karbu returned to his chair, his lips trembling. Jiri had put him into a box by agreeing to the contract. It meant their company was on the line to complete it since they offered a no-fail policy. That angered Karbu even more. He was bound by the contract as much as Jiri. They could always issue a refund, but then he would have to pay their operatives out of their own pocket. And it would weaken their reputation. All of it tightened his jaw.

Ivel moved from her chair to his lap, her arms looping around his shoulders. "He'll never let you leave, Bu," she said softly.

"I know. But what can I do? He's my brother."

"Stepbrother."

"He's my brother, Ivel."

She ran her fingers through his hair. "His arrogance will get you killed at some point, Bu. Jiri thinks violence can cure any problem."

When he thought of Jiri, he knew she was right.

She trailed a finger across his creased brow. "If you wait for him to jeopardize all of us, it will be too late."

"I thought you hated the business I'm in. Death. Killing." He looked at her. They had met on the island, and at first she had managed some of his office business. Over a year's time they had fallen in love and he had trusted her with more and more of the mundane business details such as payroll, while he spent time talking to clients. "Are you asking me to kill my brother?"

"No, of course not." She held his face gently with both hands. "Let's leave the business while we still can so we can truly live in peace." She kissed his lips for a few moments, her breath on his face when she pulled back. "Don't you want that for us, mi amor? I sell enough art for us to be happy, even without your savings and business. And you can finally breed reef fish for the upscale aquarium market. Wouldn't you love that?"

It was true. She painted landscapes of the ocean islands and with his contacts had begun to sell them quite well worldwide. That's where he had first met her, at one of her smaller art showings on the island. Her infectious smile and kindness had captivated him from the beginning. And he loved breeding the colorful reef fish. They were simple in a way, and often more intelligent than dogs. Taking care of the fish gave him a sense of peace. He had six one-hundred-and-fifty-gallon aquariums below in their house and seemed to have a skill at breeding them and keeping them healthy.

He wrapped his arms around her. "You are smarter about life than Jiri and me put together, Ivel."

"If you simply say, *I am done, Jiri,* you know he would consider it a betrayal. He might even try to kill you."

"I don't think so, Ivel. I have a complicated relationship with Jiri. But I agree. I have to get out of the business. I thought I could wait another five years, but this action by Jiri makes me feel it would be a mistake to wait. And I cannot kill my brother."

She rested her head on his shoulder. "If you could kill your own brother, I wouldn't love you as much as I do."

He would never kill his only family. Their parents were dead and he had no one outside of Jiri. He and Jiri had a long history together; through their youth, then Army, and then Special Ops. War had changed both of them. He had become more neutral toward violence, seeing it as sometimes necessary, and a way to make money. Whereas Jiri had fallen in love with having the power over life or death. That's why Jiri loved working in the field, while Karbu preferred the business side of things.

He heaved a sigh. "Without you, Ivel, my life would be dead and empty. I love you."

"Always and forever, Bu."

"I'm going to call my CIA contact and see if I can find out who runs this protection agency that killed Jiri's operatives." Karbu patted her back. "Jiri is right. No loose ends."

Ivel pulled back from him, her eyebrows raised. "You're going to send more men?"

Karbu stroked her shoulder. "No, my love. Most of our operatives are engaged in contracts, and Jiri won't listen to anyone except me. If we need help, we'll call someone in."

She nodded once. "So we're taking a trip."

"We'll leave in the morning."

"Do I get to pilot?" She smiled.

He chuckled. She had several licenses and enjoyed flying their small jet. "Of course."

"Weapons?" she asked.

"Of course."

CHAPTER 8

JIRI MOELLER HUNG UP, frustrated. His gloved hands clenched the steering wheel of the car. It took him a minute, but he calmed himself, and then sat back. Even when Karbu was upset with him, his brother backed down. Family.

He wouldn't stop working in the field until age posed a risk. He figured he had five good years left if he kept himself in shape. Perhaps then he would just oversee contracts in the field, but not participate. That would be hard, but remaining too long would be stupid. He knew he was impulsive at times, as he had been in taking on this contract, but Karbu would never accuse him of stupidity.

The only thing Karbu was wrong about was believing that he was greedy. He didn't need more money to be happy. He loved his work. The money was to allow all of them at some point to walk away from the business. And he didn't like anyone putting limits on what he could do. The American government was riddled with corruption, so he saw no problem with adding to the chaos. And his contact had promised more lucrative work if this job went well.

He looked into the rearview mirror at the man lying on the back seat on his side, zip ties on his ankles and on his wrists, which were tied behind his back. "Karbu said it was you that betrayed me and that I shouldn't harm you. Admit your guilt and we move on. But from here on out you will never tell Karbu anything again. That is our deal. Agreed?"

The man lifted his head slightly. "Agreed."

"One last thing. Why did you feel the need to tell Karbu about this contract?" Jiri had to work to keep his voice calm.

His captive said, "I am loyal to Karbu."

Jiri nodded. "I can appreciate your loyalty. That's a good trait. Because of your honesty I will show you mercy and not burn the car with you in it."

"Do you want to know why I'm loyal to Karbu and not you?"

Jiri could feel his anger rising, but he asked, "Why?"

"You both demand loyalty, but Karbu keeps his word and honors friendship. You would kill your brother if he got in your way and your word means nothing. Why would anyone be loyal to you?"

The prisoner's gun was resting on the passenger seat, and Jiri picked it up, turned, and shot him in the head. He left the car immediately. Stolen, and parked in an abandoned warehouse district in Richmond, Virginia, the body would not be discovered for some time. The black night would hide it. Burning it would only mean it would be discovered sooner, so he let that threat go.

As he walked away, he considered Karbu. His stepbrother had always looked out for him when they were younger, and helped him solve many self-created problems. In doing so, Karbu had made sure that Jiri's impulsive nature had not ruined his life. Thus Jiri loved his brother and would do anything for him. Yet his stomach tensed over the fact that Karbu didn't trust him and had company operatives spying on him. His brother's dishonesty set his teeth on edge. However, Karbu didn't excel in field ops so his attempts to control him were feeble too. But the lack of trust was grating.

In a mile he dumped parts of the gun into dumpsters spread out along the way. His gloves he dumped into another dumpster much farther on.

The brisk walk cleared his head and improved his mood. After another mile he reached a busier street and his parked rental car. He drove to the airport, already thinking about the next target.

***

Glancing around the Richmond International Airport, Jiri looked for his operatives. They were going to take a red-eye flight. Once he began a contract, he kept everyone together. It ensured people were on time and there were no surprises. The two men showed up, sitting in different sections of the boarding area, not making eye contact with him or each other. Gregory was shorter than him, clean cut, thirty, with a short trimmed beard. Laks had longer hair, no beard, and was thirty-five. Both had been in the field with him many times. Highly skilled.

Jiri had measured himself against both men in his mind before, something he did with every man he met. Gregory would be more of a threat in a fight. Even though shorter, the man was fast, with good reflexes and skills. But Gregory favored his right side. A weakness. Jiri was proficient on either side. Laks was taller, stronger, and with a longer reach, but he wasn't highly skilled against low attacks.

The third operative was a woman. Emilia. Relatively new. But Karbu had said she was very skilled and had been successful on three solo projects thus far. Jiri didn't know her, and after the recent betrayal he decided he would have to watch her. A text came in from her.

"Following targets. Report soon. License plate doesn't fit."

He would kill the people who had tried to interfere with the General Morris hit. Worse, they might have intel on the locations for the next targets—he hadn't been completely honest with Karbu. One of the men killed at General Morris' house was their operative, and that man had intel on his phone. No matter. He had faced much worse scenarios before. More importantly, General Morris had not escaped. Jiri's employer for this contract had helped locate General Morris. His employer possibly would also have intel on the man he had talked to at General Morris' house. He had already sent a text.

The man at Morris' house had seemed calm, even while knowing his friend was going to die horribly. Possibly a strong adversary. No matter. Jiri enjoyed challenges.

Rising, leaving his bag by his chair, he took a stroll, glancing at people and studying everyone without being obvious. He felt excitement over the coming field op. More complicated than killing the Secretary of Defense in his bathroom, the senator on the Senate Intelligence Committee with carbon monoxide, or General Morris with machetes. Those murders had been necessary, but not pleasing. He preferred face to face and something physically challenging. So far all he had done was put old men to rest. Karbu had often said he was like a caged tiger, pacing, waiting to be let out of his cage so he could make his next kill.

Karbu understood him perfectly.

CHAPTER 9

"EVERYONE ALERT." STEEL WAITED for Harry and Christie to fully wake up, and then said, "We need hoods."

He dug his Lycra black hood out of his pocket, as did everyone else, and pulled it over his head. "We're being followed," he said by way of explanation to Christie's inquiring eyes. "A medium-sized sedan. I've made a number of turns on county roads to verify it."

"You should have woken us up earlier, Steel." Christie sounded annoyed as she pulled her hood over her head, tucking her hair beneath it.

He glanced at her. "You both looked tired and they've been hanging back."

Christie shook her head. "Still."

"You think they're just following to see where you live?" Harry pulled out his gun, resting it on his leg which was stretched across the back seat.

"Maybe." The license plates on his Jeep were magnetized phonies that led to someone else, so Steel wasn't worried about the tail using it to find his address. But he was sure whoever was following them was linked to the death threat from the man who had killed General Morris. He had driven the highway to Rappahannock County, and was forty-five minutes from the county road that led to his house. He wanted to deal with the tail before he got any closer.

Trying to capture whoever was following them for questioning might prove dangerous so he opted for killing them. He hoped the person's ID or phone would provide a trail back to the killer he had talked to on the phone.

Heading south, he turned off the highway onto a county road that he knew intimately. The road was empty, with thick forest on both sides. The car following them made the same turn, still hanging back a quarter mile.

Steel didn't want an open confrontation, but when he ran through options there wasn't anything else that felt appealing. It seemed the safest choice, but any shootout left them at risk of drawing the attention of police, should any be nearby. Doubtful. The absence of houses and traffic—and time of night—made it unlikely for highway patrol cars to respond quickly, or even get reports.

A mile later Steel glanced into the mirror. "Harry, after the next curve I'll stop. Exit fast on the west side and get behind a tree. When we stop, you remain behind the car following us. If several hostiles exit and draw weapons, you'll have easy targets."

"Roger that." Harry straightened in the back seat, sliding closer to the rear passenger door.

Steel looked at Christie. "I'll cross the street and target the driver. You stay on the west side with Harry and cover the passenger doors. If they draw weapons or try to escape, we shoot to kill." He paused. "They know by now we're aware that they're following us. Since they haven't backed down, we have to assume they intend to find out where we live or kill us now. Whoever it is has a high level of confidence. We also don't know if we're facing one person or four."

Christie opened the glove compartment and pulled out two MNVDs—multipurpose night-vision monoculars. Handing one to Steel, she kept the other for herself. In the glove compartment were two belt pouches, and she again gave one to Steel. Attaching the other pouch to her jeans, she slipped the MNVD inside it. Then she pulled her gun and rested it on her thigh. "Ready."

Steel steered the car with his knees for a few moments, while he attached the pouch to his belt and deposited the monocular in it. He rolled down his window and Christie did the same. Cool air filled the car interior, waking him up.

The next curve had a small hill on the east side that blocked any forward view of the road. Steel drove around it, sped up for a hundred feet, and braked hard.

Harry jumped out, shut the door quietly, and ran into the forest.

Jamming the accelerator, Steel drove forward another fifty feet and pulled the Jeep over onto the side of the road. Stopping, he killed the lights. He gave a quick glance at Christie, which she reciprocated. Hurrying out, he ran across the street and down the side of the five-foot deep ditch. The snow on the bank was a foot deep, so when he neared the bottom he leapt across it to avoid any snow drift. He still landed in snow up to his calves. Stepping high, he ran up the opposite side and into the forest. He stopped behind a large beech tree. Leaning his back against it, his Glock pointed down, he gave himself a narrow view of the road and their car.

The snow in the forest was also a foot deep with a slight crust—it would make walking difficult and hard to keep quiet. Cold air bit his face. The forest floor was mostly barren this time of year, and American beech, white oak, dogwood, and eastern red cedar trees stood like skeletons without leaves. Some pin oaks were holding onto their leaves longer than the other trees. Still, the number of trees made the forest ideal for cover. The silence would also make it easy to hear hostiles, though that could cut both ways.

The sky had cleared enough to allow the full moon to shine through. Steel would have preferred the sky to remain overcast, but the longer field of vision would also make it easier to see any hostiles approaching without using the MNVD.

He glanced beyond their car at the darkened forest across the road. Christie was out of sight.

The following sedan pulled around the corner and slowed until it stopped fifty feet behind their car. Steel didn't like it. Whoever it was, they were acting too bold, not even pretending to go past their car—they had confidence for a reason. That worried Steel. He was glad he had placed Christie and Harry on the same side. They could watch out for each other.

Harry said over coms, "Car looks empty except for the driver."

"Head north, Harry," murmured Steel. "Watch the road and forest in case they've let out operatives before the turn. Scan the hill too with the monocular."

"Roger that."

A sniper seemed unlikely given that the driver didn't know they would stop here, but a pro might have anticipated their move and taken a precaution. Steel would have. His finger tightened on the trigger.

For several seconds nothing happened. Steel felt it reinforced the presence of more than one hostile—the car driver was allowing his operatives time to get closer. "Assume we've got enemy on both sides of the road in the forest. Everyone fade back fifty feet from the road. Watch your six."

Making sure the tree covered his retreat, Steel quickly stepped back into the forest a score of paces before stopping on the south side of a massive oak. He figured anyone coming over the hill from the north would be at least a dozen yards in from the road. He dug out the monocular and peered north but didn't see or hear anyone.

Not far away he heard the solitary *ooh ooh ooh* of a snowy owl. He glanced quickly in the direction of the calls. East, in a high branch of an oak, he spotted a nearly all white owl. A male. He had read that snowy owls, usually farther north, had made some inroads south in recent years, possibly due to the unsettled Arctic climate caused by global warming. He loved birds, and nature, which seemed to center and rejuvenate him. He would rather do a night nature hike than kill people. That made him angry and reminded him of General Morris, and that Harry and Christie were at risk.

The driver's door of the sedan opened. Steel used the monocular, then lowered it. He didn't need it. A woman stepped out of the car. Slender and tall, she had long dark hair and wore jeans, a black leather jacket, and calf-length black boots. She raised both of her hands into the air and slowly walked toward their car. Steel watched her for a few moments, and then scanned north again. The street was empty.

When the woman was halfway between the cars, she stopped, facing forward, her voice firm; "I just want to talk."

Steel noted the accent—Puerto Rican.

The woman took off her jacket and let it hang from one hand.

"She has a gun holstered at her back," murmured Harry.

As if on cue, the woman said, "I'm going to put my gun on the ground."

There was no way the woman could hear Harry's whispers. That made Steel wary. She had a good idea of where they were. A pro.

Turning slowly, hands in the air, the woman made sure the holstered gun at her back was visible. With two fingers she slowly drew it and tossed it back toward her car. Next she pointed to her neck and ear, indicating a possible throat mike and ear piece. Removing both, she tossed them to the side of the road into the snow of the ditch. Either the woman didn't want her people to hear or she was pretending to want privacy.

Not wanting to give away his position, Steel remained silent, closed his eyes, and listened. Faint noises to the north. Edging around the tree, about sixty feet north he saw a shadow moving between the trees. Using the night vision monocular, he spotted a figure working his way through the forest, coming toward him. He had to focus, because there were enough trees to block any extended view of the hostile. The man wore a head net with an attached night monocular device. And he was holding a submachine gun. Maybe a HK MP7. Body armor-piercing capability. That firepower startled him and he immediately worried about Christie and Harry.

"Hostile approaching me," he murmured. "Heavily armed. Night vision. Check-in now, then radio silent."

"Quiet here." Christie's voice was a whisper in his ears.

It startled him that Harry didn't come back on coms. And the woman in the street had disappeared while he had been watching the hostile. She must have run into the forest on the other side. "Track the woman, Christie."

Over coms, Christie said, "Woman is heading toward you, Harry. I'm coming in from the west."

The other thing that struck Steel about seeing the hostiles was that these were highly trained personnel. They knew how to seek and kill, carrying out strategies for boxing in opponents, and knew what to expect. He wondered if he should have just led them to his place. There he would have held the advantage with his security setup. Now he had to hope they would have an edge in ability.

His goal was to secure this side of the forest, then cross the road to help Christie and Harry. A slight noise east of him made him slide fast around the tree to the southwest side. Bullets chewed the bark where he had been standing. It sounded like a suppressed HK MP7. Two men, not one.

Knowing the hostile to the north would be coming at him fast now, he slid around to the west side in a crouch, immediately dropping to his belly on the ground, gun extended. The man to the north was running his way and by the time he saw Steel and stopped, Steel put three bullets into his chest.

The hostile took the hits but didn't go down, and instead aimed his gun. Heavy body armor. Without moving, Steel aimed for the man's legs and fired. As the man collapsed, Steel rolled left while the man's machine gun fire hit the tree and swept over his prone body. While he rolled, Steel continued to fire until the hostile didn't move.

Rising quickly, Steel backed up to another tree, keeping the oak as cover from the assailant to the east. He couldn't cross the road; if the woman was targeting him, he would take a bullet. Still he assumed Christie would be engaging her. Continuing to back up, he caught tiny glimpses of the man approaching from the east. His opponent was also using the massive oak trees for cover. This man would be more cautious and Steel was at a disadvantage going up against an HK. Yet his virtual reality training was built on finding solutions to impossible situations. Kobayashi Maru didn't exist for him. Still, he was running out of forest.

Then he had it. The ditch.

Remaining behind a massive tree, Steel walked backward until he could go prone in the snow in the ditch. He kept his head below the ground level of the forest.

It was cold on his belly. Reconsidering, he rolled over and over north twenty feet along the gully's incline. Stopping on his stomach, covered in snow, he waited, his hands cold and wet. This strategy was a risk if the approaching man turned north or south. He was counting on the fact that the man might mistakenly assume he had crossed the road and wouldn't see him until too late.

He counted off twenty seconds. A shadow several feet to his right appeared. Steel jerked his gun up, firing at the man's legs first, and then his head as the hostile fell into the ravine. Dead.

Without pausing, Steel rose—and then ducked down just as fast, twisting as he did. He still took a bullet in the Kevlar—he felt pain in his chest—swinging him around as he fell to his back. His chest ached and he blinked, unable to move for a few seconds even though his brain was screaming at him to do just that.

The bullet had to have hit him at an angle or he would be dead, but he still felt burning pain beneath his vest. He remembered glimpsing the hostile holding a submachine gun, slowly approaching the ditch. He wasn't sure where the third man had come from. Had to be from the east too. He had moments. Snow crunched nearby. Too late.

Dropping his arms to his sides, lolling his head to the left, he closed his eyes, opened his mouth slightly, and waited. His cheek was buried in cold snow.

More footsteps close by.

A soft murmur; "One down."

Steel cracked his left eye and saw a gun muzzle swinging low toward his head—he assumed for the insurance kill shot. Rolling left, he bowled into the man's legs while reaching up with his left arm to grab the HK barrel. Gripping it, he pushed it away, simultaneously swinging the Glock up. The guy kicked his arm away, and Steel released the gun and struck at the man's groin. The killer had padding there so it wasn't a crippling blow.

Groaning, the man kicked Steel in the stomach and jerked the HK free of Steel's hand. Steel gasped, the air knocked out of him, but again pushed the HK barrel away. He swiped the ground with his other hand until he found the Glock and willed himself to swing the gun up. He was going to beat the man's swinging HK muzzle.

Seeing that, the hostile fell onto Steel with both knees, pinning his arms into the snow. Steel was still out of air, saw the HK muzzle aimed at his face, and jerked his head right as the gun fired. His ears rang.

Bending his right wrist, he aimed as best he could at his assailant and squeezed the trigger on the Glock repeatedly. One of the bullets hit the underarm of the man atop of him, but the killer just jerked back, swinging the HK again. Steel kept firing as the HK muzzle was shoved into his head. He tried, but he couldn't move his head any farther.

The HK was never fired, and his assailant slowly toppled off him to the side.

Steel lay there, staring up, his chest heaving. Slowly he painfully pushed himself to sit up, seeing an upper neck wound on his assailant. The hostile's legs were still atop of his, and Steel had to push them off. More pain. His chest was throbbing now. He didn't want to check the wound. Couldn't. These men were good. Redundant backups.

Rolling to his knees, his hands planted in the snow, he sat back on his heels. Holstering the Glock, he picked up the man's HK MP7. Evening the odds.

Pushing to his feet, he stumbled out of the ditch and across the street, hearing gunfire coming from the north. Harry would be taking the brunt of any assault forces. Christie could take care of herself as well as any of them. Still his heart wanted to protect her. Swearing under his breath, he ran toward Harry's last location.

CHAPTER 10

HARRY KNEW HE WAS in trouble almost immediately after hearing Steel's warning that the hostiles were heavily armed. Already fifty yards father north, he had stopped behind an oak tree. With the monocular he glimpsed two hostiles in the forest about a hundred yards north of him. One coming straight at him, the other heading west at an angle big enough that he wouldn't be able to get behind the guy. He assumed they had already spotted him.

Worse, they were carrying submachine guns too. Even with his Kevlar vest, the submachine guns would punch through. The hostiles also had head nets with night vision monoculars attached. Handsfree gave them an advantage. He only had the handheld monocular, but of course Steel hadn't expected the three of them to be in the forest fighting killers tonight. The woman in the street had been a decoy, as Steel had thought. Where was she?

Harry glanced through the forest to the south. Long ago Steel had made sure he and Christie knew this piece of land, just in case they needed to do something like this. Harry remembered a stream south of Christie, and beyond that a hill leading to a small cliff. The water would be frigid. All of it was too far away to matter.

Over his coms he heard Christie's warning of the woman heading toward him.

Keeping his back to the tree, he considered his options. Flee south and risk a likely shot in the back or an ambush from the woman if she had grabbed her gun or had an ankle holster. Try to move west or east and risk the same thing. Stay put and hope he could take out one of them, and maybe Christie would be close enough to help him. None of it was appealing. Steel always advised operating with no expectations of help. And Harry didn't like the idea of Christie trying to advance against submachine guns either. But he knew she would come no matter what.

The idea of losing another family member was disturbing enough that he decided he needed to be aggressive. It wouldn't be expected.

Taking a deep breath, he calmed himself. Rolling slightly along the trunk, he risked a peek north. The hostile there had paused, mostly hidden behind a tree thirty feet from him. The man was waiting for his partner to get into position. They knew where he was, and expected him to remain there or run south. Either of those choices left him dead. Quickly rolling along the tree trunk he peered northwest. He glimpsed that hostile running between trees—seventy feet due west of him. He had seconds to move.

Reaching down to his ankle holster, he drew his S&W 640 .38 Special with his left hand. A small gun with five rounds, it was still accurate and powerful. He wasn't as good with his left hand as Steel or his brother Clay, but at this point he needed any advantage he could get.

Rolling back to the east side of the tree, he picked a big beech tree due northeast. If he could reach it, the hostile to the north would have to move closer to get a good shot at him. The hostile to the west, if he was lucky, would have an obstructed view with the trees between them.

He bolted, aiming the Glock at the north hostile's tree, the S&W west toward that hostile. The snow wasn't easy to run through and he found himself having to put more effort into lifting his feet to keep up his speed. Every step crunched into the snow's crust.

Halfway to the tree, a submachine gun muzzle appeared moving forward around the tree to the north—the man hiding there was tracking him. Glancing west, he saw the hostile there running at him and firing. Bullets whizzed by him. There were too many trees between them to waste shots.

He still felt he had a good chance to reach the beech, and maybe take out the hostile to the north.

Then he was flying toward the ground, limbs outstretched. Something buried in the snow had caught the toe of his left boot. A branch or root.

As he fell, two things caught his attention. One, he glimpsed the woman from the road peeking out from behind a tree to the east of him—her head edged out past the trunk. And two, the hostile behind the north tree was coming into view to watch him fall. Probably thinking he had an easy kill.

Harry couldn't disagree.

CHAPTER 11

When the woman had bolted off the road, Christie hadn't tried to shoot her. She didn't have a clear shot and she didn't want to give away her position. The woman's gun was still in the road, but she might have a second piece.

Thus Christie had worked her way northwest, knowing the enemy would engage Harry long before they reached her. If she was far enough west, she believed coming in behind the hostiles was a better strategy than following the woman.

Stopping behind a tree, she put the monocular up to her eye again. In the distance—she estimated a hundred yards—she glimpsed four people to the northeast. Three converging on one. Harry was in trouble.

That galvanized her. Perhaps Steel was facing three on his side too. She had to trust he would be all right. But Harry wasn't in Steel's class. The thought of losing her brother sent her pulse racing. She loved him. She wasn't going to watch him die here.

Running all out, she headed in the direction of the figures she had spotted, using the trees for cover. The punch of her boots into the snow on every step assaulted her ears, but the hostiles were moving too, so they might not hear her charge. She kept her breathing quiet. Lean, she was in excellent cardio shape. Her back still ached from the wound at Morris' house, but it was tolerable.

Estimating a halfway point, she rounded a tree. And nearly died.

As far as she could tell, the man on the other side of the tree was rounding the tree nearly as fast as she was moving, holding the barrel of his HK MP7 waist high. Close to the trunk, she twisted her back against the bark and ran into the side of the man's gun barrel, her right shoulder colliding with his chest. They both went down into the snow.

The man exclaimed in pain—her weight ended up on his trigger hand. Landing face first in the snow, she twisted to the left, trying to get her gun free from beneath her. Using his left hand, he swung at her. Taking a glancing blow on her cheek, Christie released the SIG and hit him in the nose with her right elbow. Blood colored the snow. Swearing, the man swung at her again. She blocked his arm with hers.

He released the HK, jerked his hand free from beneath her, and drove a knee into her side. Grunting, she pushed up to her knees. He scrambled toward her, facing her on his knees.

Steel had practiced this kind of situation with her relentlessly, face to face, on their knees, and she did as she was taught. Fingers to the eyes, palm to the nose, half-fist to the neck. Her opponent moved his head to avoid the fingers, ditto the palm to the nose, and her fist just caught the side of his neck above the body armor. His right hand must have been broken because he bludgeoned her with his left several times fast and hard; chest and inside the shoulder. Then he tried for her face. She half-ducked that, but he caught the side of her head above her ear. Even with one broken hand he was going to dominate her if she didn't do something quick

Dropping backward to her side, she sent a hard toe kick at the side of his neck, connecting solidly this time. The man looked a little dazed. That fraction of a second allowed her to rise again and do multiple hits to his neck, nose, and eyes. Glassy-eyed, he tried to move away from her.

Reaching to her ankle, she pulled her Smith & Wesson HRT12B dagger and stabbed him in the neck. He collapsed in the snow.

It was then that she registered the HK firing east of her. Thinking it was aimed at her, she ducked, going to her belly and grabbing the SIG, her fingers buried in snow. When she realized the gunfire wasn't coming her way, she sheathed her knife and pushed to her feet. Pain assaulted her shoulder, chest, and head. The cut on her back also ached.

Harry.

She rose, stumbled up to the next tree, and peered around it. Just in time to see her brother tumble to the ground. She wasn't sure if he was shot, but Harry was firing at two targets.

The closest hostile near her ran around a tree, stopped, and raised his gun to his shoulder as he aimed at Harry. Christie yelled to get the attacker's attention, while pausing to aim at his head. She fired six times as he turned toward her.

He fell to the ground, dead. Stepping farther right, she saw two guns pointed at her brother. She didn't have a clear shot at either; both shooters were blocked by trees. Adrenaline spiked her chest.

Harry was still firing at one of them from the ground.

"Harry!" she yelled, and ran.

CHAPTER 12

STEEL WAS IN A dead run, the HK held in both hands. Using the monocular, he had spotted the woman behind a tree, with two more shooters closing in on one man. Had to be Harry. Where was Christie? He couldn't believe a hostile had made it all the way to her position that fast. Which meant she had to be farther west, coming in from behind their attackers. Otherwise he would have seen her.

When he was still sixty feet away, he watched Harry bolt from the tree. Shots were fired to the west. Christie. Weaving around trees, he picked a spot ahead of him where he would have a shot at the woman—who had her gun aimed at Harry. Steel hoped Harry could take out the other man.

Harry fell, it looked like he tripped, firing his guns as he went down. But he wouldn't be able to do anything about the woman.

Christie yelled from the west.

Steel stopped, brought the HK up fast, and sighted on the woman. He hesitated when the woman shouted, "Stay down!"

She dropped to one knee, swung her gun away from Harry, and gunned down the hostile to the north with a head shot.

Steel kept his gun aimed at the woman as he strode toward her. She didn't seem concerned as she stood up, first sliding her gun into a small black ankle holster.

Harry regained his feet, dusting off snow. Christie ran up from the west.

Steel's chest heaved. Relief swept him. He realized his whole body had been tense, his chest tight—and still aching.

Ten feet from the woman, he finally lowered the HK to his waist, but kept it aimed at her. Christie stopped beside Harry, and the three of them faced the woman who calmly returned their gazes. She appeared about thirty with a strong chin and facial features that could pass for Puerto Rican.

Steel kept his voice calm, even though he felt like putting his fist into someone. "Give me a reason why I shouldn't put a bullet in your head."

"I just saved your partner's life." Her voice was level.

"That's not enough." He raised the barrel of the HK slightly. "You saw me coming, and your men falling. You could have just taken out your man to save yourself."

The woman sounded steady. "I work for the CIA."

Steel didn't like it, and didn't trust her. "Prove it."

The woman faced him. "Jack Steel, you took down a presidency not long ago. That's not common knowledge that anyone can get off a Google search. My superiors know I was going to contact you tonight." She lifted her chin to him. "You kill me and they'll come after all of you." She added, "Your services are no longer required."

Steel tensed that the woman knew his name. And it was true that the information about the presidency takedown was not general knowledge. "How do you know who I am?" he asked sharply.

Her voice calm, she continued. "I saw you earlier tonight and took photos. We know who all of you are. Jack Steel, ex-Blackhood operative now running the protection agency, Greensave." She looked at Christie and Harry. "Along with Christie Thorton, ex-Army counterterrorism analyst, and her brother, Harry Thorton, ex-Marine." She shrugged. "General Morris was the target you tried to save tonight."

Steel didn't detect any tells that indicated the woman was lying, but she could be skilled at hiding lies.

"If you're CIA, why lead the killers to us?" Christie's voice had an edge.

"The man running this operation had me followed so I had no choice." The woman continued. "The CIA does a lot of business with the organization that targeted General Morris. We don't want their whole company damaged. The Morris hit wasn't sanctioned by the primary owner. His younger brother agreed to it."

Steel felt wary. "What's the younger brother's name?"

The woman shook her head. "Classified."

Steel's voice hardened. "Not good enough. His men just tried to kill us."

"You're working for him too." Harry said it with confidence, looking at the woman.

She glanced at him. "Yes."

"What's the name of the killer's organization?" asked Steel.

The woman turned back to him. "Classified."

Annoyed, Steel asked, "What's your name?"

"Emilia."

"Hey, Emilia." When Emilia turned to her, Christie snapped a photo with her cell phone. Emilia glared, but Christie shrugged. "Seems only fair."

Steel stared at Emilia, his gun still on her. "What does the CIA want from us?"

"Stay out of the case. We'll handle it." Emilia's voice was relaxed. "We don't want a wild card involved."

Christie's voice was sharp. "Your employer murdered a United States Army general."

Emilia ignored Christie and stared at Steel. "The owner of the organization found out his younger brother had taken this contract and sent me to keep him informed. Neither of the brothers know that I'm CIA."

Steel grimaced. "The CIA did nothing to protect General Morris tonight."

Emilia nodded. "I thought he was safe at the hotel, as did you. I watched you drop him off. We were both caught by surprise."

"No one followed us." Harry's voice held certainty.

She nodded. "Correct. The CIA tracked your truck for me."

Harry scowled.

Steel considered that. He pulled the hood off his head, as did Christie and Harry. "How did you know that we would be at General Morris' house?"

"An informant who was reporting to the older brother informed me that Morris was next in line to be killed so I followed Morris all day to make sure he was safe. When I saw you pick him up, I had the Agency track Harry's truck. After you dropped General Morris off, I assumed he was safe. That's when the younger brother ordered me to watch Morris' house, to make sure the hit was successful. When you left, he ordered me to follow you and he sent his men to rendezvous with me."

Christie said harshly, "Consider yourself lucky we didn't put a bullet in you."

Emilia ignored her. "We'll make sure you're under no threat. I'll report to the younger brother that you killed everyone and I had to shoot my way out of it. He won't come after you again until he finishes the contract. We'll deal with him before then. We don't know his next targets and don't want him dead until we find out who hired him. We'll get involved as needed." Her voice was firm. "I repeat, stay away from this. It doesn't concern you."

"Why don't you just pick up the younger brother?" asked Christie. "Question him. Hold him indefinitely until he gives up his contact."

Emilia shrugged. "It's a delicate situation. We have contracts with this organization and picking up the owner's younger brother could jeopardize other important actions the CIA is counting on from them."

Harry sounded disgusted. "He's a murderer. Who cares what contracts the CIA has with his organization?"

Emilia didn't respond.

Steel shook his head. "If what you say is true, you're playing a dangerous game with this organization. You could end up dead if you're not careful."

She rested her hands on her hips, her voice confident. "I can take care of myself."

Steel nodded. "Maybe. But if you die, that puts us at risk. We could have unknown killers coming at us at any time." He straightened. "I want the name of the organization and the names of the two brothers running it before you leave."

"As I said, classified." Emilia stared back evenly.

"Then we'll just hold you until you tell us." Steel lifted his chin. "I'm guessing the younger brother expects you to report back soon, otherwise it's going to look strange and you'll have a lot of explaining to do."

Emilia's voice sharpened. "The CIA won't take kindly to your interference. Neither will the police if we tip them off. You killed four men at Morris' house alone."

"And here you are with six more dead men, one by your own gun." Steel stepped forward. "You're not leaving until we get names."

Emilia stiffened. "You're making a mistake."

"We have a spare bedroom, Emilia." Christie shrugged. "We'll just zip tie you to the bed. Maybe have a look at your phone. Make some anonymous calls on your behalf."

Emilia grimaced, quiet for a minute. "M4N."

"What does it stand for?" snapped Steel.

"Emergency Measures for Emergency Needs. Karbu Moeller runs it, his younger stepbrother Jiri Moeller runs the field work and took on this latest contract involving General Morris without Karbu's permission." She paused. "That's all you're getting from me. Either release me or take your chances."

"What are you going to tell Jiri?" Steel studied her carefully.

"The truth." She shrugged. "We tried to ambush you and we were ambushed instead. You're very good. To throw him off a little and make it sound competitive, I'll say there were five of you and two of you were shot."

"What about the bodies here?" Christie studied Emilia.

Emilia pursed her lips. "I'll have a cleanup crew take care of it tonight."

Steel nodded. "Time to say goodnight."

Emilia lifted her chin. "I need a bullet hole in my jacket. And score my side with a knife." She pulled up her jacket to expose her waist. "I'll say I killed one of you, and then had to run for it."

Steel reached behind his back to the horizontal belt-sheath built into the inside of his belt. It held a Benchmade 3300BK Infidel auto OTF knife. But before he could pull it, Christie walked up and pulled Emilia's jacket out from her torso, aiming her SIG into the edge of it. She fired once.

Emilia eyed her. "Now the knife wound. No stitches, please."

"My pleasure." Christie pulled her dagger, squatted to clean it off in the snow, and then stood and made a thin cut beneath Emilia's ribs.

Emilia didn't flinch.

Christie cleaned the blade in the snow again, drying it on her shirt before putting it away.

Emilia looked at her bleeding cut. "Perfect." She pulled her coat down and looked at all of them, her voice certain. "This will be the last I see of any of you."

"Hey." Harry lifted a hand to her. "If you're who you say you are, thanks."

"Of course." Emilia stared at him for a few moments, and then walked past Steel, her eyes on his as she passed him.

Christie and Harry came closer to Steel, and the three of them followed Emilia through the woods back to their car. As they walked, Steel pulled out his rag and wiped off and then dropped the HK.

Harry eyed Christie. "You okay, sis?"

She lightly flicked his arm. "Still ticking. You had me worried, bro."

Harry shook his head. "I had myself worried."

In a minute Steel stared at Emilia's departing car. "Let's get out of here."

Christie took the front passenger seat again, Harry in back.

Steel drove away, lights on. His chest ached and he dropped one hand off the wheel to ease pressure on it.

"What's wrong?" Christie looked at him.

"Chest wound. Glancing blow." He glanced at her. "You?"

"A few bruises besides the back cut." She smiled at him. "We can bandage each other up."

"I look forward to it." He looked into the rearview mirror. "Harry?"

"Only a bruised ego. Marine does faceplant, rescued by CIA woman."

Christie glanced at Harry. "Better than marine does faceplant and shot to death."

Steel couldn't smile.

"I agree," muttered Harry. "And CIA complicates things, doesn't it?" He stretched one of his legs out on the car seat.

"I don't trust Emilia, or whatever her name is." Christie put her seat back. "We need to verify she's CIA."

"Her story feels right, but I agree." Steel gripped the steering wheel. "If she told us the truth, the CIA failed to protect General Morris tonight, and even though they know Morris is dead, they haven't taken down Jiri Moeller and his M4N crew."

Christie leaned back. "Whatever M4N does, it's important enough for the CIA to give them a temporary pass on Morris. Any ideas?" She looked at Steel.

Steel considered that. "Murder seems to be this organization's specialty, but that would make them good at protection too. There could be a lot of situations where it's better for the CIA to hire out than to be directly involved."

"CIA doesn't want us involved, but we can't count on them to protect us either." Harry slid down onto his back on the rear seat, his knees raised so he could fit. "I gotta get some sleep before I fall over."

Steel closed his window and turned on the heat. "Morris called me *Buddy*."

"You think he was giving you a clue?" Christie closed her eyes.

"He said, *Buddy, give him your name or you're going to get me killed. Jay would never do that.*" Steel looked at Christie, following the lines of her jaw and face. "*Buddy* means a friend. Maybe Morris called someone from the hotel that was a friend and that mistake cost him his life. His friend turned him over to M4N and Jiri Moeller—the man who threatened us tonight on the phone." If true, it would make him feel slightly less guilty about Morris' death.

Christie shifted slightly in her seat. "Why didn't Morris just give us the name of whoever he called in the sentences Jiri gave us?"

Steel swallowed. "Morris knew Jiri wouldn't pass on his message if he recognized the name of his contact. And Morris wanted to make sure he got both sentences to us. At the hotel tonight Morris told me he didn't want to bring in CID, CIA, or Army intelligence. He didn't trust anyone inside."

Christie bit her lip. "Which means someone inside is dirty."

Steel felt they were on the outside looking in on a nest of rattlers.

Harry yawned. "Is there anyone we can trust? It would be good to have some logistical help."

Harry's comments triggered something in Steel. "Morris said *Jay would never do that*. He might have been telling us that Jay would never be a traitor, like his buddy." Steel considered that, running through all his contacts in his mind. "I don't know any Jay."

Christie rested her hand on his. "What if Morris meant the letter *J*, instead of the name Jay?"

Harry spoke softly from the back seat. "Brilliant, sis."

"Colonel Jeffries." Steel glanced at Christie. "He's the only contact Morris and I have in common with the letter J. Morris trusted him. So do I." Colonel Jeffries had helped them with the cartels last fall.

"Would Morris have called Colonel Jeffries?" Christie rolled her head toward him.

Steel rested his head on the headrest. "It's more likely that Morris would have called someone higher up, with more connections than Jeffries would have. Someone he trusted."

"Why would Morris break your protocol of no contacts from the Hotel?" asked Harry.

"Morris had to believe it was someone who could help him solve the murders." Steel wanted that name.

Christie cleared her throat. "If Morris used *Jay* for the letter J in Jeffries, what if *Buddy* is for the letter B for someone's name?

Steel squeezed her hand. "I like it. That's possible."

"Someone whose first or last name begins with a B that is above a ranking general in Army Intelligence." Christie pursed her lips. "That's a small list. I'll research names tomorrow."

After a few more turns, Steel was on the highway again, headed home. "What's the second date on the phone and where does the latitude and longitude put it?"

"Chena Hot Springs Resort, Fairbanks, Alaska. In three days." She glanced at him. "We don't know who the target is, what the killers look like, or if this is even the next target."

Steel considered that. "We don't, but it's our only lead. If we find the connection between the targets, what they all have in common, then maybe we'll find a trail to the traitor, B. Colonel Jeffries might also know who B might be, who Morris associated with. I'll call him in the morning. Maybe he can help with getting us photos on Jiri and Karbu Moeller too."

"How much are you going to tell Jeffries?" asked Harry.

Steel thought on that. "If we don't tell him everything, he could end up talking to the wrong people and buy a bullet. We need his help."

Harry yawned loudly. "How could M4N have ten operatives here in Richmond to take out Morris and take us on?"

"Jiri Moeller has to be here, and this has to be a staging area—they were meeting to plan out their assignments for the next three assassinations." Steel glanced at the rearview mirror at Harry. "Which means we just put a big crimp in their timetable and assets."

Christie yawned. "Looks like another road trip, honey."

Steel gave her a terse smile. "Another wonderful vacation. Can't wait."

Christie smiled sleepily at him. "Any kind of trip with you is better than one alone."

"And this one I won't have to spend in the back of a trunk," Harry said sleepily from the back seat.

Christie glanced back at him. "You can't complain when that trunk earned you a ticket to the altar with Isabella."

Harry smiled. "Might not be a church wedding."

Steel glanced at Christie, wondering what she was thinking when Harry mentioned *wedding*.

Harry passed his phone up to Christie. "Which dress do you like? Ebay or Isabella's mother's?"

Christie smiled as she looked at both. "Let's see, cheap knockoff, or original handmade mamacita's dress that honors her mother's memory. Duh, I don't know, Harry, what do you think?"

"That's what I like about you, sis, you're never direct."

Christie's voice softened. "It's a beautiful dress and it looks great on her, Harry." She reached over, showing the photo to Steel. "Isn't that sweet, honey?"

He glanced at it. "It's a slam dunk, Harry."

Sounding content, Harry said, "Yeah, that's what I thought." He took the phone back from Christie.

After that the others dozed while Steel drove. All the wedding talk made him wonder more about the ring. Maybe he should flip a coin. There was something wonderful about working with Christie in the field. But the danger was real. She could have died tonight. But he could have too. They had talked about this many times, mostly to lighten his concerns. Christie had accepted it. He could accept it. He had to. He glanced in the rearview mirror. Harry was getting married in two months.

It used to be easier on Blackhood Ops, carrying out missions with unknown operatives. Less emotional attachment. But he also knew if he had to pick a life, his current one far outweighed any satisfaction or value of his old military life and marriage to Carol. Christie had told him the same thing repeatedly. They were fortunate.

Now he just had to keep everyone alive. Or the ring wouldn't matter.

He also wanted General Morris' killer brought to justice. Morris' question about justice made sense now. Someone high up felt they were above the law—or that the law couldn't touch them—and Morris had asked him what he would do about it. He wasn't an assassin. He didn't want to jeopardize his current life. Killing high-ranking cartel officers was different than assassinating a high-ranking U.S. official.

Still, however many people were involved in General Morris' murder, he wanted them all dead. When he thought about it, what that might entail with a murder-for-hire organization like M4N that the CIA used, possibly partnering with someone high up in the American government for assassinations, he thought he might have to start a small war.

CHAPTER 13

STEEL DIDN'T COMPLETELY TRUST that Emilia wouldn't sell them out, or give his address to the enemy. Yet he doubted the enemy could have sent anyone to his house before their arrival even if she had.

Still, to be safe he drove along the south country road bordering his square mile of forest. County roads bordered all three sides, except to the west, where his land abutted the Blue Ridge Mountains.

There were no cars parked on the south road, nor in front of his property on the east side, nor on the north side when he drove by. That gave him confidence. He had security cameras and sensors along the perimeters and driveway that triggered alerts to his phone and computer. Nothing had sounded. But all security could be bypassed if you knew what you were doing.

Taking one more security measure, he dropped Harry off on the south perimeter, and when Harry crossed the perimeter, Steel received a text alert on his phone. The same occurred on the east and north side. Thus no one had disabled his perimeter security. It made him feel safe enough to use the main driveway.

Two heavy metal gates there swung on six-inch-thick metal posts, and a sturdy chain and heavy padlock locked them together. Bolt cutters wouldn't get you in, and trees prevented anyone from driving around the gates.

Opening the gates, he stared at them, deciding to leave them open. If someone came tonight, the driveway would be easier to manage than an attack from the forest. The winding half-mile gravel driveway led to a circular turnaround and his rustic four-bedroom, two-story house at the end of it.

He was glad to be home.

***

Steel grunted. The bullet had scored his chest and Christie was dabbing the wound with alcohol before she covered it with antibiotic cream and nonstick gauze bandages. He was sitting on a bedroom chair, a towel wrapped around his waist. He had just showered and Harry was asleep in one of the guest bedrooms.

"It's not bad. You were lucky." Christie winked at him when his forehead wrinkled. "I know, honey. Your training and skill kept you alive again."

He chuckled. "Thanks for the compliment. I think."

She smiled. She had a towel wrapped around herself too, her skin damp from a bath—she had elected to keep her wound out of the water. When she finished bandaging him, it was her turn to sit while he looked at the cut just above her bath towel. About one foot long, it was thin, had stopped bleeding, and didn't need stitches. She also had bruises on her face and shoulder. That didn't make him feel good, but she never complained.

After cleaning the machete wound with antiseptic, he put antibiotic cream over it. Next he fastened butterfly bandages across it to keep it closed, and then covered it with nonstick gauze and tape.

"It's not bad. You were lucky." He stepped in front of her and she made a face at him. He said softly, "I know, honey, your training and skill kept you alive again."

She stood up and pressed against him lightly. "We're just so alike, Steel. What are we going to do about that?"

Steel wondered if she was hinting at something more, like marriage, and if he should just ask her. She tilted her head up so he could kiss her, which he did. Pulling back, he murmured, "We are a good match, aren't we?"

"Perfect." She ran her hand through his hair. "What's on your mind? Did you want to take a trip? Let Harry take care of the Morris case?"

Steel smiled. "Do you think he'll mind?"

"Not at all." Christie snuggled up to him once more and they kissed passionately. They were interrupted by his phone beeping.

His cell was on the nightstand and he picked it up. One a.m. It was a text alert from his security system. The driveway.

He punched keys, pulling up cameras on the long, winding entrance. A large van with tinted windows was slowly coming down the dirt road. Immediately he worried that Emilia had lied about being CIA and had sold them out. But how could M4N get here so soon? And how many men did the M4N organization have to throw at them?

Christie's brow wrinkled as she watched the van with him.

"Get dressed," he said quickly. "Get your throat mike and ear piece. Take the lower house tunnel to the barn, come out through the barn door. Harry and I will go out the back door to either side of the house."

"Got it." She tossed off her towel and immediately began dressing. Grabbing his clothes, coms, and Glock, Steel ran down the hallway to Harry's room. He knocked once, then opened the door. Harry was already swinging his legs out of bed in the darkened room—his phone received the same text alerts that Steel and Christie did on theirs.

Steel talked fast, while pulling on his jeans and shirt. "Christie's taking the tunnel to the barn. I'll go out the back, into the woods on the north side. You go out back and take the south corner of the house near the barn. Wear coms." He put on his own coms.

"Right behind you." Harry was already pulling on his jeans.

Steel ran back to the wide stairway. Hanging onto the left side railing, he took the open-backed steps down three at a time to the spacious living room. The high ceiling interior was rough-framed in cedar, with oak and mahogany blended in. It was dark, but he didn't turn on any lights.

His two dogs, Lacy and Spinner, were lying in the center of the living room on the rug there, and did little more than raise their heads to look at him.

Rounding the bottom of the stairs, he ran across the small throw rugs to the back door, pulled on his boots, grabbed his jacket off the hook, and slipped outside into the cold air. Just before he shut the door, he heard footsteps coming down the stairs. Christie.

Heading right, Steel ran along the back of the house. Forest grew close to the house on all sides. At the rear corner he ran the twenty feet across open lawn to the trees and another ten feet into the forest. Remaining inside the tree line, he ran east parallel with the side of the house, stopping when he was across from the circular end of the driveway where his Jeep, Harry's red pickup, and Christie's green Jaguar were parked.

The van wasn't in sight yet. Near the house stood a giant sycamore, and from one of its lower branches hung a tree swing. Making a quick decision, Steel ran out of the trees and across the open ground to the sycamore. It provided good cover for him and would give him a better angle on the van. In seconds headlights appeared down the driveway, and in moments a vehicle stopped at the entrance to the driveway circle. The van's engine was still running with its headlights on.

Steel whispered, "Remain out of sight. Watch your six. Prepare to exit to the barn if we have to." He worried other men might have breached his perimeter security in other areas and the van occupants were waiting for those operatives to signal they had arrived. He realized if operatives came in behind him, he would be an easy target. He had to assume the van driver or passengers had night vision so he didn't peek at them.

He didn't see Harry at the south corner of the house, but assumed he was out of sight. Christie exited the steel barn door, which was the size of a house door and faced west. She was twenty feet ahead of the van, but also remained out of sight, her gun in both hands.

The large, rectangular red barn ran east-west. Built more like a bunker, it had a rounded roof, steel siding, and no windows. If more operatives came at them, they would make a run for the barn. Inside he had more weapons and hidden tunnel exits for escape.

Steel didn't want to wait any longer. Christie was closest to the van so he whispered, "Take out the driver's side headlight, Christie."

He knelt as she did, ready to take out the passenger headlight, but the van lurched forward into the drive. "Hold, Christie."

Steel waited, watching as the van drove up parallel to the house, just before the front door, and stopped. The white van had a sliding side door and rear doors, but no side or rear windows.

The passenger door opened, and a woman with long hair got out. At first Steel thought it was Emilia. But the woman was shorter and curvier, and wore a bulkier jacket and short boots.

Steel waited, but the van's rear doors didn't open. The woman walked up to the front door and hit the doorbell several times, and then knocked loudly. After a minute she turned to the van and raised her palms up questioningly.

Steel rose and walked forward, gun up and aimed. The woman saw him, but instead of looking worried she put her hands on her hips.

"Dad said you were a paranoid ex-military type. Keep your trigger finger steady, will ya?"

"Who's your father?" Steel lowered his gun a little.

"It's me, Steel. Mark Lerkin."

The deep voice came from the van's cab. Steel lowered his gun all the way. "We're good everyone. Guns down." He walked to the passenger door, still holding his gun. When he peeked around the door and saw his friend, he finally put his gun away. There was no one else in the van.

Lerkin was six-three and still looked strong, even though he was wheelchair bound. The car steering wheel had a hand brake and accelerator. Dressed in jeans and a T-shirt, Lerkin had short, black hair and a short, trimmed beard on his ebony face.

His voice warm, Steel said, “It’s been a long time, Mark.”

“Way too long, Jack. I’m sorry to come so late, but I need help.”

“What’s wrong?” Steel heard the stress in Lerkin’s voice.

Christie arrived at Steel’s side, while Harry talked to the woman.

Lerkin flicked a finger to the woman standing at the front door. “My daughter, Katterine, has an ex that’s stalking her, and she could use someplace to disappear for a while.” He paused. “I found out you were in the protection business and wondered if you could help Kat out. I could take care of her, but I’m limited.”

Steel had given Lerkin his address years ago. He didn’t hesitate. “I can do that. Do we have to worry about an attack tonight?”

Lerkin shook his head. “Absolutely not.”

Everyone was dead on their feet so Steel decided to sort out information in the morning. After quick introductions, Kat took the other spare bedroom on the second floor, and they made a bed on the sofa in the living room for Lerkin. Everyone was settled in a half-hour.

Steel was happy to just get back to his bedroom.

As she undressed, Christie asked, “What did Lerkin do for you that was so amazing?”

Steel threw off his clothes and wearily crawled into bed. “I was wounded in Afghanistan and he came back on his own and dragged me out of some bad country that the Taliban was holding. I’m alive because of him. That risk also cost him a bullet that paralyzed him from the waist down.”

Christie slipped into bed and whispered, “Then he’s my new best friend too.”

With bleary eyes they curled up with each other in bed. Christie fell asleep almost immediately in Steel's arms.

Just before he drifted off, Steel considered Jiri Moeller—the man on the phone—the man who had killed General Morris. Jiri could extend his threats to his ex-wife, Carol, and his daughter, Rachel. Rachel and Carol were visiting Carol's parents, so he thought they would be safe for the time being. But if Jiri learned his identity, he might have to move Carol and Rachel someplace else.

Too many unknowns, too few answers. And ten men dead already. Even if M4N was a big organization, losing ten good operatives was going to hurt. Also if Jiri was on the same timetable as the phone dates they had found, Emilia was probably right—he wouldn't be able to come at them for a while. Steel hoped to meet Jiri in Alaska and end it there.

Jiri didn't feel like someone who would back down. And Steel wouldn't stop until he had justice for General Morris. He owed Morris a debt for keeping their names safe, and for promising to keep the general safe and failing to do so. He decided two immovable forces were about to collide.

CHAPTER 14

DANIEL BAKER DIDN'T PARTICULARLY like Paul Franks, but the man was CEO of one of the largest defense contractor companies in the world, so he appreciated the man's role in his own agenda. They were meeting at a Washington D.C. dog park. Saturday morning.

Baker refused to meet Franks officially one-on-one in his or Franks' office, and avoided communicating through texts or phone calls. Nothing traceable for evidence, should things fall apart. His experience in the CIA had taught him that—never assume anything was safe and always assume the worst could happen. They had met once, set everything up, and this event was on the schedule. Meet at the dog park on evenings and early on Saturday and Sunday mornings. If there was anything to talk about, they would wander toward each other and stand shoulder to shoulder while their dogs ran. If anything was an emergency, they both had burner phones to call.

Baker had a pit bull—Max. Max never backed down to any dog. Franks had a German Shepherd named Wolf. Baker swore Wolf looked more wolf than Shepherd. Amazingly the two dogs hit it off, as if they knew they were the tough guys on the block, and spent their time running and dominating the other dogs.

Baker slowly made his way toward Franks, all the while watching Max and Wolf chase each other in the fenced dog run. Franks was five-eleven, so they were about the same height, but

Franks was ten years younger than Baker's sixty. Franks was also slowly moving toward him, watching the dogs and smiling. That annoyed Baker a little, Franks' constant smile.

Baker had a solid face and graying hair, but Franks was leaner, and his blue eyes and blond hair made him look younger. Baker had more wrinkles due to age and stress—past CIA employment was mostly responsible for the stress. His current position of National Security Advisor was actually less stressful. He thought that was because he had more control over what he did and what he wanted to have happen.

He was soon shoulder to shoulder with Franks, both staring at the dogs and talking softly to keep their conversation private from the few other dog owners standing nearby.

Franks said, "Three down. Three to go. Tragic about General Morris, wasn't it?"

"I heard about his death from contacts in the FBI. Very sad affair. But no one is buying the cartel retribution charade. That was sloppy." Baker kept his features calm. "Any other concerns?"

Franks clapped his hands to get Wolf's attention for a second, and then said, "Run, boy!"

Wolf ran, Max followed.

Franks whispered, "Small hiccup. You were right. Someone tried to protect Morris. They failed, but took out ten on our side. We don't know who it was."

"Ten?" Baker instantly felt wary, as if he'd seen a cobra near his feet. But he kept himself under control. Earlier in the week, General Morris had met with him to tell him his theory for the deaths of Secretary of Defense Marv Vonders and Senator Seldman, the ranking senator on the Senate Intelligence Committee.

And last night General Morris had called Baker from the hotel where he was staying. Baker had told Morris that he had new intel and wanted to see him immediately. Morris had given Baker the hotel address, which he immediately passed on to

Franks via a burner phone. Franks had passed the intel on to the organization he had hired.

Baker didn't like the complications. "You said this organization was good."

"The best. They have a no-fail policy or your money back." Franks squatted by the fence as Wolf came up, wagging his tail. Max was beside Wolf, looking happy. "How are you boy, huh?"

Baker didn't like Frank's cheery attitude. The man was arrogant, probably assuming money and position made him free of jail and other serious things. Baker knew better. Anyone could take a fall. "Does their no-fail policy include cleaning up their mess? They lost ten men to unknowns who might now be on to us."

"Absolutely." Franks stood. "They said not to worry. They'll handle everything. But..." He paused.

"But what?"

Franks said evenly, "You knew General Morris. Had a relationship with him. He must have thought you were a friend to call you. And yet you betrayed him."

Baker felt anger rising in chest. "State your point."

Franks smiled thinly. "Two points. One, it makes me wonder if you might betray me. So I've taken precautions, just to let you know. Should anything happen to me, you will go down hard."

"That goes both ways, Franks." Baker was more than annoyed. "We're in this together to the end, so let's stop the nonsense and get on with it."

Franks whistled to Wolf, who was running across the park. "Do you know who General Morris would have hired in the protection arena? Maybe someone highly skilled who worked under Morris in intelligence?"

Baker had learned long ago that you didn't give anyone more information than necessary that would implicate yourself. And Franks would be angry if he found out Baker's connection to Jack Steel. "No idea. But your organization, if they're as good as you say they are, should be able to figure it out." He clapped his hands, and Max ran to the fence.

"Do you think a pit bull or a German Shepherd would win in a fight?" Franks asked cheerfully.

Baker knew Franks was baiting him, and the question about the dog fight was an analogy for them. "Pit bulls are slightly more aggressive and dangerous. It would be a mistake to underestimate them." He leashed Max quickly and left without looking back.

Things were too loose. At least he had no contact with the organization Franks had hired; thus there was nothing that led back to him. Only Franks. And he had a plan for Franks if things got out of hand. But he was so close to his objective that he had to let things play out.

He knew General Morris had hired Jack Steel to protect him, so once Steel was handled everything would be okay. Still, he couldn't stop the nagging thoughts of the loose end that Steel presented.

He had known General Morris for ten years, and they had many talks, dinners, and discussions on world security. But Baker had kept an emotional distance inside, even if he had projected a more involved appearance to Morris. It had resulted in success when Morris had called him last night. Their whole relationship had paid itself off with that one call.

He decided he needed a backup plan to get rid of Steel. He thought about that. If ten men had failed, he needed a different approach. He would call his contact at the CIA. Hire an experienced assassin. They could take out anyone, since you never saw them coming.

CHAPTER 15

COLONEL JEFFRIES KEPT HIS voice level, but his disgust was obvious. "An anonymous caller sent a tip to police. General Morris was found dead in a warehouse district in Richmond, Virginia. Multiple machete strikes, with cocaine found sprinkled over his body. Last night in Morris' home they found three dead men carrying machetes and cocaine, another dead man in the street, but they didn't have tattoos and are not part of MS-13.

"Army Criminal Investigation Command doesn't believe Morris' death had anything to do with the cartel business five months ago. It looks like someone was trying to hide what the murder was really about. CID checked Morris' cell phone record. He made a call earlier in the evening, but it looks like it was to a burner phone so that's a dead end."

Steel had to shove down his guilt and anger over Morris' death, and how he had died. He saw the same tension on Christie's and Harry's faces. His cell phone was on speaker and they were all standing near the virtual reality station in his barn. Steel had called Jeffries.

Jeffries asked, "Were you at General Morris' house last night, Steel?"

Steel glanced at Christie and Harry, but they only shrugged.

"Yes." Steel felt he couldn't hold back. He told Jeffries everything, and paused to let the colonel take it all in.

Colonel Jeffries was silent for a few moments. "That's a hell of a story. Anything else?"

"I took a drive this morning to the forest site where we killed six of their operatives." Steel had already informed Christie and Harry. "The bodies were all gone. I don't think M4N has that kind of ability, at least not in Virginia, so I'm assuming Emilia is CIA and they cleaned it up."

"Anything else?" persisted Jeffries.

Christie said, "One of the men we killed had four latitude longitude locations with dates on his phone—the first was for General Morris' house last night. We think there might be three more targets, but we don't know who, just the locations and dates."

Steel added, "General Morris had to have called someone higher up in the government."

"Almighty." Jeffries was quiet for a moment. "So we can't trust anyone."

Christie asked, "Do you have any contacts in the CIA that can verify Emilia's story? She's Puerto Rican and I'm sending her photo now, along with the photos of the men we killed at Morris' house."

Jeffries was silent for a moment. "If the CIA is using M4N it's probably off the books and micromanaged by a very small group of people. I have one contact I can trust, but don't expect anything. I'll share Emilia's photo."

"If Emilia is CIA, and they are involved, then what?" asked Steel.

Jeffries voice hardened. "Screw the CIA. If they let one of our own die without taking down the killer, we don't owe them anything." The colonel paused. "Alright. What are you going to do, Steel?"

"We fly out at seven p.m. today and arrive at Fairbanks at ten p.m. Alaskan time. That gives us a day to find the next target." Steel kept his voice level. "We need to find out who General

Morris might have called that has a name beginning with B, and who the target might be in Alaska. Anyone who had a connection to the acting Secretary of Defense Marv Vonders, Senator Seldman on the Senate Intelligence Committee, or General Morris. Barring that, anyone important in the government. We don't know what they all have in common yet."

"I'll check out everyone I can." Colonel Jeffries paused. "I can't run interference for you with the law if you get yourself into a situation in Alaska."

"Understood." Steel didn't like the lack of legal cover, but he had operated without it before.

"That said," continued Jeffries, "I want these SOBs taken down, Steel. If we find out who's behind it, you'll have whatever protection and help I can give you."

***

Steel decided to work out on the virtual reality station. The large padded platform took up the front third of the barn and sensors in the barn allowed room-scale tracking. A wireless motion-tracking controller and full-body haptic suit simulated pain, temperature, uneven surfaces, and inclines. Boots, gloves, a head piece, weighted pistol, and goggles completed the sensory input.

Blackhood Ops had developed the VR program and Steel had convinced them to let him use it at home. He still used the VR equipment obsessively to develop his razor-sharp skills. For two hours he used Brazilian jiu-jitsu, kung fu, and Special Forces techniques on several attackers, increasing the difficulty up to a half-dozen assailants.

At the end of it, sweating and feeling loose, he took off the goggles, showered, and slipped into his sensory deprivation tank. He still enjoyed the privacy and alone time in it. And the silence allowed him to consider things.

Emilia's comments to him felt off. Something wasn't quite right. But when he went over their conversation, he couldn't find what it was. In the end he decided he just couldn't trust her for now. He also realized he was under stress. Harry had almost died.

Christie hadn't said anything, but after Emilia had left, he had caught Christie glancing repeatedly at Harry. He didn't know what to do about that. They had all talked about accepting the risks, but he had made an internal decision to remain cautious on the assignments he chose. Then General Morris had come to him, and it seemed like a perfect, safe way to start back in on protection assignments for Greensave. That idea was blown to hell.

***

They sat in the large dining room adjacent to the living room, around the table that seated a dozen. Kat and Lerkin had made breakfast—buckwheat blueberry pancakes, eggs, and hash browns. Kat served everything on the table. Lerkin wheeled himself from the kitchen to one end of the table. His wheelchair was manually powered. He and Kat had insisted they do work to help out. Steel appreciated that.

Lacy and Spinner lounged on the living room oak floor, soaking in the sunlight coming through the large front windows. The two dogs had already been out for a run with Christie and him in the morning.

Spinner, a chocolate lab, and Lacy, a golden retriever, had both taken to Lerkin and Kat—who had spent time brushing them and petting them in the morning. Steel took it as a good sign. Both dogs rarely barked and were friendly to a fault with everyone. Steel didn't rely on them as guard dogs—more like a friendly welcoming committee.

Steel regarded Kat. Cute and twenty-five, she was curvy but not overweight. A light-skinned mix—Lerkin's wife had been Caucasian. Kat wore ripped jeans and a black sweater over a white tee. Her curly hair was a mix of brown and black, but didn't look dyed, and she had a vulnerable look in her large brown eyes. As if she'd been through a tough stretch.

Lerkin had also been quiet this morning and appeared weary. His black hair was graying and his fifty years looked more like sixty. Steel remembered how much worry his own daughter had caused him when she went missing for two years. Lerkin's wife had also died due to cancer five years ago, and Steel hadn't kept in touch. He was glad his friend had come to him. From what he recalled, Lerkin was independent. Having to ask for help must have been hard for him. Steel didn't want to make it any harder.

Food was passed around and they ate in silence until Harry said, "Good grub, Mark and Kat. You can cook for me any day." He smiled at them, and Lerkin returned a quick fading smile.

Kat smiled too, but Steel noted pain of some sort behind it.

"Love the buckwheat cakes." Christie smiled. "Do you two cook a lot together?"

Lerkin and Kat glanced at each other, and Lerkin cleared his throat. "We haven't seen each for five years so we're kind of getting reacquainted." He reached a hand to cover Kat's. "I'm glad," he said softly.

"I am too, Dad." Kat glanced at him, and then Christie. "I was a real pain in the butt after Mom died, and I ran off to find myself." She looked at her plate and murmured, "I screwed up in marrying this guy."

"We all make mistakes," Christie said firmly.

Steel said, "We have to go away for a few days. I'll give you my cell number, Lerkin." He had thought about it, and decided after last night that he couldn't afford to leave Harry or Christie behind. He didn't know how many adversaries they would be facing in Alaska, but he already knew they would be elite operatives. Besides, he doubted either Harry or Christie would agree to stay back anyway.

Lerkin put his fork down and nodded. "We'll get a hotel in Richmond, Steel, so no worries."

"Did either of you tell anyone where you were going or who I was?" Steel looked at Kat and Lerkin.

Lerkin shook his head. "I made Kat give me her phone before we headed out here from Las Vegas, and I dumped it into a trash can."

Kat frowned at him. "You didn't tell me that, Dad."

He shrugged. "Phones can be tracked and I didn't want to bring anyone dangerous into a friend's life."

Kat sighed. "Okay, I can live with that."

Lerkin continued. "I didn't give Kat your name or address until we drove in. She had no idea where we were going and made no calls, sent no texts, no emails." He gave a wan smile. "Security first. I remember."

"Perfect. You always were careful, Lerkin." Steel gazed at Kat. "Tell me about your ex."

"His name is Ryan Randall." Kat lowered her eyes, her voice soft. "He lives in northern Utah. He owns a gun shop and online store. We're not officially divorced yet. After the last time he hit me, I just ran. I didn't really have anywhere to go, so I went back to Dad." She glanced at Lerkin, before looking at Steel again. "I thought I knew Ryan when I married him, but I found out that he hung around with a group that scared me. I was young, stupid, and naïve. Believed I was in love."

Christie said, "Did you ever run away before?"

Kat shook her head.

"Why do you think Randall is chasing you?" asked Steel.

"He called me nonstop after I ran." Kat wiped moist eyes. "He said he would never stop looking for me. He told me that wives should never leave their husbands."

"You don't have to worry about him anymore." Christie's eyes narrowed. "We'll take care of him, and keep you safe until we do."

Steel looked at Lerkin and Kat. "While we're gone, you can stay here." He was aware of Christie giving him a sharp glance, and Harry raised his eyebrows. But neither of them said anything. "I trust you, Lerkin. But there are a few conditions."

Lerkin's face looked strained, but he nodded. "Whatever you need, my friend."

Steel relaxed. "Good. I need you both to promise me now, no calls, no texts, and no emails to anyone, absolutely no one, until I get back."

Kat shrugged, her voice soft. “I’m just glad to have someplace safe to rest, so I’ll do whatever you need, Jack. Thank you for putting us up. I appreciate it.”

As she gazed at him, Steel didn’t detect any signals of lying or stress in her face, eyes, or body language. He believed her.

“We’ll do it, Steel. What else?” Lerkin stared at him.

“Stay on the property. There’s enough supplies and food for a week at least. I’ve got a security system I’ll show you both how to use so that you’ll know if anyone shows up. You can lock yourself in the barn if need be. It’s fortified, but if you’re in danger, call the police. No one can break into the barn fast, and I have weapons there.” Steel wouldn’t show Lerkin or Kat the underground tunnel system. Only he, Christie, and Harry knew about that.

Lerkin nodded slowly. “You got it, Steel.” He looked down. “I appreciate it. It’s been hard for a while so it’s good to have someone to turn to for help.” He looked up. “I haven’t had a good friend in a long time.”

“You can always turn to me.” Steel’s voice softened. “I’m glad to pay a debt that I’ve owed you for a long time, Lerkin.”

“Plus you get to take care of Lacy and Spinner.” Christie smiled. “So it’s a win-win for all of us.”

“I love the dogs.” Kat glanced at them, her eyes shining.

Lacy and Spinner both raised their heads off the floor to look at her, tails wagging.

Harry clapped his hands together softly. “Pass me some more of that food, will you, Christie?”

Steel eyed Lerkin. He detected something beneath the surface of his friend’s eyes. But the debt he owed him pushed him to let it go. Lerkin had a lot to be worried about, and he didn’t feel like piling on more pressure now.

CHAPTER 16

ZEUS SAT IN THE easy chair in front of Ritchie's desk, waiting patiently. He wore his usual denim shirt, jeans, and tennis shoes. His clean-cut dark hair matched his olive skin tone.

Ritchie, on the other hand, had his five-eleven frame covered with a black suit, his black hair swept back, also clean-cut. It made Zeus a little self-conscious and he straightened his denim shirt and shifted his six-foot-five frame upright.

Mykey sat in the other easy chair next to Zeus. Not quite as big as Zeus, Mykey wore black slacks, a black pullover, and his dark hair hung down to his shoulders. Solid face. Rock solid body. An Eastern European who had grown up on the streets and studied boxing—a past Golden Glove boxer—along with krav maga and ju jitsu.

Mykey had quick hands and he was very inventive and spontaneous in fights. Brutal. Zeus had watched Mykey take on five martial arts guys once—he obliterated them. The man was scary. Zeus had never lost a fight either, but he wasn't in Mykey's league. His own background included college wrestling and Aikido.

Usually Zeus worked alone on collections, so he wondered why Mykey was here. The few times he and Mikey had collaborated, it had been to go up against a group of guys. Mykey usually did the rough stuff, and Zeus just made sure no one else interfered. Men stared at his size and it was usually enough to dissuade them from trying anything.

Also it was a Saturday. Noon. Ritchie liked to keep business limited to weekdays so his collection people had the weekends off. Zeus at one time had found that amusing. Now he questioned why they had been called in. More than that, he had planned to tell Ritchie he was through with working for him, but he had decided to do it on Monday, and alone, not with Mykey here. He would wait until Mykey left, and then tell Ritchie he was finished. He had waited for nearly two and a half years to quit. He couldn't wait to walk out of Ritchie's office, knowing he was finally done.

Ritchie hung up the phone. "I got a job for you two. One week."

Zeus shrugged. He didn't want to be rude and anger Ritchie so he pretended to be interested. "I'm listening."

He waited. In his experience it was better to let Ritchie talk and not ask questions. Zeus' family were all talkers. He liked to talk too, but three years of working for Ritchie had made him quieter. At twenty-five sometimes he felt like fifty-five. Ritchie was forty-five, but seemed more exuberant. Mykey was thirty-five and always looked calm, but Zeus knew he could explode into violence.

"We're taking a trip." Mykey sounded certain and eager.

Ritchie nodded. "Five days of driving roundtrip. I don't want you flying because you might need to bring them back in our vehicle." He tossed a photo across the desk. "His name is Lerkin. That's him and his daughter, Kat. Lerkin owes me sixty thousand plus interest, so a hundred K. Gambling loser."

Zeus picked up the photo. Lerkin looked like a lot of the gambling addicts that owed Ritchie money. Beaten down. Struggling with life. Although seeing a man in a wheelchair didn't make Zeus feel good. The woman was pretty. That didn't make him feel good either. He knew what Mykey would want to do to her. He passed the photo to Mykey.

Mykey took it, gave it a quick glance, and then tossed it on the desk. "Just collecting?"

Ritchie swiveled slightly in his chair. "Lerkin took his daughter to see a friend out east. He's going to ask the friend for the money he owes me."

Mykey nodded. "You want us to see if the friend will cough up the hundred K to protect Lerkin and his daughter."

Ritchie smiled. "If not, then I want you to bring Lerkin and his daughter back here. She can work off her father's debt."

Zeus considered all that. He didn't want to watch Mykey put a beating on a guy in a wheelchair, and he wasn't going to kidnap a woman. Usually people took one look at him—and Mykey—and decided it was better to pay their debts. He had never needed to pull his gun. A few times he had to hurt someone, but they were creeps that hurt others too so it felt justified to him.

Zeus already knew the answer to his question, but he forced himself to ask it anyway so he appeared interested. "And if they refuse to come back?"

Ritchie stopped smiling. "Then we'll have to take more serious action." He winked at Mykey. "Tell the daughter if she wants to help her father, we'll hire her to pay off his debt."

Zeus knew what that meant. Ritchie would force the daughter to work the street. Maybe drug her up first. That made him sick inside but he kept quiet. In a way Ritchie was much more dangerous than Mykey. Ritchie had people killed for unpaid debts, something Zeus hadn't found out about until after the first six months he had worked for Ritchie.

But originally he had agreed to work for Ritchie for three years. Ritchie took verbal agreements seriously and had made it clear that Zeus couldn't leave until his three years were up. If he went up against Ritchie, he would be on the run forever. Ritchie would probably send Mykey after him, or after someone in his family to force him to return.

Mykey leaned forward. "So if they refuse to return, we put a beating on them and bring them back anyway."

Ritchie wagged a finger at Zeus, smiling again. "I know what that big Greek heart of yours is doing, Zeus. You're thinking you can't hurt a guy in a wheelchair, and you don't want the girl working the street. Am I right?"

Zeus kept his face calm, but he lifted a few fingers an inch off the arm of the chair. "Yes."

Ritchie slapped the desk lightly. "I knew it!" He beamed at Mykey and then Zeus. "That's why I'm sending you with Mykey. You convince Lerkin's friend to shell out a hundred K and no one gets hurt, and no one has to come back. Mykey doesn't have to do a thing. Mykey is just insurance if they don't cooperate." He swiveled to the other side, looking at Zeus sideways. "I figure because you're decent you'll be motivated to find a way to make it work." He leaned forward on the desk. "I'm paying a bonus on this one. Five K to each of you. Any questions?"

Zeus knew Mykey didn't care how much he got paid. The man had saved a small fortune and could quit collecting for Ritchie anytime, but he enjoyed the job. The violence. And he was good at it.

"I'm happy." Mykey smiled.

Zeus didn't have to think about it. He didn't care about another gambling addict's debt. He had to get out.

He had first met Ritchie after beating up three of his security team in front of a club one night, when one of Ritchie's men had slapped a woman repeatedly. Zeus had been on spring break the last year of college, and had stepped in to protect the woman. Ritchie had found him the next day and offered him a lot of money to collect loans from people that owed him. Zeus had been tired of going to school as a history major and doing road construction, and impulsively had taken the job. He had wanted a new start in life. Something fresh. And Ritchie paid well.

But the novelty and money had quickly worn off. And after three years he was sick to his stomach of it. He had a lot of money saved, which had always been the plan—save up a large stake and get out. Finishing college and maybe opening up a restaurant now seemed like a dream life. He couldn't believe how stupid he had been to ever think collecting money for Ritchie would be a great idea.

He had been counting down the days to this moment for two and a half years. It's all he thought about day and night. Getting out. Getting a real life like normal people, away from the violence and sick people he interacted with every day.

He nodded, as if deliberating on it. After a few moments he sighed and said, "I think I'm out, Ritchie."

Ritchie sat back, his expression calm. "I'm not surprised. I've been waiting for you to say that. You don't have the heart for this kind of work. That's fair. We agreed on three years." He paused. "Would you rather I send Mykey alone after Lerkin and his daughter?"

Zeus swallowed. Mykey wouldn't hesitate to beat up a man in a wheelchair, and he would rape the daughter. It frustrated him that Ritchie was using his empathy for others against him.

Zeus glanced at Mykey.

Mykey shrugged, winking at Zeus "I don't care either way, kid. Up to you." He stood and stared down at Ritchie. "I'm ready, Ritchie."

Zeus was frustrated but didn't show it. Spending a week with Mykey felt like adding another lifetime on this job. It made him depressed just thinking about it. But he didn't want the woman raped.

"Do you know where they are?" asked Mykey.

Ritchie smiled. "I put a tracker on Lerkin's van." He swiveled to Zeus. "What do you say, Zeus? One more job. In or out?"

"In."

PART 2

OP: CHENA HOT SPRINGS RESORT

CHAPTER 17

STEEL SAT NEXT TO Christie, her hand in his. He liked that. Harry sat on the other side of Christie, texting Isabella. They were flying to Fairbanks, where they would pick up a rental SUV. The latitude and longitude of 65.0518° N, 146.0510° W led to the center of Chena Hot Springs Resort. Due to the cold winter weather and off-peak season, the resort had low occupancy and it had been easy to book rooms. Fairbanks had five feet of snow on the ground and minus fifty Fahrenheit overnight temps.

Steel was tense. Jiri was dangerous, and might be expecting them. And they couldn't trust that Emilia wouldn't warn him. But what bothered Steel was that he couldn't see a way to ease his tension over having Christie and Harry on Ops with him. They had lost their brother Dale on their last Op, and Steel's guilt over that had almost ended his relationship with Christie. Their family didn't blame him, but he wanted to find a way to make things safer for all of them.

He was excellent at problem solving, but this had stumped him for months and it had made his sleep restless much of the previous night. But as he sat there an idea finally came to him. Simple. So simple he was surprised he hadn't thought of it before. He needed to add operatives to his team so they held more advantages in Ops like these.

Christie's green eyes were aimed at his, and he asked, "What?"

She squeezed his hand. “We’ll be okay. You have to let it go.”

“I’m working on it.” He hesitated. “We could always find something else to do.” He glanced at her and Harry.

Harry looked up from his phone. “Steel, it makes me feel good to help people. I don’t want to do anything else.”

Christie stared at him. “Someone has to protect the innocent, and we have the skills to do it, Steel.”

He sighed. “Okay, just checking in. That’s how I feel too.” He paused. “But I thought maybe we should expand our team.”

“That’s not a bad idea.” She let go of his hand and studied her laptop. “Secretary of Defense Marv Vonders, Senator Seldman, and General Morris had one thing in common.”

Steel watched her, and Harry glanced at her too.

Christie continued, “They were all war doves.”

“So a war hawk is killing the doves?” whispered Harry. “That seems far-fetched.”

“Maybe.” Steel couldn’t see someone killing General Morris and the others over just that. It was too high risk. “You find anything on M4N or the Moeller brothers?”

She shook her head. “Nothing. M4N and Karbu and Jiri Moeller don’t exist on the internet. Colonel Jeffries is our best hope there.”

Not surprised, Steel considered that. His own identity was nonexistent on the internet due to past Blackhood Ops. It further supported that M4N and the Moeller brothers had CIA support.

Christie continued. “However I did run Ryan Randall, Kat’s ex. He hangs out with white nationalists. I found a blog with him on it. Spewing stuff about taking back the country from the increasing brown horde.”

Steel frowned. “Why would he marry a black woman then? His own people would disown him.”

“Kat is light-skinned so maybe he got away with it. Forbidden fruit. Sex. And maybe he’s not a true believer.” Christie looked up from her computer. "Why did you give Lerkin the run of your place?"

He studied her. "You don't think it was wise."

She shrugged. "It just surprised me, given how careful you are with security."

"You mean obsessed." He smiled.

She batted her eyelashes at him. "I didn't say that, but since you did, yes, rabidly obsessed. Which is a good thing."

He cleared his throat. "I should have asked you first."

"It's your house, Steel." Her voice held no disappointment.

"It's our place," he said firmly.

She stared at him, a hint of a smile on her lips. "That's nice of you to say, but..."

"What if it was our place, not just mine?" he blurted. His words surprised him.

"What do you mean?" She reached a hand over to his.

Steel was aware of Harry looking up from his phone and glancing over at him. It embarrassed him that he was doing it like this. It wasn't what he had planned. But where Christie was concerned his emotions sometimes overrode his logic. "Well, I've thought about us a lot. What our future would be."

"I don't need promises, Steel." She rested her chin on her palm, her elbow on the armrest as she stared at him.

That made him pause and he wasn't sure what she was saying. "So you don't want any commitment?"

"Are you asking me?" Her voice was neutral.

This was harder than he thought it would be and felt clumsy, but he didn't see any way to recover now. "Would that make you happy?"

She rolled her eyes, released his hand, and leaned back. "Tell me about Lerkin."

Sighing, he didn't know what to make of her reaction. He leaned back too. "Lerkin was like a brother for the years I was in Afghanistan. I trust him. And what can he do to the place anyway? He needed help."

"I'm glad you trust some people, Steel. Otherwise we probably wouldn't be here together. Trust, honesty, and sincerity." She leaned in and kissed his cheek.

"If you give trust out, people can rise up to it." He glanced at her. "You picked up that something was bothering Lerkin."

"What do you think it was?" she asked.

"His daughter. I was stressed out of my mind when Rachel was missing for two years. He's worried about Kat. He knows a creep is hunting her, and he also feels guilty coming to me for help."

Christie nodded. "That sounds plausible." She glanced at him. "You're pretty insightful about people, but you need some virtual reality training in relationships."

"Wonderful." He felt even more confused about what she was trying to tell him.

"You know what I'm worried about?" Harry looked up from his phone. "Isabella wants us to pay for her family to come to the wedding, and she's been adding other items to the list. It's getting expensive."

"Elope. Vegas or Bali." Christie smiled. "Then come back for a big celebration."

Harry stared at her with wide eyes. "Isabella won't do it. She thinks it's not fair to her family."

Christie chuckled. "Good luck, little brother. You *are* marrying her whole family in a sense."

Steel thought about that. If he offered Christie a ring, and he became part of her family, how would they react to him if she got seriously hurt? Maybe she was thinking the same thing. He had never considered that she might say no to marriage. That made him wonder about their relationship. Maybe he was the one that wanted marriage.

He exhaled. One step at a time. Find a murderer first and kill him. At least that felt clear.

CHAPTER 18

THEY LANDED IN FAIRBANKS at ten p.m. The largest city in the interior region of Alaska, Fairbanks still only had about thirty-three thousand residents.

Before they left the terminal, they put on more winter gear in the restrooms. Brown parkas with snorkel hoods, thick-soled white boots, wool socks, thermal underwear, insulated snow pants, thermal gloves inside of fleece-lined Gore-Tex chopper mitts that covered their wrists, goggles, and wool pullover face masks.

It was minus thirty Fahrenheit already, heading to minus fifty, and the wind was gusting at thirty miles per hour. Minus eighty windchill. Frigid. Even with the extra clothing, Steel felt the chill in the air. They had good gear, but remaining out for any length of time would still pose a risk for hypothermia. Still, he didn't mind the cold when he could dress for it. And if they became active, body heat would be enough to provide comfort.

They had a rental black SUV reserved, and threw their luggage and weapon cases in the back. Open and conceal carry was legal in Alaska, with no firearms registration and no permit required to purchase firearms. Still, Steel didn't want to advertise their presence with guns on their hips.

They had an hour drive to Chena Hot Springs Resort, and he decided it was safer to get a hotel in town for the night and leave early in the morning. They were booked at Pike's Landing Hotel across the street from the airport. Harry drove, white knuckling it as the wind pushed against the SUV. Blowing snow reduced visibility to five feet in front of their headlights. They were forced to creep along, turning a five-minute drive into twenty. They arrived at eleven p.m. and used the extension cord from the car rental office to plug their SUV into an outside outlet at the hotel. They booked two rooms and crashed at midnight, which was four a.m. Richmond, Virginia time. They all were exhausted.

Up at eight a.m., they dressed and quickly made their way to the hotel's hot breakfast buffet. Steel was already scanning everyone in the dining area, and everyone they saw in the hotel. He noted Christie and Harry doing the same thing. His tension ramped up. They ate a quick breakfast, with plenty of calories for the waiting cold.

While Christie used the restroom, Steel looked at Harry. "Advice?"

Harry smiled. "Christie always did like blunt. Do you want to marry her, Steel?"

He thought on that. He had put so much internal focus on her feelings that he had shoved his feelings aside. "More than anything I've wanted in a long time."

"Then you'll have to say so."

Steel grunted. "How did you ask Isabella?"

"We were cooking dinner one night, and I put a rose on her plate while she was in the kitchen. When she came out, I knelt down near her chair and asked her."

Steel had to admit that sounded miles superior than his blunder. "You're better than me at this."

"I did it once before with my first wife so I had practice." Harry shrugged. "Isabella told me the kneeling was overkill, but it was funny and made it romantic." He eyed Steel. "How did you ask your ex, Carol, to marry you?"

Steel felt his cheeks warm. "She asked me." He shrugged. "She's an aggressive lawyer and felt I was too passive."

Harry winked. "Do you want to practice on me?"

Steel smiled. "That's overkill too, but I appreciate the advice, Harry."

"Hey, glad to help. You two are a perfect match, Steel. You know she'll say yes."

Steel regarded him, realizing Christie's brother was more certain of his sister's interest and answer than he was. "The plane approach was pretty clumsy."

"No kidding." Harry rolled his eyes. "You were trying to be careful, not pressure her. She probably thought it was cute and stupid."

Steel chuckled. "Thanks for that assessment."

"Anytime."

Christie arrived and they headed out.

They piled into the SUV. Harry would drive again, and he let the vehicle warm up while he brushed snow off the windshield and windows. When the vehicle was half-thawed, Harry drove it slowly in the lot and backed it into a corner. He got out to scrape off more snow on the windows. From the back seat, Christie and Steel hurriedly transferred all their guns from the gun cases to their suitcases.

The temp was still minus forty and it was dark outside. Daylight ran from ten a.m. to three p.m. Steel thought that fact alone favored their movements, but also the enemy's. Finished, Harry drove, hunched over the wheel, carefully looking for moose, elk, or bear that might be crossing the road. Steel sat in front, Christie in back.

The wind had settled so the visibility provided by their headlights was much better than the previous night. After the SUV warmed up, they pushed back their parka hoods and took off their wool face masks.

On the way to Chena, Steel received a text from Colonel Jeffries. No confirmation on Emilia as CIA, and nothing useful from Jeffries' CIA contact—except that his contact agreed M4N had to be off the books. Black budget. That's how Steel's past Blackhood Ops had been run. Everything on a need-to-know basis. Jeffries did find out that the men they had killed at General Morris' house all had prison records with histories, except the one with the phone intel with the latitudes and longitudes. That man had no record anywhere.

Jeffries also gave them a useful name gathered from flight manifests and other queries. Senator Ash Tindren, chairman of the Senate Intelligence Committee, was already at Chena Hot Springs Resort for a two-day stay. Senator Tindren was an outdoor enthusiast and wanted to see the Aurora Borealis—Northern Lights. Jeffries hadn't found anyone else visiting the resort that seemed connected to General Morris or the other deaths. Senator Tindren didn't have any connection to Morris or any of the others either, but his presence felt too coincidental to Steel. He decided Tindren had to be the target.

Jeffries texted two more names. Daniel Baker, the National Security Advisor, and Bill Bishop, head of the CIA. Both men had contact with General Morris. Both also had names beginning with B. Steel couldn't see any connection between either of them and Morris that fit.

Christie had her laptop open, and said from the back seat, "Those are the only names I came up with too. But they both seemed a stretch for someone who would hire assassins. In addition, Daniel Baker and Bill Bishop are hawks. So is Senator Tindren. So the theory of doves being killed also doesn't fit if Tindren is the next target."

"It's doubtful General Morris called Senator Ash Tindren—no B in his name." Harry kept his eyes peeled on the road.

"Okay, we find Senator Tindren and set up a watch on him." Steel considered things. "We carry at all times and we stay on coms at all times."

Christie passed up her laptop, showing them a photo of Senator Tindren. Graying hair, average height and weight, sixty years old. "He's single, seems to have a new girlfriend every other month, and just broke up with someone. No children." She paused. "Don't you think M4N will want to make Tindren's death look like an accident up here? Or at least not draw attention to it? No gunshots. They won't want a major investigation."

Steel considered that. "That favors us. But they broke that pattern with General Morris so we can't count on it. Maybe with Morris they decided an accidental death on a third major government figure would wear thin and look too suspicious. But I agree, they have more to gain by keeping it quiet and appearing to be accidental than having an outright murder investigation."

Steel was anxious to arrive at Chena. He had considered calling in protection for Senator Tindren, but then they would have to admit to at least four bodies. In addition, anyone else they contacted might take too long to respond, or might pass it up the channels to whoever had hired M4N. And they had little proof. It still seemed best they do this quietly on their own.

As they closed in on their destination, the sunrise began to shed more light on the snow-covered terrain. Hills and low mountain ranges appeared all around them. But the green conifer forest on both sides of the road remained thick and dark. Steel enjoyed the view.

At one point Harry had to stop the SUV to allow a moose to cross. Steel loved seeing the large animal close up. He snapped a photo to show his daughter Rachel at a later date.

It took an hour to reach the entrance to Chena Hot Springs Resort. Nestled in a valley surrounded by low mountains rising forty-four-hundred feet above it, Chena Resort's landscape and building rooftops were also covered in a layer of snow. The increasing sunlight first revealed eighty-plus dog houses south of the tree line bordering the road. Some of the dogs were standing outside of their houses already. Steel thought Rachel would love to take a dogsled trip up here. He would too.

The highway continued into the resort, past the Aurora Ice Museum, greenhouse, reindeer pen, and campgrounds just north of the road until they finally reached the resort buildings and lodges. They also passed an Everts Air Cargo Douglas DC-6A plane that was suspended twenty feet off the ground on three big pillars that looked like stilts. Apparently just a curiosity for visiting tourists.

Steel had read that the resort grew most of their restaurant food in their greenhouse, and geothermal and renewables powered the heating and electricity of the nearly fifty buildings. Solar heaters for their water, along with recycled plastics turned into fuel, made the Chena Resort almost a hundred percent independent of fossil fuels. The hot springs also provided geothermal energy. On another visit Steel would like to see more of it. Now he just wanted to find Senator Tindren.

He looked at Harry and Christie. "Finding Tindren is the priority. I'm assuming he'll be in Moose Lodge with us, but he might be in a cabin on his own. Anything else?"

"If someone isn't responding on coms, we assume they're talking to someone or in trouble. We give them a one-minute window to respond." Christie glanced at Harry. "Let's keep each other apprised of where we are so we can act quickly if need be."

"I like it, sis." Harry nodded.

"In this kind of cold, wear the wool face masks if you're running and breathe through your nose. Make it a short distance." Steel glanced at them. "We don't want lung damage."

They parked, put their hoods back up, pulled down their wool face masks, and grabbed their suitcases. It was a short walk to the Chena Hot Springs Resort restaurant, which was also used for check-ins. Once inside, they took off the face masks. A medium-sized building, it looked capable of seating fifty to sixty people, with a small bar at one end.

Steel pretended to look at the walls and décor, while glancing around at the few people present. Christie checked them in.

With the low occupancy, Steel expected it to be easy to find Tindren—and the enemy. The rustic, visible ceiling logs and *log-cabin* appearance of the bar-restaurant appealed to him. Wildlife paintings, rams' heads, and crossed paddles decorated the walls, along with many other wilderness objects that gave the place an outdoor feel.

The few people besides employees they encountered didn't stand out in any way.

In minutes they were outside again taking the few quick steps to the Moose Lodge. Snow crunched beneath their feet and the air was frigid.

Christie kicked some snow with her boot and looped her free arm around Steel's. "Just trying to blend in, dear."

He smiled at her. Her sense of humor, despite any situation they were in, helped ease his tension.

Their adjacent rooms were on the second floor. They were assigned an outdoor overnight plug-in for their SUV, but Steel hoped to be gone before they needed it.

Each room had two beds, a small table, dresser, bathroom, and eating table. Big windows. Comfortable and simple. The temperature was set in the sixties. Christie hadn't wanted one of the smaller cabins, given the current temps and the fact that the cabins came with outhouses, not bathrooms. Steel agreed. Not just an inconvenience, the outhouses also posed higher risk for an attack.

Harry entered his room, while Steel and Christie unloaded their gear in theirs. Steel loaded his Glock, Christie her SIG, and both strapped fixed-point knives to their ankles beneath their outerwear. Steel had brought a Browning Backlash dagger, slightly smaller and less bulky than his Marine Ka-Bar, while Christie strapped on her dagger. Steel wanted daggers up here. Smaller, thin, and easier to conceal, they could also pierce thick clothing and animal hides if need be.

The knives wouldn't be easy to get to fast but were a last resort backup. Steel still had his OTF Microtech knife in the back of his belt, but that would be even harder to dig out from under his gear. Christie had a mini OTF dagger in her belt too. She liked the idea of a hidden knife, and had asked him last year to get her a custom belt like his. So had Harry. Steel had also purchased one for his daughter, Rachel, which she loved. She seemed fully recovered from the kidnapping, but the hidden mini OTF knife in her belt gave her another sense of security.

"Hey, waterproof my back cut, honey." Christie pulled off her outer shirt and Lycra top, and pulled up her hair, while Steel dug out their first aid kit.

He pulled out large waterproof bandages, a few of which he had to cut the ends off so he would be able to apply them all the way across the wound. First he removed the butterfly bandages on the cut, and then he patted on the edges of the larger waterproof ones. "The wound is healing nicely."

He had read Chena Resort's information on the geothermal pool and they had discussed it before leaving home. Patrons were advised not to go into the pool with any cuts or sores, but Christie had argued that if they needed to find someone, the pool was an obvious place to look. Steel couldn't disagree.

He said, "You still shouldn't stay in long. The outdoor pool doesn't have chlorine and there could be some bacteria in it."

She pulled on her Lycra and top again. "I won't. Just a quick check. And I brought a swimsuit that covers my wound."

The guns went beneath their front zippered parkas in shoulder harnesses. In a minute Harry joined them and they put on coms and tested them.

Steel looked at Christie and Harry. "If we find our enemy targets, just observe. No contact. We can't assume they don't already have our photographs from Emilia. Let's see if we can find out Senator Tindren's schedule and where an attack might occur. Tonight at the Aurora Borealis event would be a likely place."

"We should remain together for a bit, Steel." Christie winked at him. "You know, couple out for a holiday, little brother not tagging along."

"Thank you for that, sis." Harry smiled. "I can live with it. Should be easy enough to walk the compound, talk to a few people. Especially if I'm on my own."

"We can check the front desk, see what excursions are occurring today, and get booked for the Aurora Borealis show tonight." Christie smiled at them. "I love this place already!" She patted Steel's arm. "I have to get into character. You should too."

Steel chuckled, but he couldn't help but feel wary as he looked at both of them. "All right, let's keep our timetable loose for now. Early dinner meetup in the lodge restaurant if nothing materializes by then. Find Senator Tindren, and alternate following him."

"What happens after we find Tindren?" Harry glanced at Steel and Christie. "We just let him hang like bait until the killers show up?"

"Emilia will be here and the CIA supposedly will intervene." Steel didn't trust her.

Christie pursed her lips. "And we already saw how the CIA handled General Morris."

Steel nodded. "I agree. If Senator Tindren dies here because we kept our mouths shut, that's on us."

Christie shrugged. "Why not give Senator Tindren a choice? He can stay or leave with us."

Steel considered it. "Alright. We'll talk to him as soon as we find him. In his room preferably or alone outside. Let's get his lodging verified."

"Let's let Harry leave first." Christie looked at her brother.

Harry nodded, winked, and left.

Christie grabbed Steel's coat on both sides and pulled him in for a kiss, which he didn't mind. Pulling back, she smiled at him. "Ready to hunt, dear?"

He smiled. "Ready." He almost broached the subject of the two of them again, but let it go. He wanted to be focused here at all times. And he didn't want to be clumsy a second time with Christie. His next attempt had to be thought out.

"Wait." Christie grabbed a small daypack and shoved her swimsuit into it. "Almost forgot."

They stepped out into the hallway, which was empty, and she took his gloved hand in hers. “We need to play the part, dear.”

“I don’t mind, honey.”

“When will we do another real vacation?” she asked.

He didn’t hesitate. “When this is over.”

“Good answer, Jack.”

He wondered where she would like to go for their honeymoon. That’s if she said *Yes* to his proposal.

CHAPTER 19

JIRI SAT IN HIS cabin with a cup of coffee, on coms with Gregory, Laks, and Emilia. They were early, prepared, and ready. Laks came over coms and said, “Three individuals arrived. Looks like a couple and tagalong relation. Suitcases.”

Jiri considered that. Amateurs often brought too much gear, and suitcases didn’t sound like professionals for the outdoors or his business. Tourists. But he wanted to be sure since Emilia had said their two teams had killed two of the protection agency’s operatives, which left three alive. “Laks, send full body photos to all of us. Emilia, see if you can match the threesome to who you fought earlier.”

“Will do,” she answered quickly.

The fact that he had lost two teams had enraged him when Emilia returned and reported it. Not only was that costly to the company, he knew Karbu would be furious. Worse, some of those men had been his friends for many years. Close relationships were difficult for him to build and took time, and overnight he had lost many.

Still, he had to stay on schedule now and finish the contract before he could seek revenge. He had underestimated the team General Morris had hired; they were elite. It made him more careful and more cautious.

He also still wasn’t sure of Emilia. She had a minor knife wound and bullet hole in her jacket. Nothing serious. Still, he couldn’t see her working for his brother Karbu and manufacturing those details. Nor could he come up with a reason for her to get their two teams killed. He considered the possibility that Emilia represented a past enemy, but didn't make sense either. M4N personnel worked like ghosts and were very anonymous in every contract they carried out. It was nearly impossible for any enemy to find them. Anything else logical stumped him for the moment.

Thus he had decided to take Emilia's story for what it was—a stupid, impulsive, and costly decision on his part that should never have happened. He should have sent the other teams off to their targets. His pride had taken over his decision-making. Now he would be forced to do the last three assassinations himself, and then go after whoever General Morris had hired. In a way that part excited him.

Emilia's voice returned over coms. "That could be them, Jiri. They all wore Lycra hoods, but the woman's build and size fits the one I fought."

Jiri straightened in his chair. If Emilia was right, his life just became much simpler. And his trust of Emilia was firmed up. "Okay, don't engage. Emilia, go to your room and stay out of sight until we're ready to move on the primary target."

"Will do," she answered in a whisper.

Jiri studied the photos. The couple looked real the way they were smiling at each other. Maybe it was an act. It would be risky to have someone you love with you on assignments like this. That made them vulnerable, and if true it made him curious how they handled it emotionally. The third man was powerfully built. All three looked fit. He had to remind himself they had taken down two of his elite crews without serious injury to themselves. That made them very dangerous. He couldn't afford to underestimate them again.

For a moment he vacillated on informing Karbu of any of this; at some point he had to anyway. And he wanted to know who these people were—names, backgrounds, and faces. Karbu could find out anything, if not through his own research, then through his CIA contact. He transmitted the photos to Karbu. A small protection agency operating in Virginia, with a woman and two men with possible ties to General Morris couldn't be that hard to identify.

It only took ten minutes and Karbu returned three names, along with three facial photos: Jack Steel, Christie Thorton, and Harry Thorton. Special Ops, ex-Army Intelligence, ex-Marine. Greensave Protection Agency. Jiri found their backgrounds impressive, but they must have had special training to take down his teams. He scanned a short summary the CIA had also sent to Karbu, but the report didn't talk about Steel's background training. Either the CIA didn't know it, or was unwilling to disclose more. He found it interesting that a brother and sister were working together. Not unlike he and Karbu in the past.

Karbu followed the information with a text, "Very skilled. Jack Steel also did highly classified black ops; information they will not release to me. That means specialized training and abilities. Be careful, brother. Assume they also have high-ranking contacts that will respond if you kill them."

Jiri felt vindicated in his assessment, and decided Christie Thorton was the optimal way to expose their weakness. Her brother Harry would be protective of her, and if Jack Steel was her lover, he would also be protective of her. That gave both men a disadvantage that he could exploit.

He gave instructions to his men, while hurriedly getting ready for what he had in mind.

CHAPTER 20

STEEL AND CHRISTIE WALKED downstairs and were quickly outside. They needed to visit the Activities Center—just north of Moose Lodge—to book events, but they headed east first.

Steel was glad to be outside again, given they were still wearing all their gear. The temp was twenty below, the windchill colder, but it was sunny, the snow bright. He wore sunglasses over his wool face mask, as did Christie.

They had their hoods up, but it was decent with the sunshine. Dressed like two Eskimos, they walked toward the pool building. Long and rectangular, it housed a heated pool, dressing rooms to shower, and provided the entrance to the outdoor geothermal pool for which Chena Hot Springs was famous. Boulders of various sizes surrounded the outdoor pool, and the melodious song of the American dipper filled the air. Steel had read that the gray wren-sized birds foraged in the stream near the outdoor pool that was used to cool the geothermal water.

Boulders and the pool building blocked any view of who might be in the pool, but they could see steam rising up from the water. Steel had read that the outdoor pool was about fifty feet wide by one-hundred-fifty in length.

Christie glanced at him. "Should I assess the pool now?"

"First sign us up for the Aurora Borealis event at the Activity Center." He wanted to be on that excursion no matter what.

Nighttime, isolated. Perfect for murder. "Then see if you can find out what else Senator Tindren is doing. I'll wait here in case he's here or arrives."

"On it." Christie strode away through a small stand of pines, heading toward the Activity Center. In fifteen minutes she returned, again looping her arm through his. He liked it there.

"I booked all three of us for the Aurora Viewing Tour. Nine-fifteen p.m. check-in. Five-hour tour."

"Great." He glanced at her.

Christie smiled. "The guy at the center was chatty and I found out Senator Tindren also booked a dogsled run late this afternoon so I booked us on that too. Two p.m. A sunset run."

"Perfect." He stared at the pool building. "Thoughts?"

Christie said, "I'm going into the hot springs, Steel. I can see who's in the building, and the outdoor pool, and get a read on everyone there."

He nodded. "Alright. I'll stay here in case Senator Tindren is already in the locker room and leaves while you're inside. Keep your coms on. Given your wound, make it a quick sweep in the geothermal pool."

She winked at him. "Back soon."

Harry's voice was a whisper on coms. "Copy all that. I'm at the dog kennels. I'm following a guy along the trail paralleling Monument Creek. Short, trimmed beard, dark hair."

***

Christie walked into the pool building. The enclosure still allowed a lot of light through the massive side windows. Warmer, she began unzipping her parka. A smiling young man sat at a small table in front of the locker room entrances. She showed him her room key, collected a towel, and went inside to change. Given what she was wearing, she wondered how much she could get into a locker.

Lockers cost fifty cents and were half-size. She had read that on the way up and had change. She opened two of them side by side. She was alone in the locker room, and discreetly threw her weapons into one locker and quickly shut it. The rest of her clothing went into the second locker. Pulling on her swimsuit, a one-piece with slits on the side, she wished Steel was going to join her in the outdoor pool. It would be fun. She stopped those thoughts. *Focus*.

"Almost out," she whispered into her coms. She only had ear coms this time. A pro in the pool might see them on her, but it was worth the risk given the attacks on them in Virginia. She tied her hair up, allowing it to cover her ears, but not wanting it to hang in the geothermal pool. Standing back a little from the spray, she took a quick shower.

Finished, she looked into one of the mirrors, liking what she saw—her body lean, hair pulled up. Cute. It was too bad Steel couldn't see her. She also made sure her swimsuit covered the new bandages. It did. She walked out. "Heading to the pool now."

She entered the indoor pool room, which was warmer. The pool looked inviting. A family of four lounged halfway down on one side, talking together. At the far end of the room a solitary individual was hunched up on a bench near one of the massive windows with a towel drooped over his head and body. It looked like an elderly person. Male or female, she couldn't tell.

She exited the pool room through a door that opened into the enclosed outdoor walkway. Windows, thin wood walls, and a cement floor that ran sixty feet down a slight incline in front of her before it turned sharply at the bottom. The air was frigid and the cement floor wasn't heated. A hose ran cold water over the cement—she guessed so it didn't ice up. Her feet were cold and she shivered.

Hurrying along the walkway, she turned at the end of the L-shaped ramp. In another half-dozen steps the walkway ended with an overhead heater in the ceiling blasting warm air downward. Then she was outside.

She blinked at the cold that assaulted her senses. The charm of the geothermal pool left her immediately. A twelve-foot-long cement ramp led down a gentle slope into the water.

The wind had erupted out of nowhere, blowing crystalline snow through the air and onto her skin. She was chilled in seconds. No. *Freezing.* The windchill took her breath away. She hustled down the ramp to the water and stepped in, quickly up to her chest.

One hundred and six degrees. It felt like salvation. Pebbles and sand formed the bottom and felt nice against the soles of her feet.

She bent her knees to sink down to her neck. The boulders and pool building blocked any view of Steel, otherwise she would have waved at him.

She knew he was worried. And she knew her humor lightened his load. They were all worried. She was just as freaked out about the possibility of Harry dying as Steel was about her. And brother Harry looked more tense than usual too. They were all on edge about each other.

She realized it then. PTSD. They hadn't fully moved past Dale's death. She and Harry mourned a brother they loved, and Steel still felt responsible for her brother's death. She would talk to them about that when this was over and they had a moment to breathe.

The water gave off a sulfur scent, but it wasn't horrible. The boulders that formed the shoreline were all covered in snow, many with icicles hanging down. Also the shoreline was irregular, with nooks and crannies that could hide someone, especially with the rising steam and blowing snow.

She decided she wouldn't stay in long. If something developed, Steel and Harry might need her out. She would find out who was in the pool and do it as quickly as possible. No patrons were visible from where she stood near the end of the ramp.

Walking through the water, she discreetly glanced at the shoreline and interior of the pool. Visibility was about a dozen feet. Thus she walked four yards from the shoreline, clockwise, which allowed her to see anyone the boulders hid, as well as being able to see anyone in the center of the pool.

Halfway around she spotted Senator Tindren standing ten feet from her. Eyes closed, he seemed to be enjoying himself. She assessed him. Five-eleven, graying hair, one-seventy pounds, lean.

"Senator Tindren is in the geothermal pool," she whispered.

"Copy that," said Steel.

"Roger that," replied Harry.

Along her walk, Christie spotted five other people in the chest-deep water. That surprised her, given the extreme cold. Three were men. Two of the men in the pool had their backs to her. The women were overweight and older.

The blowing snow glittered in the sunlight, landing on her face and hair, but the hot water kept her warm. With a few white clouds in the blue sky above, the rising steam and snow felt otherworldly.

The wind was still a bit much though, yet she didn't dunk down because she had read that freezing your hair at these temps wasn't healthy for it. Plus you could accidentally break off chunks of it. Not good for coms either. Nevertheless, her eyelashes soon felt frozen, as did the hair on her head. She was grateful that the water temperature made it pleasant for the rest of her body.

The gusting wind and snow reduced visibility even more, so she moved to within five feet of two of the men to view them. Neither seemed like potential enemies. One had a belly, and the other looked fifty—his age made him a stretch. The third man looked a youngish twenty.

"None of the men in here fits," she murmured. "And no Emilia."

"Good enough. If you're cold, get out, honey." Steel sounded empathetic.

"Okay, I'm almost finished. It's really not bad in here. What do you think the temp is?" She enjoyed talking to him.

"A very warm minus twenty Fahrenheit, with minus twenty-five-degree windchill." Steel chuckled.

***

Harry followed the shorter man down the trail nonchalantly, trying to appear as if he was out for a stroll. He decided to shadow the man for five minutes, and then head back. The short man walked briskly, hood up against the blowing snow. Visibility was shortening and Harry thought it would be easy for the average person to get lost in the woods in a situation like this.

However his family were hunters out of Montana, so he always knew the location of the sun, looked for trail markers, and made mental notes of details along the way.

In minutes Monument Creek appeared, paralleling the path. The cool water was a little above freezing, but snow and ice that had built up along the sides gave it a postcard beauty that Harry enjoyed. He'd read that the creek water was mixed with the geothermal water to cool the outdoor pool down to a hundred-and-six-degrees Fahrenheit.

The short guy disappeared around a curve in the trail, and Harry slowed a touch. The wind and crunch of his boots in the snow made it impossible to hear anyone ahead of him. He didn't want to run into the guy on the trail.

Before he reached the corner, something soft reached his ears, a touch of noise that didn't match the blowing wind or his boots against the snow. Spontaneously he went into a forward roll, rose to his knees, and turned. A man was swinging something. Not the short guy. He leaned back and avoided the blow. A short, thick stick.

The man kept coming, and Harry leaned sideways, dodging a knee to his jaw. He swung hard and fast at the man's thighs, waist, and crotch. He connected twice, but the man's clothing kept his blows from feeling like powerful landings.

The stick was swung at his head again, this time from an overhead blow. Harry ducked and launched his shoulder forward into the man's abdomen, knocking him down to his back. Climbing atop the gasping man, he finally had a better view of his attacker. A tall man. He glimpsed hair sticking out of the lower edge of the attacker's wool hood, near his neck. That was it.

A second man came at him from the side, kicking at him.

Harry rolled away, gasping, "Two men attacking me."

***

Christie stiffened over Harry's words. She had to get out. "Go, Steel. I'm almost out."

Steel quickly strode away. "Alright. Follow Senator Tindren if he leaves, else hang outside the main entrance."

"Will do." Christie quickly finished the circle. At the exit she had to force herself to step out of the water onto the ramp again. She was warm, but her body wasn't that overheated due to the limited minutes in the pool. Concern for Harry pushed her to move faster. She was surprised Jiri would attack them during the daytime.

The wind was still blowing hard, the crystalline snow in her face, and she wanted to be inside ASAP. Once out of the heated water, she hurried. Ice crystals pattered against her skin and swimsuit and she ducked her head against the wind. In a dozen steps she entered the bottom L of the walkway, past the heater at the end, already looking forward to the heat of the locker room. She made the turn, and ran into someone. Short quick punches pounded her stomach—she'd never been hit that hard or quick—knocking the air out of her immediately. Doubling over, she was unable to respond physically or speak.

She had no chance to murmur, struggle, or resist as someone shoved the side of their hip into her back and a strong arm locked around her neck and choked her out.

***

It startled Steel that the enemy would try a daytime assault against one of them, but the blowing snow along a solitary path made it viable. Concerned for Harry, he hurried across the compound. He had to rely on his memory of the resort layout because buildings weren't visible in the blowing snow until he was nearly on top of them.

He murmured, "Harry?"

No reply.

He was quickly past the Ice Museum and looked ahead for the path west. He guessed that Emilia had sold them out.

Yet if Jiri killed Harry, the police would be called and there would be an investigation. Jiri wouldn't want that. Thus Steel assumed Jiri wanted to injure Harry. Reduce their number to two. Jiri would rightly assume an injury wouldn't be enough for Steel to call in the police.

He unzipped his coat a little to be able to reach the Glock fast.

CHAPTER 21

WHEN HARRY ROLLED OFF the tall attacker, he swiped his gloved hand hard along the man's coat. He avoided taking the full force of the second attacker's kick, and his layers of clothing provided the same protection for him as it did for the enemy. The second man jumped over his companion lying in the path to pursue Harry. The man was agile and fast. But so was Harry.

He rolled once more along the path, sprung up to a crouch, and sidled sideways on the path at the same time to avoid an attack that never came. Blowing snow in the gusting wind made it a whiteout for a few seconds. He couldn't see more than a few feet in front of him.

Backing up farther, he unzipped his coat. Taking off his outer mitt, with his gloved hand he drew his Glock, holding it level with both hands. Carefully he eyed the path in all directions. The expected attack never came.

Slowly he sidled down the path, in the direction of the resort, keeping an eye west and east on the trail. The men had disappeared. Which way, he couldn't be sure. And he wasn't certain they wouldn't attack him again.

In a minute the gusts subsided a little, and he could see fifteen feet down the path in both directions. Empty. He hustled faster, still watching his six.

"Steel, they're gone. I'm good. Walking back toward the resort. Unsure of hostiles' location. Most likely they're exiting toward you."

***

Steel stopped on the pavement, his hand on his gun, peering into the snow. "I'm at the edge of the compound, Harry. Near the doghouses."

He didn't see anyone on the path or in a three-sixty view around him. The attack on Harry wasn't convincing. Or they had tried and failed, and had not wanted to risk injury. Harry was strong, fast, and skilled. They might have underestimated him.

He stood there for several minutes, waiting to see if the attackers would appear, but they didn't. Something didn't feel right. Perhaps they had bolted across the dog compound to a cabin or the Ice Museum.

He decided to regroup instead of wandering all over the resort in search of the men. "Harry, let's meet back at the pool building entrance."

"Roger that," replied Harry.

"Christie, are you outside yet?" Steel waited another minute for her to respond. "Christie?"

No response. That triggered something in him. Harry might have been a diversion. "Harry, I'm headed back to the outdoor geothermal pool."

Harry came back immediately. "A few minutes behind you, Steel."

Steel turned around, moving fast. It had been over five minutes since Christie had left the pool with no word from her. She might be taking a warm shower. A few minutes longer wasn't conclusive. Still.

The blowing snow slowed his return and it took a few minutes to reach the pool house. Along the way there was no sign of Christie, and she wasn't standing outside. At the pool building he immediately stepped inside and checked in. Forcing a smile at the young attendant, he asked, "Did you see my wife leave? Brunette-blond, checked in twenty minutes ago?"

The young man shook his head. "A man left, but that was it."

"Thank you." Steel grabbed a towel and quickly strode into the men's locker room. Empty. He hurried out into the pool area, spotting the exit to the outdoor geothermal pool.

Then it came to him. Emilia. She could have attacked Christie in the women's locker room. A family of four were wading in the indoor pool, but appeared oblivious to him.

Steel hustled to the women's locker room entrance, pausing there to call inside; "Excuse me, is anyone in here? Christie?"

No answer. He went in cautiously, in case a woman was showering and hadn't heard him. All empty. That stiffened his back.

Whirling, he ran out, and across the pool room to the door leading to the outer walkway. Pushing through the door, the cold walkway air surprised him. He estimated minus fifteen. But no windchill. In seconds he made the turn at the end of the L-shaped walkway. Just beyond the exit heater he saw Christie. Lying on her back on the ramp. Not moving. Snow crystals covered her skin and face. She lay like a white mannequin.

Scrambling out, Steel gripped his gun, but didn't pull it.

Senator Tindren was already walking up the ramp out of the water and knelt down beside Christie, touching her shoulder softly. Steel let his gun go as he knelt on Christie's other side. He touched her face. Cold.

Senator Tindren wasn't a doddering sixty-year-old. The man looked very fit, built, and strong. The wind whipped all around them, but the blowing snow didn't seem to bother the senator. The man had been in the pool a while so his body temperature was up.

Pulling off his coat, Steel wrapped it around Christie and gently lifted her. His chest wound ached, but he ignored it.

Senator Tindren's voice was deep and smooth. "She has a pulse. Shallow breathing." He rose, his face sincere. "I'll alert the attendant and get their EMT to your room. She must have fallen, hit her head."

Steel was already moving away and said, "Room 210, second floor of the Moose Lodge." He wondered if he was talking to Christie's attacker, or if Senator Tindren had been in on it.

He strode back through the walkway. Once in the pool area, he continued through the men's locker room. Assuming Christie was hypothermic, the heated indoor pool water wasn't a good idea.

Wordlessly he exited the locker room, strode past the startled attendant, and was quickly through the outer door. Tindren had followed him closely, and he heard the senator explaining the emergency to the young attendant.

Once outside, and out of earshot of Tindren, Steel said, "Harry, Christie's in trouble. Get an EMT to our room ASAP. Senator Tindren is asking the attendant for the resort EMT, just make sure it happens."

Harry's voice came back immediately. "Will do. Type of injury?"

"Hypothermia."

In seconds Steel crossed to the Moose Lodge, pushed in the door, and took the stairs up to the second floor. Hurrying to his room, he had to press Christie against the hallway wall to use the room key while he held her.

Eyes closed, she murmured something. A good sign.

Once inside he put her in one of the beds and covered her with blankets from both beds. She murmured again. Gathering towels from the bathroom, he used his fixed blade knife to cut off her swimsuit. With one towel he gently patted moisture off her skin, and then wrapped a dry towel around her torso. Using the blankets, he covered her whole body, including her head, leaving her face open to the room.

Stripping off all of his outer clothing down to his briefs, he climbed in bed behind her. He shoved the Glock beneath the pillow.

Her skin was cold, but she was shivering. Another good sign. Moderate to severe hypothermia left the body unable to shiver. He focused on warming her neck and torso. He'd read that warming legs and arms could force cold back to the core and cause complications.

He also checked her arms for syringe marks. He didn't find any. Jiri wanted this to appear like an accident, and a lethal injection would have thrown a murder investigation net around the resort. Jiri would know Steel wasn't about to tell everything to the police for an accident report.

"Christie, can you hear me?"

"S...Steel." Her voice was faint.

"You're safe, Christie."

Her voice was a halting whisper. "S...someone...gut punched me...choked me out."

Anger and concern welled up inside him. "I found you outside, near the walkway exit at the pool."

"Cold."

"You need to stay awake, honey." He figured if Christie had been choked out, with the air knocked out of her, the cold had done the rest. Maybe she had been kicked in the stomach too. He hoped he had reached her before hypothermia was severe. He couldn't be sure. Wearing only a swimsuit, while lying outside at minus twenty, left her open to hypothermia in minutes.

Jiri was shrewd. The man had tried to incapacitate two of them, and had succeeded with one. Though Steel wasn't sure of Harry's health until the big man opened the door and hurried in with a young brunette carrying a medical bag. Harry's brow furrowed as he stood at the foot of the bed, while the young woman walked to Christie's side.

"Christie, my name is Suzanne. I'm Chena's EMT. I'm going to take your temperature and check you for injuries." She quickly took Christie's temperature with a forehead thermometer. "Ninety-two degrees. Christie, can you hear me?"

"Yes," murmured Christie.

"We have to assume you were down to ninety degrees." The EMT continued, "I'm going to check your eyes, Christie, and your scalp. Do you remember falling?"

"No." Christie's voice was faint, sleepy.

The EMT took her pulse and glanced at Steel. "She's on the border of mild to moderate hypothermia. Her pupils are responsive. Her breathing and pulse steady. And I can't find any abrasions or bumps on her scalp. My deeper concern is that she might have suffered a seizure, stroke, or heart attack."

"I tripped." Christie's voice was faint, her eyes closed. "I'll be okay."

Suzanne looked at Steel and Harry. "I don't think she should be moved in this cold right now." She turned back to Christie. "Christie, my advice is that you slowly get your body temperature up, drink warm liquids like no caffeine tea or hot chocolate, and head into Fairbanks for a more thorough assessment tomorrow morning."

The EMT glanced at all of them. "No outside activities for at least thirty-six hours. Then several days of R&R. For now she needs to take it easy, get some calories, and later get a good night's rest. Stay awake for now."

Steel cleared his throat. "Thank you very much, Suzanne."

"Of course. I'll get her some warm liquids and check back shortly. I'll also have someone check the path where she fell to see if anything dangerous needs to be changed." She patted Christie's shoulder. "You need to stay awake until we get your temp back to normal, Christie."

"Okay," she murmured.

Suzanne left, and Harry moved closer, eyeing his sister. He sat on the bed across from her. Reaching over, he gently touched her cheek. "Stay awake, sis."

"I am," she whispered, her eyes still closed.

"She said someone gut-punched her and choked her out." Steel watched Harry, knowing how concerned he was for his sister.

Harry's eyes narrowed.

"I didn't see who," murmured Christie.

Harry clasped his hands tightly, staring at Christie. "They tried to take out two of us for the day."

"You didn't take any damage, Harry?" Steel eyed him.

Harry shook his head. "A partial kick. I think as soon as they saw it wasn't going as planned, they bailed."

Steel considered that. "Senator Tindren is signed up for a dogsled ride at two. If we're out of the picture, Tindren is vulnerable."

Harry said, "We're saved there. The dog musher told me the blowing snow forced them to cancel the dog sledding today. Ditto the northern lights unless it calms down. They had no snowmobile excursions planned for today. Not enough interest."

"Senator Tindren was taking Christie's pulse when I found her." Steel paused. "I'm unsure if we can trust him or not."

"It wasn't Tindren," murmured Christie.

Steel chewed on that. "Jiri or one of his men saw the three of us arrive and Emilia told them that there were three of us left, one a woman. Or Emilia sold us out."

Harry's hands were bunched into fists. "Which is it?"

Steel considered that. "I think they had help if they ID'd us based on photos with our wool hoods on. We haven't been anywhere for them to see our faces. Jiri would be looking for a protection agency off the grid in Virginia. I don't think M4N could find us."

"CIA." Harry's voice held disgust.

Steel nodded. "And Emilia might have been in a box with Jiri and felt she had to ID us. Or the CIA decided we were expendable given they had warned us to stay away." Steel eyed Harry. "The locker room attendant said a man left the pool area ahead of my return. It's likely Christie's attacker was already inside."

Harry nodded. "Christie, are you hearing all this?"

She mumbled, "I think a guy p...pretended to be an old man in the pool area. Missed that. Sorry."

"Don't be," Steel said softly.

Harry stood. "I met Tindren in the pool building and he gave me his room number. First floor, room one-twenty, Moose Lodge. He offered any help available."

Steel looked at Harry. "After you talk to him, if Senator Tindren decides to leave the resort with us, tell him we can't leave tonight. But one of us could stay in his room with him from here on out. He'll be safer here with us than on the road alone."

Harry lifted a hand. "I'll try to talk Tindren out of the Aurora Viewing Tour. Though why should he believe me? I have no credentials he can check on. I could give him yours, but do we connect him to Colonel Jeffries for verification?"

"No, that puts Colonel Jeffries at risk since Senator Tindren is still an unknown." Steel thought on it. "See if the senator will join me for dinner. You can watch Christie. I'll bring you two some food."

A soft knock sounded on the door, and the EMT entered again. Suzanne had a tray of hot chocolate and chamomile tea, and set it down near the bed. She took Christie's temperature again "It's up another degree, ninety-three, so that's good."

Steel lifted his chin. "Thank you. How long do you advise I stay beside her like this?" He didn't mind, but he wanted to be in a stronger position when Harry left, in case the enemy tried anything else.

Suzanne regarded him. "How about waiting until I check her temperature one more time in another hour?"

"Sounds fine to me." Steel was overheated, but that was the least of his concerns.

"Christie, want to try some hot chocolate?" Suzanne lifted the cup off the tray and knelt beside the bed.

"Sure." Christie still sounded sleepy.

"Okay, I'm going to lift your head a little, sis." Harry did, and Suzanne slowly poured a little of the chocolate into her mouth.

Christie swallowed it. "Mmm. More."

Suzanne gave her a little more, and after Christie said, "I'm good."

The EMT set down the cup. "Keep up the warm liquids." She smiled at them and left.

Harry stared at Christie. "If I can't find Senator Tindren, how about I eat early and get some food for you and Christie?"

"Works for me," said Steel.

"Yum," murmured Christie.

Harry patted Christie's shoulder. "I'm glad you're okay, sis."

"Thanks, bro."

Harry turned to leave.

Steel stopped him. "Harry?"

Harry turned and Steel said, "They know we're vulnerable now. Stay close to the lodge. No excursions. Christie will be alright." He hesitated. "I know you're angry, like me, but we can't afford to act on that or we'll make another mistake."

"Harry." Christie's eyes opened a crack, her voice soft. "Nothing stupid, bro."

"Got it." Harry waved them off and left.

Steel stared after him. He heard a rare edge in Harry's voice. He recognized it because his own nerves were on edge. If he had chased after Harry a few minutes longer, Christie might have suffered severe hypothermia, organ failure, needed amputations, or died. Minutes.

Christie placed her hand on his wrist near her chest. "I'll be okay, Steel," she murmured.

"I know." He kissed her cheek. "How are you feeling?"

"Cold. Weak. Better," she murmured.

"Good. Want some more hot chocolate?"

"Yes."

He reached over her, positioned himself on one elbow, and helped lift her head while tipping the cup. She used one of her hands to brace the cup too as she sipped a little.

"Okay," she whispered. "Starting to wake up a little."

"That's good."

"Harry worries me." She settled down in the bed again, nestling against him.

"He's concerned," said Steel.

Christie sounded apologetic, talking slowly and sleepily. "Whoever hit me was fast. Very experienced. I wasn't ready."

"You were coming out of minus twenty temps and blowing snow. It was a bold move on Jiri's part. He takes risks, which makes him dangerous." Steel thought about that. The man would not back down in going after Senator Tindren either.

"Harry has a protective side." Christie held his arm close to her. "I remember a boy in grade school pulled my hair once. Harry dragged the poor boy around the classroom floor by his hand for a minute."

Steel considered that. "He's wiser now, right?"

"I hope so. My left ribs are sore. Where the guy hit me. I didn't want to tell the EMT."

Using his fingertips, Steel gently applied pressure on her side, asking her where and how much it hurt. She didn't respond sharply, so he guessed the ribs were bruised, not broken. Still. He wanted to hurt someone.

After the next EMT check-in and after Harry returned, Steel felt he had to even the score. Christie couldn't go on any excursions, and one of them would have to stay with her. That meant Jiri's team had to take some damage before tonight.

CHAPTER 22

HARRY KEPT SEEING CHRISTIE in bed next to Steel. She had almost died. But Steel was right. He had to keep a level head. He also knew he had to step up his game. He couldn't leave it all to Steel. Jiri had effectively reduced them to two, maybe one operative, in one bold move. Which meant Steel would take over the Aurora Viewing Tour if Senator Tindren still decided to go, though Harry couldn't imagine the senator doing that after Steel talked to him.

He went cautiously into his room first, to make sure no one had entered while he had been gone, and that no one was hiding there now. Gun in hand, he found it secure.

After putting his gun away, he walked down to the first floor. He found Senator Tindren's room, but there was no answer when he knocked. He waited two minutes, knocked again, and then left. Tindren knew their room number, so maybe the senator would seek them out at some point.

Still on coms, he murmured, "Senator Tindren isn't answering at his room. Headed to the restaurant."

Steel's voice came back in a whisper. "Got it."

Harry decided the restaurant was a likely place for anyone wanting some respite and diversion from the cold. Maybe Tindren was there. When he stepped outside it was three p.m. and darker already. The wind had subsided and the sky was already showing some stars. The Aurora Viewing Tour would be on tonight. Nine p.m. Lots of time.

When he entered the quaint restaurant, he decided eating would be a good excuse to hang out for a bit too. Warmer inside, soft background music with muted lighting made everything easily visible, while giving it a restful quality. Pushing back his hood and taking off his face mask and gloves, he opened his coat a little.

He scanned the few patrons. No Senator Tindren, nor any other potential suspects. Outside of wandering around the compound, he couldn't come up with a plan.

He ordered a beer, picked a corner table, and waited for a fish and salad dinner. The fish was braised salmon, the salad large and full of greens, sweet peppers, cucumbers, and tomatoes they grew at the resort. He was surprised how hungry he was. The salad was tasty, and along with the fish was the kind of lean meal he enjoyed. He sipped the beer in between mouthfuls, taking his time to enjoy the ambiance, but also to give himself longer to remain inside.

"Salmon and salad, both recommended, Christie," he whispered.

"Get me that and a potato or fries," she responded on coms. "And another hot chocolate."

Her appetite suggested she was recovering. That helped relax him.

"Double that order," whispered Steel.

"Will do." Harry looked up when the door opened.

Two couples entered, one middle-aged, one younger, behind them a family of four, but no one that could have attacked him. Thinking of ways to find those men seemed impossible. He would try the Activities Center next. Wandering around the cabins would expose him to more risk that he couldn't afford to take with Christie out of the mix. Yet he couldn't stop thinking of her being hit, choked out, and left like trash to die on the cement ramp of the geothermal pool.

He enjoyed the meal, finished it, and left half the beer in the bottle. Walking to the counter, he put in two orders to go, and then returned to his seat.

While he waited, a tall man came in—a wool hood hiding his face—and made his way to the restroom. Harry didn't see the man's face, nor anything distinguishing.

Leaving his beer and gloves, he got up and entered the restroom. Small, two stalls, one urinal. The man was in a stall. Outhouses posed risks here. So even if Jiri's men were in a cabin, they might be using indoor restrooms.

Harry washed his hands at the sink, then drew paper towels, stepped to the door, opened it, and allowed it to shut while he quietly remained inside.

The toilet flushed and the man came out of the stall, still wearing his wool hood. Harry turned partly away, keeping the man in view though. The man didn't glance at him, and walked to the sink to wash his hands.

Harry had immediately noted two details. One of the upper buttons on the outside of the man's parka was torn off. During the attack, he had slid his hand over the tall man's coat on the path for that very purpose. The other was a touch of hair visible from beneath the man's wool hood near his neck. Similar to his attacker. The man glanced briefly in the mirror at Harry.

Harry suspected that the man would assume an attack in a public restroom in the restaurant would be low risk—better than an outhouse. Any noise here would draw the attention of patrons.

Taking one step closer to the man, Harry kicked sideways hard, hitting the side of the man's knee. It would ruin the knee and throw the man's back out of alignment. Gasping, the man tried to turn to him, and back up, but Harry was already hitting him hard in the neck and face repetitively, aiming for the carotids, jaw, and nose. The man collapsed. Harry bent over and hit him three more times. He stopped, realizing he was breathing hard, his whole body tense. He had to get out before someone came in.

Quickly stepping behind the man, he grabbed his shoulders and dragged him into the farthest stall and sat him on the toilet.

Rifling through the man's coat, he found a holstered SIG and a driver's license. He snapped a photo of the license with his phone. Likely a fake. The man groaned. Harry stepped back and kicked hard into the man's lower ribs with his boot. The man half slid off the toilet, propped up by the wall. Perfect. He checked the man's pulse. Still alive.

Harry exited the stall, shut the door, and looked beneath it. You could see the man's boots, so no one would bother him. Walking out of the restroom, he quickly assessed everyone in the restaurant.

No one seemed to have noticed what had occurred, because all the patrons were either seated or ordering food and drinks at the bar. The background music probably helped.

Leaving the beer, he waited at the counter for the orders. It didn't take long, and the food was boxed up and in a paper bag. Putting on his hood and gloves, he grabbed the two orders and left.

The restroom door never opened. When the man came to, he wouldn't want to draw attention to himself and most likely would need to call for help to walk out. One down.

"Coming back now," he whispered.

When Harry stepped outside, he paused near the door, his gaze sweeping his surroundings. He carried the food with his left hand, his right inside his parka near his gun. Cat and mouse. Now Jiri and his crew might feel some of the same wariness he felt.

Striding to the lodge, he was quickly inside and up to the second floor, walking to Steel's room. "Walking down the hallway to your room."

He reached the room, knocked, and Steel let him in, dressed with a gun in hand.

CHAPTER 23

STEEL LISTENED IN SILENCE to Harry. Harry had taken a big risk in the restaurant, but it had paid off. Given their situation, he couldn't help but feel good over it.

Harry sat on the edge of Christie's bed, talking as he methodically cut up Christie's fish—at her request. Finished, he handed the plate and fork to her.

"Thanks, bro." She smiled weakly at him.

"Anytime, sis." He gave a brief smile.

The EMT had visited one last time for the night, and Christie's temp had been ninety-six. Closer to normal. She was still covered up in bed, propped up with pillows, weak but hungry. The EMT had said she would check on Christie in the morning before they left.

Christie eagerly started in on the fries.

"Good job in the restaurant, Harry." Steel was impressed. It made his task easier for later. Senator Tindren's absence from his room didn't feel right though. Maybe Jiri had already killed him. But that didn't fit either. It was too risky. Unless they found a way to hide the body.

Harry leaned back, his palms on the bed. "I'll send Colonel Jeffries the photo of the man's ID, see if he can get his real name."

Christie eyed Harry. "You took a risk, little brother."

Harry glanced at both of them. "I figured if we didn't even up the odds, we had no chance."

"Jiri still has the short man that attacked you, plus Emilia. Three." Steel regarded Harry and Christie, setting his scoured plate aside. He thought on the night. "I think for the Aurora Viewing Tour, if we don't locate Senator Tindren beforehand, if Tindren shows I go up too. You two stay here."

"No." Harry and Christie said it together as they looked at him.

"I can hold a gun." Christie eyed Steel. "I'm going with you."

"No." This time it was Harry and Steel that replied together.

"That's out of the question, Christie." Steel shook his head. "Tomorrow morning you're headed home."

Christie frowned.

Harry put a hand on her arm. "He's right, sis. No arguing on that."

She stared at both of them. "Alright, but no one is staying back to babysit me. You need someone with you, Steel."

Harry raised an eyebrow at Steel. "She's right, Steel."

Steel looked at both of them. "Okay. I'm going to see if I can talk to Senator Tindren and Emilia now."

No one objected so he rose to put on his outerwear gear.

There was a knock on the door.

Steel drew his Glock. Harry got off the bed and stepped to the wall adjacent to the door, gun in hand, and Christie pulled her SIG from beneath the covers.

"Who is it?" asked Steel.

A soft voice replied. "Senator Ash Tindren, chairman of the Senate Intelligence Committee." There was a pause. "I'm here with Emilia, CIA representative."

Steel didn't like any of it. He looked through the peephole. Tindren and Emilia, dressed in an indoor fleece jacket and pullover, respectively, stood in the hallway. He gestured Harry farther away from the door, unlocked the deadbolt, and moved farther back too. He lifted his chin to Christie, and she rested her SIG on a knee and aimed it at the door.

"Come in." Steel kept his voice calm.

Senator Tindren came in first, followed by Emilia. Tindren raised his eyebrows when he saw the guns. Yet he strode with confidence toward Christie. Steel watched Emilia. Lithe build, Hispanic dark eyes and facial features, attractive, and Steel felt dangerous. Her form-fitting pullover and jeans left nothing to imagine for weapons—she wasn't carrying.

Senator Tindren walked up to the bed, smiling down at Christie, his deep, smooth voice gentle. "How are you feeling?"

Christie lowered her gun. "Better. Thank you for your help."

"My pleasure." Tindren sat on the bed next to hers, and looked at Harry and Steel.

While Harry locked the door, Steel grabbed Emilia's arm and pushed her to the end of the bed until she was forced to sit on it, the barrel of his gun against her forehead.

"You gave us up," snapped Steel.

Emilia glared up at him. "They took your photos when you arrived, and Karbu was about to ID you to Jiri. I said Christie fit the woman's size I fought, and you three were a likely fit. If I hadn't, I would be dead by now." She shrugged. "You were told to stay away."

Steel didn't know what to make of it, nor what she had told Tindren. He backed up, but didn't put away his gun. Everything Emilia said made sense, but something still bothered him about her.

Steel looked at Tindren. "Senator, what have you been told?"

Tindren turned serious. "You're trying to take down the group that killed General Morris, and want to know who's behind all of it. I've agreed to help."

Steel frowned. "It will be dangerous. We could take you out of Chena tomorrow morning."

"That's what Emilia said to me." Tindren nodded slowly, as if deliberating. "I knew General Morris. A decorated hero. Besides, if I run, these killers will just come at me somewhere else when I'm not protected."

Steel couldn't disagree, and he felt better knowing Emilia had told the senator to leave with them.

"How do you want to help?" asked Harry.

"I'll do the Aurora Viewing Tour and try to get this Jiri to talk." Tindren looked at each of them. "I have a conceal carry, and I've been assured by Emilia that the CIA will be dialed-in on the cliff to protect me."

"That's too dangerous." Steel glanced at Emilia. "You're willing to risk his life?"

"As he said, I offered to have him taken out of here, but he wants to help." Emilia sounded confident. "We have two snipers standing by in position, and Karbu wants this contract ended. He contacted us. My CIA handler said we're to do whatever is necessary to stop his brother, Jiri." She stared at Steel. "We're going to end it all tonight."

"Sir?" Steel looked at Tindren.

Senator Tindren lifted a hand from his thigh. "I'm more than happy to help bring down this rogue, Jiri, who killed General Morris. With the CIA, along with you and your team, I should be more than safe."

Emilia said sharply, "Senator, we don't need Steel and his team—"

Tindren cut her off with a raised hand. "I'd feel better about them being there on Charlie Dome tonight, Emilia. I knew Morris and he told me about Jack Steel. One of the best. Excuse me for not going along with the plan we agreed on, but extra security can't be a bad thing, can it?"

Emilia stared at the senator but didn't reply. Steel looked from Tindren to her. "What if the senator doesn't get the name you want from Jiri?"

Emilia shrugged. "Orders are to end it here, one way or the other. The plan is to take Jiri alive. We'll take him out of the country if we have to and get the name of his employer from him sooner or later."

"You could have taken Jiri in Virginia." Steel eyed her.

Emilia lifted her chin. "I don't make the decisions. They felt a more isolated area would favor less attention and less likely a public shootout. And they talked to his brother, Karbu. Karbu signed off on getting Jiri's employer name, but not on killing his brother."

"Why should we trust you?" asked Harry.

Emilia glanced at all of them. "I took a huge risk going to Senator Tindren, and another risk coming to you." She turned to Steel. "I assumed you checked—we cleaned up the mess in the woods in Virginia."

"I checked." Steel watched Emilia carefully. "What are Jiri's plans on Charlie Dome?"

Emilia looked at Tindren. "Get the senator to walk close to the western edge, or force it, and shove him over the side. It has to look like an accident. No guns. There will be at least one Chena Resort employee and other guests up there tonight. Jiri doesn't want it to look like a murder."

"You knew he planned to attack us today." Christie eyed her.

Emilia stared at Christie. "He wasn't going to kill any of you, just disable you for tonight. There was nothing I could do about it. Giving you a heads-up would have put my position at risk. Again, you were told to stay away. The Agency kept tabs on you, and told me you were coming." She paused. "Jiri still plans on taking revenge against you, but not here. He doesn't want the police or anyone else in law enforcement investigating in Chena for any reason."

"How are they getting up to Charlie Dome?" asked Christie.

"Jiri wouldn't tell me." Emilia shrugged. "I'm to go up with the senator on the Aurora Viewing Tour and get him to the western edge, away from everyone else."

Tindren smiled at Emilia. "I'm a sucker for beautiful women."

Steel thought on all of it. "Then we'll see everyone tonight." He nodded to Emilia. "You leave first. Once you're in your room, Senator Tindren can leave."

Emilia frowned, but she got up, cautiously opened the door, checked the hallway, and left. Steel watched her walk down the hallway and enter a room. He made a mental note of the door. He wondered if she was in the room alone. He would find out soon enough.

Senator Tindren rose, but Steel raised his palm and shut the door. “We need to talk, Senator.”

Tindren spread his hands. “I’m listening.”

“We found this latitude and longitude and date on the phone of one of the killers who tried to kill Morris in his house.” Christie spoke deliberately. “You’re the only one that fits for an assassination up here, Senator Tindren.”

For the first time Tindren’s eyes clouded over and he looked concerned, maybe even shaken. He stiffened. “I’m still going. What do you advise?”

Steel moved away from the door to the side of it. “First, bring your gun tonight. If anything looks risky, you can use it. If you end up shooting Jiri, we can cast him as an assassin, which he is, in any police investigation. Jiri doesn’t want to use guns, but you can.”

Tindren nodded. “I like it.”

“Secondly, don’t trust Emilia.” Steel walked closer to Tindren. “The CIA let General Morris die, and still didn’t move in on Jiri, because they wanted to find out who hired him, but also because they have running contracts with his organization, M4N. We can’t trust they won’t do the same here. And we can’t verify with certainty that Emilia is CIA.”

“I come from a family of hunters.” Tindren looked thoughtful. “I learned a long time ago when you’re hunting dangerous prey to expect the unexpected. I’ll be careful.”

Steel considered having Tindren on their coms, but decided against it. There were risks no matter what he decided. But if things fell apart, better that Tindren wasn’t in the loop.

Tindren raised an eyebrow. “What’s your plan?”

Steel smiled tersely. "Better you don't know it, sir."

Tindren nodded. "I can live with that."

Before the senator left, Steel checked the hallway again to make sure it was clear. Tindren's room was on the first floor, and Steel walked him down, making sure his room was clear before the senator entered it. "We'll come for you shortly before tonight's tour," said Steel. "Keep your door locked and gun handy. Don't open for anyone except myself or Harry."

Tindren waved him off. "Emilia will pick me up. Whatever her role, she has to get me to Charlie Dome tonight." He smiled. "Our cover story is that she's my new girlfriend."

Steel couldn't argue with the senator's logic. "Alright."

He returned to their room. Pulling out a chair, he sat in it. Christie was finishing her dinner. Harry was sitting on the other bed, his back against the wall, his legs stretched out.

Steel said, "Jiri and his crew might have already left Chena, and be planning to helicopter or snowmobile in to Charlie Dome." Chena had snowmobiles, but he doubted Jiri would use those if they planned to exit on snowmobiles. "I don't think they'll be riding up with everyone else on the tour tonight. Same with the CIA." He paused. "If the CIA plans to have snipers, it sounds bulletproof." He looked at Christie and Harry. "Does anyone else have a bad feeling about this?"

Christie chewed on a piece of salmon. "It feels risky. We're set, *if* the CIA are really behind protecting Tindren at all costs."

"That's the *if* I'm worried about too, sis." Harry ran a hand through his hair.

"Okay, we play along, trust no one, ready for anything." Steel glanced at Christie.

Christie shrugged and leaned back into the pillows. "I'll be on coms at least." She sounded disappointed.

"We've got a few hours." Harry smiled. "I'm going to my room to talk to Isabella. She's been texting me all day and I've been ignoring her. I'll stay on coms. I'll just pretend you're not listening."

Steel nodded. "Pick me up at nine p.m., Harry."

Harry left, and Steel locked the door behind him. He sat near Christie on her bed, staring at her.

"I lived, Steel."

"That's a relief." He didn't want to tell her how much he had worried about her, and how much he wanted Jiri dead because of it.

"My swimsuit is ruined." She eyed the scraps still lying on the other bed.

"That expense is coming out of your salary."

She rolled her eyes. "You love it when I don't have to go with you on an Op, don't you?"

"Who's going to watch my six?" He winked at her.

"Exactly." She studied him. "Anything else you want to talk about?"

He looked at her, frowning with exaggeration. He had decided to wait until they returned home to ask her to marry him. "No."

She looked puzzled. "Really, you're sure?"

"Absolutely. Nothing at all to talk about." He rose. "I'm going to take a warm bath. Relax a little. When I'm done, I'll give you a light back massage."

"Mmm."

But when he came out later, she was sleeping. He let her continue. She had to stay awake while they were gone, so it was better she rested now. He doubted Jiri was going to send anyone after her, but they had to expect the unexpected with this man.

He sat in the dark with the lights off, staring at Christie's face in the shadows. He was a very lucky man. And he sensed that Harry had left out some things in his story about the attack on the tall man in the restaurant restroom. Harry had beat the man hard. He understood. He didn't care what the CIA wanted. Jiri was as good as dead.

CHAPTER 24

STEEL STRODE DOWN TO Emilia's room and knocked on the door. He had his hand inside his parka, ready on his gun. A large daypack with gear hung over his shoulder.

Emilia opened the door and stepped aside to let him in, her voice and face calm. "I've been expecting you. My coms are put away."

Entering cautiously, Steel was quickly convinced she was on her own. She stood, hands on her hips, staring at him, her dark eyes on his.

"I don't blame you for not trusting me, but you can." Her voice betrayed no lies. "I've been straight up with you from the beginning."

"Jiri told you nothing specific." He said it with doubt obvious in his voice.

"He told me to stay in my room until tonight, which I haven't done." She moved to the side of the bed, her dark hair hanging down the front of her shoulders. "I've taken risks. To be blunt, the CIA doesn't care if you live or die. You're interfering."

"I believe you." He lifted his chin. "Okay, what are you bringing tonight?"

"I don't need to tell you anything. If I'm not there, they will be suspicious immediately." Emilia lowered her voice. "I'm saying that so you understand I am trying to help. I'll be on coms with

Jiri, and I'll be carrying a Glock 19 Gen4, CQD knife, and a night monocular." She hesitated, her voice slightly sarcastic. "Anything else you want to know?"

"How many men does Jiri have with him?"

Emilia nodded. "Two men and myself, and I heard on their coms that you've disabled one of them."

Steel moved closer to her. "Who are you really working for? Karbu or the CIA?"

She smiled. "I receive paychecks from both. It's quite lucrative. But my final orders are from the CIA. They wanted someone inside Karbu's organization to make sure everything is okay, given how much they use him."

"How is Jiri planning to leave Charlie Dome?" he asked.

She shook her head. "Jiri always operates on a need to know basis. I'm not sure. Snowmobiles or helicopter. CIA is sending a chopper." She stiffened. "Let's be clear. We take Jiri alive. You don't kill him."

"Got it." He stepped to the door.

"It's cute."

Turning to her, he raised an eyebrow. "What?"

"A brother and two lovers on the same Op." She studied him. "A very risky combination that Jiri saw immediately to exploit. He's always ahead of his enemies."

"How can you be sure he won't toss you over the cliff tonight too?" he asked.

Her lips pursed, a moment of vulnerability showing. Steel didn't know what else to say to her, so he turned and left, heading for the top of the stairs where he waited.

In seconds Harry joined him, also carrying a full daypack, and wearing white boots but all brown in parka and peripherals, as did Steel. Besides holstered guns and knives, they were both carrying backups in the bags too.

"Everything set?" asked Steel.

Harry gave a thumbs up. "We're good."

"Good luck, boys." Christie's voice was soft over coms.

They made their way outside, the night air frigid. Had to be minus thirty already. No one else was out. The bar-restaurant had some people in it, visible through the windows, but Steel guessed that outside of food, the cold weather was going to keep everyone else inside tonight.

Besides the crunch of their boots on the snow, it was quiet. The stars above lit up the sky.

Steel had seen the aurora borealis lights before, but not this far north. Maybe he could take Rachel up here during the summer, when it was much warmer.

They made a quick trip to their SUV and plugged it into an outlet. Due to Christie's health, it was guaranteed they were staying the night.

In the Activity Center they checked in, and then stood around. The family of four were present again; husband, wife, and two young teens—a boy and a girl. Senator Tindren arrived with Emilia hanging onto his arm. Dressed as warm as they were, Emilia also had a sling bag over a shoulder. Steel thought it was a smart move—Emilia pretending to be Tindren's latest girlfriend. After checking in, the senator and Emilia chatted with the family. Steel preferred that too.

Jiri and his associates didn't show. Steel wasn't surprised.

A smiling young man in his twenties arrived at nine-thirty and introduced himself as the Chena tour guide. Lean, six feet, short hair. Chad. He told them to expect a twenty-minute trip up to Charlie Dome. The Chena yurt on Charlie Dome would have a fire for heat and warm cocoa, tea, oatmeal, or ramen snacks for everyone while they waited for the northern lights to appear. No guarantees.

"Any questions?" No one responded, and Chad smiled. "Good, let's get the show on the road."

Everyone followed Chad outside to the path that would take them up to Charlie Dome.

Chad pointed at their waiting transportation. "SUSV—Small Unit Support Vehicles—are full-tracked, articulated vehicles designed to support infantry platoons during military operations in arctic and alpine conditions. Barely heated, and loud as a tractor, the SUSVs can be used in all types of terrain, such as snow, over rock, boulders, bog, marsh, and even underwater." He smiled. "These were old Swiss Army vehicles from the sixties. The forward unit has one bench seat behind the driver, and the rear unit that's hitched to the forward unit has bench seats that hold ten."

Steel chose to sit in the forward unit with Harry and the driver. That forced the family, Senator Tindren, and Emilia to pile into the rear SUSV unit. Windows in the SUSVs allowed visibility of the sky above the trees surrounding both sides of the path.

Chad checked everyone in both units, and then returned to the forward unit and started it.

Steel leaned forward, talking loudly over the engine. "Do you have binoculars or night vision of any kind in the SUSVs or at the yurt on Charlie Dome?"

"I have binoculars to look for wildlife during the day." Chad smiled and shook his head. "You won't need night vision to see the northern lights."

Satisfied, Steel sat back as Chad began driving the SUSV forward.

Harry doubled over in his seat. "I'm not feeling well," he muttered.

Chad stopped the SUSV immediately, letting the engine run. "Where do you feel sick, Harry?"

"Stomach." Harry groaned. "I have to stay back. Maybe food poisoning or the flu."

"That's horrible, Harry." Steel frowned at Harry and then the driver. "I'll stay back, make sure he makes it to his room. I'll contact the EMT if need be."

"I'm sorry to hear that." Chad nodded. "Maybe you could go up tomorrow night, Harry."

Harry groaned, holding his stomach, as Steel opened the door and helped him out. They exited, with Harry bent over, and quickly hurried off the path to the side of one of the buildings. The SUSV rambled past them up the trail. Steel thought it was fifty-fifty that someone in the second unit would have seen them exit the forward SUSV unit. Good enough.

As soon as the SUSV was past them, Harry straightened and led Steel through the compound at a fast clip to a rectangular shed not far from the doghouses. A padlock on the outside didn't provide much trouble as Steel shook his gloved hands out of his choppers and picked the lock.

Once open, they slid the door back and walked inside.

Harry used his phone as a flashlight. "The guy I talked to made it sound like they never have theft here and weren't concerned. We can start them without keys, but it will be easier with them." He swept the light around the shed.

Steel's gaze followed Harry's flashlight, which revealed a workbench, tools, and a key rack. He grabbed one, as did Harry, and they quickly walked to the half-dozen snowmobiles that were lined up side by side.

Before getting on, they took off their snow pants, parkas, and choppers, and reversed them from the brown exterior to the other side, which was all white. From their day packs they pulled out white goggles, which they both slipped on.

Hurriedly they sat on the snowmobiles, turned the keys, pulled the chokes, and pulled the draw starts. Both vehicles started immediately.

"He told me they're rigged to not go past twenty-five miles per hour," said Harry. "Family friendly."

Steel nodded. They eased them out, and Steel shut the shed and locked it again. They steered wide of the compound on low speed, aiming for the trail of the SUSV. Once on the tracks, they turned on the lights and revved up the speed. Steel took the lead. He wanted to keep the SUSV in sight so they didn't lose it.

In minutes the interior lights of the rear SUSV unit appeared as a bright dot on the trail up ahead. Steel cut his headlight, as did Harry. They eased down on the speed slightly, and hung back. There was enough light from the sky and the trail ran fairly straight, both facts making it relatively easy to stay on the packed surface. The few times the trail wound around an obstacle, trees on both sides made it obvious where to aim their machines.

In fifteen minutes the ascent was steeper, climbing higher until in about twenty minutes the terrain leveled off. Steel stopped his snowmobile and quickly angled it off the trail in among trees in the woods. Harry pulled his sled up alongside Steel's.

From their backpacks they pulled out white taped snowshoes, and quickly put them on. In a minute they were walking through the trees, their backpacks on their shoulders, heading west. The snow was deep here, at least five feet, and deeper in gullies. Without the snowshoes it would be near impossible to get through.

The goal was to parallel the plateau to the western edge where Emilia said they planned to kill Senator Tindren.

In minutes the loud engine of the SUSV turned silent. Harry kept going, but Steel stopped and dug out his night vision monocular. Looking back, he spotted the SUSV parked close to a traditional yurt near the entrance to the plateau. The yurt's small, round structure was about thirty feet in diameter with a round peaked roof. Steel had read that it was made of all wood, instead of a wood frame covered with animal skins or wool like those in Asia. Smoke exited the top. A fire had to be burning inside—most likely a wood stove. That would be inviting later.

Remaining among the trees, he watched the family, Emilia, and Senator Tindren disappear into the yurt.

Steel studied the plateau. Big enough to hold four football fields. Conifers ran up to the eastern edge of it and were scattered across it. Not many hiding places. If the CIA had snipers in position, they could be dug into the snow anywhere. Even with the night monocular's infrared ability they might be hard to spot.

Warmly dressed as he was, the cold was still biting. Steel could feel it through his parka, clawing at the edges to get to his skin. He started walking again, toward the western side. Even with the snowshoes his feet sank nearly to his knees. No running in this snow.

Emilia and Senator Tindren might remain in the yurt for hours, but Steel doubted that. If the aurora borealis show began, the family and any Chena employees would come out on the plateau. He guessed that Jiri wanted things finished by then. It made more sense that Emilia had been given instructions to coax Tindren out as soon as possible to the far end of the plateau, away from the yurt, where a plausible, unwitnessed accident could occur.

Zipping his parka down, he pulled his Glock, shoved it into an outer pocket, and rezipped his coat. Thinking ahead, he also pulled his fixed blade knife from his backpack, and put it into his other jacket pocket. Ready. He and Harry wore Kevlar, but it wouldn't mean much if a sniper fired at them with a high-powered rifle.

"Harry?" he whispered.

Harry came back immediately. "Almost ready."

"Stay warm. Quiet here." Christie's voice came faintly over coms.

Steel kept going. He passed Harry, who had found a place to his liking, but Steel wanted to be much closer to the western edge. It took him twenty minutes to arrive there, and he stopped and looked back again at the yurt with the monocular.

A snowy owl was making a sound like a coarse bark somewhere behind him. He didn't look, but found it interesting that he had heard one in Virginia just days ago.

He focused on the yurt. Two people exited it. Senator Tindren and Emilia. Arm in arm, they were walking toward the west end of the plateau along a packed track made by previous SUSV trips. Steel finally hoped to put a face to Jiri's name. And then kill him.

***

Harry was in great shape and the exertion felt good in the cold, generating heat he knew he would need. Finding the right position was key. He required an unobstructed view of the western edge, and as much area as he could see north and south. The yurt was visible in glimpses from among the trees, and the thick smoke exiting its peaked roof gave it an eerie quality. Wood stove, he guessed.

He finally found what he was looking for. Almost too good. A snow-covered slab of rock among the trees, rising five feet off the ground. Walking around it, he studied the ground on all sides before returning to the back of it.

After taking off his snowshoes, he climbed up its backside. Once atop it he knelt and pulled the HK G28 hybrid CSASS sniper rifle out of the bag. Taking off his choppers, he quickly assembled it. Steel had it modified so the stock and barrel came off easily so it didn't have to be carried in a big bag. The rifle had also been painted white.

In seconds Harry assembled it and dialed in the night vision scope. The cold was biting his fingers so he put his choppers back on. Lying on his belly, elbows propping up the rifle, he scanned the plateau east to west and quickly spotted Senator Tindren and Emilia walking west from the yurt. He looked, but couldn't find Steel among the trees. That was good.

Swinging the rifle farther, he also didn't see any sign of Jiri or anyone else. That bothered him, but he wasn't going to give up his position to go looking for them. This was as good a spot as he was going to find. Now he just had to track Senator Tindren and wait for Jiri to show.

He could guess what Steel was planning, because he was planning the same thing. Screw the CIA's plan. Jiri would die tonight.

CHAPTER 25

CHRISTIE HAD HER GUN barrel resting on her knees, which were bent, her feet flat on the bed. She still had blankets pulled over her legs and torso right up to her chin. She felt warm and comfortable. The truth was she hated being out of the night's Op, and worried about Harry and Steel. The odds were stacked against them, and she didn't trust Emilia any more than Steel did.

But she also recognized she was beyond going back out into the cold and having strength to be highly active. That felt dangerous and wearying just thinking about it, even with her stubborn desire to be with Steel. Thus she hadn't argued with either of them when they refused her offer. Jiri was a dangerous man. Clever. Willing to take risks. Unpredictable. She was glad Steel was on their side. That was their edge.

She smiled over Steel's refusal to talk about what he had been trying to say on the plane. His clumsy attempt to ask her if she wanted to commit to him had annoyed her then. Now she thought it was cute. Knowing Steel, he would have talked to Harry about it. Gather intel, learn, improve. That was Steel.

No wonder he had been acting weird around her lately. As obsessed as Steel was with perfecting fighting and safety measures, he was sometimes pretty ignorant of how to talk about some things.

She had to cut him some slack though. He was concerned about her feelings. Still, she wanted him to state what he wanted, not try to figure out what she wanted. She didn't care about how he did it, or if he gave her a cardboard ring, but if he wanted to marry her, he had to say it, not fish around for her interest. That made her chuckle. She also realized it was something that her heart deeply wanted. She didn't need it to confirm anything between her and Steel, but she wanted to celebrate their relationship with their families and friends in a way they would understand, just like Harry was doing with Isabella.

She listened for any telltale sounds. Anything out of the ordinary. Steel and Harry had been gone close to an hour and she was sleepy. It would be a long night, but not as long as Steel's and Harry's. She just had to make sure she didn't fall asleep. She heard them checking in on coms, and she responded, glad to hear their voices.

She nodded off before she knew it. Drifted into a deep, satisfying sleep. Dreaming about her and Steel running together, not quite out of range of danger, holding each other's hands. Something was chasing them.

Telltale sounds woke her up. Groggy, she rubbed her eyes. Small rasping sounds were coming from the hallway door.

Swinging her feet out from beneath the covers, she walked unsteadily to the door and placed her ear against it, listening carefully. She was dressed in layers; PJs, flannel shirt, fleece jacket, slippers. She still felt a little chilled. Exhausted. And her ribs ached where she had been hit.

The other room door was being opened. She barely heard the click.

Quietly and quickly she opened her door, gun up, and very carefully checked the dimly lit hallway in both directions. Empty. She stepped out and took the two steps to the next door over which was open just a crack. Toeing it open with her left foot, she held her gun up with both hands and aimed for the bed. The small bedlamp was on, enough to light up things clearly.

The back of the man came into view first. He stood between the two beds and was pulling back the covers on her bed with his right hand, his left holding a gun.

Christie remained in the doorway, her voice cold. "If you so much as breathe, I'm going to put bullets into your back and head. Entering a woman's room at night with a gun makes for an easy self-defense case if I kill you. Drop the gun on the bed, very slowly, then clasp your hands behind your head.

He complied.

Christie said, "Turn slowly."

The man obeyed. He wore a parka, pullover, snow pants, and wool hood.

"Down to your knees," she added. "Then lie down on the floor."

He followed her directions, and she slowly pushed the door open all the way so she could see the rest of the room. Empty.

Stepping in, she turned on the overhead light and shut the door with her foot. "With you left hand pull off your hood and look at me," she said.

The man complied, and Christie snapped a photo of his face with her phone. Five-eight, one-sixty-five pounds, solid build, dark hair. The short man that had attacked Harry on the path.

She wanted to hurt him.

Steel had been right about expecting another attack on her. When he had visited Emilia, Harry had kept watch in the hallway while Christie had moved into Harry's room. In her bed in Steel's room they had stuffed all their pillows beneath the covers to make it appear like a believable figure.

"I have him, Steel and Harry, as you expected," she whispered.

She saw the coms in the man's ears and knew that meant Jiri would know too that his operative had been captured. Couldn't be helped. Jiri's man might be a bargaining card and thus she couldn't kill him outright. She doubted a man like Jiri would care if one of his operatives lived or died, but he would care about someone in custody that could ID him and his M4N organization if someone such as Senator Tindren was murdered. Thus Steel had told her not to kill him, and to leave him with his coms.

She pulled a desk chair to the wall beside the door, sat down, and kept the gun aimed at the man's head. "One down," she whispered.

CHAPTER 26

FROM INSIDE THE TREE line, Steel watched Emilia and Senator Tindren. The fact that Jiri had sent his man after Christie, most likely to force them out of cover, meant that he might have other men up here too.

Emilia and the CIA were wildcards. Still an unknown. CIA snipers? Doubtful. Maybe the CIA was still trying to get a name out of Jiri. Worse, perhaps the CIA wanted Senator Tindren dead. That seemed beyond what they were capable of, but a special offshoot of the CIA, operating out of black budget ops, might not be above letting M4N do whatever they wanted. But allowing them to kill a senator seemed far-fetched even to him.

"Harry, watch your six," he whispered.

"Got it." Harry's voice was steady.

There was a lone, large tree on the far western edge of the plateau, and from behind it stepped a man. Steel believed it had to be Jiri. About his height, also dressed in an all-white outfit of parka, hood, goggles, and choppers. No gun in hand. No weapons visible.

Emilia and Tindren had stopped and were talking to the man .

Steel whispered, "Harry, getting any of this conversation?"

"Nothing."

Steel studied them through the monocular. He could read lips, but at night at fifty yards with wool hoods and goggles it was impossible.

Tindren drew his gun and pointed it at Jiri. Emilia drew her gun and also pointed it at Jiri.

Jiri dropped to his knees, his hands locked behind his head. Steel began moving closer through the trees. What he was seeing fit Emilia's story about the CIA's plan to take Jiri alive.

***

Harry had Jiri sighted in. At least he believed it was Jiri. He wanted to squeeze off a shot into the man's head or back, but he held off from firing. They had to be sure. Plus the man was kneeling and thus wasn't a risk at the moment.

Faint sounds. He rolled along the rock and off the western edge of it, landing on his back, his rifle pointed at the forest behind him. He couldn't see anything and remained motionless. Someone camouflaged was likely approaching the other side of the rock, which blocked his view. He didn't want to sit up—his head would be a target if the man was on the other side of slab.

By the time he heard the faint footfalls, a voice reached his ears.

"Don't move, finger off the trigger, lay the gun on the ground or you're dead, Harry."

Harry felt a gun barrel press into the top of his head. The slight Caribbean accent meant most likely that Karbu Moeller had found him. He slowly released the HK. The man stood in front of the slab.

Harry noted the wooden snowshoes near his head. Wood was quiet in the snow.

"Now get up, Harry, put on your snowshoes, and we'll walk to Senator Tindren and have a nice chat."

***

Steel saw Harry walking out of the trees on his snowshoes, the HK G28 absent from his hands. He had heard the exchange over coms. Which meant Christie had heard it too. Emilia still had her gun aimed at the kneeling man, as did Tindren.

The man walking out with Harry remained on his opposite side, so Steel couldn't squeeze off a shot at him. The hostile was also dressed in all white like the other man that Tindren and Emilia had their guns trained on. Even the hostile's gun was nearly invisible, probably painted white.

Steel's chest tightened. Given the accent, Harry's captor was likely Karbu Moeller.

He guessed Karbu hadn't shot Harry because they didn't want to attract any attention to what was going to happen, and because Harry's captor knew Emilia, Tindren, or Steel would shoot the kneeling man.

"I'm going to kill their man if they hurt Harry." Christie's voice was ice.

"Keep him alive, Christie." Steel heard her concern and anger—mirroring his own feelings. He walked up to the edge of the tree line, choppers off, gun up and aimed at the kneeling figure, while watching the man escorting Harry. That man was still being very careful and Steel didn't have a shot at him.

The aurora borealis arrived then. Bright ribbons of green, blue, and violet streaked the sky above the plateau. It was stunning, but Steel ignored it.

In seconds faint, excited voices drifted across the plateau as the family and Chena Resort employee emptied out of the yurt to point skyward in their direction. The visitors couldn't see Steel's or Jiri's crew in the darkness, especially since they were dressed in white. That was also the reason Steel had asked the Chena SUSV driver if he had night vision binoculars. However, it was dead quiet across the plateau so they would hear a gunshot.

Steel heard the faint chop of helicopter blades in the distance. The CIA coming to take Jiri, or the Moeller brothers' escape plan. Supposedly Karbu Moeller was against the contract his younger brother had taken, and Steel hoped it was another reason he hadn't shot Harry.

The kneeling man didn't rise, so he was still under Emilia's or Tindren's orders to stay down. That gave Steel hope that Emilia was on their side. And that the helicopter was CIA. He scanned the plateau and trees east of him once more, unable to see anyone else. He doubted anyone else was here. Either Emilia had lied about CIA snipers, or they were waiting on her orders.

He walked out of the trees toward the others, wary of everyone, his gun leveled. Even though his hand was still gloved, the cold was numbing his fingers. He had no conclusive evidence that a sniper wasn't dialed into him. It was a risk, but he had to take it. His gut said there wasn't anyone else here. His snowshoes dug into the snow about two feet, but he kept his eyes forward.

When he reached the tracked path, he kicked off his snowshoes without looking down. The man beside Harry had his gun barrel tucked into Harry's side, and had waited for Steel's arrival, stopping on the opposite edge of the groomed track ten feet away. Harry separated them. If the man tried to shoot Steel, Harry would be ready to take him down.

Walking toward them, Steel used his left hand to unzip his backpack and pull his second gun. A SIG.

The man holding Harry captive continued walking toward the others, still keeping Harry between himself and Steel. Steel followed, one gun aimed at the kneeling man, the other aimed in the direction of Harry's captor.

When they were all gathered six feet from the edge of the cliff, everyone's gloved hands held guns—except the kneeling man. Steel waited, both guns still on the Moeller brothers. The cold had to be hurting everyone's fingers as much as it hurt his.

Harry's captor spoke first, sounding confident. "I want my man at the hotel released."

"Negative." Steel looked at him, recognizing a slight Caribbean accent. But it didn't sound like the man on the phone at General Morris' house—thus Harry's captor had to be Karbu. "I'll kill your kneeling brother, Karbu, and Harry will take you down to the ground. I'll have shots at everyone here."

Steel noted Harry tensing. He didn't want Harry to do anything. There wasn't any doubt Harry would take a bullet if he tried to take Karbu down.

The kneeling man finally spoke, sounding excited. "A stand-off."

Steel recognized his voice. The man from the phone conversation at General Morris's house. Jiri. Steel tensed. He would kill both brothers as soon as he had a chance.

The helicopter was closing in. Steel noted Emilia wasn't paying any attention to it. Maybe a good sign.

Steel assessed everyone, and saw fingers curled around triggers. Emilia and Tindren could take Jiri, he would take Karbu by leaping backward—the angle would give him a shot. He would also shoot Jiri, and Emilia if she turned on Tindren. Harry might still take a bullet.

The helicopter was an unknown.

Another thing bothered him. Intuition. Something felt off with the whole situation. And his ability to read facial tics and eyes was a nonfactor since it was dark and everyone wore wool hoods. A slight panic touched him that something had been hidden from him.

His cold fingers curled tighter on his triggers.

CHAPTER 27

"LET'S PUT THE GUNS away." Karbu spoke calmly, with authority. "No one needs to shoot anyone, and with witnesses, no one wants gunshots to draw police up to Chena." He shrugged. "Otherwise most of us are going to take bullets."

"You first, Karbu." Steel glanced at him.

Karbu shrugged. "Of course." He slowly withdrew his gun from Harry's ribs and shoved his gun inside his parka pocket, his hand in his pocket too, still on his gun.

Harry backed up several steps from Karbu, kicked off his snowshoes, and stuck his hand in his pocket, ready. Emilia put her gun away. Jiri stood up from his kneeling position, one hand loose at his side, the other shoved into a pocket.

For a moment Steel considered shooting Karbu and Jiri, but one of them would put a bullet into Harry, Senator Tindren, or both before they went down. And Emilia was still a question mark. Also the helicopter would be here before they could get off the plateau; without the HK G28 they wouldn't stand a chance against what he believed the chopper was bringing. Maybe the CIA—which would be in their favor. But if it was Jiri's escape plan, they had no quick exit strategy or place to hide. And neither Moeller brother seemed concerned about the approaching chopper.

Steel gave in to reason, and put both of his guns in his parka pockets, but kept his hands on them. At least the pockets gave his hands a chance to warm a little. As soon as Senator Tindren moved away from Jiri, and was safer, he would shoot Karbu and Jiri.

Senator Tindren still hadn't put his gun away.

"Senator, please." Karbu looked at Tindren.

Steel readied himself. Maybe Tindren had decided to shoot Jiri now.

"Sure." Tindren slowly lowered his gun and shoved it into a pocket.

Steel didn't know what to make of Tindren backing down. Maybe he was playing for time, to see if they could find out who had hired Jiri. If so, the man had guts.

"Now everyone pull their hands from their pockets, empty of guns." Karbu looked at all of them, including his brother. "Jiri."

Jiri pulled his empty gloved hand out of his pocket, as did Karbu and Emilia. So did Harry. Steel followed suit. That left Tindren with his hand still in his pocket. Karbu didn't seem to care about the senator, but Steel thought he had it right. Tindren was hoping to get the name of who had hired Jiri before he shot him.

"Good, we all live to fight another day." Karbu looked at Steel. "Tell Christie to release our man."

"I need to hear him on our coms," said Jiri.

Steel considered the options, still uncertain of what was going on. He glanced at Emilia, but she was staring at Tindren. "Christie, release the man, as we discussed."

***

Christie had heard everything. Her back was stiff over the odds her men were facing. "Are you the one who attacked Harry?"

The man didn't answer.

She rose from the chair, keeping her gun aimed at him. "Put your hands out in front of you."

The man complied, and Christie stepped forward and stomped down hard into the back of the man's left hand, hearing it break beneath her foot. Crying out, the man rolled onto his right side, cradling his hand. "Now slowly get to your knees and tell them your situation. I want to hear everything you say clearly."

The man spoke into his coms. "I'm still in the room with a gun on me."

"Do I let him go, Steel?" asked Christie.

"Negative for now," answered Steel.

***

Steel looked at Karbu. "We need Senator Tindren safe, out of range from here, before we let your man go."

"Our helicopter is coming." Karbu shrugged. "You won't win this fight. My brother and I agree to allow Senator Tindren remain alive for today."

Karbu's voice sounded genuine, but that meant nothing to Steel. He glanced at Emilia, but she continued to ignore him and stared at Tindren, who still faced Jiri.

Steel focused on the Moeller brothers, but said, "Senator, step over to my side."

Tindren pulled his hand out of his pocket, still holding his gun, but turned and aimed it at Steel. The senator smiled. "I can claim self-defense, as you said."

Steel swore under his breath, tense, ready to pull his guns and dive sideways.

"Release Karbu's man," snapped Senator Tindren.

Steel wondered what was motivating Tindren. He had missed something in all of this. Yet he had no doubt that Tindren was ready to shoot him. The senator might know guns, but movement in their multiple layers of clothing made everything more awkward and Tindren didn't have his training. Thus Steel was fairly confident that if he dove sideways, he could get a gun out before Tindren killed him. Still, he said to Christie, "Release their man as we discussed."

***

Christie heard the exchange, which amped up her worry for Steel and Harry. She motioned to the door with her gun, and said to the man, "Get up slowly, take a few steps, stop at the door."

The man got up, slowly stepping to the door, still holding his broken hand.

Christie kicked hard at the man's ankle, hearing something snap.

The man exclaimed and stumbled into the wall near the door, barely able to stand.

"Tell them I'm freeing you," she snapped.

The man gasped. "She's letting me leave now, but I'm injured and she has a gun on me."

Christie motioned to the door with her gun. The man opened it, and slid along the wall out into the hallway, needing to brace himself against the wall as he slowly hopped away.

"He's leaving," said Christie.

***

"Your man is badly hurt." Steel lifted his chin. "If anything happens that we don't like, Christie can easily track him down, bring him back, and call the police."

Karbu stared at Steel. "That's unfortunate."

Senator Tindren's deep voice was calm and smooth. "Tell Christie to go back into the hotel room and shut the door, or I'll shoot you and claim self-defense."

Steel assessed everyone on the plateau. Karbu and Jiri were still not making any motions to draw weapons. Emilia continued to study Tindren. The senator was either the head of this Op or being manipulated somehow. It didn't matter.

Steel said, "Do it, Christie."

"Affirmative," she responded.

Steel stared at Tindren. "You're part of all this."

Tindren didn't lose his smile. "Of course. The plan was always about you, Steel. I'm leaving on the helicopter with them after we kill you. My visit to you with Emilia earlier tonight was a nice touch, wasn't it? You bought all of it."

Steel glanced at Emilia—she was still focused on Tindren. She had lied about everything. He still hoped for one edge. He believed the senator had it wrong, and said, "Again, this location and date was on the phone of one of Morris' killers, and you're the only one at Chena Resort that fits. Do you really think they plan on letting you walk away from here alive? If you shoot me, then they toss you off the cliff and the authorities are left with me as the assailant, who died while killing you. Karbu, Jiri, and Emilia will helicopter out, unknowns in all this."

Tindren lost his smile for a moment, and glanced at Karbu. "The latitude and longitude on the phone was just to get Steel up here, right?"

Karbu didn't answer, and Tindren swung his gun to him. "I'm leaving on the helicopter with you, correct?" He glanced at Emilia and Jiri. "Our contact called me in the yurt, and asked me to inform the SUSV driver that I'd be leaving in the helicopter. I was told Steel was going over the edge."

Jiri and Karbu didn't reply, but didn't seem concerned about Tindren's gun either. It confused Steel.

"Who called you, Tindren?" Steel wanted that name.

Tindren raised his gun to shoulder level and pointed it at Karbu. "Tell me I'm leaving on the helicopter or I'm going to put a bullet in your head, Karbu."

In that same instant Emilia stepped forward and chopped hard into the front of Tindren's neck. Wide-eyed, the senator choked for air, his arm dropping.

"Secure their man, Christie!" Steel went for his guns, but Jiri came at him fast, throwing hand strikes at his head. Steel was forced to forget about drawing his pistols so he could block Jiri's hands. The man was fast, strong, and skilled.

Karbu attacked Harry with fists and open-handed strikes. None of them were moving very efficiently with all the clothing, which also softened their blows.

Harry took two body hits, stumbled back, blocked Karbu's flying hands aimed at his head, and counterattacked.

Emilia hit the senator's arm hard and Tindren's gun fell out of his hand. Without hesitating, she pushed the senator with both palms. Tindren stumbled backward, close to the edge of the cliff, his arms spread out. Emilia stepped forward and kicked him solidly in the chest, sending him flying backward, crying out as he disappeared into the black night.

Harry swung at Karbu, but the stocky man blocked his strikes with open hands and stepped back calmly, hands up in a fighting stance.

Steel faced Jiri in a sideways stance as Jiri's foot flashed at his knee. Raising his leg, Steel blocked it, and kicked at the man's thigh.

Jiri was already withdrawing his leg, his hands flashing forward in finger strikes at Steel's eyes and a knife-hand at the side of his neck. Steel slid his head sideways, blocked the knife hand, and flicked his bent wrist at Jiri's nose.

Jiri was already moving out of the way. Steel noted Jiri's smooth, very fast movements. The man was testing him, trying to find weaknesses and strengths.

Harry and Karbu were trading strikes to the side, while Emilia tossed Tindren's gun over the side of the cliff and then ran away from all of them, back toward the yurt. The helicopter appeared from below as it rose above the plateau on the southern edge.

***

Christie exited her hotel room, gun up, and aimed it down the hallway. "Stop."

The man hopping along the wall paused.

"Come back to me," said Christie.

Ahead of the man, at the top of the stairway leading to the first floor, two hooded men appeared, both with guns up, facing her. Christie knew she could take one or both, but that would mean police and she wasn't sure Steel wanted that. "Two of their men are here, Steel. Gunfight in the lodge or I let them go."

Steel's voice came back immediately. "Let him go. Track him."

Christie edged back into the room, her gun still on the men.

One of the men stepped forward and looped his arm under the injured man's shoulder, while the other kept his gun aimed at Christie. In a minute they disappeared around the edge of the stairway and out of sight.

Christie ran down the hallway after them.

***

Steel blocked another low kick from Jiri, aimed his own kick at Jiri's legs, and only partially connected. Jiri had circled Steel so that he had his back to the helicopter that was descending onto the plateau a hundred feet from them on the path, landing between them and the people back at the yurt.

"Another time, Jack Steel." Jiri smiled, whirled, and ran.

Karbu gripped Harry by the front of his parka, rolled backward onto his back, and threw Harry over him. Then he sprang to his feet and ran for the helicopter. Steel pulled his guns.

Two men in the side of the helicopter held automatic rifles, aiming at them but not firing. A warning. Steel kept his guns aimed at the men in the helicopter, but also didn't fire.

Harry scrambled to his feet and hustled to Steel's side, gun in hand.

"Let's get out of here, Harry. Cover me first." Steel rapidly put on his snowshoes, while Harry covered him, and he covered while Harry put on his.

The helicopter took off. Emilia stared down at Steel, and then they were gone in the night.

Steel and Harry made a beeline for the trees to the north. In all white, at this distance, Steel knew the people at the yurt wouldn't be able see them in the darkness. They would assume Senator Tindren and his girlfriend Emilia were leaving in the helicopter. As far as they knew there was no one else here.

"Steel? Harry?" Christie sounded anxious.

Steel spoke as he hurried through the snow. "We're okay. Emilia kicked Tindren over the cliff edge, and she, Karbu, and Jiri left on their helicopter."

Once back in the trees, Steel and Harry pocketed their guns and put on their choppers, walking as fast as possible for the snowmobiles. "Christie, do you still have their man in sight?"

"He's gone, Steel," she replied. "I followed them all the way to the first floor and outside, but they had a car waiting. I saw them take off."

"Back to the room, Christie."

Steel thought on all of it as they made their way back to the snowmobiles. It took twenty minutes of hard work. On the way, Harry recovered the HK sniper rifle. They quickly took off the snowshoes and packed guns and gear in the backpacks. Keeping the snowmobiles on low revs, they made their way down the trail until they were far from the plateau. Then they turned on their lights and traveled at maximum speed.

In another twenty minutes they had the snowmobiles back in the shed, the door locked, and they were walking back to the Moose Lodge. It was after midnight and no one was outside. Steel assumed guests or employees were all in their rooms or cabins sleeping. Christie advised them that the hallway and stairway were clear before they entered the lodge.

In minutes they were back in their room. Silent. Taking off gear. Letting the chill evaporate. Steel was tired. So was Harry.

Christie walked up to Steel then, kissed his cheek, and held him tightly. He gripped her back just as fiercely. She released him and hugged Harry.

"I was going nuts." Christie sat down on her bed and pulled the blankets over her, looking weary. Steel sat near her, while Harry slumped on the other bed, his big frame sagging.

“Karbu could fight.” Harry glanced at Steel. “It looked like Jiri could too.”

“Both pros.” Steel acknowledged that much. Karbu and Jiri would provide tough matchups with either of them. Steel felt like they were David playing against Goliath. “I think Jiri is the one who attacked you in the geothermal pool walkway, Christie.”

Christie flicked her fingers. “I figured as much. So now we all want him dead.”

Steel couldn’t argue. "Jiri is still going to come after us.”

“What do we do now?” Harry ran his hands through his hair and looked at them.

“The tourists atop Charlie Dome won’t know the senator’s missing, and will think he left on the helicopter.” Steel glanced at them. “They might not find Senator Tindren for days, or even begin looking for him if he doesn’t have someone waiting for him somewhere. Even then they probably won’t look for him anywhere near the plateau. No gunshots, no evidence of wrongdoing, and a story that the senator gave that he was leaving on the helicopter with his girlfriend. The senator might be buried in a snowdrift at the bottom of the cliff and not be found until spring. That’s also why Karbu and Jiri didn’t want a shooting match, or shoot at us from the helicopter. Emilia was honest about that. They didn’t want bodies or gunshots drawing police attention for now.”

Steel continued. “If we tell anyone, all we would have is our word—Senator Tindren was shoved over the edge by a shadow organization that we can’t find.”

Harry shook his head. “They outgunned us. And Emilia played us.”

Christie pulled her knees up to her chest and rested her chin on them. “So they got what they wanted. Tindren dead, and no attention for now.”

“Someone Senator Tindren trusted called him, manipulated him to do what he wanted, and set him up for murder.” Steel thought on it. “The same person that General Morris called.”

"And we still don't know the connection between all of the victims—why Tindren was killed." Christie half-closed her eyes. "Emilia?"

Harry looked at Steel.

Steel shrugged. "She lied to us multiple times. She killed Tindren. She has to be Karbu's asset, or CIA, or both."

"How could she be CIA?" Harry frowned. "And if Tindren knew the person who hired Jiri, why not take Tindren alive?"

"Maybe the CIA learned Tindren was part of the Ops to kill the others, including General Morris, and they wanted him dead. Maybe they're protecting M4N." Steel shrugged. "Whatever the reason, we can't trust Emilia." He twisted to Christie. "Where are the next target locations and dates?"

Christie flicked her fingers. "Fiji. Viti Levu, the main island. I asked Jeffries for names and he came up with the Director of Homeland Security, Ryan Singer, another dove. He'll be there in two days for four days of snorkeling and diving. The one after that is Chairman of the Joint Chiefs of Staff—Carl Wyman. He's a spelunker, like you, Steel. He'll be at Carlsbad Caverns National Park in the Chihuahuan Desert of southern New Mexico in one week." She paused. "Another dove."

Steel clasped his hands. "Senator Tindren was the only one that didn't fit, everyone else does. We have to assume killing doves is the motivation. We also have to assume Senator Tindren was part of all this and whoever hired Jiri saw Tindren as a risk and dumped him. Maybe Emilia was given orders by the CIA to kill Tindren."

Harry cracked his neck. "So we're looking for a hawk who wants the doves in this administration gone."

"Most likely Daniel Baker, the National Security Advisor, or Bill Bishop, head of the CIA." Steel felt disgust sweep him. "Maybe both after what happened to Tindren tonight."

"Are you sure killing doves is the motivation?" asked Christie.

Steel thought about it. “Hawks want wars. So a zealot, or someone who stands to profit off war, or both. I’d say the zealot part is primary, because all these high-profile murders are high risk for any amount of money.”

“People get stupid where money is involved.” Harry stretched his arms.

“When do we leave for Fiji?” Christie eyed Steel.

Steel shook his head. “You’re going home to recuperate, Christie.”

She squinted at him. “I’ll be fine by tomorrow, Steel.”

Steel frowned. “I’ve seen you favor your ribs and you’re exhausted. Besides, I’m calling Colonel Jeffries tonight. We’re done. Ryan Singer and Carl Wyman need protective custody until we can find Jiri and end this. There’s no sense playing Jiri’s game anymore. The only reason to come to Chena was to take out Jiri, but we can’t put two more targets at risk for that goal, and two of us are not enough to be a protection detail. Plus, if I was Jiri, I’d be changing the schedule now.”

Harry looked at him. “So we’re all going home?”

Steel nodded. “Unless someone has a better idea. We have to find a way to locate Jiri and Karbu’s base of operations and hit them there. If Singer and Wyman are protected, that’s the end of things for now. Colonel Jeffries has to find some way to act, and we still can’t go to the police or anyone else at this time because we don’t know who we can trust, and we would have to admit to killing the four at Morris’ house, which exposes us to possible charges of not coming forward, among other things. I’d rather not.”

“I second the idea of all of us going home.” Christie smiled at him.

“Amen to that.” Harry looked at Christie. “The aurora borealis was beautiful tonight, sis. Sorry we couldn’t enjoy it.”

"Another time." Christie yawned and slid down beneath the covers. "I'm sorry, guys. I'm spent. And we have early flight times out of here."

"We could change the times." Steel looked at her.

Christie murmured, "Better to be home early, in case Jiri or Karbu head there."

Harry rose. "Get some sleep, sis."

"You too." Christie closed her eyes. "Night, Steel."

"Good night, honey. Harry, if you don't mind, I'll call Jeffries from your room."

"No worries." Harry left, and Steel with him.

Harry lounged on his bed, chatting with Isabella, while Steel sat in a chair and called Colonel Jeffries.

Jeffries sounded tired and annoyed, but he listened to all of it. At the end he said, "I'll find a way to get protective custody on Singer and Wyman ASAP without bringing attention to them. I still want Jiri dead, Steel."

"So do I, Colonel."

Jeffries continued. "No ID on the photos Harry and Christie sent me of the two M4N operatives."

As expected. Steel thought of one more precaution. "Would your CIA contact be able to find out if any personal jets belonging to Karbu or Jiri are scheduled to fly out from Fairbanks? We're headed home in the morning and I want to make sure the Moeller brothers aren't headed to Virginia now."

"Give me little bit." Jeffries hung up, but called back in fifteen minutes. "No jets or planes with a manifest headed to Virginia. My contact said CIA can hide that kind of thing under their security umbrella, but he managed some access. One personal jet is headed to Hawaii, and one to Denver for a scheduled layover. But I couldn't get a passenger or owner list for either."

That made Steel feel better. "Jiri might be trying to get to Homeland Security Director Ryan Singer in Hawaii instead of Fiji."

"I'll make sure he doesn't. Good night, Steel." Colonel Jeffries hung up.

Steel relayed the conversation to Harry, said goodnight, and returned to his room.

Christie was already asleep. He quietly propped a chair beneath the doorknob and took the other bed, lying on his back, his Glock beside him.

Senator Tindren's death didn't bother him. Tindren had been associated with Karbu and Jiri somehow, and with the man behind General Morris' murder. How they were all connected was the key, and he didn't have it. He felt he was operating blind, and he knew Karbu and Jiri were going to come at them again—at least Jiri would. He wondered how the Moeller brothers would respond when their last two targets went MIA under protective custody.

The whole thing felt like a complicated puzzle that could only be explained by one person who was still hidden. General Morris' comments to him about justice felt a little lost on him now. He didn't know if he could get justice for the general's murder.

But he could still find Jiri and Karbu. He would find a way. And he would make them pay.

He closed his eyes, glad that at least for tonight he could rest in peace.

He slid his hand over his Glock.

CHAPTER 28

KARBU LOOKED AT JIRI, who sat across from him in the limo. Emilia sat next to Jiri. She was speaking with Ivel in Spanish. Karbu could only decipher fragments of some sentences. He had never put much time into learning Spanish, and neither had Jiri. Ivel would tell him later what they talked about, but it was usually just friendly conversation.

He was glad Ivel had a friend in Emilia—the two had seemed to hit it off when they first met. They both had Puerto Rican heritage and long dark hair, but Ivel was shorter, with softer facial features. Emilia had a stronger chin and her eyes held more caution. The CIA had recommended Emilia, a freelance contractor they used, and Karbu had grown to trust her. She was loyal to him, not Jiri, but he had impressed upon her to never allow that to show.

Karbu had also been impressed with Emilia on Charlie Dome. She had played things perfectly. And probably saved them from a mess. She sat calmly, a little distant from Jiri, which told Karbu she wasn't sleeping with his brother. That was for the best too.

They were sitting on the runway, waiting for the hired jet that Jiri would take to Seattle, and then Hawaii. Ivel sat next to Karbu, her arm looped through his, her long dark hair on his shoulder. The air was frigid outside, but none of them were dressed for it. The car was warm and they would soon be on jets.

Karbu struggled to keep his fury at bay. Jiri had just informed him that his stupidity had cost them two teams. He glared at Jiri, who lounged in his seat next to Emilia. "I want this to end."

His brother didn't answer.

Karbu continued. "That could have been very ugly on Charlie Dome. We were fortunate. Tell the client we're done, and they can have their money back. Leave the last two targets go."

Jiri's forehead creased, and then he sat up. "That will affect our reputation and we will lose ten million."

Karbu stared hard at his brother. "Even the CIA told me that Jack Steel is a hero, a man of integrity. You need to let go of your vendetta against him."

"And allow him to find us and kill us?" Jiri shook his head. "You read the CIA report on him. This is a man who also doesn't let go. He took down a president. He will come after us until he finds us."

Karbu felt impatience burning in his chest. "Then we find a way to make peace with him."

"I killed a friend of his." Jiri took a sip of his water. "There is no way to make peace with him now."

Karbu stared out the window. "If Ivel and I had not come to Charlie Dome, Steel would have killed you there."

"Perhaps." Jiri smiled. "Without you on the ground, and without Ivel flying the helicopter, it would have been much more difficult, but still workable. I thank both of you."

Ivel nodded slightly, but Karbu's voice was hard. "You lost two more operatives to serious injuries. We're not losing any more men to Steel."

Jiri spread his hands. "It's just me now, brother. I'll take care of the next two targets with Emilia, while you find another leverage to use against Steel."

"This man is no fool." Karbu lifted a few fingers off his thigh. "Your targets won't be in the open now. You may not be able to get to them."

"True. Then we will have to inform the client that we have to delay things." He paused. "Does Steel have family? Children?"

"We're not killing children." Ivel stiffened beside Karbu.

Jiri lifted a hand. "Of course not, Ivel. But they can be used as leverage against a man like this."

Karbu thought on everything. Jiri would not let go of killing Steel any more than Steel would let go of killing Jiri. He was stuck, for now. "Alright. You finish this contract, under one condition, Jiri. Otherwise we are finished."

Jiri waited calmly. "I'm listening, brother."

"This Op is the end of U.S. operations. No more contracts with the man that hired you. No more contracts with anyone on U.S. soil. Every contract needs my approval from this point forward." Karbu leaned forward. "I love you, my brother. But if you don't agree, we're finished. Now. Here."

Jiri lifted his chin. "Agreed. I can live with it. You're right. It was impulsive to take this contract, and it has cost us too much. We finish, we clean up the loose ends, and I walk away."

Karbu leaned back. "Then Ivel and I will get the leverage we need on Steel. We're going to get some rest in Denver and organize there. I'll call you around noon."

"Talk soon." Jiri exited the limo, and Emilia left with him, speaking in Spanish to Ivel, and nodding slightly to Karbu as she did.

When the door was shut, Ivel said, "I'm not kidnapping Steel's child, Karbu! That is beneath us!" She turned away from him. "Why do you let Jiri push you around like this?"

"We're not going to kidnap Steel's daughter." Karbu touched her arm softly. "I don't let Jiri push me around, but he's stubborn. He's finally agreed to what I want. We just have to find something, someone, that will force Steel to let Jiri go at the end of all this."

Ivel turned, her dark eyes on his. "I've said this before, but Jiri is putting all of us in danger, Bu."

"I agree." He sighed. "Do you know how many times he saved my life when we were both in Special Ops?"

"You never said."

He nodded. "Three times. He risked his life three different times to save me."

"I'm sure you did the same for him."

"One time. I did once." He stroked her arm. "This will be over soon and we can move on. When we return home, I'm going to make plans to cut all ties with everyone in six months. At that point I'll give Jiri the option of getting out, buying me out, or just give him the business. We have enough money. I want out."

Ivel gripped his arm. "You're serious?"

He nodded. "We owe Jiri a favor for making us both feel this way."

"And if he won't accept that? Then what, Bu?"

"He will have no choice, Ivel. He wasn't being honest. He was dead on Charlie Dome without our help. And without our help now, Steel will probably find a way to kill him. I told you, I am very skilled at assessing people. Steel is highly trained, smart, and doesn't have Jiri's weakness for impulsive decisions. If I help Jiri this last time, I will have paid my debt to him. We're finished. If he cannot handle that, I'll deal with him then."

She snuggled closer to him. "I've dreamed of this for years, Bu. Just us. No more business ties to violence and death."

"I'm finally feeling it too." He stroked her face. "Tonight on Charlie Dome we came close to a shootout. Jiri and I could have both died. I don't want that kind of risk in my life anymore. I have too much to live for." He paused. "My fish and your art."

She made an exaggerated face. "Just fish and art?"

"Well, maybe more."

"Finally." She kissed him lightly. "It took you a while to get here, dear."

"I'm a slow learner." He smiled. "One more action on Steel, then it's over."

"You know how much I love you, and how much pain I would go through if I lost you, Bu."

"Always and forever, Ivel."

PART 3

OP: STEEL'S HOUSE

CHAPTER 29

CHRISTIE WAS GLAD TO be back in Virginia. She realized as she and Steel unpacked and put things away in the master bedroom that this really felt like home. It had from the very beginning over a year ago. It made her even more happy that he wanted it to be hers too. A few times she caught his eyes as they passed each other, exchanging smiles while silently putting guns and gear away in the closet safe, or hanging up clothing.

Lerkin and Kat had been sitting with the dogs in the living room when they arrived, and though Steel owed Lerkin, Christie wished they had the house to themselves. Harry was never a bother. But he was family.

Steel finished first, changed into jeans and a shirt, and looked at her. "I'm going to check supplies, groceries, and make a run before I shower and settle in."

"It's late, honey. Do it tomorrow," she said.

"I don't want to do anything tomorrow except R&R. Besides, stores are empty this time of night."

"Do you want me to go with you?" She set her insulated snow pants on the bed.

"No, just relax, go to bed early. I'll be back soon."

She walked up to him and held him tightly, and he reciprocated. Pulling back, she smiled and kept unpacking her suitcase.

"What was that for?" he raised an eyebrow. "Not that I minded at all."

She shrugged. "It feels good to be home, Steel."

He nodded. "It does, doesn't it?"

She stopped to look at him. "You're home for me, Steel."

"I feel the same way, honey." He smiled warmly at her, and then turned and left.

She stood at the window to watch him drive the Jeep out of the turnaround in a few minutes. She felt blessed to have found someone who loved her like Steel did. She would never take it for granted.

In five minutes she was finished. Humming to herself, a bath sounded good. Then bed. She had slept fitfully on the plane and dozed off during the ride back from Richmond International Airport. But she needed one long night's sleep in her own bed.

Sitting on the bed, she pulled a photo album off the bedstand. Pictures of her. Steel. Rachel. A few with Harry and her other family members. They didn't have that many printed photos of each other, but they had enough. Sometimes they looked at it together. She paged through, deciding she would print some of the few she had taken at Chena. For fun.

Rising, she went into the bathroom and began running the water.

Her phone rang and she pulled it out, expecting Steel. It was his daughter, Rachel.

"Hi, Christie."

"Hey Rach, what's up?" Steel hadn't informed his ex-wife Carol or his daughter that they had gone to Chena Resort. He always tried to insulate them from worrying about what he was doing. Christie liked Rachel and was happy to be part of her life.

"Mom is in the city working on a case, and Grandma isn't feeling well. Grandpa is dropping me off at the front gate and I'm walking in." Rachel sounded excited, as she always did when visiting her father, which was often.

Christie frowned. "Did you call your Dad?"

"I wanted to surprise him. Mom said he's home."

Christie thought about it. Steel could decide what to do with Rachel when he came home. "Honey, he's out shopping, but he'll be glad to see you. When will you get here?"

"Fifteen minutes."

Christie didn't hesitate. "I'll walk down the driveway and meet you at the gate."

"That would be great, Christie. See you soon."

Christie didn't mind. She never turned down a chance to bond with Rachel. Also she tended to sleep better with some light exercise before she went to bed. She turned off the running water. The bath could wait until she returned. She tucked her SIG into her belt at her back and sent a quick text to Steel explaining things. She ended with, "Act surprised when you see Rachel!"

Steel sent back a swift, "Thank you! I will!"

In a minute she was downstairs, pulling on a light winter coat. Lerkin was sleeping on the couch already, and Kat was in her room. Harry was probably talking to Isabella while taking a bath—he was different that way. Most men liked showers. Not Harry. It was fine with her that everyone was busy. She wasn't feeling like chitchat anyway.

It was cool outside, dark already, but compared to Chena Hot Spring's minus thirty-five Fahrenheit, it felt like summer. The air temp was forty. Fresh. But the forest surrounding their house kept the ground cooler, protected from the daytime sunlight. Thus there was still a foot of snow on the ground. Stars had joined the moon. A great horned owl hooted. Hanging around Steel and Rachel had developed her skill of identifying different owl sounds.

She walked a relaxed pace down the winding half-mile driveway. The dirt and gravel had a small layer of snow over it. In a dozen minutes she reached the county road. Tired, she leaned her butt against one of the gate posts. Steel had left the front gate open, which was a relief. She felt too weak to struggle with it.

She hadn't fully recovered yet from hypothermia and would be happy to be in bed as soon as possible.

In minutes Rachel's grandfather, Tom, pulled up parallel to the driveway on the county road in his station wagon. Wearing a baseball cap, with graying hair, he was tall and thin. He smiled and said hello to her. Christie hadn't visited with him often, but he had always been pleasant.

Both grandparents respected her, and Steel's decision to move on. After all, it was his ex—Carol—who had initiated the divorce with Steel. At the time it was also Carol who had entered into an affair that had ended badly. To her credit, Carol had made sure Christie hadn't been painted as *the other woman*. Christie had always appreciated Carol's honesty and taking responsibility for her actions instead of blaming her.

She talked to Tom for just a minute while Rachel got out with a small overnight bag. Tom apologized, but said he felt like he was coming down with the flu too. He looked tired. Christie thanked him and he left.

"Good to see you, girl." Christie gave Rachel a quick hug.

"You too, Christie."

"Your hair is getting long." Christie liked it. "You're also getting taller!" She guessed a lean five-four.

"I know, right?" Rachel smiled at her.

They started back, both of them quiet. But it wasn't awkward. That was one of the things Christie liked about Rachel. She was Steel's daughter. Independent. Confident. Calm. Observant. It was relaxing to be around her. But she was still a teenager.

Car tires on gravel made Christie glance over her shoulder. Her first thought was Tom had come back for some reason. High beam headlights were in her eyes and she had to shield them. Then she saw the car aiming right at her. Pushing Rachel to the side, she flung herself out of the way to the ground as the car skidded to a stop.

Rolling into a tree, Christie yelled, “Run, Rachel!”

Before she could do anything, a dark figure stood above her, his boot pressed hard on her chest. A Lycra black hood covered his head, only revealing his eyes and mouth. His silenced gun was aimed at her head, and his voice was factual. “Call the kid back or I’m going to put a bullet in your left leg for starters.”

***

Zeus watched Mykey almost run the woman and kid down, and he wasn’t sure if they hadn’t jumped out of the way if Mykey would have.

“Get the kid!” Mykey was out of the car smoothly nearly before it had stopped, striding toward the woman.

Zeus jumped out of the car and ran. It was dark, but the moon and stars gave him enough light to see the girl’s shadow in the woods. She was fast, but big as he was, he had been a sprinter in high school and was no slouch.

He was glad to hear the woman calling out, “Come back, Rachel! Come back!”

It meant Mykey wouldn’t put a bullet in the woman. Mykey never gave people second chances. Do what he asked or pay a price.

Still, the girl didn’t slow down or seem to care that the woman was calling to her.

Zeus’ heart was pounding. Teenagers always had phones. And if the girl called the police, he was going to jail. Worse, Mykey might kill the police, and then he would be up for a murder charge. It scared the hell out of him, making his legs work harder.

The girl seemed to have a specific destination in mind, because she never hesitated or looked back at him.

Still, he was gaining on her. Filled with shadows, the forest gave him glimpses of her. It was enough. As a child he had spent a lot of time in the Florida Everglades and other wildlife areas. He was sick of Las Vegas, the never-ending concrete and pavement.

The girl glanced over her shoulder at him once, then immediately veered west. She had decided something. He made a calculation, veered sharper west, and gained some more on her. In a minute she dropped to the ground. Maybe she had stepped in a hole. Charging forward, he almost tripped over her. She had pulled something out of the ground. A plastic bag, and she was taking something out of it. Raising it.

His heart in his throat, Zeus leapt at her, landing on the ground near her, his hands tearing the small pistol out of her hands. That's when he saw her eyes and face for the first time clearly. Nice features, hair to her shoulders. She kicked out hard at his side.

Rolling away from her, he sprang to his feet. His Aikido and wrestling skills kicked in as he charged her. She was already on her feet, in a sideways stance, hands up, no fear in her expression as she kicked out at his forward knee.

Zeus rolled to her side, one hand sweeping at her back foot. He would never try this with an adult with any weight, but she weighed a hundred ten pounds if she was lucky. But she was lean, not skinny.

She hopped over his sweeping hand, which surprised him, and instead of running, kicked out at his head. Dropping the pistol, he caught her foot with both hands and used his weight to twist her. He didn't want to hurt her, but her skill left him with little choice. She rolled with him, to avoid injury, and landed on the ground.

She tried to kick him with her other foot, and Zeus caught her ankle, trapped it against the ground, and was quickly atop her. She still managed to throw two strikes at his neck and head before he pinned her arms down. Both of her blows failed because of his longer reach and the fact that he jerked his head out of the way. His two hundred fifty pounds made resistance futile at that point.

Zeus shifted his weight back a little so she couldn't knee him. "Stop. Please." He said it softly. "I won't hurt you, Rachel, I promise. But you have to stop."

Her whole body relaxed then as she stared up at him. "If you're not going to hurt me, then why are you wearing a hood and attacking me?"

Again he detected no fear in her voice. "It's complicated. Look, I need you to come with me, but you have to understand something. My partner won't hesitate to hurt you or the woman you were with. So let's go back and make sure that doesn't happen."

That seemed to quiet her and she gave a little nod.

"Stay put," he said.

He reached out with one hand, sweeping the ground for the pistol. He found it, and stared. Ruger LC9 9mm. Ritchie had taught him all about guns. It was perfect for a girl. Small, compact, seven rounds. He saw the plastic bag, put the gun back in and sealed it, and then looked for the hole. It was actually a coffee can buried in the ground, with an attached round steel lid with sticks and leaves glued to it.

Zeus hurriedly put the gun in the can and closed the lid over it. When he looked at it, he realized he would never have noticed it if he was walking through the woods here. The lid was perfectly camouflaged. How the heck did the girl find it so fast?

He saw the girl staring at him, not fighting to escape. "If my partner sees the gun, or knows you went for it, he'll break your arms to make sure you can't shoot anything. You understand?"

He swallowed. He was exaggerating, and he was also taking a risk talking to her about Mykey. But he didn't want Mykey to hurt a child, and he wanted her scared of Mykey. "You understand, Rachel?" he repeated.

She nodded.

"Give me your cell."

She slowly pulled it out of a back pocket and handed it over.

Carefully Zeus rose, gripping her upper arm in one of his massive hands, and they began walking back.

"Is your dad here, Rachel?" Zeus hoped the answer was yes, that the man had money, and they could just collect it and go.

"No," she answered. "But you're going to meet him."

Her voice was strong when she said that, and it made Zeus wonder who the man was. Who buries a gun in a camouflaged can for their daughter, or trains their daughter to fight like her? He wished he had said *No* to Ritchie, but now he was committed.

It took them a few minutes to walk back. Mykey was in the driver's seat, and turned to stare at them.

At first Zeus thought Mykey had killed the woman and dragged her body into the woods. He relaxed when he saw her in the back seat, sitting quietly, a hood over her face and zip ties on her wrists behind her back and on her ankles. The hood on the woman was looser than theirs with no eye or mouth slits. He wondered if Mykey had beaten her.

Rachel immediately opened the driver's side passenger door, but Zeus said, "Stop, Rachel. Hands behind your back." He pulled a zip tie out of his pocket and put it tightly on the girl's wrists. From a jacket pocket he pulled out a hood and slid it over her head. "Okay, get in."

Rachel climbed into the back seat, slid over to the woman, and put her head on the woman's shoulder.

The woman said, "I'm okay, Rach. Are you?"

"Yes." The girl didn't sound scared.

"Good."

Zeus got into the front seat and looked at Mykey, who smiled at him.

"Gun out, kid. Silencer." Mykey started driving.

Zeus took out his Glock, pulled the silencer from his jacket pocket, and screwed it on. Then he rested it on his thigh. The few times he had held his gun it was for self-defense during dangerous collections. He had never shot anyone. It made him jittery to have it out now.

Mykey studied him. "Glad you're here after all, kid. What took so long with the girl?"

Zeus lifted a hand. "She's fast and I had to slap some sense into her."

"Good." Mykey glanced back at Rachel and said calmly. "Now listen, Rachel, I already told Christie this and now I'm telling you. I don't need to hurt you, but I won't hesitate to put a bullet in either of you. Do as you're told, and you'll be fine. I never repeat myself or ask twice. If I have to, there will be pain involved. Got it?"

Rachel nodded, turning her face into Christie as if she was scared. Zeus didn't buy it, but Mykey did because he smiled and winked at Zeus as he drove.

"What's the name of the home owner?" Mykey sounded casual.

"Jack Steel." Christie answered quickly.

"Rachel his kid or yours?" asked Mykey.

"His." Christie's voice was steady.

"Perfect." Mykey looked into the rearview mirror. "I saw the perimeter cameras and sensors. Nice. They're along the whole driveway too, right?"

Christie didn't answer, and Mykey braked hard to a stop, picked up the gun in his lap, and swung it over the back seat. He used his right hand, but Zeus had seen Mykey use either hand with guns. Ambidextrous.

Mykey's voice was cold. "I have my gun on the girl, and I'm going to shoot her. So let's only play this game once; you answer or I shoot."

"Yes," answered Christie. "The cameras are along the whole driveway."

"Who's monitoring it in the house?" asked Mykey.

"Harry, my brother. Everyone else is asleep." Christie's voice was steady.

Zeus found it interesting that, like the girl, the woman didn't sound afraid either. "Who else is in the house?" he asked.

"A wheelchair friend and his daughter," answered Christie.

"We already knew that." Mykey grinned at Zeus. "Where's your squeeze, Christie? The owner."

Christie didn't hesitate. "Out shopping."

"Late to be shopping." Mykey didn't sound concerned as he faced forward again and continued driving. "I checked your phone out, Christie. Quite the security setup you have here." He flicked Zeus' arm and nodded to the console between them. A SIG lay there. "She had a SIG tucked into her jeans. Can you believe that?"

Mykey looked into the rearview mirror. "Who were you afraid might come by, Christie?"

Christie said, "We're a protection agency and we're always prepared."

"What's the name of the agency?" asked Mykey.

"Greensave."

Mykey glanced at Zeus. "Google it."

Christie spoke up quickly. "Our business is from referrals only. You won't find us listed anywhere."

"More and more interesting." Mykey seemed intrigued.

They drove down the driveway to the house and Mykey parked behind the van in the circular turnaround.

Christie spoke quickly. "We have two dogs. They're friendly, not barkers."

Mykey looked at her and Rachel. "Good to know. From here on out, both of you keep your mouth shut unless I ask you a question." He looked at Zeus. "We'll have to shoot the dogs."

Rachel spoke up, sounding panicked. “I can get them into the basement and keep them quiet. They’ll listen to me. Please don’t shoot them.”

Mykey stared at her, and for a moment Zeus was afraid he’d beat the girl.

Mykey said evenly, “You know, you’re lucky I like dogs. I had a few in foster homes growing up. They were always honest and kind.” He hesitated. “You get a pass this one time, Rachel. But shut up now.” He looked at Zeus. “You take Rachel in first, very quietly, and get the dogs into the basement. They bark, they run around, shoot them.” He looked back at the girl. “And I expect you to whisper, Rachel.”

Zeus gently guided Rachel out, holding her arm while they waited for Mykey. Mykey tucked Christie’s SIG in his jeans, grabbed Christie by her upper left arm, and dragged her out of the car. Her lower body fell to the driveway and Mykey pulled her across the dirt like a sack of trash, as if she weighed ten pounds, not a hundred-thirty plus.

At the door, Mykey stopped, his voice quiet. “If either of you have anyone you love in here, and you try to warn them, you get a bullet and they get a bullet. That’s after I give you some pain and have fun with you, Christie. So lie on your stomachs and keep your mouths shut.”

Zeus listened, chilled because he knew Mykey meant every word he spoke. Mykey used prostitutes, but he never hurt them. However on a collection once Mykey told Zeus he didn’t mind beating or killing women that owed Ritchie money. Mykey believed it was only fair to treat women equally. Zeus had been happy never to go on those collections with him.

As far as Zeus knew, the only ethical standard Mykey had was regarding pedophiles. On a collection once, Mykey had found out a man was a pedophile and he just shot him without collecting any money. Then he had reported to Ritchie what he’d done, telling Ritchie to take the money the pedophile owed him out of his paychecks. Oddly enough, Ritchie had agreed with Mykey’s decision and absorbed the debt, saying, *We're on the same page there, Mykey.*

Mykey tried the front door and found it unlocked. Pulling his Glock from beneath his leather waistcoat, he paused and whispered to Zeus, "Get the dogs."

Zeus walked in first with Rachel, still holding her arm. He left her hood on. He immediately recognized Lerkin on the couch, sleeping. The dogs were lying on small throw rugs on the wood floor near the couch.

Rachel extended her hand and whispered, "Come on, Spinner and Lacy, let's go."

Both dogs rose and wagged their tails as Rachel continued to call to them softly. She whispered to Zeus, "The basement door is straight ahead by the back door."

Zeus guided her down the open hallway, past the open stairway leading to the second floor. He was happy when the dogs followed Rachel to the rear door, and adjacent basement door. He opened the door, and Rachel told them to go down and the dogs obeyed. Zeus shut the door behind them.

By the time Zeus returned to the living room with Rachel, Mykey had dragged Christie in. He had dumped her so she lay parallel to the couch Lerkin was sleeping on, halfway between it and the front wall of the house.

Mykey put a finger on his lips to Zeus and headed up the stairs.

Zeus gently pushed Rachel down beside Christie, zip tied her ankles, and whispered, "Not a sound from either of you. My partner meant every word he said." He hoped to hell that they listened.

***

Harry had his phone set for alerts from the perimeter security just like Steel and Christie, and the first alerts set off were Christie. He checked to make sure as Isabella kept talking.

Rachel arrived, and he saw her and Christie on the camera walking back down the driveway. All good. He ignored the ensuing driveway alerts that were set off; Christie and Rachel walking in. Besides, it was highly unlikely the Moeller brothers would be attacking them already. If Jiri had flown to Hawaii as they suspected, he would be at least a day away from them. And Steel thought any attack would have to include Jiri. Though he said they should be prepared to expect anything from the Moeller brothers.

He was lounging in the bathtub, listening to Isabella talk about her time with her family. It had all gone better than expected. Her father, Carlos, approved of him, was happy for her, and would attend the wedding. He felt warm inside. Everything was working out perfectly. Except for the wedding bill. He decided to let that worry go.

Footsteps. He heard them softly coming up the stairs, then down the hallway. Christie and Rachel, headed to their bedrooms. Rachel was a great kid. If he had one like her, it would be fun. But he was satisfied to be a cool uncle to her and to his brother Clay's twins. Isabella felt the same way. Neither of them wanted kids, at least for now.

A slight knock sounded on the bathroom door, and he answered, "Yeah, sis? I saw Rachel. I'll be out in a bit and say hello."

The door opened and a man stepped in, wearing a hood and holding a Glock. Harry didn't move. The man's build didn't fit Jiri or Karbu. He looked bigger. The intruder put a finger over his lips. He strode up, gun and eyes on Harry, and with the toe of one of his boots he nudged the phone off the bathtub edge. It slid into the water, and the man backed up.

When the man spoke softly, Harry was certain it wasn't one of the Moeller brothers. No accent. A cold, calm voice. A pro. Maybe he worked for Jiri and Karbu. That fit. Harry listened.

"Get some clothes on. Then put this hood over your head and lie on your stomach on the floor. I'll zip tie you." The man had pulled a hood from his jacket pocket and tossed it on the floor.

Harry studied the man for a moment, assessing if there was anything he could do.

The man aimed his gun at Harry's legs.

Harry nodded and slowly, deliberately, stood up to follow the man's directions. Better to stay healthy for an opportunity later rather than take a useless bullet now.

The man backed up, cautious and not allowing any surprise attacks.

Harry did as requested.

CHAPTER 30

STEEL HAD SEEN THE original alerts from the driveway—it made him happy to see his daughter Rachel on the camera shot with Christie. He sympathized with Carol's grandparents. They were always responsible, so if they were sick and Carol was busy, it made sense they would drop Rachel off with him. However he would have to send Rachel to Carol tomorrow anyway, even if she was busy. Until Jiri was out of the picture, he didn't want Rachel on his property.

As other alerts came in, he checked them. All driveway—so he ignored them without pulling up the camera feeds. He continued to head into Richmond. Glad to be out of Chena Resort's frigid temps, he rolled down his window an inch. The cool air of the evening was refreshing and woke him up. Last thing he needed was to fall asleep at the wheel. Tired, he could sleep in tomorrow and then figure out their next move.

In fifteen minutes a WhatsApp call came in. Isabella from Mexico. He took it with a smile. "Hi Isabella. It's good to see you."

She smiled back, her chiseled features, high forehead, and narrow chin all framed by her straight, jet black hair. "Hi Jack, how are you?"

"I'm good, Isabella. Just heading into town to get some food and supplies. Harry's back at the house."

"I know. That's why I'm calling. I was talking to him on WhatsApp, and the phone just tipped into the bath water, and then it died."

Steel smiled. “Harry knocked it into the bathtub, huh?”

“Jack, I think he was staring at someone else in the bathroom when it happened. I can’t be sure, but I waited fifteen minutes and he never called back.”

Steel’s blood ran cold. He pulled onto the shoulder and thought about it. “Alright, Isabella. I’m going to ask you for a favor. I have to check security and the house. Whatever you do, please don’t call or text any of us if you don’t hear from me, alright? And if you don’t hear from me in one and a half hours, call Harry’s brother, Clay. I’m an hour away from home, so I won’t have anything sorted out immediately.”

Her forehead creased, and he said, “Rachel and Christie were walking down the driveway, so maybe Rachel walked in unexpectedly on Harry in the bathtub and he moved suddenly and knocked the phone in.”

“That’s probably it.” Isabella sounded hopeful. “I’m sorry to bother you, Jack.”

“Don’t be. Thank you for being careful and cautious, Isabella. Talk soon.” He ended the call and quickly went back to the driveway alerts—and saw the car captured on cameras along the driveway. A man wearing a hood was driving. Another man wearing a hood sat in the front passenger seat. He swore. How could Karbu and Jiri attack them again this soon? Or even find operatives that fast?

The cameras also picked up two shadowy figures in the back seat. Christie and Rachel, he guessed.

Wheeling the Jeep around, he floored the vehicle to ninety in seconds. It didn’t make sense that Jiri had come for them this quickly. Still, the man was unpredictable. He must have sent more of his men. How did M4N have more resources available this quickly? He had thought he had at least a day to prepare for any arrival of the Moeller brothers. And according to Colonel Jeffries’ CIA source, the private jet likely to have Karbu had overnighted yesterday in Denver.

The brothers' M4N organization had experienced operatives, and would easily bypass his perimeter sensors. He had to plan on multiple hostiles in different locations on his property. His best plan of attack would be the tunnels. He would run west on the county highway into the Blue Ridge foothills, then south, then back east on the county road bordering the southern edge of his property. It was highly unlikely Jiri or Karbu knew about the lot west of his property. That lot had been purchased under an anonymous LLC so it couldn't be traced back to him. That would be his point of entry.

He assumed he was the primary target. But Jiri would kill Christie without hesitation. And Rachel was at risk. They would use his daughter against him. When he thought of the two girls in his life that he would do anything for, now both at risk, his stomach churned. He wanted the brothers dead more than ever now.

Every idea he came up with to attack his own house ended with him either captured, dead, or failing a rescue. He hunched over the steering wheel. Even at high speed it would take an hour for him to reach his land.

***

Zeus watched Mykey herd the hooded and zip-tied man and woman down the steps. He recognized Kat from her photographs. Pretty figure. She was wearing PJs, while the man wore jeans and a flannel shirt. Harry, Christie's brother, was big, not as big as him, but powerfully built. Tough in a fight.

Mykey told them to lie down on their bellies near Christie and Rachel, and to shut up or take a bullet. They did as they were asked. Then he asked Zeus to zip tie their ankles.

Zeus complied.

Casually Mykey walked behind the closed front door and hit an overhead light switch for the adjacent dining room. It cast light over the table, but kept the prisoners a little shadowed.

Lerkin finally woke up, and pushed himself up to a sitting position, swinging his dead legs off the sofa so he could sit upright. His face was drawn as he stared at them. Haggard and looking guilty.

Zeus didn't care what happened to the old man. What kind of father would place his daughter and friends in this kind of danger? Loser gambler.

Mykey sat on the arm of the sofa, smiling, his Glock resting on his thigh. Zeus knew Mykey reveled in this kind of situation. Risky, chaotic, with the possibility that it could turn very violent if Mykey didn't get what he wanted. Mykey seemed to live for these moments.

"Ritchie wants his money, Lerkin." Mykey held his Glock loosely in his hand, looking relaxed. "What's the name of the guy you came here to see?"

Lerkin didn't respond, and Mykey casually aimed the Glock at Kat.

Zeus was leaning against the front door. He impulsively stepped between Mykey's gun and Kat on the floor, and said harshly, "Lerkin, your daughter's going to take a bullet, so you have one chance to answer!"

Lerkin paled and said, "Jack Steel."

Mykey frowned up at Zeus, who stepped back again. "You get in the way of my gun again, kid, and I'll put a bullet in you."

"Sorry." Zeus spread his hands, his mouth dry. "Just trying to help."

"Good cop, bad cop." Mykey flashed a cold smile. "No worries. Just don't do it again." He turned to Lerkin. "I'm happy to hear you and Christie agree on that. How do you know Steel?"

"Army," said Lerkin.

Mykey studied his fingernails. "Special Forces?"

Lerkin nodded.

Mykey looked at Christie on the floor. "Christie, does Steel have a hundred K on the premises? If he does, we'll take it and leave."

Christie said, "Eighty."

"Where?" asked Mykey.

Her voice was calm. "In several safes in the house."

"That's sounding better." Mykey stared at her. "Okay, where's the security set up? Cameras etc.?"

Again Christie didn't hesitate. "In the barn."

Mykey stood up. "Cover them, kid. And if anyone talks, put a bullet in them. I'm going to take Christie to the barn and check out the security setup. See what the hell else this guy has going on."

One thing Zeus found odd about Mykey, given his job and the man's enjoyment of violence, was that he rarely swore. *Hell* was as far as he went. Mykey had told him years ago that he considered swearing lazy English and low class. But after hanging around Mykey for a while, Zeus could tell when he was angry. His voice became quieter and controlled, like a wolf baring its teeth and ready to charge.

Zeus held his gun loose in his hand. "How long before you're back?"

"Soon enough." Mykey grabbed one of Christie's ankles and dragged her out between Rachel and Harry. Then he gripped one of her arms and effortlessly dragged her across the floor to the front door.

"Don't touch her." Lerkin's voice was steady.

Mykey dumped Christie on the floor near his feet and slowly turned. His voice was quiet as he leveled his Glock at Lerkin. "What did you say, old man?"

Lerkin stiffened. "I owe Ritchie a hundred K. Nothing else. You'll get your money."

Zeus blinked, not wanting to watch what was coming.

"After what I just said, you've got balls, Lerkin, I'll give you that." Mykey lowered his gun. "Shooting a cripple is unethical."

He stepped forward quickly and pistol-whipped the old man twice on the head, sending him groaning onto his side. "We don't get the full hundred K, you're taking another trip back to Las

Vegas. With your precious little Kat. We'll drug her up and farm her out to every man we can find who'll pay until your debt is paid off. With interest."

Lerkin slowly pushed himself back upright, wiped blood off his lips, and stared defiantly at Mykey.

"Tough too. I respect that." Mykey looked at Zeus. "Zip tie the old man's wrists behind him and hood him." He paused. "He can stay on the couch, given his legs."

Zeus tucked his gun into his belt, and while Mykey watched, he zip tied Lerkin's wrists behind his back. He hoped Lerkin would just shut up. Something about Lerkin's eyes made him feel the old man wasn't scared to die or stand up to Mykey. But his big mouth could get his daughter raped and killed. Zeus pulled a hood over the man's head. Then he drew his gun again and looked at Mykey.

"You hurt Christie, you might as well kill all of us, and you'll be running for the rest of your life," said Harry. "Jack Steel is connected to Army Black Ops and a special group of friends. They will hunt you down."

Mykey aimed his gun at Harry's back.

Zeus tensed, expecting him to pull the trigger. Accessory to murder. He swallowed.

Mykey said, "Pow." He smiled, his voice cold. "Talk again, Harry, without me talking to you, and you'll wish you hadn't." He stepped forward and kicked him twice in the ribs.

Harry groaned and doubled up on the floor.

Mykey stared down at him. "That's for not keeping your mouth shut. Doesn't anyone listen to me? You talk without permission and there's going to be pain."

Mykey's voice hardened. "New rule. If anyone opens their mouth or doesn't do as asked the first time, or lies to me, I will hurt the kid. Little Rachel. Maybe kick her teeth out, choke her out, break an arm. Something serious. Got it? I'm not repeating any of this again."

Everyone was silent, and Mykey smiled at Zeus. "That shut them up."

Zeus watched Mykey drag Christie out the door and across the driveway like a sack of garbage, wondering if he would rape her in the barn. He felt sick to his stomach.

"Whoever you are, thank you for protecting my daughter." Lerkin looked in Zeus' direction. "If you untie all of us now, we can take your friend down."

From the floor Harry said, "We'll trade. Your freedom, no charges, if you help us now."

Zeus stared out the window, worried Mykey would come back and find them all chatting. "Shut up. The man who sent us, Ritchie, has resources. If I run, he'll hunt me down or hurt my family."

"We have resources too," said Harry. "Way more dangerous than a two-bit loan shark with a few men to beat people."

Zeus shook his head. "Stop talking. I don't want to see you hurt, but I can't help you."

Kat lifted her head and spoke softly through her hood. "Thank you for protecting me."

Zeus stared at her, thinking of Mykey's promise to take her back and sell her to men. He would do it. Ritchie would do it. "My partner will let you all live if we get the hundred K. Then we'll leave."

Rachel spoke up, sounding encouraging. "You lied to your partner about slapping me. And you didn't tell him I had a gun." She lifted her head in his direction. "Thank you."

Zeus glanced out the window again.

Harry lifted his head. "Kid, whatever your name is, your partner is smart. He now knows Jack Steel is connected. I told him that so he won't hurt Christie. But there's no way he's going to let any of us live to hunt him down, or to send others after him. He might take Lerkin and Kat back to Las Vegas, but the rest of us are as good as dead."

"Just shut up, all of you!" Zeus stared at Harry, Rachel, and Kat on the floor. Murder. He was adding up the years in prison. Life sentences. Also these were normal people, not the violent scum that Ritchie dealt with, or gambling lowlifes like Lerkin.

For the last three years he had been lying to his parents and three sisters, telling them he was making great money as a bouncer in a Las Vegas club. His parents lived in Tarpon Springs, Florida, and ran a Greek family restaurant. His sisters had college degrees, but still helped his parents out at times in the restaurant. That restaurant had put them all through college with no debt at the end of it. Zeus visited them often in Florida, but no one in his family really cared for Vegas and hadn't visited him. That had been for the best.

Still, his lie about his job had been eating away at him. And while his family might forgive him for working for a loan shark against violent men and lowlifes, they would be disgusted with him for being part of this. Hurting women and a child, and a man in a wheelchair. Murder would cost him their respect, and their love. Family was important to him. When he thought of that, he wondered suddenly what he had become.

In the past sometimes he had thought Mykey was lucky. Mykey had grown up in foster care, abandoned when he was ten years old. No siblings. No one that he needed to lie to. But Zeus suddenly realized that he was the lucky one, and he was making a mess of it. How would he feel if his sisters were Rachel, Kat, and Christie? His stomach was in knots.

He considered bolting as soon as Mykey entered the barn. He could take the pickup out front and drive away. Call the police and FBI on the way out. But he would always be looking over his shoulder for Mykey. And contrary to what Harry said, Ritchie did have considerable resources and could find anyone. Worse, Ritchie wouldn't hesitate to send Mykey or someone else after his family to hurt them. That would be one of the first things Ritchie would do.

Zeus felt hollow inside. He was stuck here with Mykey, and with whatever Mykey decided to do. It was either that or die.

CHAPTER 31

CHRISTIE FELT GUILTY OVER her sloppiness. Allowing herself and Rachel to be captured. The two men must have been parked on the county road, waiting for an opportunity. At first she had thought they were the forward crew of Jiri and Karbu, waiting for the brothers to arrive before they did anything.

But as she listened to the lead man talk to Lerkin, she realized Lerkin had brought this mess to them. It answered the uneasiness she and Steel had sensed in Lerkin. Steel had made a mistake, thinking Lerkin had just been worried about his daughter.

Christie didn't blame Steel for his loyalty to Lerkin, but she was furious with Lerkin for putting them all in danger. Lerkin had brought these killers to them, without giving them any warning.

She had known from the start that the man dragging her to the barn would do as he said. His voice had told her that, and his acts of violence against Lerkin and Harry only served to back up her assessment. She wanted to hurt him for hurting Harry. Lerkin deserved whatever he got.

She had also seen enough in the initial attack in the driveway to know the man dragging her stood six-three, weighed about two-thirty, and sounded in his mid-thirties. From the very first his eyes and voice told her that he wouldn't hesitate to hurt or kill, and she felt he wouldn't think twice about killing all of them if he had to. This was a man who had killed many times before.

The man's partner was even bigger, in height and weight—she had glimpsed him from the ground when he ran after Rachel. Massive. But she sensed from his voice that he was at least ten years younger—mid-twenties—and more sensitive. The fact that he had placed himself between his partner's gun and Kat said a lot. He wasn't a killer, while the man dragging her was stone cold. An odd pair.

Steel would know about the alerts, would have seen the car, and would be coming. But he could be as much as an hour away. She felt responsible to find a way out of this.

When she thought about what she could do, it was very unlikely she would have a chance against this man in a fight with her wrists tied. With her ankles zip tied, it would be impossible. Not just ruthless, the man was very careful. The hoods, zip ties, and the killers not using their names backed up that perception. But that might also give the killer a reason not to murder them if they couldn't ID him.

Plus he was dragging her around as if she was a small cat. He was strong. Maybe stronger than Harry. The way he had exited the car to put his boot on her chest had also displayed speed and agility.

She had one ace that she hadn't played yet; the mini OTF knife in the back of her belt. The man had missed that when he had groped her for weapons. She could use the OTF dagger to cut the zip ties. In the car, with two guns in front and Rachel in back, she had decided against any attempt to use it there. In the house, same issue.

She didn't think she could kill this man one on one. Especially because she felt a deep sense of weariness and fatigue in her body. She hadn't fully recovered from hypothermia in Chena, and the lack of sleep was fatiguing her even more. But if she and the others were left alone, even for a minute, she could cut herself and Harry free and then they could kill this SOB together.

She wondered if the man's younger partner would go along with murder. He had protected Kat from a bullet without even knowing her. She didn't know if Harry was wearing his OTF knife belt. Rachel was wearing hers. So they had at least one more knife between them.

The man stopped dragging her. Her hip hurt from being dragged over the driveway gravel and stone, but she ignored it.

"Give me the code," he said.

The barn's single steel, house-sized door faced west and was always locked. The code was for the keypad to the side of the barn door. Christie gave it to him.

Next the man wanted the key for the deadbolt lock. She told him it hung around her neck on a light chain, and he bent over and ripped it off her. In seconds he dragged her inside.

Christie couldn't see anything out of the black hood, but light suddenly played at the lower edges of it. The killer had turned on the lights.

The man whistled. "This place is like Fort Knox. The door is solid steel, an inch thick, with three thick deadbolts. Reinforced steel walls. No one is getting in here." He squatted down beside her. "But what's in here that I can't see? What is your man protecting?"

When she didn't answer right away, he pushed one knee into her chest hard and wrapped one hand around the front of her neck, squeezing slightly, with the Glock pressed into her forehead. "If I have to hunt for things, and I'm very good at finding everything in a room, and you haven't told me about it, then you're up for whatever I want to do to you. Understand?"

"A virtual reality station, exercise station, and shooting range at the far end," she said.

"No kidding." His voice was sarcastic. "So Steel is also very good at everything necessary to kill people." He squeezed her neck hard.

His hand was like iron. Maybe stronger than Steel's grip. She couldn't breathe and realized she was going to black out. Still she didn't try to resist, knowing he would just hurt her more.

At the last moment he released the pressure. She coughed for a minute, gasping for air.

"Next time I'm going to choke you out, Christie. And have fun with you while you're unconscious. Now cut the bull. What's Steel hiding here?"

She wouldn't tell him about the tunnel system. That was the best chance Steel had to help them. However, after seeing Wyatt's barn setup last fall, Steel had installed a safe on this floor three months ago, similar to the one in the master bedroom closet and the one in the barn's lower hidden level. She hoped it was enough for the man to not search for anything else. The hidden stairway to the downstairs level was hard to find anyway. She had to risk it.

She babbled, "There's a safe in the wall with money and weapons."

"Tell me where it is and how to get in."

She did, and he dragged her across the cement floor, beyond the virtual reality station and across the barn to the opposite wall. There she told him to tilt a picture frame, which exposed another keypad. She gave him the code for it. She heard the wall slide up, and the man used the combination she gave him to open the four-foot-by-three-foot horizontal safe door.

The man whistled. "He's ready for a war. Love it. You get bonus points for telling me."

Christie heard him rifling through the banded money that was in the safe.

"Twenty K here. A good start," he said.

Christie listened as he pulled out weapons and loaded clips, maybe packing all of it into one of the duffel bags in the safe. In minutes the safe was closed again.

"What is Steel, a survivalist?"

She tried to sound afraid. "He obsesses about security. This is his safe room." The last sentence was a partial lie, but she thought it worth the risk.

"Safe house more like it," he scoffed. "What's in the locked cabinet across the room?"

"Burner phones, security sensors, and extra cameras," she said quickly.

"I believe you. He's not going to keep something important in a cabinet. Anything else he's hiding, Christie?"

"No."

"Alright." He dragged her by her arm, her hip hitting the six-inch-high raised and padded virtual reality platform, where the computer and wall monitors were located. Dumping her near his feet, she could hear him hitting keys on the computer.

"Give me the computer password."

She did and the man entered it and whistled. "Love it. Great perimeter camera set up. And let's delete these pictures of our car and arrival."

In a minute he slid his hand down to her knee and ran it along her inner thigh. She didn't react but felt sick to her stomach.

"We might have some time together later if your man doesn't come up with the money. I bet you're a feisty one, right? Itching to hit me, hurt me, aren't you? It would be fun. Maybe we'll have to make time anyway."

Removing his hand, his tone changed and became brisk. "First, business. Let's text your man, Steel, on your phone. See if he wants to pay Lerkin's debt."

Christie heard him texting, wondering what he was saying. He could be guiding Steel into a trap. The man was right, she wanted to kill him, but she doubted he would give her the opportunity. The man's matter-of-fact approach to violence scared her. And she felt rape was just another item on his list that he had done often in the past. But she forced herself to focus on solutions, not fear.

A text came back, and the man said, "Steel backs up your story. Says he has eighty thousand here, but he can get the other twenty tomorrow at a bank. He wants to know how to proceed. He also says if you or anyone else is seriously hurt, he'll call the police and SWAT. He wants proof you're okay. Facetime with you, Rachel, and Harry."

The man laughed. "A guy like this doesn't call the police. Plus, if he does, he knows I might decide to kill all of you anyway." He paused. "Let's make that an affirmative."

He starting talking. Christie assumed he was sending a voice text.

"Hey, Steel. I see any sign of police, SWAT, or any other men besides you on your property—and I'm looking at your security cameras right now—you can assume Christie and Rachel are going to experience a lot of pain and then buy bullets. I've been in prison before, so if I'm going back for this it's probably going to be for a long time and I might as well make it worthwhile. Don't disable the security system in any way. Another no-no." He nudged Christie's leg with his boot. "Christie is quite the looker. I'm tempted. Don't push your luck. I'll have instructions for you soon."

The man chuckled. "That should make him cautious."

Christie's phone beeped, and the man said with humor. "Yeah, Steel agrees to all of my demands. Big surprise."

The computer beeped several times.

Christie heard the man punching keys to bring up camera feeds.

The killer sounded annoyed. "What's Steel playing at? I just warned him, and eight men are breaching different areas of the perimeter."

"We don't have that many employees." Christie instantly thought of Jiri and M4N. "More likely an enemy. I can't be sure who they are unless I can see them."

"Who have you pissed off lately?" asked the killer.

"It's a long list," she said.

He pulled her up to her feet, sat her in the chair, and faced her toward the computer. "If you try anything, I will kill you. And just so we're clear, if you turn around and see my face, you're definitely going to die."

She nodded. "I get it."

He pulled off her hood. Christie looked at the camera shots on the computer monitors. He was right. Men were walking in cautiously from the north and south, and east along the driveway. Wearing fatigues, carrying automatic rifles, and wearing night vision. They looked ex-military, but they weren't dressed like Karbu's and Jiri's men.

She said, "Kat has a husband she's running from. Ryan Randall. He's part of a white nationalist group. These men look the part."

Just seeing them made her even angrier at Lerkin. He and his daughter had brought them here too. Kat's husband or one of his friends had tracked down Lerkin, followed them here, and then called in their friends.

The killer scoffed. "Weekend wannabe warriors."

A text came in on her phone.

The killer's voice was calm. "Steel is saying the same thing. Well, I don't want to get stuck in here when all the fun is going to be out there. How long before these guys get here?"

Christie was unnerved by his excitement to face eight armed men with only his partner. "Ten minutes max. They're about a half-mile away."

"We have to hurry then." He pulled the hood back over her head, and dragged her unceremoniously off the chair so she fell onto the padded virtual reality floor. He pulled her fast. When he reached the end of the raised platform, her butt fell onto the concrete floor.

She heard him opening the barn door, propping it open with something, and then she was dragged outside, the cold air on her face again, the ground rough against her jeans as he dragged her over snow and gravel again to the house.

In seconds they were through the front door and he dumped her there.

The killer said, "Kid, you got two minutes. Take Rachel, have her leash the dogs, and put them in the barn. When you leave make sure you shut the barn door. Hurry up."

Then the killer dragged Christie back to her spot next to Harry, twisting her so she lay on her stomach again. Harry touched her shoulder with his and she nudged his shoulder with hers to let him know she was okay.

Christie assumed Steel would use the tunnel to the house basement below them. Then Steel would bring these men hell. But she didn't know how close he was, nor what the man would demand of him.

She heard Rachel talking calmly to the dogs as she left with the younger man. They were back in minutes, and then Rachel was lying beside her again. Rachel nestled up beside her, nudging her forehead against her other shoulder. Christie turned her head, resting her chin lightly on top of Rachel's head. There was little else she could do for Rachel, and she hated that too.

"Get ready, kid," said the man. "We've got guests coming. And look what I found for us in the barn. Check the duffel bag. Mossberg 500s, mags for our Glocks, MPK5s with thirty-round magazines. Tons of ammo. I even got a Kevlar vest for both of us. We can take on an army. I'm in heaven, kid."

CHAPTER 32

STEEL GOT THE TEXT from the man holding Christie, demanding a hundred thousand to clear Lerkin's gambling debt. That made him swallow. He had been so eager to pay his life-debt to Lerkin that he hadn't listened enough to his gut about what Lerkin was uneasy about. A gambling debt. That didn't fit the Lerkin he knew, but neither did lying about why he had come out here.

The killer sent him the warning about calling the police, SWAT, or reinforcements, and Steel responded with an affirmative that he would comply with his request.

That's when Steel received multiple alerts of perimeter breaches to his property south, north, and east via the driveway. When he pulled up the alerts, he decided it had to be Ryan Randall and his white nationalist buddies. Dressed in fatigues, some looked and moved like ex-military, and some looked like amateurs. Either way, Karbu or Jiri's men wouldn't be dressed in fatigues. Ryan Randall must have followed Lerkin from Las Vegas. Lerkin hadn't been as careful as he thought.

Steel sent a quick text to the man holding Christie saying the intruders were not his men.

He was still twenty minutes out and these men would be at the house before he reached the shed. As upset as he was with Lerkin, he didn't want Kat handed over to these men. They might beat or rape her.

Steel swallowed. Harry, Christie, and Rachel. He loved all of them deeply. Family. Now that he had one again, he didn't want to lose it. There wasn't anything he wouldn't do to make sure that didn't happen.

In twenty minutes he pulled up to the southwestern edge of his property. A half-mile ahead he saw a Jeep and SUV parked on the county road.

He turned north into a short dirt driveway and quickly had to stop in front of a locked metal fence. A sign read, *Private Property. Keep Out.* He unlocked the fence, drove in, and locked it behind him. He drove another hundred yards up to a large steel shed hidden from the road. After punching a series of numbers into a keypad on the side of the garage, he pulled the shed door up, drove the Jeep in, and shut the door again. He hit a light switch.

To the side was a black and blue Yamaha SR400 motorcycle with a black tinted helmet and black leather coat on the seat.

He ignored the bike and walked up to a locked cabinet. Using a key to unlock it, he stared at the supplies inside. First he changed into an all-black outfit. Lycra pants with multiple magazine sleeves built into it, pullover, light jacket, and a black Lycra hood that he kept rolled up to his forehead for now. There was a holster and silencer for his Glock, both of which he put on, and more magazines for the gun which he pocketed in the Lycra sleeves. He removed his belt with the OTF knife from his jeans and slid it through the Lycra waist loops.

There was also an HK MPK5 in the cabinet with a carry strap and night scope, also with a silencer that he screwed on. He swung the carry strap over his head so the gun hung near his hip. He grabbed four spare magazines for it, along with a night vision monocular. Lastly he strapped a fixed blade knife to his ankle.

He hoped he wasn't too late. But he decided to get some insurance and sent a text to the killer. *If you want the hundred K, Kat stays with Lerkin.*

No reply.

Opening the shed door, he pulled it closed after he exited and ran into the woods.

***

Zeus wondered what Mykey planned to do. Eight or more highly armed men were coming to get Kat, and yet Mykey seemed relaxed as he sat on the edge of the sofa. Mykey always seemed calm in situations that would panic Zeus. In the past he was unnerved by it, but after going with Mykey on just a few collections he realized that Mykey always had a plan. The man was very shrewd and unpredictable in how he problem-solved situations, just as he was in fighting. And his solutions always included violence.

"Christie, where are the other safes?" Mykey stared at her.

Christie spoke quickly. "Kitchen cabinet, study floor, and master bedroom closet. They all have money and guns, but the upstairs closet one is loaded like the barn."

"Wonderful." Mykey lifted his chin. "Kid, turn off all upstairs lights, make sure all the windows are closed and locked. I'll wait. Do it quick."

Zeus hustled up the stairs and checked the bathrooms and bedrooms. In one of the bedrooms there were stuffed animals on the bed and plush birds lining a book shelf. Rachel's. He didn't want to see any of it. He was back downstairs in two minutes.

"Kid, I'm going to recheck entrances on this level, lock everything down, and check the basement." Mykey toed Christie's foot. "Christie, anything you want to tell me about the basement?"

She lifted and shook her head. "No."

"Okay, back in a minute or two, kid." Mykey left, checking the rear door and window locks, and then disappeared into the basement. He was back in two minutes.

He walked up to Rachel's feet. "I found a door leading to a tunnel downstairs. Behind the bookshelf. The tunnel door is locked so I can't get in. You all know what I said would happen if you break any of my rules. Lying wasn't smart, Christie. So this next punishment is on you. Rachel, turn over onto your back. I'm going to break one of your legs."

Rachel silently turned over onto her back.

"I didn't know!" Christie sounded scared. "If you want to hurt someone, hurt me."

"Don't worry. You're next." Mykey lifted one of his boots over Rachel's lower leg.

Zeus swallowed, not wanting to watch, not wanting to be here. He was going to be sick to his stomach. For one wild moment he considered shooting Mykey.

"Christie's telling the truth!" Harry spoke fast. "She didn't know. Steel and I are the only ones who know about the tunnel system. Steel is a little sexist about stuff like that."

Mykey hesitated, and then lowered his boot. "Okay, tell me all about the tunnels, Harry. You have thirty seconds."

Harry rattled off, "The tunnel in the house basement leads to a hidden room beneath the barn, from there two tunnels lead southwest and northwest to exits in the woods."

"Superb!" Mykey sounded delighted. He looked at Zeus. "You hear that, kid? We have a way out of here if we need it." He turned back to Harry. "What's in the lower hidden room beneath the barn, Harry?"

Harry spoke fast again. "Food, security computer, a safe room, and another hidden closet safe with tons of stuff."

"Steel is my kind of guy. Great escape exit or attack entrance." Mykey shook his head in admiration. "It's your lucky day, Rachel. Uncle Harry bought you a stay on your leg. You can turn back over onto your stomach again." He paused. "But Christie, just in case you were lying..." He stepped forward and kicked her left thigh once hard, and then her stomach once with the point of his boot.

Christie groaned and doubled over.

Zeus felt ashamed just standing there watching. He had beaten three of Ritchie's men for slapping a woman in front of a casino in Las Vegas, and now he was a bystander to watching Mykey do worse to a woman right in front of him.

"That makes me feel better, Christie, just in case you were lying." Mykey sat down on the sofa arm again and studied Christie's phone. In another minute he stood up. "Okay, they're here, kid. Time to put on the Kevlar."

Zeus obeyed. His fingers were shaking as he did it. Turning slightly, he hid that from Mykey. He didn't want Mykey to see that he was scared. Worse, if Mykey sensed at all that he was conflicted over hurting their captives, he didn't doubt that Mykey would kill him.

Mykey put his vest on quickly and then turned off the overhead light in the dining room. It was dark inside. He put his back against the front wall adjacent to the front door. "Kid, grab one of the MPK5s and a shotgun. Then crack open the door, but stand behind it so you don't get shot."

Zeus' hand felt clammy on the Glock as he slung one of the MPK5s over a shoulder. From the duffel he pulled out one of the Mossberg shotguns and leaned it against the front wall behind the door. Gripping the door knob, he cracked it open a few inches, and then stepped behind it so the wall would be his buffer against any bullets.

Mykey slid close to the door, Glock in hand, and called out calmly, "Ryan Randall, you can have Kat without a fight if you want her. I represent someone who her old man owes money to, so we have no beef with you or her. Come on in with one of your men and let's talk about it."

"This is Ryan Randall speaking. You bring Kat out here, or let her walk out on her own."

Mykey replied, "We're not coming out there to get shot, and we want to make sure you're Ryan Randall. She's tied up and can ID you."

There was a pause of almost a minute before Ryan shouted back, "How do we know you won't just shoot us the moment we walk through the door?"

"And have six or more of your men light up the house with automatic rifles? I'm not stupid." Mykey leaned forward past the opened door and grinned at Zeus.

Zeus peeked out a nearby front window and saw two shadowed men conferring with one another behind the pickup.

Ryan shouted, "Okay, two of us are coming in, armed, fingers on triggers. Turn on some lights."

Mykey yelled back. "We're waiting, armed, fingers on triggers too. But we just want to talk." He looked at Zeus. "Stand near the wall behind the door with the shotgun, so when they come in, you're at their back, kid. Anyone starts shooting, they're easy targets. And turn on the dining room overhead light again."

Zeus hit the switch for the light. Sliding the Glock into his belt, he grabbed the loaded shotgun and stepped back. The Mossberg was light in his sweaty hands. He made sure the safety was off. He felt different about shooting these men. They were coming for Kat. And if they planned to hurt her, or kill him and Mykey, he had no problem with self-defense.

Mykey returned to sitting on the arm of the sofa, still smiling, his gun resting on his thigh. He winked at Zeus as he dialed a number on Christie's phone.

It was picked up in silence.

Mykey said, "Steel, the phone's on speaker. Keep your mouth shut unless I ask you a question or I'll hurt your daughter Rachel before you ever see her again. Thanks for the text about Lerkin's daughter. Nice to know you care about Kat." He put the phone on the sofa arm.

"Coming in now, slow and easy." Ryan Randall sounded uneasy. In a few seconds he slowly pushed the front door open to ninety degrees and stepped in with another man behind him. They both held leveled automatic rifles.

Zeus stepped out from the wall, shotgun leveled, so the door wasn't completely between them, but added some protection for him.

Both men glanced over their shoulders at him.

"I'm Ryan Randall."

Ryan looked thirty, short brown hair, Caucasian. His partner had a short, trimmed beard. Average height, lean, about forty. The two men stopped just past the door, standing back to back, with Ryan facing Mykey, the other guy facing Zeus, their guns aimed at them.

"Well, there she is, on the floor, hooded, tied up, ready to go." Mykey chuckled, keeping his Glock resting on his thigh, but aimed at the floor. "Her old man, Lerkin, owes the man I work for a hundred K. But Kat doesn't owe my boss anything."

Mykey looked at Ryan. "Okay, first order of business, you step over, pull off her hood, and she ID's you. Then put the hood back on. You'll like that hood on, because then she can't ever ID any of your buddies."

Ryan nodded. "Alright." Half-facing Mykey with the rifle, he slowly stepped forward and squatted near Kat's head. He pulled the hood off, and Kat looked at him, wide-eyed, her lips trembling.

"Time to go home, Kat." Ryan said it sternly.

Zeus didn't want Ryan taking Kat, but he didn't see that he had any choice. It made him sick to see her treated like a piece of property.

"Kat, is this your husband, Ryan?" asked Mykey. "And remember, all I have to do is ask for Ryan's ID to confirm who he is. So if you lie, Daddy Lerkin is buying some pain."

Kat's voice was hushed, but full of fear. "He's my husband."

"Good enough for me." Mykey looked at Ryan. "Put her hood back on."

Ryan slid her hood back on and straightened. "Okay. We'll be taking her now. We'll leave you to whatever you have going on here."

Mykey nodded. "Just out of curiosity, when a woman runs off from a man like you, what do you do to teach her a lesson? Pass her around to everyone? Beat some sense into her?" He shrugged. "That sounds only fair."

Ryan gave a terse smile. "That's what we planned. We have a long ride back to Utah."

Ryan's partner gave a slight smile too, making Zeus want to smash his face in.

Mykey shook his head. "Yeah, I bet you can't wait to get Kat into the back of a truck on her back, right?"

Zeus listened, feeling sick just hearing it. He didn't know if he could let them leave with Kat. But what could he do? Nothing.

Mykey smiled. "Sounds fun. I'd join you if I didn't have this mess to clean up."

"You can't let them take my daughter!" Lerkin's voice was strong. "Please don't! You tell Ritchie I'll pay whatever he wants to let her stay here. I'll pay you whatever you want to keep her here! Please, mister, do the right thing."

Mykey smiled again. "Lerkin, that's a nice gesture, but you don't have any money so you're just blowing smoke up our asses. And you broke the rule. Now Rachel has to take some pain." He stood up. "Not only are you a terrible father for your daughter, Kat, now you've gone and put someone else's daughter into harm's way too."

Steel said over the phone, "I'll pay whatever you want to stop that from happening."

Mykey looked at everyone. "Fathers! What are you going to do?" He paused. "Okay, one thing at a time." He faced Lerkin and kicked him in the shoulder with the heel of his boot. "That's for opening your mouth, Lerkin."

Lerkin grunted and half-slid down, but used his other arm to push himself upright.

"You are a tough old bird." Mykey returned to sitting on the arm of the sofa. "Now, Steel, I said I'd hurt your daughter if you spoke, but since you made an offer, that's more interesting. How much more are you willing to pay me to not hurt Rachel?"

Steel answered immediately. "Twenty thousand. For the duration of the time you have her."

"That sounds fair, Steel. That's a deal. But everyone has to still keep their mouths shut or that price is going higher." Mykey looked at Ryan. "Now, Ryan, just one more thing before you take Kat. My boss said if Steel doesn't have a hundred K, we're to take Lerkin and Kat back to Las Vegas to have them work off the debt. Kat on the street, and Lerkin doing who knows what. We got eighty K here in this house. You wouldn't happen to have another twenty, would you?"

Zeus tensed as Ryan and his partner glanced at each other. Ryan turned back to Mykey, his eyes narrowed. Gripping the shotgun, Zeus curled his finger around the trigger and slowly aimed the shotgun higher at the man in front of him. He knew enough about Mykey that he could see where this was going.

Ryan sounded impatient. "Kat's my wife. I'm not paying you anything to take her."

Mykey nodded. "That makes sense to me. How about you, Steel? You got eighty here. We need twenty for Lerkin, twenty for Rachel. That's one-twenty so far. How much more are you willing to pay me to keep Kat here?"

Steel's voice came over Christie's phone. "Twenty. I'll get sixty at the bank tomorrow morning, so one-forty in all."

Mykey slowly nodded. "That sounds nice. But I'm facing eight guys with automatic rifles. You're asking me to risk my life for twenty K."

"That's an extra forty for you," said Steel.

Mykey chuckled. "We can't count the twenty to not hurt Rachel."

"Ten more," said Steel. "One-fifty total."

Mykey sighed. "Still, thirty for me to risk my life."

Ryan and the other man regripped their guns while keeping them aimed at Mykey and Zeus.

Mykey lifted his chin. "Ryan, can you match the thirty Steel is offering? What's Kat worth to you and the boys for that fun ride home?"

Ryan's partner glanced at Mykey. "Are you deaf, mister? Like Ryan said, we're not paying you anything to take Kat, but we will kill all of you if we have to."

Mykey didn't flinch, his voice cool and quiet. "The big guy behind you is about to put a hole in you with the shotgun he's holding, so I wouldn't get trigger happy right now."

Ryan and his partner glanced at each other, and in that instant Mykey raised his Glock and shot Ryan in the forehead. Zeus fired the shotgun, aiming high so he didn't hurt anyone else, sending the other man to the floor with a lethal neck and head wound. Ryan had already collapsed.

Kat shrieked.

Mykey leapt to the floor and yelled, "The door and light, Zeus! Get down!"

Zeus kicked the door shut, hit the light switch, and went to his belly as automatic gunfire blew through the windows and walls, spraying everywhere. His arms and back were tense as he glanced sideways and saw Lerkin had already rolled off the sofa to the floor. He avoided looking at the corpse of the man he had shot and was thankful it was dark inside.

He'd never shot or killed anyone before and it made his hands sweat. The police wouldn't look at a kidnapping situation as self-defense on his part either. It felt like his whole world was collapsing before his eyes.

Mykey held Christie's phone in his hands, and said, "Steel, the situation now requires that you help protect your women from these guys. No tunnels. You try to come up through the basement into the house, or through the back door, and I guarantee a lot of bodies inside the house. Stay in the woods. Do your thing."

The guns kept firing from outside, and Mykey grinned across the floor at Zeus. "Beautiful, isn't it, kid?" He turned his head. "Kat, in case you're wondering, you just got divorced."

Zeus gaped at Mykey. The man was crazy. He hoped Steel was as good as Mykey thought he was.

CHAPTER 33

STEEL CROUCHED BY THE open manhole cover in the woods—which led down to the tunnel leading to the room below the barn. Before he could climb down, he heard the two shots. Gunfire erupted in the distance. Silenced guns, but still easy enough to hear.

The killer immediately warned him against using the tunnels. He wondered how the killer had found out. Maybe he had threatened Rachel or Christie, or was just good at finding things. It didn't matter. Either way, the tunnels were out now. He shut the manhole. It had a layer of leaves and twigs glued to it, with seasonal snow on it too, so it would remain hidden.

He had six men to deal with, but he didn't think they knew he was here. Pulling his Lycra hood down, he ran west through the woods, wanting to make up as much ground as possible before the gunfire stopped. It would provide cover for his footsteps crunching in the snow. The tunnel entrance was halfway between his house and the shed, so he estimated he had a quarter mile to go.

While he ran, he was assessing the killer in the house. Without the advantage of the tunnels he had no way to get in for a rescue. He also knew the killer was going to place more demands on him either way. He needed backup, but he didn't have anyone close he could call. It was a mess. He had to hope Christie or Harry had some way to get to the killer from the inside.

The guns kept firing for over a minute, and when they stopped, he stopped. He doubted Ryan Randal's friends really wanted to die for Ryan. More likely they had wanted a chance to play weekend soldier and rape Kat.

He pulled out his monocular. Behind the house, two men knelt beside trees, their guns aimed at the back door. Fifty feet from him. He holstered the Glock, raised the MPK5, and sighted on both men to get range. Squeezing off the first shot, he killed the closest man with a head shot. Swinging the rifle, he shot the second man—who was turning toward him—in the thigh. He was already running as the man went down.

The man yelled, "I'm hit! I'm hit! Joe is dead!"

Steel stopped by the man's feet, his MPK5 aimed at the intruder's chest. The man had dropped his rifle and was gripping his bloodied thigh. He looked about thirty, scruffy beard, average build.

The man raised his head. "I don't want to die here, mister."

Steel nodded. "Good. Because legally I could kill all of you for coming onto my property armed like this, shooting at my house." He paused. "Are you all on coms?"

The man nodded.

"Okay, listen up everyone. Here's what's going to happen. I know there are four of you left. You're going to collect your dead and wounded and carry them off my property and leave. Two of you come to the back of the house unarmed, hands in the air. I'll tell the men in the house that two of you are coming in, also unarmed and hands in the air, to get Ryan and his friend. You get one chance to get this right, or I'm going to kill your buddy here, and then the rest of you."

He thought on something. "Wait." He knelt and rifled through the injured man's pockets until he found a billfold and ID, and the man's cell phone. He studied the ID. "Dan Northfeld." He replaced the billfold in Dan's pocket, but kept the phone. "I never forget a name or face, Dan, nor an address. I'm going to do some research on you and your friends. You're safe as long as you stay in Utah. Got it?"

Dan nodded, his face taut as he groaned. "I will. I promise."

Steel added, "All of you are going to exit on the driveway to the east county road. When all of you are at the beginning of the turnaround, I want your driver's licenses, including those of your dead, put on the ground next to each other, and a clear photo taken and sent to Dan's phone, which I'm going to keep so I know who all of you are. You have two minutes to get Dan before I kill him."

Steel backed up twenty feet to a tree and listened as Dan begged his friends to do as asked. Satisfied, he called the killer in the house and told him two unarmed men—with their hands in the air—would come into the house to get the bodies. He also added that he would shadow them down the driveway to make sure they left.

"Excellent," replied the killer.

In a minute a voice called out, "Coming back now, hands in the air!"

Two men appeared, slowly walking around the south corner of the house without their guns, their empty hands raised in the air. They glanced from their prone friends to Steel's raised rifle, and then back to their friends. Neither looked aggressive.

One of the men quickly tied a piece of cloth around Dan's leg wound, and then helped him to his feet. With Dan's arm draped over his friend's shoulders, Dan hopped away on one foot, while the other man dragged the dead man by his wrists around the south side of the house.

The killer in the house also confirmed that Ryan Randal's buddies were dragging the bodies out.

Cautiously Steel ran to the woods north of the house and watched the hostiles with the monocular. All eight were accounted for as they made their way around the driveway turnaround. They stopped at the entrance and took a photo of their licenses on the ground. Steel checked Dan's phone to make sure the photo they sent to it was clear. Then the men gathered their IDs and continued down the driveway, the injured man helped by one of his friends, while the other three dragged the bodies. Steel checked; the front house door was closed. He noted the killer's car parked behind Harry's pickup. A Malibu.

Remaining deep in the forest, Steel shadowed Ryan Randall's buddies all the way down the driveway. In part he wanted to make sure they left, but he also needed time to consider things. At the driveway gate, which was still open, the men stopped. Two vehicles were parked on the county road in front of Steel's place, one a sedan, the other an SUV. The men threw the three bodies into the back of the SUV. Then all five men piled into the two vehicles, one headed north, one headed south.

Sighing, Steel sank to his butt in the snow. He needed help. But anyone he could trust or call was a long distance away. This situation affirmed what he had already realized. His past self-reliance and obsession with a small outfit for security purposes for his protection agency was also a major weakness that he hadn't assessed properly. That flaw, of having so few operatives in Greensave, had put them at risk in Chena, and now at even more risk here. Rachel was at risk. Christie. Harry. Everyone he loved could die here.

The other thing was fatigue. Christie had to be feeling it. Harry too. He had less sleep than both of them in the last twenty-four hours since Christie and Harry had napped on the drive home from the airport while he drove. And he felt it. Weary.

He took a deep breath. Screw Kobayashi Maru. *Stay calm, assess options, wait for a solution.* If he didn't see a way out of this now, he would. He was going to kill the man in the house.

While he waited for the killer's instructions—which he knew were coming—he worked through every scenario he could. One thing was certain, the killer in the house planned to murder all of them. There was no way the man would let them live after all this. The killer wouldn't risk retribution from him. But the man might risk keeping everyone alive overnight to get his fifty grand. And he seemed like a dog with a bone regarding returning to his employer with the hundred K. Both factors could work in Steel's favor.

Steel considered who he could call that could get here on a red-eye by tomorrow morning.

Isabella would have already called Harry and Christie's brother, Clay, in Montana. It had been over an hour and a half. He hated doing it, but he texted Clay the situation and asked for help. Clay had a wife and two kids. The man had helped him last fall with the cartel mess, but had lost a brother in the process. They were on good terms, but he wasn't sure how Clay would respond to another request from him for help. Clay would come to help his sister and brother, no matter what, Steel just didn't know how pissed off Clay would be at him. And he wanted to marry Christie. *Hell.*

Clay sent a text back immediately; he had already booked a red-eye and was at the airport. He would land at eight am. That left a two-hour drive to Steel's home.

Steel thanked Clay via text, but his phone rang and he answered it. It was Clay.

"How bad is it, Steel?" asked Clay.

Steel couldn't lie to him. "The guy running this is a killer and very good at what he does."

Clay asked quietly, "Will I be there in time?"

The drive-through at Steel's bank didn't open until seven a.m., so that might work. "Yes, Clay, it could save us."

Clay exhaled sharply on the other end of the phone. "Alright, see you soon, Steel."

Steel ended the call. He was glad Clay was coming, but he needed something more than one ex-marine sniper on the perimeter. He hoped Harry and Christie had something planned.

The killer in the house called on Christie's phone. "Where are you, Steel?"

Steel lied. “Watching them leave near the driveway entrance. A few more minutes and they should be gone.”

“When you return, walk the center of the driveway back. No weapons in your hands. When you get to the turnaround, stop and I’ll tell you what to do next. It better not be more than ten minutes from now, Steel.”

Steel rose, stepped out of the woods to the driveway, and started walking.

CHAPTER 34

CHRISTIE FOUGHT OFF HOPELESSNESS. The killer was expertly orchestrating everything in a way that gave him complete security, even from Steel. And the fact that he had killed Ryan Randall and one of his men with no hesitation fit what she thought about him. Cold killer. Smart. In minutes he had turned an eight-man assault into a nonstarter.

She worried about Rachel, thirteen years old, going through this, and dying here. All of them dying here.

That made her angry. She wouldn't let it happen. Steel was counting on her, she knew it. She had to be ready. The mini OTF knife in her belt was the key. The one mistake the killer had made—missing it when he had been more interested in groping her. It gave her hope.

Cool air was coming in through the shot-out windows. The house furnace was going to work overtime to keep the place warm. And the furnace created a small background noise that worked in their favor too.

Her thigh and ribs ached—the killer had kicked the same ribs that her assailant in Chena had punched. She could take pain, but she had doubled up in exaggeration to give the man any sense of weakness she could. When she attacked him with the knife, it might give her a tiny edge of surprise.

Steel had often said when they trained that the tiniest of edges could mean the difference between winning and dying in this kind of a situation. He trained them obsessively with the virtual reality system and in person to hone those tiny edges to perfection. Sometimes she thought it had been overkill. Not now.

Another thing she thought the killer hadn't assessed accurately was how much his younger partner was against hurting them. The younger man had protected Kat spontaneously, and lied to protect Rachel. She hadn't given it as much weight at the time as she should have. Given the killer's dangerousness, and his recent killing, she had a deeper understanding of how brave those moves had been by the young man. It meant he was concerned about women. He had to be even more concerned about a young girl like Rachel. Christie wondered when the time came if he would act on that concern.

The killer said, "Looks like we're spending the night, kid. We'll trade off on watches, but I brought some rope from the barn so we can make sure they're all tied up securely while we trade off sleeping."

Christie was aware of the killer threading rope beneath her arm pits and across her back. She felt Harry's and Rachel's shoulders press up against hers on either side. The killer was tying them all together like logs in a raft so they wouldn't be able to slip their hands beneath their feet and break the zip ties. The rope was pulled taut. She guessed both ends of it were tied to something heavy. Maybe the other sofa across the room. He wasn't finished. He used another piece of rope to thread through their ankles, above her zip ties, again tying them all together in a raft. She could feel Harry's and Rachel's feet press against hers from either side. As her legs were pulled taut, she assumed he was tying the rope ends from their ankles to one of the dining room table legs.

He was done in minutes. "Kid, use the bathroom, then I will. Hurry."

Christie heard the younger man hustle down the hallway to the small bathroom near the back door. He returned in a minute, and then the killer left, quickly back again too.

"Kid, turn on the outside floodlight. And get behind the door again with the shotgun, but back up five feet." Punching a number on a phone, the killer talked calmly. "Steel, I'm staring at you. Lose the guns, the knife, the ammo. Pull off your jacket, hands raised high, so I can see everything, and turn around slowly."

In a minute the killer added, "Okay, walk slowly to the front door, no sudden moves or Rachel takes a bullet. You know now that I won't hesitate to do it. Keep your mouth shut. You don't speak unless I ask you a question, otherwise Rachel is going to be hurt. When you reach the front door, we'll open it, you enter very slowly, take two steps in and stop, hands still in the air."

"Kid, turn on the light switch behind you again."

Christie saw the light from the dining room creeping in at the lower edges of her hood. In another minute she heard Steel enter the house. She felt comforted by his presence, and that he could see they were alright. She knew when he left to go shopping that he had been wearing his belt OTF knife. Another edge.

The killer sounded happy. "Pull off your hood and turn around slowly, Steel." A slight pause, and then, "Okay, Steel. We're going to overnight it, then you'll go in and get the money from the bank and return alone. No phone. Toss yours onto the floor now."

Christie heard the phone *thunk* on the floor, and then slide when the man kicked it away.

The killer said glibly, "Okay, you followed directions admirably. Take two more steps forward and drop to your knees, arms still in the air."

Christie suddenly feared the killer would shoot Steel, kill all of them, take the eighty thousand, and leave. Why not? He could still have Kat work off the debt in prostitution. Tying them all together was just to make it easier for him when the time came. A mass execution.

***

Steel wasn't surprised by what was happening. It's how he would manage a situation like this. Whoever the man behind the Lycra hood was, he knew what he was doing and was good at it. He didn't seem like ex-military the way he nonchalantly sat on the arm of the sofa, with the Glock pointed at him, but the killer was street smart in every way imaginable. Much more dangerous than Ryan Randall's misfits. This man lived in the real world of expedited violence.

From what Steel could see of his body type, the man was built like a bull. Rock solid. Formidable and confident. Probably had a hair trigger on the Glock he was holding too.

Steel had scanned the room immediately, seeing everyone zip tied so they couldn't budge. Ready for an easy execution. That unnerved him.

Still, it was such a relief to see Rachel and Christie alive, along with Harry, that Steel wanted to go to them. Instead he knelt down as asked and kept his eyes glued to the killer. He glanced to the side once, at the even bigger man holding the shotgun. An obvious amateur with a gun, the way he held it, but massive. Bigger than Harry and the killer. Strong.

Steel knew in a fight against both of these men it was unlikely he would come away without a serious injury, if he won—which was questionable. But he wasn't scared or worried. All he wanted was the opportunity.

Both men were six feet away, making any kind of lunging attack on either of them a nonstarter.

Another thing bothering him was the absence of the dogs. Spinner and Lacy were like a welcoming committee to everyone. He wondered if they were both dead in the basement.

The killer smiled. "I have to tell you, Steel, the way you handled those six out there was very clean and efficient. I couldn't have done better myself, and I'm pretty good at those kinds of situations. But in my book that does make you dangerous." He lost his smile. "Lie down on your belly, ankles crossed, hands outstretched past your head. You so much as wiggle and the kid is going to put a hole in your back."

Steel complied.

The killer threw something soft on Steel's hands. "Pull the hood over your head. Slowly."

Again, Steel did as asked. He was glad to do it. It meant the killer might be serious about him going to the bank in the morning. More opportunities.

"Hands behind your back, Steel."

Steel followed directions.

"Kid, lean the shotgun against the wall, put a knee on his back, and zip tie his wrists and ankles. Two on each. Make them tight. Steel, you so much as breathe and I'm putting a bullet in your head. Then Rachel's and Christie's, because if you're dead, there's no money coming from you."

Steel felt the full weight of the younger man in the knee settling into his back. The young man had to be two-hundred-fifty-pounds. Harry had dropped some muscle mass to be leaner and quicker, down to two-hundred-twenty pounds, and this guy weighed more and didn't look like he carried any fat.

After Steel was zip tied, the younger man took his knee off him. Steel waited.

The killer said nonchalantly, "I have to check on something everyone, so hang on." He punched a number on a phone and said, "Hey, Ritchie, sorry to call so late. Yeah, I figured you'd be up. Hey, the kid and I have Lerkin, Kat, the man they were going to see, Jack Steel, and his daughter and girlfriend and one male friend tied up on the floor, all hooded. They can't ID us, but Lerkin blabbed who you are so they know your name.

"Steel has eighty K here, but can go into the bank in the morning and bring back the other twenty. He's going to bring back fifty more for me too for protecting Kat against some white supremacists that showed up." Pause. "Yeah, it's been a real shitshow. And Steel is connected. Army Black Ops. What do you want me to do? Because we could just bring the eighty and have Kat work off the rest."

Steel's blood ran cold. There was another significant pause.

The killer continued. "We think alike, Ritchie. Okay, see you soon."

The killer was quiet for a few moments. "Well, you're all in luck. The boss says to wait for the seventy K from the bank since it's late anyway. And he says me and the kid have earned the extra fifty." His voice lowered. "So Steel, everyone stays alive as long as you don't screw up and no one else arrives."

Steel didn't believe him. They wanted him to go to the bank, but then they would kill all of them. The fact that the killer had used his employer's name also indicated that, because he would be concerned that a black ops man like himself would track Ritchie down. Which he would.

Next, the killer wound rope beneath Steel's arm pits and over his back, pulling it tight as he tied it most likely to one of the sofa legs. Steel's ankles were next, pulling him in the opposite direction, stretching him taut—probably tying him to a leg of the dining room table as he had with the others. The amount of effort it would take even with the OTF knife would slow down any escape. Thus if either of the killers were watching him, they could easily put a bullet in him.

The killer sounded happy. "Okay, kid. You're the night owl. I'm dead on my feet. You take first watch. I'll set my alarm for four hours. Six a.m. Leave that light on, and stay far away from Steel."

He added, "Now listen up, everyone. I'm taking Rachel upstairs with me. I'm not a pedophile, so no concerns there. But let's say the impossible happens, and you figure out a way to get free, or my partner here falls asleep. I'm a very light sleeper. All my partner has to do is yell once, or I hear anything I don't like, and I'll kill Rachel first. Got it?"

The killer continued, "Kid, keep the Glock, but put the rest of the guns in the duffel. I'm taking them upstairs for safekeeping."

Steel heard the younger man grunt, throw the guns in the duffel, and the killer headed up the stairs. Steel heard him dragging Rachel, her feet bumping on each step. To her credit, she didn't make a sound. It sickened him to think about her in the same bedroom, maybe even the same bed, as the killer.

This would be their opportunity, but with a Glock on him, tied up like this, it didn't seem like much.

The solution came to him then.

All he needed was a distraction. Steel hoped either Christie or Harry could see that and do something that would give him thirty seconds to a minute. That's how long it would take to cut himself completely free. Then he would kill the younger man quietly with the OTF knife, take his gun, and go kill the other man holding Rachel. It was all high risk, but an actionable plan. Better than waiting for Clay. One way or another, they had to end this in the next hours.

CHAPTER 35

HARRY KNEW THIS WAS the only chance they would have. Christie, Steel, Rachel, him. He didn't care what happened to Lerkin after the mess the man had brought them, but he couldn't blame Kat. An abused woman who needed help, she had unknowingly put her faith in her gambling addict father.

Harry wished he had his belt OTF knife, but the killer hadn't allowed him to put his belt back into his jeans in the bathroom. Harry had taken the belt out, intending to wash the jeans. At first Harry thought the man had seen his OTF knife in the sleeve built into the inside back of it. But then he realized the man just viewed the belt as a possible weapon if Harry picked it up. Still, it reminded him that Christie had a mini OTF dagger in her belt. So did Rachel. So did Steel.

What they needed to get free was a distraction that didn't push the younger guy to call his partner upstairs. Harry had thought this through, but wasn't sure it would work. He had to try. He concluded the man guarding them wouldn't want his partner to come down, especially not to kill Rachel in front of him—the young man had shown some empathy for women and children.

Harry waited an hour. Given how tired he was, he had to work at not falling asleep. Light sleeper or not, the killer upstairs would be sleeping soundly by now. And the furnace was running so it would disguise whispers and soft sounds. It was now or never. Harry lifted his head slightly, and whispered, "I need to go to the bathroom."

All he got back was a soft, "No."

"Come on, please." Harry just started mumbling stuff, continuing to whisper, ignoring the young man's commands to stop talking. He wanted the young man to come closer to him, at least a few steps, to focus solely on him so that Steel and Christie had a chance to cut themselves free. They had practiced this many times in the virtual reality training, cutting themselves free fast and quietly. In practice sessions Steel had tied them up securely in dozens of different ways with their hands tied or zip tied behind their backs. Steel had also made them do it blindfolded. Again Harry had thought it had been overkill at the time. He was glad for all that practice now.

"Come on!" he said more sharply, still keeping his voice a whisper. "If you don't let me go, I'm going to make a mess." He had no expectation that the young man would free him, but he hoped the man would come closer, maybe to hit him. He was right.

The man had moved quietly, and pushed one large hand down against the side of Harry's hooded head, his knee pressing down on Harry's back. "Shut up or I'll call him. And he'll kill Rachel. You don't want that, do you?"

Harry kept babbling softly, mumbling, and the man slid his hand over the hood until his palm covered Harry's mouth. "You need to shut up or I'm going to tape your mouth shut. You're almost free. A few hours more."

Lerkin lay between Harry and the sofa, and he got in on it then, talking very softly and slowly. "He's going to kill all of us as soon as Steel returns from the bank, son. You'll be running from multiple murder charges for the rest of your life. Your boss told him to kill us. Even I know that. You know Ritchie, what he's like. He won't risk a black ops guy or his people coming after him."

The young man just listened, his hand still covering Harry's mouth. Then he said softly, "I'm sorry, there's nothing I can do.

This wasn't supposed to happen like this. It was supposed to be just a simple collection."

"Are you a murderer, son?" Lerkin asked softly. "You saved Kat and helped Rachel. Now be brave and save the rest of us. You can do it. I feel it in your heart. You need to trust in the right thing to do, son."

The young man's reply, still a whisper, was sharp. "Shut up, old man! You're the reason we're all here. A loser gambling addict. You don't care about anyone, especially your daughter."

"Son, my wife had cancer. I used Ritchie's money to pay for medicine and doctors I couldn't afford. I told Ritchie it was gambling money just so he had a better reason to give it to me. And I lied to him about going to a friend to get money. I just wanted Kat safe, and didn't care what Ritchie did to me."

Kat whispered then, her voice trembling, "Mom did die from cancer, and my father couldn't pay the bills. He's never gambled a day in his life."

There was silence as everyone took that in.

***

Steel listened to all of it, not focused on the words, but the sounds. He had the OTF knife out, had cut through the zip ties on his wrists, and had slipped off his hood and the rope beneath his arms. Because of the rope through his ankles he had to push himself up quietly until he almost sat on his heels. That was the only way he could cut the zip ties there. He watched as Harry kept mumbling, and Lerkin kept talking. Then Kat.

Christie was cutting her zip ties too, but she had to work slower. Her body was more in the shadows, not in the light like he was, and the young man was turned to Lerkin, so his back was partially exposed to her. Still, the man was much closer to Christie and might hear her.

Lerkin's confession surprised Steel as much as it did everyone else.

By the time everyone quieted he was free, rising straight up to his feet and assessing everything in one sweep.

Christie had her hood off, her wrists and arms free, and barely lifted her head to glance at him over her shoulder. She just stared at him. He knew she was waiting on him.

The young man was squatting, holding the Glock in his right hand, his left hand over Harry's mouth as he stared at Lerkin.

If Christie lunged for a kill strike, she might not succeed. Steel made a jabbing motion into the back of his hand. Then he quietly strode toward the young man. The longest ten feet of his life. He noted the man still wore the Kevlar vest.

Christie rose a few feet in one quick motion, leaned over, and stabbed her OTF dagger into the back of the gun hand of the young man.

The man gasped and dropped the Glock. It hit Harry's back and slid to the floor. Christie reached for it with her left hand and picked it up, but the man hit her hand with his bent wrist, knocking it out of her grasp so it slid across the floor into the far corner beneath a bookshelf.

Steel leapt forward to slice the man's throat from behind.

The man sensed Steel's attack and rolled forward very quickly and smoothly, coming up in what looked to Steel like an Aikido crouch. Aikido wouldn't match his Brazilian jiu-jitsu, kung fu, and Special Forces techniques, but Steel couldn't afford to grapple with this man, given his weight, strength, and speed. That would take too much time and make too much noise.

Steel threw the knife. The younger man twisted sideways, lifting his left hand for protection. The knife flew by him, hit the far wall, dropped, and clattered on the floor.

"What's happening?" whispered Kat, still tied up.

Steel stepped past Harry and Lerkin—aware of Christie cutting Harry's zip ties—as the young man rose from the floor into an Aikido stance, backing up toward the corner and the gun, still continuing to face Steel. His lips were pursed. The man had taken a knife wound to the hand and still hadn't called out to his partner. It showed high pain tolerance, control, and unwillingness to see them all murdered.

"Get back or I'll yell for my partner," whispered the young man.

Steel knew he had seconds. Given the big man's speed and size, it might take more time than he had. He had one other option.

He whispered, "You haven't done anything I can't forgive. Help us now and we'll kill your partner. I'll take care of Ritchie. You'll never have to worry about running or for your safety. Ever. Guaranteed. I don't care who Ritchie is connected to or who he knows. I'll pay him off, and if that isn't enough, I'll kill him and everyone connected to him."

The man backed up carefully, still moving toward the gun beneath the bookcase.

Steel heard a creak. He glanced over his shoulder, ready to bolt into the kitchen to get the Glock in the cubbyhole there.

Halfway down the steps, the killer stood motionless. No hood on his head. Eyes glinting. Hair to his shoulders. Eastern European. A solid face. With his right hand he held Rachel's upper left arm, with his left he held a Glock that he aimed at Steel. His voice was calm and cold like his smile. "Well well well. This is going to be fun."

CHAPTER 36

KARBU CLIMBED BACK INTO the rental SUV and quietly shut the door, tossing the night vision binoculars into the back seat. "I've disabled all the camera and sensor feeds on the driveway. Steel is careful, like myself."

"Are you sure about this, Karbu?" Ivel's voice held uncertainty.

He looked at her, never tired of her dark eyes, her black hair, and the soft features of her face. "The other two targets Jiri was supposed to kill are safe. Untouchable for now. I texted Jiri and told him the contract is over. He needs to refund the money. Ten million. He takes the loss, but I'll be open to sharing it out of M4N's budget if he objects. If he doesn't accept my terms, I told him we're through."

"I'm so happy that you're standing up to him!" Ivel gripped his arm. "When did you do this?"

He smiled. "While you were sleeping on the car ride out here." He chuckled. "Are you all caught up?"

"Yes, jet lag is gone." She smiled. "You're the one with little sleep."

"I never seem to need as much as you, dear."

She frowned. "You don't think this man Steel will just kill you?"

Karbu shook his head. "He's black ops. He knows how things can get out of control. I'll give him options he can't refuse. Emilia told Steel I had nothing to do with this contract. He'll have worked out that Senator Tindren was part of it all. Thus I won't be on his list. Just Jiri and the man who hired him. It's worth one conversation. My CIA contact said Steel is reasonable, not a mindless murderer. I saw that on Charlie Dome in Chena too. I read people very well, Ivel. That's what has kept me alive in this crazy business we're about to leave behind."

"I'm so excited, Bu!"

He chuckled. "I am too, Ivel. I am too."

"So we're just going to knock on his front door this early in the morning?" Ivel sounded happy.

Karbu nodded. "Something happened here. The front windows are shot out, and the outside front wall of the house is riddled with bullets. There's a light on in the living room. We have to see if he's still alive. I think he has more enemies than just Jiri."

Ivel looked out the windshield. "How can you be sure the men who shot up his house are gone?"

"Footprints in the driveway and snow lead out, and it looks like they dragged bodies out too. Steel killed some of them, forced the rest to retreat somehow." He thought on that. "Who knows? One of our options might be to offer help from M4N to him before we retire from it."

"I like that!" Ivel sounded positive. "Turn an enemy into a friend."

Karbu drove the SUV off the shoulder of the county road and turned into the driveway. He kept the engine quiet at a low speed, and turned off the lights halfway down the driveway. Pausing at the end, he slowly drove the SUV into the turnaround and double-parked beside the pickup, in case they needed to leave in a hurry. The van parked ahead of the pickup also blocked any view of their SUV.

Exiting quietly from the SUV, they walked up to the front door. Karbu looked at the cars. Porsche, Jeep, van, pickup, and Malibu. He again noted the shot-out windows and bullet-riddled front wall of the house.

Noises came from inside. A fight. Shouts. Karbu suddenly didn't want Ivel here. But she would never stay outside. And she was very capable with her gun and hands. Still. *Damn.* He deliberated for a few moments. They could retreat, wait things out.

Ivel cut off his thoughts with a whisper, "If we help Steel out, Karbu, we can end everything right here."

He pulled his Glock, and Ivel pulled her SIG. Placing his hand on the front door knob, he slowly turned it. Surprised to find it unlocked, he pushed it open. What he saw made him step inside quickly, Ivel right behind him.

CHAPTER 37

STEEL FROZE FOR ONE moment, staring as the killer on the stairs kept smiling and swung the Glock toward Rachel's head. "No," he breathed.

Rachel swung her right arm.

Steel saw a flash of silver.

Rachel tried to hit the killer's side, but the killer reacted instantly, tossing her down the steps. Thus her mini OTF blade ended up in the killer's forearm. The killer dropped the Glock, which bounced through the open steps to the floor below him.

Rachel tumbled down the remaining ten steps.

Harry was already up and charging the man full throttle. Christie rose and was on his heels. Steel turned and faced the big man blocking access to the Glock. "Choose now or die."

The young man didn't reply.

Steel stepped forward with speed, his hands flashing at the man's neck and face.

***

Harry wanted the killer dead so badly he could taste it. By the time he reached the bottom of the stairs, the killer had pulled Rachel's blade from his arm and was stepping down quietly and calmly, blade in hand.

Christie raced three feet away from Harry to not crowd him. She went up two steps on the far side, still holding her knife.

Harry knew why she didn't go for the gun on the floor behind the stairs; it was close to the killer's side. If the man jumped the rail, he would have it before she could get to it. At least here they had him trapped from it.

Rachel was slowly pushing up to her knees, looking wobbly. She looked hurt from the fall. It enraged Harry further to see her hurt.

Three steps from the bottom, the killer threw Rachel's knife at Christie, gripped the handrail with both hands, and leapt up sideways, still hanging onto the railing as he kicked both feet at Harry. Christie jumped up one step, avoiding the thrown knife, and rushed the killer from the side.

Even though Harry was ready, the man was very fast and Harry took a partial blow to his chest. He stumbled back. But when the man landed at the bottom of the stairway, Harry was already stepping in, hitting him with short, sledgehammer blows on the shoulder, waist, and one on the side of the head.

The killer absorbed them, twisted away, bent down, and kicked out, hitting Harry in the abdomen and sending him flying. Harry had half-expected it, but not the speed again. And it felt like he'd been kicked by a mule.

Turning, the man blocked Christie's low kick at his knee with his leg, and blocked her forearm and slashing knife with his right arm. Jabbing at her with flashing fists, he hit her arm, shoulder, and jaw. She dropped the knife and staggered back to the opposite railing.

Harry landed on his back but was quickly up.

The killer sat down on the first step, leaned back, and kicked a charging Christie in the leg. She took a partial blow, but it was enough to send her off balance. Rachel was crawling around the stairs, headed for the Glock there.

Christie regained her balance and attacked.

Harry ran forward and gripped the killer's neck from behind as he rose from the first stair. Ducking out of Harry's hold before it was locked, the man twisted and gave a back kick—hitting Christie's stomach—while aiming a low fist that caught Harry near the groin. Harry stepped back, intense pain forcing him to pause.

The killer whirled and was on him in seconds with open hands flashing at his head and neck. Harry took one hard blow to the neck and staggered back. Managing to block further strikes, he swung back, hitting the man's midriff—which felt like hitting iron.

Stepping around him fast, the killer forced Harry to turn until he had his back to Rachel and the gun. Another quick blow to his neck made him slump down. As Harry fell to his butt on the floor, half-dazed, he leaned back, keeping his legs up for defense, effectively blocking the killer's access to the Glock. Rachel was almost there.

Christie charged the killer, kicking at his leg—missing when he lifted it. But she hit him in the side and back with fists.

Whirling, the man elbowed her twice—chest and inner shoulder—and then shoved her away to the floor. He turned and kicked Harry in the jaw, sending him into Rachel, which knocked her back away from the Glock.

***

Steel had the young man staggering, but not down. The big guy blocked half his strikes, and absorbed the rest. Steel glanced over his shoulder, and saw Christie take the elbow strikes, and Harry take the kick to the head. The man would kill them in seconds.

Steel rushed the young man and went low onto his hands, able to kick the big man in the groin this time, finally sending him to the floor, but in front of the bookcase and gun. Glancing back again, he saw Rachel reaching for the Glock.

The killer glanced over his shoulder and grinned at Steel.

In that instant Steel realized Harry, Christie, and Rachel, his whole family, would be dead before he could get past the young man to reach the Glock beneath the bookcase. And before Rachel could shoot the killer.

Rising, he ran across the room, charging with hand strikes, low kicks, and body blows. The killer was as fast as him, if not faster, and body blows did nothing to him. He kept smiling as he backed up, dropped to one knee, and tried to hit Steel between the legs. Steel sidestepped the effort.

Grabbing one of the small throw rugs on the floor, the killer tossed it up into Steel's face. Steel backed up, but was hit by the man charging him like a bull.

They grappled, and Steel felt the strength of the man, his power, and speed. He tried to take the killer down to the floor by tripping him, but couldn't. The killer tried, but couldn't take him down either. A few times Steel gripped the man's left wrist, but the knife wound had made it slippery with blood. The killer had unbelievable pain tolerance.

Steel glimpsed Rachel, both hands on the Glock, rising unsteadily and limping out from under the stairs on the other side, aiming it. Aware of her too, the killer swung Steel around to block any shot at himself, and pushed Steel toward Rachel in a rush. Steel couldn't stop the man's legs. Too much strength. Worse, Steel felt like he had hit a wall with his fatigue.

Rachel backed up, trying to move to the side of Steel, but the killer just angled his push on Steel to keep blocking her aim at him. Normally Steel would have rolled backward and thrown the man over his head. But not with Rachel there. The gun might go off and he would take a bullet from his daughter. He glimpsed Harry struggling to his feet.

A man and a woman walked in the front door, guns up.

Rachel saw them, turned, and dropped to one knee as she had been taught, just as Steel bumped into her.

Rachel's gun fired.

The woman slumped to the floor. The man with her stepped forward, kicked the gun out of Rachel's hands, and grabbed her hair, dragging her hard to him. He pushed her ahead of him to the door. "If you run, I'll shoot you, girl." He picked up the woman with both arms and hurried out the door, his gun beneath the woman and aimed at Rachel.

Karbu. Steel recognized his voice and accent. Panicked, he worked harder but still couldn't get a grip on the killer's body to send him down. Anything he tried the killer countered.

Four shots from outside turned his efforts into a frenzy.

From the floor, Christie made a lunge for the Glock. The killer kicked her in the side, sending her rolling and gasping. Lerkin was there then, on the floor, gripping the killer's ankle. Yanking his foot free, the man stomped Lerkin's head twice and Lerkin went motionless.

Steel used those moments to trip the killer and take him down. But the man was just as skilled on the ground, quickly escaping Steel's hold and punching and kicking Steel from the side. Steel rose to his knees as the man threw strikes at him with both hands, still smiling. Steel took a blow to the head, but delivered one back.

A roar sounded.

The killer looked up. So did Steel.

The young man picked up the killer by the back of his neck and waist belt, in one quick motion dead-lifting him above his head.

Writhing, the killer struck at the young man's head. "Put me down, Zeus, or your whole family is gonna die!"

Zeus ducked against the blows, turned, took three steps, and slammed the killer hard onto the wood back of the sofa, breaking the man's spine.

Steel heard it.

Zeus followed up with a lethal strike to the front of the killer's neck, and the killer's body slowly slid off the sofa.

Not waiting, Steel ran outside, but didn't see Karbu's car. Their cars all had at least one tire shot out.

His phone rang. He scrambled back inside, finding it where the killer had left it on the floor. He picked it up, his heart pounding.

Rachel. He heard Karbu talking softly in the background.

Rachel's voice was steady, but cracked a few times as she relayed the messages Karbu gave her. "Just listen, Dad. No talking. If you follow, he'll kill me. Call the police or anyone and he'll get protection from the CIA. Immunity from anything he does. Try to stop his plane, same result. He'll be in touch. If his wife Ivel dies, he's going to kill everyone you love. I'm okay, Dad. I'm holding cloth over the woman's wound..."

The phone went dead.

CHAPTER 38

"WHAT'S GOING ON? DAD, are you okay?" Kat's voice was strained.

Christie limped over to cut her free, while Harry staggered toward the bookshelf hiding the Glock. Zeus was sitting on the sofa, hunched over, his face in his hands, his left hand covering the wound in his right, not moving, not making a sound.

Steel knelt beside Lerkin and took his pulse. He had one, but was unconscious.

Once free, Kat crawled to her father and stroked his face as tears ran down her cheeks. "Dad! Dad!"

Christie retrieved her phone from the dead killer's jeans and dialed 911. She spoke calmly, saying they had a wheelchair man who had fallen down and was unconscious. Finished, she said, "Kat, the ambulance is twenty minutes out from us. Get blankets upstairs to put over your father and a pillow for his head."

Kat wiped her eyes and ran up the stairs.

Steel dialed Colonel Jeffries and explained his daughter's situation. "Can your CIA contact track the private jet that flew from Fairbanks to Denver to Virginia? And can you ground that plane somehow?"

Jeffries answered the second question first. "Normally I couldn't override CIA protection to ground a plane if Karbu has been given some kind of blanket immunity. But kidnapping a U.S. citizen, especially a minor, is major. Even the CIA isn't going to go along with that. What about the FBI?"

Steel had already considered that. "They'll want to come to my house and interview me and it's a mess here with too many questions I don't want to answer. Also I have concerns that if they find and try to stop Karbu, he'll kill Rachel." He assumed Karbu had come here to kill him. Jiri might be waiting for his brother in the jet and wouldn't hesitate to hurt Rachel, especially since she had shot Ivel.

"I'm sorry, Steel. I'll call you back on tracking the jet and the CIA response." Jeffries hung up.

Steel hung up, his whole body tense as Christie eyed him. "Jeffries will call when he hears anything." He picked up the Glock, and he and Christie held each other a few moments before separating.

Harry stood up beside the bookshelf without the Glock. "The gun grip is stuck between the wall and the back leg of the bookshelf. We'll have to move the shelf to get it out."

Steel stepped over to Zeus, aiming the Glock at the man's head. "Take off your hood."

Zeus obeyed the request, keeping his head down. He bunched the hood over his hand wound. Clean-cut dark hair, olive skin tone, mid-twenties. Steel wanted to put a bullet in him.

Christie walked to Steel's side, pushing his gun arm down. "He saved Kat at one point and tried to protect Rachel. We can't shoot him."

Steel heaved a breath. He wanted to shoot someone. Fatigued, and numb over Rachel being taken, he sat on the sofa, resting the Glock on his thigh, pointed at Zeus. His chest wound ached, as well as several other places where the killer had pummeled him. He ignored it. His heart ached more over what had happened to Rachel. His fault.

Christie sat beside him and gripped his hand. "We'll get her back, Steel."

He gripped her hand and glanced at Harry. “Harry, we have to move the killer’s body to his car and drive it to the south county road. I’ll call the cleaner we use. Let’s do it now.”

“Sure.” Harry’s voice betrayed as much distaste as Steel felt. “What about Lerkin? The ambulance comes in here, sees the shot-out windows and outside wall, they’ll have questions.”

Steel thought on it. “We’ll have to move Lerkin first. Crank the heater on his van. We’ll make a stretcher, put him in back. Kat can drive him down the driveway.”

“I’ll make the stretcher.” Harry slowly walked up the stairs to get a blanket. In a minute he came down with Kat, talking softly to her, both of them holding blankets. Kat had slipped on jeans, a flannel shirt, and her jacket. She handed Harry the van keys, and he went out to start it up.

Steel studied Zeus, too upset to talk to him yet. Still half wanting to shoot him. He needed sleep, which would be difficult knowing Rachel was with the enemy.

Harry returned and in minutes had a makeshift stretcher made with a blanket tied to broom handles. Steel handed the Glock to Christie, and rose to help Harry carry Lerkin out.

Harry said, “My ribs ache. Zeus, get up and help Steel.”

Zeus rose, bent over, and held the hood down on the floor with his foot and yanked it hard with his left hand to rip it in half. Wrapping it around his right hand wound, he tucked it in at his palm. Then he stepped over, barely glancing at Kat as he said softly, “I’m sorry for everything.”

Kat didn’t even look at him. Steel and Zeus gently transferred Lerkin to the makeshift stretcher. Then Zeus gripped the stretcher by using his left hand and bent right forearm to lift and carry it with Steel. Kat walked ahead of them to open doors.

Christie followed them out, Glock in hand. They slid the stretcher into the van and Kat covered Lerkin with blankets.

Steel said, “Zeus, get out the spare tire and jack. The front wheel is shot out.”

Zeus found both, and began changing the tire, working fast. He had the spare on in a few minutes. He never made a sound over the pain it must have cost his hand.

Kat jumped into the front seat. "I want to drive Dad in. Can you call 911 again and ask them what road they're taking to get here? Tell them I'll be driving toward them in a white van. Give them my phone number so I can tell them what mile marker I'm at and don't miss them."

While Steel did that, Christie said, "Kat, call us as soon as you know something."

Kat wiped her eyes. "I will." When Steel was off the phone, her voice softened. "I'm sorry, Jack. About everything."

Steel nodded. "It's not your fault, and your father tried not to bring any trouble with him." It was the best he could do. "Wait a minute." He turned to Zeus. "How did you track Lerkin to my house?"

Zeus gestured. "Ritchie put a tracker on Lerkin's van."

"Let's find it." Steel began at the front end, kneeling on the gravel and snow, but it was Zeus who found it beneath the back of the van.

"Is this it?" Zeus held a small, black oval device. Magnetized.

"Yeah." Steel took it. "You're good to go, Kat."

She nodded and pulled away.

With Christie watching, Steel made Zeus change the front shot-out tire on the Malibu, and then help him dump the killer's body into the trunk—the car keys were in the dead man's pocket. Dropping the tracker on the ground, Steel stomped on it and tossed the remnants into the trunk.

"Back on the sofa, Zeus." Steel walked back in, and Zeus settled onto the sofa again.

Christie sat on the other sofa, Glock in hand.

Steel regarded Zeus for a moment, then went upstairs and found the twenty grand the killer had left on the bed in the master bedroom, along with the duffel bag of guns. He slid the duffel bag into the bedroom closet, and shoved the money into one of the magazine sleeves of his Lycra suit. When he went back downstairs, he said, "Harry, can you ride with me? No lifting."

"Sure." Harry joined him in the Malibu. Steel drove. They were both quiet.

Steel managed to say, "Isabella gets credit, Harry. She warned me something was off when your conversation ended abruptly."

"I'll have to call her when I get back." Harry touched Steel's arm. "We'll take them apart to get Rachel if we have to, Steel. Whatever it takes."

"Thanks, Harry." Harry sounded as sick as Steel felt about Rachel.

In minutes they had the car parked on the county road. Steel called the cleaner, and they walked away from the car, standing off the shoulder of the road. In thirty minutes a pickup showed up, driving from the east. It stopped on the shoulder, a quarter mile back from the Malibu.

Steel waved once, then walked to the Malibu, threw the twenty K into the front seat, and walked into the woods with Harry. In a few minutes they heard car doors opening and closing.

Steel glanced back, seeing the Malibu drive off with the pickup.

"I'm debating killing Zeus." Steel said it matter-of-factly.

Harry spoke softly. "I know you're angry, and worried sick about Rachel. But Zeus saved Kat, and he killed his partner. Rachel also said he protected her."

Steel heaved a breath. "Christie said the same thing. I needed to hear it from you too."

They were back at the house in ten minutes.

While they all sat in the living room, Harry used Steel's phone to text Isabella. Steel sat next to Christie, Harry on the other end of the sofa Zeus was seated on. Christie held the Glock, but had it aimed at the floor. Her eyes were barely cracked open and she looked half-asleep.

They all needed sleep, but Steel had to wait to see if Jeffries could find Karbu's jet. If so, he would need help going up against the Moeller brothers.

Colonel Jeffries called back and Steel put it on speaker. Jeffries sounded apologetic. "I'm sorry, Steel. My contact can't get anything on a flight plan for a personal jet that went to Virginia. He said someone reported his interest in flight plans out of Fairbanks yesterday and he's shut out now. I think if M4N is off the books, they don't want anyone investigating any avenue that would lead to them. You have a lot of airports in Virginia, and if the CIA is blocking information on the plane, we won't get any intel calling the airports either. When Karbu's jet leaves U.S. mainland airspace, I might be able to use Army resources to track personal jets, especially if he's headed to the Caribbean as you suspect. I'll let you know."

Steel slumped into the sofa, not seeing any way to take action for his daughter at the moment. He felt devastated.

Zeus had his head hung, his hands clasped in front of him.

Steel leaned forward, his voice sharp. "Your real full name, kid, and your relation with Ritchie. Anything you know about him. Start from the beginning."

The young man kept his head down. "Zeus Gataki."

Steel frowned. "Zeus is your real name?"

Zeus nodded. "I was a big baby."

"Figures," murmured Harry.

Zeus kept talking, his head still bowed as if he was giving a confession. "I did collections for Ritchie for three years, from violent men or gamblers usually. He's a loan shark, but runs prostitutes and sells drugs on the side. I met him when one of his men was slapping a woman in front of a club in Vegas. I told the man to stop, and he and his buddies came at me so I beat them up." He paused. "I have three sisters and can't tolerate violence to women." He glanced in the direction of Christie but didn't make eye contact. "It made me sick to watch Mykey kick you." He looked down, his face red. "I was too scared to try to stop him."

"Mykey would have killed you." Steel said it matter-of-factly.

Zeus nodded and continued. "Ritchie liked that I could handle myself so he hired me to do collections. I never killed anyone, but I beat a few bad men. I've wanted out of this job for two and a half years, but I made a three-year commitment and Ritchie wouldn't let me out. Just before this job my contract was up. But Ritchie showed me the photo of Lerkin in a wheelchair and Kat and gave me the choice of this being my last job or quitting. I came because I was worried about what Mykey might do to Lerkin and Kat if I wasn't here." He barely looked up. "Are you going to kill me?"

Steel's appraisal of the man softened one notch. He raised an eyebrow. "No."

Zeus heaved a deep breath. "My family is in Florida. They think I'm a bouncer."

"Ritchie," Steel said firmly.

Zeus twisted his hands together. "He's connected to the mob, some mob guy. He has people killed when they can't pay or if they threaten him. He's dangerous."

"What do you think he told Mykey to do?" Steel studied the man.

Zeus looked down again. "Get the money, kill everyone, except maybe bring Kat back to work the streets. When he finds out I killed Mykey, he'll have my family hurt or killed, and put a contract on me." He looked up. "I have to go back so Ritchie doesn't hurt my family. He'll kill me, or put me into the business for a decade on no salary. He still might hurt my family. Kidnap one of my sisters and put her into prostitution." He seemed to choke up over that. "Mykey was his favorite collector, so I think he'll kill me."

"What will Ritchie say if I offer to pay Lerkin's debt, or give him the hundred-fifty K?" Steel could guess, but he wanted to hear Zeus say it.

Zeus shook his head. “He’ll take the money, but he’ll ask for a lot more to cover his loss on Mykey. Or he’ll act like everything is good and then put a contract out on you and your family.”

“What if we tell him we killed you?” asked Christie.

Zeus glanced at her. “He’ll want proof. He’ll still check out my family from time to time. Eventually he’ll find out I’m alive. He always finds out.”

“I figured as much.” Steel thought on that.

Harry looked up from his phone. “Is Ritchie guarded? In a secure place?”

Zeus nodded. “Yes.”

Steel added, “We have to stall Ritchie until I get my daughter back. Any idea on the best way to do that?”

Zeus was quiet for a few moments. “One time, when we were out of state, after we collected from a customer, Mykey wanted to celebrate.” He cleared his throat. “Prostitutes and drinking. I don’t do those things. After three days we returned to Vegas. I think Mykey told Ritchie first about not coming back right away. Ritchie didn’t seem to care.”

Steel assessed that. “Would Ritchie take that message from you, say at noon today? You call him, tell him Mykey’s drinking, wants to take the long road back through some southern, warmer states and party with some women. Three, four days. It’s just you and him—if Ritchie acts surprised that Kat’s not with you—you just say Mykey decided he had to kill her. Tell him Lerkin and the rest of us are dead.”

Zeus nodded. “I called in once before for Mykey for something like that. Not the killing part.”

“Okay. You’re going to make the call in front of us on speaker.” Steel studied Zeus. “I haven’t decided what we’re going to do about you yet.”

Zeus glanced in his direction. “I understand. I’m responsible. I’ll do whatever you want, Mr. Steel.” He paused. “What will you do about Ritchie?”

Steel didn't hesitate. "He's as good as dead."

Zeus paled. "What about the mob?"

"We'll figure that out," Christie said sleepily.

Zeus nodded and sat back. "Can I call my family?"

Christie said, "After we take care of Ritchie, not before. No calls, texts, or emails to anyone. Nothing. Do you understand?"

Zeus nodded. "I'm not a professional or anything so I'll do whatever you say." He cleared his throat. "Thank you for the help."

"We're doing this to protect ourselves, you fool," snapped Steel. "If you don't do exactly as you're told, any slight slip-ups, and we'll send you on your way with lots of pain first. You'll crawl out of here with nothing but your clothes and be on your own."

Zeus swallowed and nodded. "I'll do everything exactly as you want, Mr. Steel."

CHAPTER 39

KARBU'S FINGERS TREMBLED ON the steering wheel. Usually he was efficient and calm in any situation, but not where Ivel was concerned. He was doing ninety on the county road, and had called his M4N coordinator to have a team of doctors and nurses standing by at the local municipal airport where his jet waited. He had set this up ahead of time in Denver as a possibility. It was expensive, but he always prepared for every possible outcome.

Their jet had a copilot, but he also had another pilot en route since Ivel had been the pilot. Days ago he had insisted that the CIA blanket information about his flights while he was in the U.S. He was also glad he had chosen a smaller airport that was much closer than Richmond International Airport, which was almost two hours away. Ivel would have help nearly as fast as driving to the nearest emergency room—he had also planned all of this ahead of their arrival.

He turned on the inside dome light to look at Ivel. Her face was pale, her breathing weak like her pulse, her eyes closed. Steel's daughter had her hands glued to both wounds with cloth ripped from his shirt and the girl's. The girl was in the back seat, leaning forward, not buckled in and not moving, her hands applying pressure on Ivel's front entry wound and the back exit wound. As far as Karbu could tell, she was doing a good job.

"Hang on, Ivel. We'll be there soon." He was taking a small risk, driving her to the airport instead of the nearest hospital or emergency clinic, if the doctors couldn't do what was needed on the plane. But right now they had to get out of the country ASAP. He wasn't sure what Steel would do, or how far he would go to get his daughter, but the sooner he was out the better.

The CIA would shut down any police involvement. FBI involvement was trickier, but he doubted Steel wanted the FBI involved any more than he did. Steel certainly didn't want them viewing his bullet-riddled house, nor risk his daughter's death. The FBI wouldn't be able to find him before he was airborne anyway.

He glanced at the girl. Tomboyish, cute, long reddish hair, freckled. Lean. In the house he had come within a tenth of a second of putting a bullet in her. Instinct had saved him. Ivel would have never forgiven him if he had killed the girl. Instinct had also made him grab the child and leave. But the girl could have run off in the dark. Instead she had run ahead and opened the car door for him.

Her face was pale and she was biting her lip. She was as concerned as he was. She hadn't meant to shoot Ivel—him possibly—but not Ivel. It had been chaotic in the house, from what he had seen, and the girl had just reacted—her father under attack had bumped into her—then the gun had gone off.

He felt sick to his stomach. Ivel had warned him for a long time about Jiri putting them in danger and it had taken him much too long to see it. And now she was paying the price for his timidity and stupidity with his brother. He wanted to scream over that.

"You're doing a good job, Rachel."

She glanced at him. Vulnerable, scared. He saw it in her eyes.

"She'll be okay?" Rachel asked timidly.

"I hope so." He wasn't sure. It depended on internal injuries. Ivel had lost a lot of blood.

Rachel said in a whisper, "I didn't want to shoot her."

"I know." Yet he wanted Steel to pay for the accident anyway. Anger filled him, but when he thought about it, he had to be honest and blame himself. "We're going to go far away, and then we'll call your father together. I'm not going to hurt you." He paused. "Who was attacking all of you?"

"A killer who wanted money from a friend of Dad's."

Karbu wondered how Steel justified having his daughter involved in situations like this. It was precisely why he had refused to raise children with Ivel. But over the last days he had thought about adoption again if they got out of M4N. It would make Ivel happy. It would make him happy. He realized then that Jiri would never be a good influence around any children. A protector, yes, but not someone to give advice about life and healthy relationships. His brother was a broken spirit in those areas.

"Who taught you how to handle a gun like that?" He already knew the answer, but he needed to talk about something to keep from screaming about Ivel. It might help the girl calm down too.

"Dad. After I was kidnapped for two years, we moved from self-defense into practicing with weapons."

Karbu swore in his mind. Kids were usually kidnapped by perverts and pedophiles. Those people deserved to be shot. And now he was traumatizing the child with another abduction. Ivel would yell at him if she could. But he needed the girl's help now. "Who kidnapped you for two years?" He glanced at her. "You don't have to tell me if it's painful to talk about it."

She took a big breath. "A woman had lost her daughter so she wanted someone to take her place. I escaped after two years."

He swore out loud. "Sorry, but that makes me angry. It must have tormented your father."

"He and Mom got a divorce. But he's very happy now with Christie." The girl glanced up at him. "Do you think we could call and find out if everyone is okay?"

Feeling empty inside, he said, "We'll call from the plane and let him know you're okay, and you can ask if everyone at the house is okay."

"Thank you," she whispered.

He noted something odd about the angle of her left arm, and she was wincing. "What's wrong with your arm?"

"I think it's broken."

The girl was tough too, and her injury made him feel worse about taking her. He decided to call Jiri from the plane too, but in private. He already knew Jiri's response. His brother would be like a tiger wanting revenge now. Jiri would want the girl dead for shooting Ivel, and Steel dead for certain. Jiri wouldn't accept his responsibility for all that had happened, and instead would push his guilt and anger onto Steel and the child.

A tear rolled down his cheek as he looked at Ivel. "Hang on, Ivel. Hang on."

PART 4

OP: M4N;
ST. CROIX ISLAND

CHAPTER 40

STEEL DROVE THE SUV, while Harry, Christie, Mario, Clay, and Carlos checked and loaded their weapons. The winding dirt road they were on was dry, and ran at a forty-degree incline as it ascended the mountain. The mountaintop was only eight hundred feet up, but the road was a mile long due to the number of switchbacks.

Tropical forest bordered it on both sides. It was dark, a starlit sky, the air warm. Gray tree frogs were trilling loudly in the jungle, and Steel could hear the long *Whooooooo* of a barred owl in the forest.

Karbu had said he would send his private jet to pick them up in Richmond, Virginia on Friday, if Steel agreed to come peacefully. However Colonel Jeffries had been able to track Karbu's jet to St. Croix Island. The colonel had given them a military flight a day early for the six-hour trip to the island. The only stipulation was that they kill Jiri. Once on the island, it had been easy enough to find out where Karbu lived—Christie had pretended to be a reporter doing a travel piece on the secretive rich and famous of St Croix Island.

Steel wanted to surprise the man, and wanted control over their meeting, instead of Karbu having that element in his favor. He couldn't trust the man at this point. Nor could he trust that Karbu could control his brother, Jiri.

Christie sat in the front passenger seat. Steel glanced back at his passengers. Harry, Harry's future father-in-law—Carlos,

Harry's future brother-in-law—Mario, and Christie's brother Clay had all arrived in time for the flight.

Mario and Carlos both had some of the same chiseled features as Isabella. Mario was in his thirties, strong and lean, and Carlos in his fifties, stocky and wearing a moustache. Clay had short hair, was in his late forties, and also had a moustache. Carlos' other son, Pedro, had wanted to come, but he was still recovering from serious injuries from the cartel mess. Steel would have refused Pedro's help anyway. The youngest son had no military training and was too inexperienced and unpredictable.

Steel didn't know how he felt about putting future in-laws at risk, but they had all insisted on coming. And he needed all the help he could get to go up against M4N. Worse, Harry, Christie, and Clay had lost their brother, Dale, five months ago, and Steel worried about them losing another sibling here. Carlos had also lost a son—Mario a brother—in the cartel business last September. Steel didn't want to add to their family loss either. *Hell.*

Christie still favored her ribs. Harry had injuries too, but he and Christie had demanded to come. Steel had some bruises and aches from his fight with Mykey, and the cut on his chest had to be rebandaged again after his last fight. However no injuries would be enough to sideline him from getting Rachel back.

Carlos glanced at him. "You need not worry, Steel. I'm doing this for Isabella and Harry. It's my duty to help if I can. I can't have Harry die before he's married without helping him or my daughter would never speak to me again." His eyes glinted with humor as he glanced at Harry. He became serious and said, "I also wanted to help for what we put you through six months ago."

"Me too." Mario smiled, a toothpick in his mouth, a small cowboy hat on his head. "Isabella told me I better help or else I wouldn't be invited to her wedding."

"She's tough, right?" Harry chuckled.

Clay cleared his throat. "You're like a brother-in-law to me, Steel. I'm glad to help. And there's no way I'm letting my little sister and brother do something like this alone. Besides, as snipers, Carlos and I will be at a distance, so we're out of the danger close situation."

Steel nodded in respect, looking into the rearview mirror. "I owe all of you." Everyone was ex-military. No amateurs. And Clay and Carlos were superb marksmen—another thing in their favor. Everyone was dressed in black Lycra, hoods off for the moment. All of them wore Kevlar vests and were linked with coms.

A stream ran down the mountain, leading up close to the villa, and small wooden bridges crossed over it on the way up as they drove. Harry, Mario, Clay, and Carlos would walk in the water up the mountainside, hopefully bypassing sensors and cameras. Clay and Carlos would leave the others near the top of the mountain to go wide of the villa and set up as snipers.

As soon as Clay and Carlos were set up, Steel and Christie would infiltrate the jungle close to the road, take out any guards along the way, and try to reach the villa more directly by paralleling the road. There were risks with all of it, but they had to try.

The only other plan of attack was to hike up the mountain through the jungle. Steel had felt that someone like Karbu would have multiple and redundant sensors on the mountain in all approach directions. They wouldn't be able to spot them all, and any attack would fail. This plan might also fail, but he felt it had a better chance to succeed.

Christie had her eyes glued to the night vision binoculars. "Nothing up ahead, Steel. But we're halfway. We should unload here, do a check."

Steel pulled the vehicle a few feet into grass along the side of the road, stopping fifty feet before the next hairpin turn in the road. A small wooden bridge was just ahead of the Jeep, running over the stream the others would walk up.

Getting out quietly, Steel drew his silenced Glock. Christie exited on her side, and everyone else exited the SUV, getting ready to head up the mountain.

Steel walked with Christie over the small bridge and eyed the stream. Rocky and very shallow. Not too difficult a hike. They continued another thirty yards to the next curve in the road.

Steel stopped before it, unable to see around it, or be seen by anyone on the other side. Kneeling on one knee, gun up, he waited.

Christie strode into the trees a few yards to look ahead at the next stretch of road with the night vision binoculars. She quickly returned. "A Jeep is fifty yards down the road. Two guards. No gate." She looked at him. "One of the guards is waving us ahead. They know we're here."

Steel frowned. They were still a half-mile from the villa. "A camera feed much farther down the mountain?"

Christie shrugged. "And why the invitation instead of an ambush?"

Steel stood up. The advantage of placing snipers might be lost. And Karbu might have his own snipers already in position. He considered that as he walked with Christie ahead to the bend in the road, guns leveled, and cautiously peered around it.

One of the guards was walking toward them, arms in the air, motioning them forward with his empty hands. Instead they waited, allowing the guard to come to them. The man was dressed in black Lycra, Glock holstered, an HK machine gun on a carry strap on his back. No nonsense. And he moved fluidly.

When the man reached them, he said with an Hispanic accent, "Karbu wants no trouble. The gate is open. Drive up to the villa, go in through the front door. They are waiting on the roof for you. He will talk to you first."

Steel lowered his Glock, but didn't trust the message. The guard's cell phone rang from an upper Lycra pocket, and the man slowly pulled it out and handed it to Steel. It was Karbu. Steel put it on speaker.

Karbu's voice was calm. "Steel, I have many friends on this island. Did you really think any inquiries about me would go unnoticed? I also thought you might arrive early and extended my security perimeter. No matter. I'm glad you are here. Come up to the roof as my man said. You have my word. No shooting, no ambush, none of my snipers targeting the roof. Here is your daughter."

"Dad?"

Steel had a lump in his throat. "Rachel."

"I'm okay, Dad."

Her voice sounded relaxed and excited, instead of nervous or afraid. That meant something to him. "Okay, honey. I'm coming."

Karbu came on again. "I wish to talk, Steel. Not fight. This is my home. Respect that."

The call ended.

Steel handed the phone back, and the guard nodded to him and stepped to the side of the road. Steel walked back to the SUV. He and Christie still gripped their guns and alternated on watching the guard behind them.

Everyone formed a small circle with him and Christie near the SUV.

What was that all about?" asked Harry.

Glancing at everyone, Steel said, "We have an invite to the villa roof. No choice."

"Hell." Clay frowned. "Danger close after all."

"At least we'll all be together, mis amigos." Carlos smiled. "I wasn't looking forward to spending the night moving through water and jungle anyway."

"Amen to that," said Harry.

"We have no choice." Steel grimaced. "Karbu knows we're here, and he'll have Rachel on the roof."

Steel got in behind the wheel. Thinking. In one move Karbu had removed their snipers and given himself an edge over them. Very dangerous. He didn't like it. "Windows down, guns ready just in case."

Everyone in the SUV complied.

Steel drove past the first set of guards, and in a hundred yards a ten-foot-tall thick chain-link gate across the road was opened by two more guards that waved them through. Steel kept his eyes peeled, and Christie had the night vision binoculars up the whole time, checking the jungle for any apparent ambush. Harry did the same from the back seat.

The gate was closed behind them.

Except for lights shining through the treetops, the winding road hid most of the villa from them until the last curve revealed it ahead, well-lit on all levels, including the roof. It looked like a concrete wall bordered the top of the roof, with potted plants atop it obscuring even more of it. The villa was on the top of the mountain, facing north.

In minutes Steel parked by several other SUVs adjacent to the villa. The sweet perfume of frangipani filled the air. Strangler fig, mahogany, flamboyant trees, cacao, and wild orchids surrounded it. Karbu's love of nature mirrored Steel's.

Before getting out, Steel said, "I think things are going to develop as expected. Remember what we talked about. Questions?"

Everyone was silent.

Steel put out his palm, and Christie opened the glove compartment and handed another Glock to him, and grabbed a SIG there and handed it to Clay. No one said anything as they exited the SUV. Steel holstered the extra Glock, keeping one in his hand. Clay also had two guns; one SIG in hand, another at his back. Clay and Carlos also strapped the HK G28s to their backs. Harry and Mario held Glocks, Christie her SIG.

They walked into the first level, all of them holding guns ready just in case. Steel noted the six massive aquariums with tropical fish, potted plants and flowers, a casual dining space, and a large kitchen. The entire space wasn't separated by walls and looked pleasant, beautiful. A few closed doors signaled possible bedrooms. He didn't think Rachel would be here. Karbu would use his daughter against him and have her on the roof.

They took stairs up to the second floor, which had a smaller kitchen, an open living area again, and a half-dozen closed doors to what Steel assumed were also bedrooms.

The same open stairs led up to another short hallway that ended with a glass doorway, which opened onto the roof.

Before he stepped out, Steel pulled his other Glock and scanned the roof through the glass door. Flat, seventy-five feet square, with lounge chairs pulled to the sides. Potted frangipani, hibiscus, and bougainvillea flowers sat on the perimeter four-foot-high wall. Overhead lighting on twelve-foot poles around the perimeter gave it all good visibility. Steel guessed it was set up for outdoor dinners and parties.

Across from them, on the far side of the roof, Karbu stood facing him. Emilia stood to Karbu's right, Jiri to his left. Six other men stood on Jiri's left side, all holding guns in their hands, but pointed down. Karbu's gun was in a holster and he wore shorts and a flowered shirt, while Emilia wore jeans and boots, her long dark hair hanging over a denim blouse.

Jiri and his men were dressed similarly to Steel and his crew, and all wore Kevlar.

Steel walked out first, both guns pointed down. Steel took the center, with Christie and Harry on either side of him, while Clay, Mario, and Carlos floated to the edges of their line.

Steel stopped forty feet from Karbu. He didn't like the number of opponents they were facing on the roof. Nine against six. He suspected that element had been chosen by Jiri, who showed at Chena and Charlie Dome that he always favored operating from a position of strength over his opponents. But Steel had expected that. He and Clay shot equally well with either hand, which made it nine guns against eight.

Still, in a shootout Steel knew his side would take bullets, and possibly lose the fight. He also felt a needle of anxiety over not seeing Rachel. He was wrong; she was being held in one of the lower rooms with someone probably holding a gun to her head.

Karbu's ace in the hole. Now he wished he had checked the lower rooms of the villa.

Steel studied Jiri, who stared at him. The man was built like himself, looked confident, wore a moustache and trimmed beard, and seemed relaxed. General Morris' killer.

Emilia gave no signal to Steel, and he didn't acknowledge her.

Karbu's voice was calm, but strong. "Everyone here is highly skilled and trained. I'm sure we could all kill each other, but what would be the point?" He spread his hands. "So can we begin with civility and put our guns away?"

"Agreed." Steel lifted his chin. "You first, we'll follow."

Karbu lifted a palm, and Emilia, Jiri, and Jiri's men holstered their guns. Steel and the others followed suit.

Karbu walked to the side a short distance, pacing slowly, eyeing Steel. "Rachel is safe with Ivel in a bedroom on the first floor. My wife is going to live, so I am strongly motivated to end this, Steel. I didn't invite Rachel up here because she is a child and doesn't need to be involved with what the adults are talking about. You can take her home when you leave. She is not a prisoner." He paused. "In fact, I am impressed that you have such a healthy, strong daughter, given what she has been through. She told me."

Steel relaxed over Karbu's words, and felt more respect for him. He assumed the man might also be lying, even though he saw no indication of it.

Karbu continued. "What is it that you need to leave us alone permanently, Steel? How do we end this?" He raised a hand. "Before you answer, everyone here is going to have to compromise. None of us is going to get everything we want."

Steel had discussed this very issue with Christie and Harry on the plane ride to St. Croix. Mario, Clay, and Carlos had also given their views. Steel had felt since everyone was risking their necks, they all had the right to weigh in. He had also wanted objective viewpoints. In the past he had sometimes obsessed with outcomes, and this time, especially since Rachel was involved, he wanted to make sure he wasn't focused on an outcome just out of stubbornness.

However, Morris' words about justice had been on his mind a lot in the last days. He lifted his chin. "I want the name of the man who hired Jiri." He looked at Jiri. "And your brother has to pay for killing General Morris."

Jiri just smiled.

Karbu nodded. "A good starting point, Steel. We offer clients full confidentiality and anonymity. M4N is based on that premise. We also offer a no-fail policy or your money back. We refunded the money to Jiri's client. Ten million. The last two targets, as you know, are safe."

"Your brother murdered the Acting Secretary of Defense, Marv Vonders, Senator Seldman, a high-ranking senator on the Senate Intelligence Committee, and General Morris, the head of Army Intelligence." Steel looked at Jiri. "General Morris was also my friend."

Jiri didn't lose his smile.

Karbu nodded. "True."

Steel continued. "I think Bill Bishop, head of the CIA, would also like to know the name of the person who ran a conspiracy to kill high-ranking American government officials for a secret agenda." He glanced at Emilia, wondering again where she fit into all this, and more importantly, where the CIA stood. Why hadn't they just forced Jiri to talk?

Karbu nodded. "Also true. We can meet you halfway, Steel, and give you the name of the person who hired M4N, with the promise that M4N would leave you, your family, and anyone important to you alone permanently. Then could you walk away?" He gestured to him. "We can also throw in a bonus. We can offer M4N's resources to help with problems you currently have with any enemies."

Steel was surprised over the quick compromise. It wasn't everything he wanted, but he could live with it. "I accept the name and the bonus."

Karbu spread his hands. "Then we are finished here?"

"Not quite." Steel's next point had taken up most of the discussion between himself, Christie, Harry, and the others. "Jiri also has to pay. He can turn himself in to authorities stateside."

Karbu shook his head. "That puts M4N and all our clients at too much security risk. And the CIA will not support it."

Steel shrugged. "Let's find out."

Karbu turned to Emilia. "Emilia, you're CIA and report to them. Tell Steel why the CIA doesn't want Jiri to turn himself in to authorities."

Emilia stared at Karbu.

Karbu smiled. "I have known from the beginning, Emilia. The CIA referral of you to M4N was too obvious. Besides, I did not mind having the CIA check up on me with an insider."

Steel watched Emilia's reaction closely and thought her surprise was genuine. That made Karbu even smarter in his eyes.

Jiri glared at Emilia, then Karbu. "You never told me."

Karbu nodded to his brother. "I didn't want you to kill her, brother. She's CIA. We do a lot of contracts for them." He turned back to Emilia. "Now let's not waste time. Tell Steel."

Emilia gazed at Steel. "Jiri is running many CIA contracts and they can't afford to have them disrupted or ended." She glanced at Jiri. "However, they want to know who hired you, Jiri. They consider that a matter of national security. That name has to be given. But they will leave you alone if you stay off U.S. mainland soil for the rest of your life."

Jiri continued to glare at his brother. "I'm not giving up my contact's name, but I agree to stay off U.S. mainland soil."

Karbu said softly, "We talked about this, Jiri."

Jiri scoffed. “You knew all along that Emilia was spying on me, yet you said nothing. You trusted her above me!” He turned to Emilia. “You tell the CIA if they want the name of the person who hired me, then all contracts with them are finished. I already know how that conversation will go.” He faced Steel. “Steel is the only one truly pushing me to give up a name.”

Steel sensed tension building on the roof. Several of Jiri’s men had their hands closer to their pistol grips. He didn’t want his friends shot over this, and he had thought it through. “Then, Jiri, let’s settle this between us. You and I fight. I win, you give me the name or I kill you.”

Jiri smiled. “I thought you would never ask, Steel. I win, and you die here and your men and woman leave.”

Steel doubted that anyone would leave here alive if he lost.

“You can’t kill Jiri.” Emilia stared at Steel.

Steel was aware of Christie and Harry glancing at him. They had talked about this too, him fighting Jiri, even though no one had been happy about it. His plan before he arrived, if this situation developed, was to permanently damage Jiri—the minimal price for killing General Morris—and then get the name of who hired him. He didn’t want Karbu reconsidering releasing Rachel, or have a gunfight on the top of the roof if he killed Jiri. Christie and the others had forced him to accept that Jiri might have to be allowed to live.

He nodded. “Agreed.”

Jiri looked at Emilia. “If I win, the CIA leaves us alone.”

Emilia lifted her chin. “I can’t vouch for that.”

Jiri’s voice hardened. “Call them now.”

Emilia hesitated. But she pulled her phone from her pocket and dialed a number. Talking quietly, she spelled out the terms to someone on the other end. She pocketed her phone. “The CIA can live with the result of the fight as agreed. But if you lose you agree to give up the name of who employed you.” She looked surprised, but she turned to Steel, barely lifting her chin.

Steel sensed she hadn't told them everything. And given her previous lies, he couldn't trust what she would do on the roof.

"Then it's settled." Jiri looked satisfied. "No Kevlar, Steel."

Steel looked at Karbu. "You agree to this, along with your men?"

Hesitating, Karbu looked at his brother.

Jiri gave a grim smile to his brother. "Have I ever lost, brother?"

Karbu nodded to Steel. "Agreed."

"Oh, just in case you do manage to defeat me, Steel." Jiri smiled, looking past him.

Steel turned, and swallowed.

Rachel was shoved through the rooftop glass door by a man who held one arm wrapped around her throat, while holding a gun to her head. Three more of Jiri's men walked through the glass door, facing Steel's team from behind.

CHAPTER 41

RACHEL WAS WEARING WHITE shorts and a colorful print blouse with fish on it. Her left arm was in a cast, which had signatures and colorful fish on it. *Karbu and Ivel*, thought Steel.

Steel's arms tensed as he met Rachel's eyes. She didn't look afraid, but he had no doubt of the result Jiri wanted. All of them dead. The fight was just to satisfy Jiri's ego. He turned back to face Jiri.

"Jiri!" snapped Karbu. "I can't let you do this." He pulled his gun, but kept it pointed down.

Jiri smiled at his brother. "Put your gun away, Karbu, or my man kills Steel's daughter now."

Everyone's hands on both sides drifted to their gun grips. Steel gripped both of his, eyeing Jiri's men.

Karbu paled, and slowly holstered his weapon.

Steel released his weapons as did everyone else. He turned and met Clay's eyes. Clay barely nodded.

As Steel pulled off his Kevlar vest and dropped it to the roof, Christie came up close and said softly, "Don't lose, Steel."

"That's the plan." He had no doubt what Jiri's men would do if he won. Jiri would never bring anyone up to the roof that wasn't loyal to him. He glanced at his team. No backing out. "On my mark, everyone," he whispered.

Harry's eyes narrowed. Mario and Carlos stared calmly at Jiri's men across the roof.

Jiri walked forward twenty feet and stopped. He took out his gun, walked over to the side of the roof, and set it down near the perimeter wall. "You too, Steel."

Steel walked to the edge of the roof, stopping fifteen feet from Jiri. Slowly pulling the Glock from his belt, he set it down on the rooftop, followed by the holstered Glock. Walking slowly back to the roof center, he faced Jiri and began walking in a circle, studying his opponent. Concern for Rachel flooded him, but he had to shove it aside to focus.

Jiri walked in the same shrinking circle as Steel, moving smoothly. Steel had already learned from Charlie Dome that Jiri handled low attacks as well as high and seemed proficient with both hands and legs. The man had trained hard at some point in his life to be very good.

Jiri kept making the circle smaller, reversing course twice, studying Steel. He had lost his smile and his gaze was focused, attentive.

Steel closed the gap, brought his hands up in a sideways stance, waiting as he slowly inched forward. Jiri stopped moving, facing him, and slowly raised his hands. They were ten feet apart when Jiri rushed, disappearing into a roll directly at Steel. Jiri's feet flashed out at Steel's legs.

Steel wasn't able to jump back, so he leapt sideways. One of Jiri's feet caught his ankle, and he twisted, coming down on the side of his foot. He went with it so he didn't injure the ankle, rolling sideways away from Jiri.

Even as he rolled, he was aware of Jiri scrambling over the ground in a low pose and kicking out at his back. Steel took a hard hit in the side but kept rolling until he faced Jiri. Then he spun on the ground and kicked out to keep Jiri at bay.

Jiri jumped back, moving like a cat, and straightened.

Steel rose immediately as Jiri ran at him again. This time Steel went down low to kick at Jiri's legs.

At the last moment Jiri leapt high and kicked Steel's shoulder. Steel rolled forward, but Jiri was already charging him again. Steel rose, forced to use defensive blocks against a half dozen hand strikes Jiri sent at him.

Jiri abruptly backed up again.

Steel's side and shoulder ached where Jiri had kicked him. Jiri was as unpredictable in his fighting as he was in his field ops. His strategy was to find holes in his opponent's defense and exploit those.

Steel decided he couldn't let Jiri control the fight. Like himself, the man was in top physical condition. Allowing Jiri to continue to run his unpredictable attacks would favor Jiri—he would eventually land a serious blow. Thus Steel had to take control of the fight.

Without waiting he went straight at the man. Finger strikes to his face, knife hands to his neck, a twisting elbow to his midriff—Jiri blocked or countered everything. But Steel didn't let up, aiming low kicks at Jiri's ankles and knees, and multiple punches, strikes, and blows at his torso and head. Yet Steel couldn't land anything solid, and Jiri countered with his own strikes.

At the end of one exchange, Steel pretended to go low, but instead slid in sideways and used his bent wrist to strike at Jiri's stomach and face, and then twisted and palmed Jiri's lower ribs.

Stumbling back in surprise, Jiri righted himself, but Steel was already charging forward with more of the same. Jiri blocked everything successfully, and Steel hesitated one moment on purpose.

Jiri threw two quick open hand strikes at Steel's neck. Steel ducked, wheeled, and grabbed Jiri's neck from behind. He stomped on Jiri's right ankle, hearing something snap, and then swept his foot and brought the man to the ground, where he locked up Jiri's legs with his and put a choke hold on him.

Then it became a test of strength, and Steel had better position and leverage. In thirty seconds he could feel Jiri's effort to escape weaken. "The name or I break your neck now," said Steel.

"Do you want your daughter to live?" whispered Jiri.

Steel applied more pressure, but Jiri still didn't say anything. He looked across the rooftop, and saw Jiri's man pressing his Glock against Rachel's head.

Emilia said loudly, "The name as agreed, Jiri. And the CIA has looked into this, so we have a short list of suspects."

Jiri still hesitated, but then gasped, "Paul Franks."

Emilia got out her phone and made a quick call. She nodded once at Steel. "It's likely."

Steel shoved Jiri away, and Jiri heaved for air from the ground.

Tired, Steel stood up. He glanced at Karbu and Jiri's men, his chest heaving. Karbu wasn't moving, but Jiri's men in front of them and the three near Rachel all had their hands on their pistol grips.

Jiri rose to his feet, glaring and favoring his right leg that Steel had injured, a thin dagger in his hands. Steel figured Jiri had the knife hidden in an ankle sheath beneath his Lycra. He noted Emilia was gripping her gun, as was Karbu. He still wasn't sure whose side they were on.

"It's over, Jiri!" snapped Karbu. He held up a palm to Jiri's men.

"This is my company now, brother," snarled Jiri.

"No!" yelled Karbu. "It's over, Jiri."

Steel turned away from Jiri, exposing his back. "Now," he whispered. He hoped the tiny edge he was giving his team was enough.

His friends all flung themselves to the roof on their bellies or knees, already firing, while Steel made a dash for his Glocks.

"Kill them all!" snarled Jiri.

Emilia fired at Jiri's men from where she stood. Karbu flung himself down, gun in hand, also firing at Jiri's men.

Christie fired at the men near Rachel, as did Clay—from his back. Carlos fired across the rooftop from his knees. Mario and Harry were already prone and firing in the same direction. One of Jiri's men across the rooftop took a shot in the back and went down; Steel saw that shot couldn't come from any of his team. Emilia fell to a knee, still firing, a wound in her side.

Nearly twenty guns firing pounded Steel's ears as he reached for one of his Glocks. A flash of steel in his peripheral vision made him jerk back as Jiri's blade just missed his neck. He pulled his OTF blade, watching the gunfight, wanting his gun, seeing Rachel still standing. If he killed Jiri, he assumed Rachel was dead. He had told his team the same thing.

Steel decided to take a knife wound from Jiri to get his gun. Swiping wildly, he then jabbed at Jiri, who stepped back and slashed his arm.

His arm burning, Steel threw himself down on the roof, grabbed a Glock with his left hand, twisted, and aimed. The man holding Rachel was crouching behind her, shooting at Clay who was rolling away. Steel couldn't take out Jiri's man.

Someone opened the glass roof door. One hand on a side bandage, Ivel limped out. Raising her arm, she shot the man holding Rachel in the head and then slumped against the wall near the door. One of Jiri's men turned to her, and Steel shot him in the head. He glimpsed Christie and Carlos taking hits.

Aware of Jiri already aiming a gun at him, Steel rolled away, expecting a bullet in his back. But when Steel stopped and faced him, Jiri convulsed as a bullet hit him from the side, in the upper chest. He went down silently. Lifeless.

The shooting stopped.

Steel lifted his head. Christie was down, on her back. He rose and ran to her, as Rachel ran to him. "Christie!" He knelt by her side, and she looked up at him. "Just hits on the Kevlar, Steel."

"Dad!" Rachel was in his arms then, and Christie slowly joined them in the embrace. Tears ran down their faces.

Steel scanned the roof. Carlos was holding a bloodied right arm. Harry was helping him. Mario hurried to his father. Clay rose to his knees, his guns still up, quickly glancing at his siblings.

Steel glanced at Emilia. She holstered her gun as she stared at him, her left side bloodied.

"Almighty." Clay stood up, slowly lowering his guns to his sides.

Harry sighed. "Likewise."

"We'll all make it to the wedding, mis amigos." Carlos rose to his feet with the help of Mario and Harry.

Karbu tossed his gun on a lounge chair and strode to his brother. Sitting beside the body, he cradled his brother's head. "Jiri," he whispered. "My brother."

Ivel managed to stumble across the rooftop, and she collapsed to her knees beside Karbu, where he wrapped his arms around her.

"Always and forever, Bu," she said softly.

Karbu had tears running down his face. "Always and forever, Ivel."

Steel said, "Clay, make sure no one comes in from the road. Mario and Harry secure the roof door, and the house."

"I can do that, Steel." Clay put away his SIGs, cradled his HK G28, and walked to the edge of the roof overlooking the driveway. He knelt there, rifle up.

Mario and Harry moved toward the glass roof door, guns up. Carlos followed them, gun in hand, his arm in a makeshift sling from his HK strap.

Steel pulled back from the two women in his life, and said, "Rachel, can you tell Christie what you've been doing here? I have to talk to someone and I'll be back in a few minutes."

Rachel bit her lip. "Okay, Dad."

"Come on, Rach." Christie put an arm around Rachel's shoulders and walked her a short distance away, near some potted flowers, to avoid staring at the bodies on the rooftop.

Steel walked to Emilia, who was sitting on a lounge chair holding a phone to her ear, her left side already bandaged with a section of material torn from her ripped blouse.

Tough woman, thought Steel.

Emilia got off the phone, ran a hand through her hair, and faced him squarely. She waved a hand to the side of the villa. "The men on the road are loyal to Karbu. It's safe to leave anytime you wish."

"You put my daughter at risk." He bit off the words.

Emilia frowned. "That was never the plan. Karbu didn't want her hurt under any circumstance and told Jiri that Rachel was to be left with Ivel." She shrugged. "Jiri had other plans." She paused. "Here is the message I am to deliver to you from the CIA. We'll verify and take care of Paul Franks. You will leave M4N alone, completely."

Steel said, "The CIA had a sniper here to kill Jiri once he gave up the name."

"The Agency knew you were coming, so we hoped you would find a way to force Jiri to talk. Karbu wouldn't allow us to take Jiri in for torture." Emilia's expression remained steady. "Karbu knows the sniper wasn't anyone from your team. He also knew the CIA couldn't allow Jiri to live, given who he had killed in the U.S. government."

Steel studied her. "The CIA ordered you to kill Senator Tindren on Charlie Dome for the same reason."

Emilia didn't flinch. "I can neither confirm nor deny that."

"I wondered why you didn't try to get the name of the person who hired Jiri on Charlie Dome." Steel watched her. "You had to kill Senator Tindren earlier than you wanted because he was going to shoot Karbu, and the CIA didn't want the owner of M4N killed, given the contracts he's running for them."

Emilia lifted her chin slightly. "You know I can't comment, Steel."

"You're here to make sure M4N carries out the contracts they have with the CIA." Steel regarded her with more respect. "You're going to take over Jiri's role."

Emilia expression didn't waver. "Again, can you leave M4N alone?"

"Paul Franks wasn't at the head of this conspiracy." Steel crossed his arms. "I can agree to your terms, but I can also help you solve who was behind Franks."

Emilia's eyes widened. "How?"

Steel heaved a breath. "In return for my help, I'm going to need three things from the CIA and Karbu."

Emilia tilted her head slightly, an eyebrow raised. "Three?"

PART 5

OP: JUSTICE

CHAPTER 42

A FEW DAYS LATER STEEL received a call on his cell. He didn't recognize the number, nor the voice, but he listened intently.

"Your problem is taken care of. I also wanted to give you a professional courtesy heads-up. I work for both organizations and another person is shopping a contract for you."

Steel said, "Thank you. And thanks for the help on Karbu's roof."

"No problem."

Steel hesitated. "Why didn't you take the contract on me, and why the heads-up?"

"I know who you are, what you've done. I'm not just a mindless killer."

Steel thought on that. "If you ever want to work with a team, I'm looking to expand."

"I keep things simple. One job at a time."

Steel added, "If I ever need help, how do I get in touch with you?"

"Emilia knows how to reach me."

"I owe you." Steel meant it.

"I know."

The phone call ended. Steel knew what the call signified. His first request to Emilia had been honored. The caller—the sniper who had killed Jiri—did contract work for M4N and the CIA, and had taken out Ritchie. It got Steel off the hook from any connection with the loan shark, and any possible retribution from his mob connections.

His second request arrived later in a call from Emilia. She confirmed it quietly, "We looked into what you asked. You were right. We'll take care of it." She paused. "Your third request was granted too, but this is the only window for it." She gave him a location, day, and time.

***

Daniel Baker walked his pit bull Max toward the dog park. He looked ahead, but Paul Franks wasn't there. Instead he saw a tall man dressed in jeans, tennis shoes, and a light black jacket. The man didn't seem to notice him, and stared at the dog park. A few other dog owners were closer to the fence.

Baker wasn't sure where Franks was, but he decided to wait a few minutes before he left. Franks was a liability now that he couldn't risk. But before he acted on that instinct, he wanted Franks to confirm a few things about the *no-fail* organization that had failed miserably. Stupid Franks. He released Max into the dog park, and Max looked around too, expecting his buddy, Franks' dog Wolf, to be there.

Before Baker realized it, the tall man was close beside him, talking calmly and quietly while facing the dog park.

"General Morris was my friend, so that made it personal."

"I'm sorry, do I know you?" Baker was instantly on guard, and looked for Max, to see how far away his dog was. He glanced at the man again, and then recognized him. "Jack Steel. General Morris used to talk about you quite a bit." He looked at Steel. "You got a friend of mine killed. William Torr."

"Don't call the dog. I'll be gone in a minute." Steel still didn't look at him. "Morris wanted justice. He made sure I would deliver on it, and I will."

"Are you threatening me at a dog park?" Baker scoffed. "I'm the National Security Advisor, Steel. How far and how fast can you run?"

"The organization that Paul Franks hired to kill General Morris and the others gave up Franks' name."

"Who's Paul Franks? This doesn't concern me. I suggest you leave, Steel. Last warning."

Steel glanced at Baker. "You're a rabid hawk. You desperately want a war with Iran, North Korea, and several other countries. You needed the doves gone."

Baker scoffed. "Our country has grown soft, unwilling to do what's necessary even to save ourselves."

"You were willing to murder anyone in your way to implement your policies." Steel's voice remained steady.

Baker backed up slightly. "That's nonsense. You'll never prove that."

Steel nodded. "I agree. So I had the CIA do a check, to find out how much you had invested into Paul Franks' defense contractor company. War drives arms dealer investments up quite a bit. You invested a million of your own money into Franks' company, and Franks gave you thousands of shares too."

"Millions of people own stock in defense contractors." Baker pulled out his phone.

Steel kept talking. "What I couldn't figure out is why General Morris thought he was the next target. There's only one way that could have happened. He went to you, explained his murder theory, and you said you would look into it discreetly with people you trust. You told Morris that your CIA sources told you that he was a likely next target. You also told Morris he couldn't trust anyone inside at this point, and you suggested he call me for protection. You wanted me dead because you blamed me for getting your friend William Torr assassinated—another CEO of another defense contractor company, and another rabid hawk.

"The hit on General Morris was supposed to also be a hit on me, but you didn't tell Franks that part. He would have objected to your personal motive to go after me. You just told Franks that General Morris had hired a protection agency, so he would make sure more men were sent to kill Morris. It just didn't turn out the way you wanted."

Baker shook his head. "All nonsense. I'm calling the police for harassment."

Steel ignored him. "The only piece I wasn't sure about was Senator Tindren, another hawk. He was in on this from the beginning, yet you had him killed. I'm guessing he introduced you to Paul Franks, and then got greedy. Wanted more money. It was you who called him in Chena. You convinced him to shoot me on Charlie Dome and to not give up your name."

"Again, I have no idea what you're talking about." Baker sounded smug. His finger hovered over the 9 for 911. "Do I need to call the police?"

"I'm leaving now. Just two more things I wanted to tell you." Steel turned, facing Baker squarely now.

Baker stared at him. "You're going to be arrested for your threats, Steel."

Steel kept his voice calm. "Before he died, General Morris gave us a clue about the friend he called the night he was murdered. He said it was someone with the letter B in their name. Someone he knew and trusted. We concluded it had to be someone farther up the ladder than General Morris. Either Bill Bishop, head of the CIA, or you—Daniel Baker, the National Security Advisor. Bill Bishop has no investments in Paul Frank's company, nor any contact with Paul Franks, which leaves you. You met General Morris once a month for dinner for ten years. Same restaurant, same time. Secondly, Paul Franks had a car accident last night. That's why he's not here." He paused. "General Morris knew I would pursue justice at all costs. I just wanted to see the man who had him killed face to face."

Baker gaped at Steel. "You think you can make accusations and they will amount to anything? No court will ever convict me on that flimsy evidence. You can't touch me."

"I agree." Steel kept his voice level. "But the CIA knows who you are now."

Baker lowered his phone, still sounding smug. "The CIA is forbidden to operate on U.S. soil. They would never sanction a hit on someone in my position for unproven allegations."

Steel pulled out his Jeep keys. "They can hire out. You did. How far and how fast can you run?" He walked away.

Baker swung around, looking everywhere. He called harshly for Max to come. He watched Steel get into his Jeep and drive away. His stomach sank and he swallowed hard. He remembered Franks saying he would go down hard if he died an untimely death. More unnerving, he knew what was coming next. Not the when, where, how, or who. Or how much time he had left.

He thought of flying out of the country or disappearing in Mexico. But intuitively he knew it was already too late for that.

Max came up to the fence, barking lightly, waiting for Baker to let him out.

"Who's going to take care of you, Max?" murmured Baker.

CHAPTER 43

At General Morris' funeral at Arlington National Cemetery, Steel felt at peace. He had made sure Morris' death received justice. Harry and Christie stood beside him.

It was a full military funeral with hundreds of military personnel in attendance. Morris had made a lot of friends over the years and was highly respected. A cannon boomed in a salute. The folded flag was presented to Morris' grandson. Morris had requested that in his will.

Steel said goodbye in his own way, wishing his friend eternal peace.

***

Later, when they were all comfortable in casual clothes, sitting in Steel's living room, Steel watched Rachel lounge with their two dogs, Lacy and Spinner. Rachel, still wearing her cast, was brushing both dogs, and they seemed content to lie in the sunlight.

Christie sat beside Steel, legs curled up on the couch, while Harry chatted with Isabella on the phone. Lerkin relaxed in his wheelchair in the sunlight coming through the front windows. The windows had been replaced, but the wood siding still had bullet holes. They had scrubbed and sanded the living room floor.

Kat sat next to her father in a chair, talking softly to him.

Mario and Carlos had flown from St. Croix back to Mexico—and Isabella—and Clay had returned to Montana. Steel had never been happier than to see them all off alive and well.

Steel took it all in, feeling warmth in his chest. They had all come out of this stronger, wounds minimal. He had a few stitches from Jiri's knife wound, but the Lycra had given him some protection. He was lucky and blessed in so many ways. He cleared his throat. "Lerkin, I made a decision."

Lerkin slowly wheeled his chair around, looking serious. "And what is that, my friend?"

"First, thanks for babysitting Zeus while we were gone." Steel leaned forward. "I'm going to give you fifty thousand for a new start. Wherever you want to go."

Lerkin gaped at him. "I can't take it, Steel. Especially not after what happened."

Steel smiled. "Lerkin, I'm here because you saved my life. Now it's my turn to give back."

"Just so you know, Lerkin, he talked to me about it and I agreed." Christie smiled at him.

Lerkin swallowed and glanced at Kat. She smiled too. "Just say yes, Dad. You can't turn down help like that."

Lerkin looked at Steel. "Thank you, my friend."

"Any idea where you would like to go?" asked Steel.

Lerkin looked at him. "Well, it depends on Kat, but would it bother you if I stayed close to a friend, maybe in Richmond, Virginia?"

Steel smiled. "I need more friends in my life, Lerkin."

Lerkin looked at Kat.

She smiled. "I'm happy as long as we're not going back to Las Vegas or Utah, Dad."

Harry got off the phone. "This wedding is getting out of control. It's up to twenty K already." He stared at Steel and Christie. "Well, Isabella will be happy at least."

Christie chuckled. "Harry, you have to tell her how you feel."

Steel slowly nodded, a slight smile on his lips. "Seems to me you gave me that advice once too, Harry."

Harry ran a hand through his hair. "Shoot. You guys are right. I've been a wimp." He started texting on his phone.

Rachel looked up at Steel, her hazel eyes determined. "Dad, when I get older, I'm going to be part of Greensave."

Everyone looked at her with horrified expressions and gave a chorus of, "No!"

Steel laughed. "Honey, do you know how hard it was to tell your mother what happened?"

Rachel lifted her chin stubbornly. "I want to help people too, and I'm tough enough."

Steel smiled at her. "You are tough enough, Rachel. And it's a good thing you want to help people."

Rachel's voice softened. "I didn't like hurting Ivel."

"That wasn't your fault, Rach." Christie leaned forward. "Accidents happen."

"And Ivel said she loved spending time with you." Steel felt he owed Ivel for saving Rachel's life. "Karbu said you were amazing with taking care of his fish."

Rachel smiled. "So when do I get an aquarium?"

Steel chuckled. "As soon as your cast is off."

Rachel's eyes sparkled. "I'm going to start looking up fish to get ready."

"I like it." Steel nudged Christie with his shoulder. "Want to take a walk?"

She smiled. "Love to."

They needed light coats, but the sun was shining. Robins, rose-breasted grosbeaks, and black-throated blue warblers were singing. The air was cool, but not chilly. They walked in silence for a while along the running path through the woods, just listening and enjoying the forest.

Christie said at one point, "Zeus talked to me for a few minutes about our business before he left. He went home to talk to his family and ask for forgiveness. He feels like he owes us."

Steel looked at her. "You really think we should consider him?"

"Let's see. Good heart. Massive. Will train hard. Commit to at least three years. Saved our bacon instead of frying it." Christie chuckled.

"Almost got us all killed. Watched you and others take a beating." Steel saw her eyes glinting in humor. "I had Mykey on the ropes before Zeus grabbed him."

"Of course you did, honey."

Steel laughed. "We'll have to talk. What did Harry say?"

Harry said, and I quote, "A guy that big and strong, what's to think about?" Christie became serious. "Zeus was ready to take a bullet for Kat, someone he had never even met before. Besides, you were right. We need to expand the team."

"You make a good point." Steel shrugged. "Let's see if we even hear from him again."

He sighed. "You know, I still worry about the team." He glanced at her. "Even at Morris' house and Chena, I was going crazy with worry sometimes."

"We all were." Christie chuckled. "I talked to Harry. Little brother can be wise sometimes."

"What did he say?"

Christie looped her arm through his. "He said we always pull through, and we'll always have each other's back. Worry is part of that."

"Harry is wise."

"No one knows how much time they will have together, so we have to enjoy what we have, Jack." She smiled at him.

"I agree, honey."

They kept walking, eventually arriving at the small wooden bridge that crossed the stream running through the southern part of his property. A coffee can was upside down on the bridge. Steel stopped there beside it, staring at the sunlight sparkling on the water.

"Remember that first run we had here?" he asked. "The day we first met?"

Christie laughed. "How could I forget? You pointed at a bear upstream, I had to jump over a six-foot rat snake lying in the sun, and Spinner was running next to me, not you. Also you had a gun in your belt and I didn't know if you were crazy or a killer."

"True." He turned over the coffee can and picked something up, keeping it behind his back. He turned to face her as she faced him. "Christie Thorton." He smiled, never tired of seeing her heart-shaped face and shining green eyes. "What I want is to spend the rest of my life here with you." He brought out a rose to hand to her. "Will you marry me?"

"Absolutely, Jack Steel." She put her arms around him, gently pulled his lips down to hers, and they kissed in the sunlight for a while. She took the rose from him, beaming.

"Did I do better this time?" he asked.

"Much. It was very romantic." She smiled mischievously at him. "But I was hoping you were going to kneel down."

He laughed. "Do you want me to redo it?"

"Maybe tomorrow."

* * *

While you're waiting for the next Jack Steel novel?

How about trying my 1st hi-octane Alex Sight thriller?

SKIP THE FOLLOWING EXCERPT AND
BUY KILL SIGHT ON AMAZON.

Alex Sight uses psychic visions to hunt terrorists, and falls in love with his partner. Both may cost him his life.

(*Special Author's note:* This is not a paranormal, crystal ball book. The main character has a special heightened sense, similar to people the author has met.)

* * *

AUTHOR'S NOTE

The Jack Steel series is in development
for a major motion picture!
Hooray! I can't wait...

Thank you for reading Steel Justice! It was a joy to write, and to take the characters to the next level in their journey. I hope you enjoyed it as much as I did!

Reviews help me keep writing, and encourage other readers to take a chance on a new author they haven't read before. So if you enjoyed the book, please leave a review! Every review, even a few words, helps!

Thank you!

~ Geoff

While you're waiting for the next Jack Steel thriller...

Turn the page to read an excerpt from

Geoffrey Saign's Book 1 in the Alex Sight series,

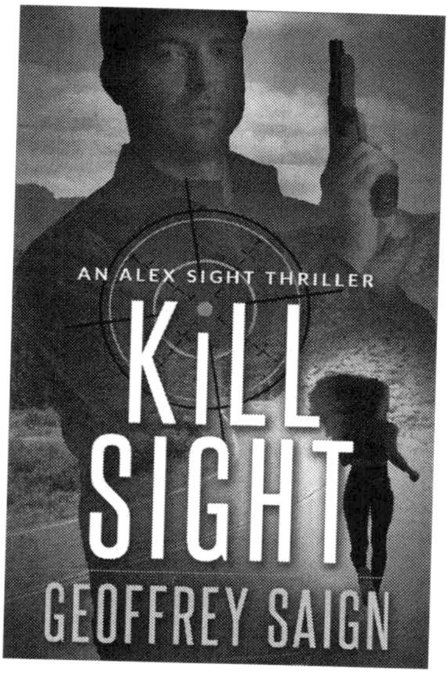

A psychic ex-detective hunts terrorists,
and falls in love with his partner.
Both may cost him his life.

(*Special Author's note:* This is not a paranormal, crystal ball book. The main character has a special heightened sense, similar to people the author has met.)

Excerpt from KILL SIGHT

CHAPTER 1

THE LATE MAY SOUTHERN California sun was a raging fireball in the clear sky, sending sweat running in rivulets beneath Odysseus' black Lycra suit. The other three men also wore black hoods that covered their faces; goggles covered their eyes. They observed Odysseus carefully.

Odysseus checked his watch. Noon. He took a deep breath, the image of Kristen tightening his jaw.

Reaching up, his fingers and toes found the small indentations and outcroppings he had already spotted. Years of climbing gave him strength to move fast. He quickly inched his head above the ten-foot stone wall.

His heart pounded. Laughter and a splash came from the distant pool. The guard was approaching from the far left on the grounds, walking along the inside of the wall. The guard's suit jacket was open, his holstered gun visible.

Lowering himself back down, hanging with one hand with his toes dug in, Odysseus pulled the silenced Glock from his waist pouch. After counting to ten, he silently swung himself atop the wall, and waited until the guard walked by just below him.

Jumping down from the wall, Odysseus' knees bent when his feet hit the plush grass. Straightening, he jammed his gun barrel against the whirling guard's neck and held a finger over his lips.

The guard's eyes widened and he nodded slightly.

Odysseus pulled off the guard's ear piece and throat mike and tossed them to the side. Then he whispered, "If you want to live, on the ground, on your stomach."

The guard paled and complied.

Odysseus put a knee on the guard's back and said softly into his neck radio, "Go."

Rubber-coated grappling hooks made soft sounds as they sailed lightly over the top of the wall and snugged into the stone. In seconds the others joined him. Six-foot-four, Menelaus' rounded shoulders and square back bulged beneath his Lycra. Patroclus, five-eight, had a thick torso, and Achilles stood six feet, his lean frame approximating Odysseus' height and size.

From his backpack Achilles pulled a Glock. Patroclus already held a Heckler & Koch MP5 submachine gun. Menelaus dug out a syringe and injected its contents into the guard's arm, and then armed himself with a Desert Eagle. All the weapons had silencers.

The guard went limp. Achilles zip-tied his wrists and ankles, and then gagged him.

Odysseus led them across the tennis court single file in a crouched run to the six-foot-high patio wall. Built out of designer cored brick, it separated the court from the pool area.

Odysseus looked through the brick, past the pool, at the glass doors at the back of the house. He prayed there would be no surprises. Waiting until the girl was swimming away from them, her head down in the water, he strode around the north side of the patio wall, his gun level. Patroclus followed him.

Achilles and Menelaus rounded the south end of the wall and headed for the house doors, running undetected behind Wheeler and his wife.

Wheeler was in his bathing suit, lounging on a chair and listening to his iPod, while watching his daughter swim. His plump body revealed his easy lifestyle. Sunbathing in a chair next to him, Wheeler's trim wife wore a yellow bikini. Her eyes were closed and she looked asleep.

Odysseus' lips pursed. The good times were over for Wheeler. It took Wheeler five seconds to notice them. By then Odysseus was in front of him.

"What the..." Wheeler sat up, looking at each of them. His face quickly turned several shades of darkening red, before turning pale. Sweat beaded his forehead. He didn't reach for the cell phone on the table by his drink, but he did pull out his earbuds and tap his wife's arm. She woke up and sat rigidly, her eyes wide.

Standing in shallow water, Wheeler's teenage daughter had stopped swimming. Her face blanched as she crossed her arms across her chest.

A twinge of pity struck Odysseus. The girl reminded him of Kristen. Innocent.

Muffled shots of the MP5 came from the house. Achilles and Menelaus. Odysseus listened, relieved when the gunfire stopped. Menelaus' whispered voice came through his ear piece; "House secure."

Odysseus glared at the two terrified people in front of him. "Mr. And Mrs. Wheeler, you're going to reap what you sow."

CHAPTER 2

ALEX SIGHT FELT DEATH hanging in the air—like a fading memory. He wanted to ignore it but couldn't. Pausing in the living room, he stared out at the patio, swallowing over what was coming.

Persian rugs, expensive wall art, and pottery on pedestals betrayed Wheeler's wealthy lifestyle. None of it meant anything to them now. He wondered what they thought it had done for their lives.

Taking the last few steps to the patio doorway, he stopped when his senses exploded with sensual details. Like the million bursts of sunlight dancing off the surface of the swimming pool in the backyard, and the hundreds of fiery points the late-morning sun created on his arms and face. Even the holstered Smith & Wesson M&P Shield 9mm in the inner waistband of his jeans felt extra hard against his skin, as did the ankle sheath holding his OTF Microtech double-edged blade. The notes of a nearby singing warbler seemed acutely crisp and sharp.

Walking through the open glass doors, he noted a large blood-red numeral 5 spray-painted on the patio. *They were making a game of it.* His arms stiffened over the chalk outlines of the victims beside the pool.

He walked to the left.

FBI Deputy Director Joseph Foley was sitting with a woman at a small white table with an enormous purple umbrella shading it. Three glasses of pink liquid were on the table, coffee and a manila folder in front of Foley.

Alex reached the shade of the umbrella and stopped, staring at Foley.

Foley took off his sunglasses. Smudges beneath his eyes indicated a lack of sleep, but his six-three, solid frame seemed alert. Dressed in a dark blue suit and tie, his graying hair swept back above commanding eyes and a jutting jaw.

Alex hadn't seen Foley for nearly a year. Wrinkles lined the corners of the man's eyes and mouth, betraying his forty-eight years and lack of sleep. Alex wondered if at thirty-eight he appeared older too, and if his lined forehead gave away his own weariness.

Foley extended a hand. "Good to see you, Alex."

Not wanting contact, he kept his hands to himself and nodded.

Retracting his hand, Foley's eyes narrowed. "Alex Sight, I'd like you to meet Special Agent Megan Detalio. She's an information analyst. One of the best."

In her mid-thirties, she wore an expensive blue suit and white blouse. An olive complexion added to her striking, unconventional appearance. A mix of Caucasian and maybe Pacific Islander, long, dark curly hair framed her soft-featured face. Alex found her attractive, but what held his attention were her dark eyes. Smoldering emotion.

Something threatening surged at him from her, details that he couldn't quite grasp. It felt oddly out of place with the calm woman who sat in front of him. Try as he might, it was an elusive thing, evaporating before he understood it.

"I'm pleased to meet you." Her voice was slightly husky, her tone genuine and easy to read. She stood, five inches under his six-foot height, and extended a hand.

Ignoring her, Alex turned back to Foley. He was aware of the woman frowning. "Get on with it."

Foley cleared his throat. "Megan, could you please wait inside the house?"

"Of course." She looked annoyed, grabbed her sunglasses from the table, and left.

As she walked away, Alex noted that her athletic frame made a distinct V to her waist. Loose fitting slacks tightened around her ankles, above low-heeled shoes. She moved like an athlete, with good balance and a smooth stride.

Alex skewered Foley with his gaze. "The case. Show me."

Foley put on his sunglasses. Rising fluidly, he strode around the pool, taking several mints from a small tin. He didn't offer Alex any.

Foley gestured at the stone wall surrounding the estate. "The killers came over yesterday at noon. Maybe from Avenida Primavera. They knew the layout..."

As Foley talked, Alex's eyes were drawn to the wall, and settled on one round, coarse stone. *Anger*. It leapt at him, clamping on his throat like a vise. He grasped at the word, trying to hang onto it. The emotion changed subtly, expanded, and he felt the rage as it swept into his chest like a hot brand. *Revenge*. That emotion slowly withered away as he listened to the deputy director.

Foley handed over a sheet of paper. "Here's the statement this Threshold terrorist group put on the Internet. A blogger informed us last night of the possibility of foul play with the Wheelers. I happened to be in Los Angeles. Thanks for taking a late flight."

Alex glanced over the words, looking for anything that might trigger a reaction. Some phrases he absorbed, while others slid out of his perception like water through open fingers. *Denton and Patty Wheeler...selling toxic agricultural chemicals...toxic deaths and sickness... victims avenged...no compromise until guilty... brought to justice.*

Nothing jumped out at him so he handed it back to Foley. They strode back to the table.

Foley continued talking. "The killers left footprints made by climbing shoes and wore black Lycra with hoods and red-tinted goggles. Wheeler's teenage daughter said they talked to each other using Greek names from the Trojan War. Menelaus,

Patroclus, Achilles, and Odysseus. She had a course in Greek history so the names resonated.

"She said Achilles dragged one of the dead dogs into the pool, but Odysseus stopped him from throwing the second one in. Achilles made some sarcastic remark. Then Odysseus gave the sentencing speech, accusing the Wheelers of poisoning the planet. They sedated and removed the daughter so she didn't have to watch her parents die. One guard and the maid were tranquilized too."

Foley grimaced as he sat down again. "So we have one slightly compassionate killer and at least one psycho who enjoys it. And they don't like each other. The daughter described Odysseus and Achilles as slender and tall, Menelaus big and strong, Patroclus short and stocky."

Sitting at the table, Alex closed his eyes, not focusing on anything, letting his gift have its way with him. He heard Foley's words in snatches and listened for something beyond them.

"Two guards killed...Heckler & Koch MP5 machine gun... Glock..."

Billings. The word hung in his consciousness and had deep anguish attached to it. Before he could explore it further, black and white images filled his mind, surrounded by darkness—*bullets spraying everywhere, men and women toppling over, shouts...*

Desperately he grasped at the vision, trying to return to it, wanting more of the small taste he had.

However his senses abruptly closed down, shrinking back to the mundane as he dropped out of his state. He made a feeble effort to cling to the fading imagery, but it dissipated like rising smoke.

Dismayed, he opened his eyes. Joseph Foley sat in front of him, seeming a bit more solid and perturbed than he had been aware of earlier. Waves of heat rose from the surrounding patio stones.

The atrocity he had witnessed, a small-scale massacre, curled his hands on the arms of the chair. He always witnessed death or its possibility in his imagery, but never of this magnitude. And never precisely where it would occur. Not knowing the details always left him feeling anxious. The word *Billings* wasn't attached to the site of the massacre, but made him curious.

Relaxing his shoulders, he sagged into his chair, his throat parched. Sweat ran beneath his casual short-sleeved pullover and his tennis shoes suffocated his feet. Lifting the glass of lemonade in front of him, he drained half of it, and then looked at the lawn. "I bet that takes a lot of water in a heat wave like this."

"I know you like print for your skill set." Taking a pencil from his shirt pocket, Foley rested its eraser against the manila folder on the table. "Threshold named several hundred company executives and owners that they're holding personally responsible for national and international environmental crimes. Climate change, toxic chemicals killing people and wildlife, GMO pesticides and herbicides, and plastic pollution. They also faxed details of Wheeler's company operations to the press. Obviously to sway public opinion. We've had quite a few panicked calls from the named CEOs."

"Why did Wheeler have armed guards?"

Foley shrugged. "He was a billionaire living in Del Mar with the Pacific Ocean for a backyard view. I guess he thought it came with the territory."

"Cause of death?"

Foley grimaced. "Respiratory failure. The Wheelers were forced to swallow a cup of glyphosate and clothianidin. Glyphosate is a common herbicide used worldwide, clothianidin is a neonicotinoid pesticide. Both are used on genetically engineered crops. The terrorists blame clothianidin and glyphosate for killing pollinators and insect populations worldwide. Glyphosate is linked to cancer."

"Wheeler's company manufactured them?" asked Alex.

"Yes. In Asia." Foley lifted a few fingers. "Glyphosate is available at lawn and garden stores. Roundup, a common brand from Monsanto, relies on glyphosate. Farmers also use it and clothianidin. We'll talk to Wheeler employees, see if anyone stands out."

"They went to some effort to spare the guard, maid, and daughter." Alex didn't ask how the daughter was doing. She would have to live with this hell for the rest of her life.

Foley's eyebrows arched. "Some twisted idea of killing only those they claim are guilty. The two guards who resisted and the dogs were expendable. They tasered the live-in maid, then sedated her. The sedative used on her, the guard, and the daughter was a mix of ketamine and xylazine. Both are used illegally for recreation, and used as sedatives by veterinarians, among others. Someone had to know what they were doing to mix the two."

"A veterinarian." Intuitively that fit for him.

"Or someone who works with big animals." Foley tapped his pencil's eraser once against the folder. "We pulled together a list of large animal vets in California and neighboring states that use xylazine, alphabetical by states and last names. We'll interview many of them in the coming days."

"How about an environmental extremist file?"

"We're working on it." Foley pushed the folder across the table. "There's also a dossier on Wheeler's company. Phone calls for the last year, acquaintances, friends, and business contacts. We've already moved on a lot of it, but it seems Wheeler was a random target. He just happened to be in the wrong business. In the folder there's a Bureau credit card, FBI photo ID, and the number to my office manager in Washington. She'll be able to locate me immediately."

Alex opened the folder and quickly scanned the list of company executives and owners, letting his eyes wander down pages. Nothing. He moved through the Wheeler company information just as fast. Lastly he scanned the veterinarians listed by state, pausing on California. *San Diego.* It felt intuitive too, and obvious. He stared at the names listed beneath it. *Dr. Frank Crary* stood out, but no images came.

He looked up at Foley. "I want to see phone records on veterinarians around San Diego, especially Dr. Frank Crary."

Foley raised an eyebrow. "Good. We'll get warrants."

Alex sat back. "Why kill Wheeler's wife?"

"She ran the business with him so they considered her equally responsible." Leaning on the table, hands clasped, Foley's steady voice matched the firmness of his expression. "Megan Detalio is your partner."

Alex clenched his jaw. He should have guessed. He recalled sensing something threatening about her. The idea of a partner brought a sour taste to his mouth and memories of Jenny flooded him. Recovering, he tried to sound nonchalant. "What's her history?"

"Phenomenal information analyst. Out of the San Diego office. She volunteered and convinced me of her assets."

Alex kept his voice calm. "Great. Tell her to review the information you have. I'll call her daily to see what she's put together."

"She'll be with you in the field. It's nonnegotiable."

Alex sensed Foley wouldn't budge, so he said, "Look for a motive of revenge."

Foley frowned. "Don't you think that's obvious?"

He shook his head. "A personal motive. Beyond the environmental concerns, and not necessarily directed at Wheeler. Has Billings, Montana, come up in your investigation?"

"Why?" asked Foley.

"Keep it in mind." Alex paused. "I saw a massacre, but it wasn't there. They're connected somehow though."

"A massacre?" Foley pursed his lips.

Alex turned in the direction of heavy footsteps.

A burly, nearly bald man approached them from the house. A tan suit stretched over his wide shoulders and thick arms. He held an unlit wooden pipe. The man stopped at their table, chewing gum and squinting against the sun.

Alex looked at Foley expectantly.

"Alex, this is Bill Gallagher. He directs the FBI's counterterrorism division and will be your contact if I'm busy or detained elsewhere."

Noting the man's surly frown, Alex stuck out his hand. "Nice to meet you."

Gallagher grunted and took his hand in a quick shake. "Likewise."

"I wanted Gallagher to meet you in person." Foley fidgeted in his chair. "You need to work together as the case develops."

"I look forward to it." Alex didn't see any friendliness in the man's eyes. "I'm sure we'll be a great help to each other."

"It should prove interesting." Gallagher nodded, wheeled, and walked back into the house with heavy steps.

Alex shook his head. "Did his dog just die?"

"It seems to be contagious, doesn't it?"

Alex waved a hand. "Sorry. Earlier...that wasn't personal. Hand contact would have interfered with my ability to focus—"

"Don't worry about it." Foley straightened. "Gallagher's the best intelligence analyst we have. He doesn't appreciate bringing in an outsider. You can understand that, can't you?"

"Of course. No one likes to have a partner forced on them."

"Alex, I brought you in because of your ability to deliver fast results." Foley tapped his pencil's eraser rhythmically against the table. "But I want everyone on this case communicating with each other. Understood?"

Foley's words carried a bite and it annoyed him. "Perfectly."

"You need to toe the line too, Alex. Nothing except standard procedure unless you check with me first."

"Fine." He had to work to not react, reminding himself that Foley, besides having a need to spell everything out, always had to tap his stupid pencil like a drumbeat everyone was supposed to march to. Not much had changed in the last year.

Foley leaned back. "I want immediate updates on anything important, and I'll contact you if anything significant develops from our other efforts."

Alex picked up the folder as he rose. He waved at the painted numeral five on the patio. "It's a countdown. The next murder will be tonight and will have a four, the next murders three, two, one."

"You're certain of this?" Foley gaped at him. "Then what?"

Alex grimaced. "Maybe they disappear or go out in a big battle."

Foley rose stiffly. "And you're sure the next one is tonight?"

"I'm guessing after sunset. They did this first one in daylight, but now they'll need to be more careful." He eyed Foley. "A lot of people are going to die before this is over, Joseph."

Foley's eyes widened. "Is that written in stone?"

"I'd bet on it." He strode past the pool, his own words filling him with revulsion. Drained, he needed rest. And his thoughts churned over Megan Detalio.

Walking through the cooler house, he noticed Gallagher talking to several agents. The man avoided his eyes as he went by. Alex wondered how Foley expected him to have good communication with someone who didn't even want him on the case.

Worse than that, the images he had experienced reverberated deep inside. He abruptly realized that he didn't want to do this kind of work anymore. For the first time ever, he wanted off a case. Wanted to walk out of this mansion and forget about it. His curse was that it was too late for that. His conscience wouldn't let him.

CHAPTER 3

JENNY YELLED FOR HIS help from the room, her voice frantic. He ran up the wooden stairs of the old house, knowing he wouldn't be in time, gripping the handrail with one hand, his gun in the other. There were too many steps and he was too far from the room...

Alex woke up, the nightmare fading but leaving him edgy. He leaned back in his seat. Soft music played—Pink singing *Just Give Me a Reason*. Sitting stiffly, Megan was driving his rental Corolla, sleek black sunglasses hiding her eyes. She had taken off her suit jacket, which lay on the back seat next to her laptop. She turned down the music on her iPod.

After telling her what he had sensed at the Wheeler estate, he had crashed. Bringing his seat vertical, he glimpsed the Pacific Ocean through the trees out his open car window. That surprised him. His sunglasses gave the water a greenish tint. A red-tailed hawk circled in the sky.

The AC was off and hot air roasted his skin. His watch read eleven a.m. The promise of another murder tonight sent his thoughts racing. He had to work to calm himself.

His eyes widened as a black and white CHP Charger pulled up alongside them in the opposing traffic lane, lights flashing. No siren.

Megan slowed down and moved their car over to the right side of the lane, biting her lip. The shoulder on their side of the road was nonexistent, with trees and shrubs growing right up to the edge of the pavement.

"What happened?" he asked.

Not answering, Megan stared at the police car keeping pace alongside them as she braked to a stop. The police car stopped beside them, the passenger window open, two male officers in front.

The passenger police officer, wearing sunglasses and tight-lipped, flashed a palm down at Megan. His sun visor was against the window and hid part of his face.

While Megan searched for her driver's license in her small purse, for one instant the driver of the police car leaned forward and scowled.

Alex wondered what Megan had done to make the officer angry—his expression didn't fit a speeding ticket. Maybe the guy was having a bad day.

The CHP quickly accelerated and disappeared around the next bend.

Megan took a deep breath and sagged into her seat. "I was going a little fast. They probably ran the plates and found your name on the rental agreement. And I'm not you."

He glanced at her. "They must have another call. Lucky you."

"No kidding." She tossed her purse into the backseat.

"Where are we?" he asked.

Turning off the music, she pulled back into the lane and continued driving. "Torrey Pines Park Road. The county highway had road construction. We'll pick it up halfway through."

He clutched the armrest as she took the next corner. Twisted pine and chaparral covered the dry countryside. Dust filled the air. He could taste it. Just west of their lane, the rugged landscape dropped three hundred feet. In his side mirror he watched a Subaru Outback with tinted glass roar up fast behind them.

The speed limit was thirty, but Megan pushed the sedan to thirty-five to accommodate the following car. Double solid yellow lines prohibited passing on the winding road and there wasn't a shoulder she could use to let the car pass.

The Subaru hugged their bumper for a few moments, and then dropped back twenty feet.

Alex glanced at Megan, surprised she was speeding again after just being stopped. "Thanks for driving. I needed a rest. Want a break?"

"I'm good." Wind played with strands of her hair while she fingered a silver dolphin at the end of a thin necklace.

He wiped sweat off his brow. "Can we turn on the AC? We're in the middle of a heat wave."

"Sure." She powered up the windows and turned it on.

He opened the glove compartment, which was half-filled with mini dark chocolate bars. "Want one?" She shook her head, and he unwrapped one and started eating.

"I like milk chocolate." She smiled. "One of my few vices."

He winked at her. "Better than drugs and alcohol."

"It goes to my butt."

"Yikes."

Alex's phone played the U.S. Army's *Call to the Post* bugle riff that began every horse race. Taking it out of his pocket, he answered it. A *WhatsApp* call. A man with red curly hair, thick eyebrows, ruddy cheeks, and a reddish beard appeared on the screen.

Alex smiled. "Hey, Harry. What are the names?"

Harry had a deep Irish accent, and Alex murmured the names after him, "Passion, Best Yield, Down Under, Snowball, Spring Step, Constant Effort..." He paused, his forehead wrinkling as he closed his eyes. "Ten on Passion to win, Harry." Two to one odds.

"Don't worry, lad," said Harry. "We'll do her."

"Thanks, Harry." As he put his phone away the Subaru closed on their bumper again and honked. "Impatient," he muttered.

Megan accelerated to forty. "Seems like a lot of effort to bet ten dollars." She brushed strands of her long hair off her cheek and gave him a quizzical look.

He felt an unexpected tug on his emotions. He hadn't had a relationship for three years. Since Jenny. Even so, his reaction bothered him. "Ten thousand." He immediately regretted telling her that.

She gaped. "I never liked gambling. I hope you're not playing with your pension. Do you gamble on everything?"

He smiled. "Just horse racing. There's always one running. Harry does the work for me."

She studied him for a moment. "What you detected at the Wheeler's today, well, are you always right?"

Looking out his window, his mouth was suddenly as dry as the parched air. He grabbed his water bottle from the floor and took a sip.

"Most of the time?" she prodded.

"Yeah, too often."

She glanced in the rearview mirror. "How long have you been able to do it?"

He looked out the window. "I have a vivid memory of an old person dying in my neighborhood when I was ten years old."

"Wow. Must have been a rough childhood." She sounded empathetic.

"Highs and lows, like most." Finished with the chocolate, he tossed the wrapper into the glove compartment and settled back. He remembered the guilt he felt when he was young, having visions of people dying, and then witnessing their actual deaths. Sometimes running to a house to see if he was right—hoping he wasn't. In his teens he tried to prevent the deaths from coming true, but he had always failed.

"That would have been a nightmare for anyone that age," she added.

"Understatement." He wondered how much Foley had shared about him. Megan was an analyst so she might have investigated him. That idea made him uncomfortable.

The Subaru dropped back fifty feet, but immediately raced up to their bumper again.

Alex pushed his feet into the floorboard. Maybe it was a stupid teenager playing around—or on drugs. "How long have you worked for the FBI?"

"A few years as an analyst," she said.

"Any field experience?" He eyed the sideview mirror.

"Not with the FBI." She glanced into her rearview mirror. "I can take care of myself."

Surprised, he turned to her. "What did you do before the FBI?"

"Not now, all right?" Her voice had an edge.

"What's the big deal?" His throat filled with words he wanted to spit at Foley for forcing her on him. "I like to know who I'm working with."

"Megan Detalio," she said stiffly.

"Great."

She glanced at him, her voice changing gears from irritated to curious. "How do you do it? You know, get your information."

"A crystal ball."

She frowned. "Is it only related to cases? What you're focused on?"

"Gambling's intuitive. The other stuff is triggered by my emotions or what's left over at a crime scene. I don't have any control over it." He swallowed. "Once I'm focused on a case everything is related to it. I usually see people die or who are going to die, but never the exact kill site."

"That frustrates you."

"Of course." The Subaru honked again and he looked into his side mirror. "Someone's in a hurry."

"So are we," she quipped.

He pursed his lips. Stubborn too. Damn Foley.

Her voice softened. "I'm glad you care enough to get involved. You could have remained retired on disability."

"You investigated me." It pushed his irritation further.

She glanced at him. "It's called Google. You came up fast through the ranks and earned a rep as a detective who always solved his cases. You retired from the force after you were wounded and only work freelance now. The last case you solved for the FBI on missing women in Seattle is well-known, as are your psychic abilities."

"Are they?"

She added, "This case will be explosive for the nation. Threshold is murderous, but getting attention for legitimate concerns."

His eyebrows arched. "Sympathizing with murderers?"

"No, but Wheeler wasn't much better. The chemicals he made are carcinogens for humans and killing our pollinators. Many countries and U.S. cities have banned glyphosate. I wouldn't eat GMOs."

The Subaru finally dropped back a reasonable distance and remained there.

Alex didn't know who he was more annoyed with, Megan or the Subaru driver. He choked back a comment about her driving. "You're an environmentalist."

"Activist all through college. The USDA, EPA, FDA, Congress, and the presidency are in the pockets of corporations so people feel they have no representation. We're back to the rich and elite running everything. That's what started the American Revolution, and that's why GMO test plots have been burned. It was only a matter of time before something worse like Threshold evolved."

She gazed at him. "I suppose you're a conservative?"

"I eat organic, worry about climate change and endangered species, and gave twenty grand to Greenpeace last year."

She began to say something, but clamped her lips shut and braked before a turn. "When are we going to Montana? And why bother with San Diego?"

"San Diego felt intuitive."

She waved a hand. "You had a clairvoyant hit on Billings. How does intuition trump that?"

Not used to being grilled, he had to admit the question was insightful. "Billings wasn't attached to the kill site. The goal is to stop the next murder tonight, and it won't be at Billings. Maybe Threshold is based in San Diego. If Wheeler was a random target, as Foley thinks, it makes sense the killers would use a convenient location like Del Mar. People know their own backyard best. I also want to meet Dr. Frank Crary in person to see if I get any further insights."

"I like that logic." She looked at him, her voice eager. "Are we going to Dr. Crary now? Foley showed me the veterinarian list and I memorized their addresses and phone numbers, along with California street maps."

"Really?" Alex stared at her. Foley hadn't exaggerated her abilities. "Foley is obtaining warrants for phone records. Let's see if Crary has any connection to Billings before we approach him."

"Sounds good."

He glanced again at the sideview mirror. The Subaru was closing in again and pulled up within a few feet from them. His stomach tightened as the car crept closer in the mirror. "Geez."

"Idiot." Megan glanced at the rearview mirror.

The car smacked their bumper with a crunch, jerking Alex against his seat belt. "Damn."

Megan scowled and eased off the accelerator. "Great. Just what we need."

The Outback pulled into the opposing traffic lane as if to pass them.

Alex wanted to snap at Megan for not letting the car go by earlier, but instead said, "Probably underage kids drinking. Get the license plate if they don't stop."

A road sign showed a hairpin curve up ahead. Megan braked and drove their car partly onto the narrow shoulder.

The Subaru was taking a huge risk if it was going to pass them now. Alex turned to glare at the driver, and saw something protruding from the car's open passenger window.

"Get down!" He gasped and spun around, hunching low in his seat.

Already ducking, Megan punched the gas pedal.

A blast struck the rear passenger window, scattering glass shards throughout the interior. A burst of warm air swept through the car.

Taking off his seatbelt, Alex drew his 9mm. A hill loomed up in the windshield and he shouted, lifting his free arm in front of his face.

Megan looked over the dash and twisted the steering wheel. The tires bit into dirt, jerking the sedan left.

Turning around, Alex looked between the seats. A man in the front passenger seat of the Subaru wore a nylon stocking over his head and gripped a shotgun. The Outback accelerated into the opposing traffic lane.

"He's coming again!" snapped Alex.

Megan jerked the sedan left and cut off the Subaru. She powered down her window.

Half on his knees, Alex fired three shots, shattering their car's rear window. The reports rang in his ears and bullet holes appeared in the front windshield of the Subaru. The Subaru veered back into the right lane.

Megan swung the sedan sharply right to keep the swerving wagon behind them. Alex slid sideways. Megan drew a SIG Sauer P320 and set it on her lap. She swung the car left again to block the Subaru.

They entered the hairpin curve in the wrong lane, the Subaru following.

Alex scanned ahead as the Toyota's tires screamed around the corner. "Hey!" he yelled.

An oncoming red minivan sounded its horn—the woman driver gaped at them.

Megan wrenched the sedan right. Wheels squealed on pavement. Alex slid against her shoulder, jamming her against the door. The minivan clipped their back fender, jolting their car a few feet sideways.

"Get off me!" yelled Megan.

Their Toyota veered across the road with Alex's weight still trapping Megan. The Subaru veered out of the way of the van, which ran off the road and crashed into a tree.

Turning, Alex shouted as pine trees loomed over them. Gripping the wheel, he wrenched the sedan left. The turn slid him against the passenger door and he swore. Tilting sharply, the Corolla fishtailed briefly before Megan steadied it.

Alex glanced back. The Subaru had lost ground to avoid the minivan.

When they rounded the curve, relief swept him. Fifty yards ahead of them, the CHP Charger was parked in a tourist lookout on the right shoulder.

CHAPTER 4

MEGAN SLAMMED ON THE brakes and spun the steering wheel. The tires screeched and their sedan did a one-eighty in the road and jolted to a stop. The engine died.

Alex gaped. The Outback was approaching them head-on.

Megan stuck her arm out the window and squeezed off three shots.

"Get down!" shouted Alex.

Megan leaned sideways. Alex threw himself over her as a hard jolt pushed their car toward the east side of the road amid crunching metal. Air bags exploded, pushing them against the front seat.

An engine whined.

Alex peered over the dash. The Subaru was racing backward, its engine hood crumpled like a camel's hump. Three bullet holes marred its windshield. The car made a reverse turn in the middle of the road, and then sped around the hairpin curve, quickly out of sight.

Alex sat up. The front end of their car was pushed in on the passenger side and their car rested at an angle in the road.

Partially rising, Megan peered over the dashboard out their windshield.

Wiping a forearm across his forehead, Alex said, "California drivers."

"Get out of the car with your hands on your head!"

One of the CHP officers stood in the turn-off twenty feet from them, a Smith & Wesson M&P pistol held stiffly in his extended hands. Dressed in a khaki shirt and pants, the trooper wore a wide-brimmed tan hat. A radio hung over his shoulder. The driving officer stood behind his open car door, his left hand already on his radio as he talked into it.

Alex was irritated at the officer holding a gun on them. But the patrolmen had seen Megan shooting at a car. Maybe they assumed it was road rage. He hoped the officers were calling to intercept the other car.

He slid his gun back into the holster beneath his shirt. Taking a deep breath, he opened his door and stepped onto the road, holding his badge above the hood. Dust and the scent of steaming blacktop hit his nostrils. Sweat coated his skin.

"FBI," he said to the officer. "We need you to get on the radio and set roadblocks at the..." He looked in at Megan. "Do you know where?"

She spoke softly. "South end of Torrey Pines, and both directions on the 5 and Ted Williams Freeway out to ten miles. Better do Camino Del Mar ten miles north of the park too."

Alex repeated the information to the officer.

The officer didn't lower his gun, and instead lifted his chin at Megan. "I want to see her badge too." His voice was hard.

Megan cracked her door, still hunched over in the seat.

Alex glanced in at her. She was moving slow, appearing a little dazed. Softly, he said, "Holster your gun, Megan."

Straightening, he shuffled to the rear of the car. The trooper in the road eyed him closely, but had his M&P trained on Megan's door. Megan sat motionless, her door still only cracked opened. Alex stopped near the trunk, wondering why she wasn't getting out. Maybe she was hurt.

The officer in the road swung his gun from Megan to him.

Alex frowned. "Hey, are you deaf? We're FBI." He spotted the SIG Sauer in Megan's hands behind the door as she stared at the trooper.

At the same moment, the standing officer swung his gun back to Megan, his face hardening. "Show your badge and hands."

Alex blurted, "It's all right, officer. I'm a special investigator on assignment with—"

An explosion cut him off.

The trooper crumpled, red darkening the belly of his brown shirt, his arms dropping as he stumbled back.

Alex gaped, lowering his badge. He swung to Megan; she lay on her back on the front seat, arms extended, her gun aimed at her window.

"Get down, Alex!" she yelled.

The officer standing behind the open CHP car door held a MP7 silenced submachine gun. The nonstandard weapon sent adrenaline into Alex's chest.

Megan shot three times at the officer, who ducked down while firing the MP7 at them through his open window.

Alex crouched behind the rear tire as bullets ripped dull pops along the car's frame. Twisting to sit behind the tire, he drew his gun and pushed his back against the hubcap, keeping his head down. His shoulders and arms were rigid and he jammed his shoes into the tar. Bullets punched through the rear car door near him and bit the road past the trunk.

Megan belly crawled out of the front passenger door down to the asphalt, and then scrambled behind the front passenger tire.

Alex rose slightly and risked a look over the trunk.

The wounded trooper was falling into the back seat of the police car. The other officer rose and sprayed them again with the MP7.

Alex ducked as bullets ripped into the sedan in dull thuds. When the shooting stopped, he glanced at Megan. She was still crouched behind the front passenger tire.

Tires spewed gravel.

Alex glanced over the trunk, and then scrambled around the car to the driver's side to get a better line of sight on the fleeing patrol car. He stood and fired three shots; Megan didn't fire.

After the cruiser disappeared around the corner, his shoulders slumped, the sudden quiet at odds with his emotions.

He leaned against the car, his left knee aching. His shirt was drenched and his stomach heaved. "Megan?"

No response.

"Megan!" He quickly limped back around the trunk.

She stood up near the front end, her face ashen, her gun holstered. Blood dripped from her left hand, staining the cuff of her white blouse.

Walking along the car in a rush, he stopped in front of her. "You're shot?"

"Just grazed my forearm." Using her right hand, she took off her sunglasses and ran her gaze over him. "Are you all right?"

Relief swept his limbs and he exhaled. "I'll make it to dinner. Sit down, keep the arm elevated. I'll call it in."

Dialing 911 on his cell, he gave a quick report while retrieving a clean T-shirt from his suitcase in the trunk. He strode back to Megan.

She sat sideways on the front car seat, her feet on the pavement. The sleeve of her blouse was mostly red.

Pulling out his OTF knife, he cut her sleeve to make it easier to pull back. She had a thin, jagged scrape along the forearm. He folded the tee into a rectangle and gently laid it against her wound. "Put pressure on it."

As she placed her palm against it, her eyes searched his, the emotion in them reaching him. "Thank you, Alex."

He stared down at her. "How did you know the cops were fake?"

The corners of her mouth turned down. "I caught a glimpse of the MP7 that the officer was hiding in his right hand. When he lifted it, I fired."

"I should have seen that." She was sharp and it impressed him. Or was he getting sloppy?

Sirens blared in the distance.

He thought about Threshold. "It's a big risk for the terrorists to attack us. But if not them, then who?"

Her face darkened and she didn't answer.

The set-up had been so elaborate that it felt bigger than a personal vendetta. Also why not just shoot them earlier instead of playing bumper cars? None of it seemed logical. And when he ran through his past, he came up empty for suspects. "Do you have anyone in your past that would try something like this?"

"I ran through possibilities," she said. "Nothing fits. You?"

"Nothing that makes sense."

She looked up at him. "I saw you limping."

"Left knee acts up sometimes. An old wound." One of the bullets he had taken from Jenny's killer.

He gestured to her. "Thanks."

"For what?"

He shrugged. "Saving my life."

She reddened with an awkward glance that didn't quite meet his. "You're welcome, Alex." Her voice lowered. "I've never shot anyone before."

"You had no choice." He wondered again what she had done before. Maybe she had never been in the field. Still, she had handled herself well.

In a moment her intense eyes probed his.

"What?" he asked.

"I guess this means I now have field experience."

Read all the Jack Steel and Alex Sight Thrillers.

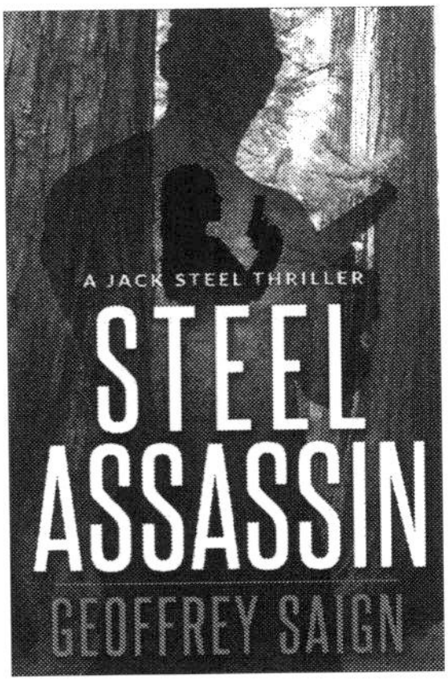

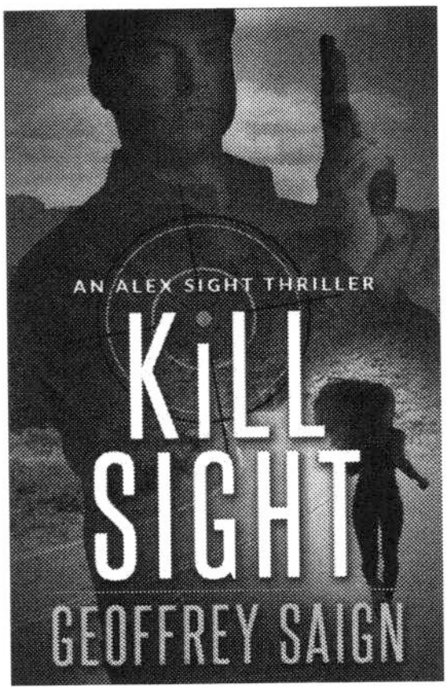

ACKNOWLEDGMENTS

I WANT TO THANK my good friend Stanley Blanchard who used his extensive military background to give Jack Steel the nuances he needed to play the part. Any mistakes or omissions in anything military is my fault alone. Fellow writer, cousin, and walking buddy Steve McEllistrem gave the book a read for grammar. Sailing and swimming buddy Mark Olien helped with the descriptions and accuracy of the Chena Hot Springs Resort and Charlie Dome. I also wish to thank my parents for their critiques—they have always had a sharp sense of what makes a great action thriller. I grew up reading Mom's thrillers, and she's my best critic.

Jack Steel is a character whose discipline gives him advantages over his enemies. As someone who did four-hour workouts nearly daily for five years in kung fu, I thought it would be interesting to create a character who used virtual reality to hone his skills to the nth degree, and then throw him into trouble.

The character Jack Steel follows his values above all else. Doing the right thing is something you learn from the adults around you. My parents did a great job of teaching that to me.

Lastly I wish to thank all the men and women who act heroically every day to ensure our safety. We owe you our thanks, gratitude, and support.

AWARD-WINNING AUTHOR GEOFFREY SAIGN has spent many years studying kung fu and sailed all over the South Pacific and Caribbean. He uses that experience and sense of adventure to write the Jack Steel and Alex Sight thriller action series. Geoff loves to sail big boats, hike, and cook—and he infuses all of his writing with his passion for nature. As a swimmer, he considers himself fortunate to live in the Land of 10,000 Lakes, Minnesota.

For email updates from Geoffrey Saign and
your FREE copy of ***Steel Trust*** go to
www.geoffreysaign.net

See how the Jack Steel series began!

Printed in Great Britain
by Amazon

62799566R00194